Critical acclaim for Tori Phillips

"…historical romance reading at its absolute best."

—*Affaire de Coeur*

"A delightful Elizabethan romp."

—Ruth Ryan Langan

"A great read!"

—Dixie Browning

"A delight to read…charming."

—Suzanne Barclay

"…packed with love, adventure, history…I enjoyed it immensely."

—Rebecca Hagan Lee

"I loved this story!…Tarleton (the hero) is pure magic!"

—Martha Hix

"A stunning debut for Ms. Phillips…"

—*Rendezvous*

Dear Reader,

Tori Phillips's first book, *Fool's Paradise,* won her a prestigious Maggie Award even before she sold it to Harlequin Historicals for release during our 1996 March Madness promotion of talented new authors. This month Tori Phillips returns with another unforgettable story, *Silent Knight.* Despite *his* vow of silence and the fact that *she* is promised to another, a would-be monk and a French noblewoman fall in love on a delightful journey across medieval England. Don't miss this wonderful book.

The Wastrel introduces a new series of Victorian romance novels from award-winning author Margaret Moore, featuring a trio of "most unsuitable" heroes that she has aptly named MOST UNSUITABLE.... *The Wastrel* is the magical story of a disowned heiress and a devil-may-care bachelor who learn about love with the help of her colorful relatives.

A Western by Rae Muir, another author from our 1996 March Madness promotion, *The Trail to Temptation,* about a star-crossed couple who fight their attraction on a trail drive from Texas to Montana, and *The Devil's Kiss,* a romantic comedy from longtime Harlequin Historicals Western writer, DeLoras Scott, round out a terrific month.

Whatever your taste in reading, we hope Harlequin Historicals will keep you coming back for more. Please keep a lookout for all four titles, available wherever books are sold.

Sincerely,

Tracy Farrell
Senior Editor

Please address questions and book requests to:
Harlequin Reader Service
U.S.: 3010 Walden Ave., P.O. Box 1325, Buffalo, NY 14269
Canadian: P.O. Box 609, Fort Erie, Ont. L2A 5X3

TORI PHILLIPS

Silent Knight

Harlequin Books

TORONTO • NEW YORK • LONDON
AMSTERDAM • PARIS • SYDNEY • HAMBURG
STOCKHOLM • ATHENS • TOKYO • MILAN
MADRID • WARSAW • BUDAPEST • AUCKLAND

ISBN 0-373-28943-X

SILENT KNIGHT

Copyright © 1996 by Mary W. Schaller

This edition published by arrangement with Harlequin Books S.A.

® and TM are trademarks of the publisher. Trademarks indicated with ® are registered in the United States Patent and Trademark Office, the Canadian Trade Marks Office and in other countries.

Printed in U.S.A.

Books by Tori Phillips

Harlequin Historicals

Fool's Paradise #307
Silent Knight #343

TORI PHILLIPS

After receiving her degree in theater arts from the University of San Diego, Tori worked at MGM Studios, acted in numerous summer stock musicals and appeared in Paramount Pictures' *The Great Gatsby*. Her plays, published by Dramatic Publishing Co., have been produced in the U.S. and Canada, and her poetry is included in several anthologies. She has directed over forty plays, including twenty-one Shakespeare productions. Currently she is a first-person, Living History actress at the Folger Shakespeare Library in Washington, D.C. She lives with her husband in Burke, VA.

My heartfelt thanks and bags of chocolate kisses to:
my agent, Mary Sue Seymour; and my editors,
Tracy Farrell and Karen Kosztolnyik, for
believing in me;
my guardian angels, Kathryn Falk, Lady Barrow;
Carol Stacy; Kate Ryan and Karen Armstrong for
pushing the "Start Now" button;
my mentors, Suzanne Barclay, Linda Castle and
Martha Hix for keeping me on the right track;
my writer friends, Jenny Bates; Katie Beach;
Margo Columbus; Margot Early; Gwynne Forster;
Sharon Frye; Karen Gromada; Loree &
Threasa Leatherman; Ammanda McCabe;
Rita Madole, Debbie Martin; Marlene Million;
Betsy Morgan; Ginger Rapsus; Kimber Rowe;
Shelia Sampson; Karen Skuce; Karen Smith;
Debbie Staley; Mara Segal; Audri Taylor;
Cindy Walker; Karen Webb and all the ladies of the
Society of the Purple Prose for your warmth, humor,
encouragement and love; and to the Write Knight,
Steve Sandalis, for his heroic inspiration,
his great letters and his fantastic smile.

Chapter One

Tie up my love's tongue and bring him silently.
A Midsummer Night's Dream

October 1528
On the Bristol-to-Chester Post Road

"*Mon Dieu!* Aunt Marguerite, are you much hurt?"
Heedless of the pelting rain, Lady Celeste de Montcalm
knelt in the viscous black mud of the roadside ditch beside the limp form of her aunt. The brown rivulet that
filled the bottom of the ditch quickly soaked the skirts of
Celeste's burgundy velvet gown. With trembling fingers,
she lifted the soggy headdress and sheer veil from the older
woman's graying hair, then unfastened the heavy woolen
traveling cloak that pulled against her neck. She held the
wet garment over them both, in an attempt to shield them
from the downpour.

"Aunt Marguerite?" Celeste swallowed back the iron
taste of apprehension that rose in her throat. Her beloved
companion's face, usually so rosy, now looked the color of
yesterday's ashes. "I pray you, sweet Aunt, speak to me!"
Far from answering her niece, Marguerite barely breathed.

Strong hands grasped Celeste's shoulders. "By the sword of Saint George, my lady, come under the cover of the trees. You'll catch your death in this damnable English weather." Gaston, his voice grown hoarse from years of commanding green-willow youths, spoke with gruff gentleness in her ear. "I shall attend your good aunt."

"Non!" Celeste shook herself free of his grip. "I will not leave her side for a moment. I cannot let her die!"

Swearing a string of colorful words heard more usually in the taverns of Paris, Gaston vented his frustration upon the five men-at-arms and the white-faced driver who strove to lift the overturned wagon off the unconscious lady.

"Move, you filthy lice! Put your backs to it! What are you? Coney rabbits?"

Ignoring her sergeant's language, Celeste focused her attention on the faint rise and fall of Marguerite's spare bosom. The good Lord be praised! She lived yet! Clasping her aunt's hand in hers, Celeste willed her young strength into Marguerite's fragile body. The side of the baggage wagon that pinned the woman against the wall of the ditch barely moved, despite the combined efforts of the men.

Shielding her eyes against the cold, driving rain of the autumn storm, Celeste scanned the flat countryside about them. Farmers' fields, recently harvested, lay in dark boggy patches, relieved here and there by sheltering trees, whose black dripping branches released the last of this year's leaves. She gnawed her lower lip as her gaze swept across the unpromising scene. If a troubadour wove this latest misadventure into verse, several handsome knights would come galloping down the road any minute, led by the darkly handsome Sir Lancelot. Alas, this was no story sung by a hearth fire or illustrated in one of her father's precious books. The rain pelting against her face hid the tears Celeste couldn't stop from rolling down her cheeks. She must not let her men know how truly frightened she was. A dark, square building, half-hidden by a rise in the landscape, suddenly caught her attention.

"Gaston, regardez!" She pointed across the flooded fields. "A house, and of goodly size, I think."

Gaston let go the near wheel and squinted in the direction his mistress pointed. *"Oui,* my lady. And pray God they understand French, for there's not a man among us who speaks this bastard country's tongue." He motioned to the young driver who attended the horses under a roadside copse of elm trees. "You, Pierre! There's a house of some sort ahead. Don't snivel and ask me where. Mount up my Black Devil and ride for help."

The slim boy nodded, then flung himself into Gaston's saddle.

"And if you value the hide on your skinny arse, do not return without goodly company!" Gaston shouted after Pierre as the boy urged the great stallion into a gallop. "Pah! I may skin him like a coney if he mistreats my horse!" the sergeant growled into the gale.

Celeste shook the droplets out of her eyes. "Please, good Saint Catherine. Let whoever they are understand Pierre!" she prayed, her words snatched from her lips by the wind. Her veil whipped into her face, wrapping her features within its wet white folds. Angrily she snatched the bothersome thing off her head, allowing her raven tresses to fly freely about her. A low groan returned her attention to her aunt.

Marguerite's eyelids fluttered, blinked, then opened. For a scant moment, the woman stared past Celeste, and then her face crumpled into a portrait of pain.

"I am dying!" Marguerite wheezed. Then, in a clearer tone, she snapped. "What happened?"

Celeste's heart leapt with joy. If Marguerite could complain and question at the same time, she was certainly not dying.

"Hush, sweet darling," Celeste crooned, in much the same way Aunt Marguerite had often comforted her and her sisters when they were younger. "Don't try to move. The wagon hit a rock in the roadway. It broke one of the wheels and bounced you out. Then the wagon fell on top of you. Are you badly hurt?" she added, hoping to sound calm and in control of the situation.

Marguerite rolled her eyes. "*Oui,* silly child! Of course I am hurt! And what is that ox Gaston doing about it, one asks? Swearing death and destruction, as always? Fah! We never should have set foot on this cursed island! Why couldn't you have stayed in the Loire and become a nun?" Marguerite groaned loudly again.

Celeste kissed her aunt's hand and murmured foolish endearments, all the while hoping to hear the sound of horses approaching. Where was that laggard Pierre?

"*Bonjour,* Lady Marguerite!" said Gaston, peering over Celeste's shoulder. "We shall have you free in no time."

Marguerite glared at the rough-hewn soldier. "In no time? Ha! You speak true, you slug. Time will run out before you can manage to relieve me of this burden. Then where will I be, eh? With the angels in heaven, that's where!"

"I predict your good aunt will recover," Gaston muttered in Celeste's ear. "Her tongue still holds a sharp sting."

The wagon shifted slightly. Gaston threw his weight against it, growling down a great number of oaths upon drivers, horses, English roads, English weather, and England in general. His scarred brown leather boots slid down the muddy embankment as he fought against the unwieldy weight.

"Courage, good Aunt. Pierre has gone for help."

"Bah!" Marguerite grimaced. "A great heap of good that will do! 'Tis like sending a tortoise to market!" She groaned again, though Celeste could not tell if it was more for effect than from pain. Aunt Marguerite's convenient headaches and mysterious stomach disorders were legendary among the extended Montcalm family. This time, however, the older woman indeed had something to complain about.

"I am not surprised this happened. A witch put her curse on us from the moment we landed, I am sure of it." She sighed. "Why must your parents send you to this godforsaken country simply to be married?" Marguerite continued, her voice growing weaker. "Just wait until I next see your father! I tell you truly, Lissa. I shall deal him such a blow upon his ear, he will see stars at midday!"

Celeste smoothed her palm across her aunt's brow, as if she could wipe away both the pain and the ceaseless rain. "Hush, sweet darling. Save your strength. Pierre will return soon."

"Ha! When the devil speaks the truth!" Moaning softly, Marguerite closed her eyes.

Celeste cast an anxious glance at Gaston. Raindrops hung on his bushy eyebrows and dripped from his salt-and-pepper beard. He gave her the ghost of a rueful smile. "It will take more than an upset cart to silence Marguerite de la Columbiare. Wipe away your fear, my lady." The old soldier squeezed her shoulder, then renewed his fierce exhortations to his laboring men.

Thank the good Lord her father had sent Gaston with her when Celeste and Marguerite left their chateau, L'Étoile, two months ago! Two months? Nay, it seemed like two years, and the journey to her unknown bride-groom was only half-over. Celeste pulled the cloak closer over Marguerite, trying to block the worst of the storm. Gruff Gaston had been her father's faithful sergeant during his youthful campaigns. Now he served his master's youngest daughter with equal devotion. Celeste promised herself to commend Gaston's steadfastness to her parents as soon as she was safely at Snape Castle—wherever in this wretched land that odd-sounding place was.

"By the holy cross, it is about time!" Gaston bellowed. "Take heart, my lady. Pierre returns, and brings help, as well!"

Shaking the rain out of her eyes and the heaviness from her heart, Celeste peered through the gathering gloom. Pierre rode Black Devil as if the true fiend of hell were after him. Behind the boy, she could make out a number of figures, accompanied by a two-wheeled cart. Knights, come to aid two ladies in distress!

"Praise be to the guardian angels," Pierre panted as he reined the great stallion to a halt. "There is a small monastery ahead, full of good brothers. And they speak a passable French. Look you, Lady Celeste. They come."

Out of the rain, a half-dozen men dressed in the simple brown woolen robes of the Franciscans hurried toward them. The creak of their cart's wheels made welcome music to Celeste's ears, though the plain-garbed monks were a far cry from her knight-filled fantasy. Without pausing, the new arrivals leapt into the ditch and took hold of the wagon. Celeste saw their bare feet, shod only in open sandals, sink into the clammy muck.

One, taller by a head than the rest, shouted a quick command in English, and then everyone heaved against the wagon together. Miraculously, the cumbersome vehicle lifted away from Aunt Marguerite's body. With the groaning of splintered wood and the creaking of the wet leather springs, the heavy conveyance regained the road-bed once more, where it came to rest in a woefully canted position.

"Peace be with you, my lady." A gentle voice, warm as summer honey, spoke flawless French in Celeste's ear. "Let me tend to your companion and ease her suffering."

Celeste looked up at the speaker, then gasped when she beheld him. The tall blond monk had the shining face of the archangel Gabriel himself!

Guy Cavendish had seen many pretty women in his twenty-eight years, but never one whose eyes flashed the color of purple violets in springtime and whose midnight black hair blew in a silken cloud about her. A hot stirring fluttered below his knotted rope belt. He clamped his teeth tightly together. Jesu! The girl was temptation incarnate—the very thing he had renounced when he entered Saint Hugh's Priory six months ago and pledged himself to a life of poverty, obedience and chastity—especially chastity.

Her eyes widened with that old familiar look of awe that he hated to see on anyone's face. Guy ducked his head lower, hiding from the lady's glassy-eyed expression. By the Book! When would people—especially women—cease to stare at him like that? All his life, the word *beautiful* shadowed Guy. Though his body had shot up to six and a half feet, filling out at the proper time into a man's form, his face had never roughened as his brother's did, but had retained the look that his old nurse once told him reminded her of the stained-glass windows in York Minster. Guy's blond curls had not darkened to brown, as Brandon's had done. Despite the bald patch in his novice's tonsure, his short hair fell about his face in a bright golden halo, which only accentuated the deep blue of his eyes.

Disgusted by his unwanted beauty, he had thrown himself into the harsh training of warfare. The years of riding at the quintain and wielding a heavy two-edged sword had not marred his cursed looks, but instead, hardened his muscles and broadened his shoulders so that men held him in respect and women openly admired him.

Singly and in battalions, ladies at the king's court had sighed at his beauty, fought for his attention at tournaments and boldly proffered their own special favors in return. Being a mere mortal, without saintly pretensions, Guy had taken what was so enthusiastically offered. But in the secret hours of the night he had wondered if the lady who slept beside him would have been so generous if he was less comely.

As his hands gently probed through the soaked velvet gown of the semiconscious woman, Guy strove to ignore the disturbing feminine presence only a whisper away from him. The injured lady cried sharply when he touched her left hip.

"Softly, good mother," he murmured as his fingers continued their necessary search. He felt her stiffen as his hand hovered over her thigh. "I will be gentle. You will feel better anon, I promise."

The old lady's eyelids fluttered open. "I am in torment!" she groaned. Then she got a good look at him, and her mouth dropped open. "Sweet Saint Michael! Am I in paradise already?"

Guy sighed softly to himself. "Nay, good lady, unless you call a foul mud hole heaven."

The woman surprised him by giving a weak chuckle. "Would that I were twenty years younger and not so sore in body. I'd make a heaven of any spot on earth, if you were there to share it with me.''

The lady of the violet eyes gasped. ''Hush, Aunt! You are speaking to a priest. Pay her no mind, Father. I fear my aunt's tongue runs faster than her wits. It is the pain that makes her prattle, *n'est-ce pas?*''

Reluctantly Guy allowed his gaze to light upon the speaker. A mistake of the first order! He felt as if a dart from a crossbow had shot through him, rendering him speechless.

''A priest! *Quel dommage!* Such a pity, eh, Lissa? Did the maidens tie black ribbons in their hair when you professed your vows, handsome Father?'' The aunt's eyes twinkled with faint merriment before they closed against another wave of pain.

Despite being the subject of this uncomfortable conversation, Guy allowed a faint grin to touch his lips. ''As to that, I know not, my lady, though my mother cried and wondered what she had done wrong in my upbringing.''

''I daresay she did right well,'' murmured the aunt before lapsing into a faint.

''Oh, please, don't let her die,'' the younger woman begged, her purple irises shimmering in the raindrops.

''She'll not die—not this day, at least.'' As he spoke, Guy removed the rope from around his waist and used it to lash the aunt's lower extremities together. ''She has merely fainted, which is a blessing. The trip back to the monastery would be an agony, were she awake.'' Averting his eyes from the young lady, Guy called in English to one of his fellow novices.

''Brother Thomas! Your strong arm is needed here. The old woman has broken a bone or two and must be gently carried.''

"Aye!" The younger monk, little more than a boy and robust in nature, slipped through the mud at Guy's command.

The girl rose and made a space for Thomas, who barely gave her a second glance. Guy wondered how the boy could be so immune to the bewitching spell of her dark, loose hair and the purple fire in her eyes. Then he chided himself. Of course Thomas saw nothing rare in her. The lad was far saintlier than Guy could ever hope to be. No doubt Thomas had never tasted the sinful pleasures of the flesh. Angry at his own weakness, Guy vowed to spend that night in humble prostration before the altar, on the freezing stones of the chapel floor. He knew from experience that such a penance would cool the ardor of even Great Harry himself.

"Slip your arms under the lady and grasp my wrists," Guy instructed, hoping his voice would not betray the turmoil of the emotions seething inside him. "Good. Now, on my word, lift her gently, holding her as level as possible."

"Aye, Bother Guy," Thomas answered. "I am ready."

"On the count of three." Guy gripped Thomas' wrists. "One . . . two . . ."

"Be careful. She is most dear to me," the girl at Guy's elbow whispered in French.

Despite the chill of the rain, Guy's blood warmed as if turned to liquid fire; his heart raced. He gritted his teeth. "Three!" Acting as one, Thomas and Guy lifted the injured lady from the ditch and carried her quickly to the monastery's cart. Brother Cuthbert, a brother skilled in the healing arts, lifted the makeshift canvas covering, allowing Guy and Thomas to place the lady on a bed of dry straw.

"Did you say she suffers a broken bone?" Cuthbert asked Guy in a quiet, professional manner.

"Aye, her left leg for sure, and perhaps her hip, as well."
Cuthbert nodded. "'Tis a blessing she is unconscious."

"Amen to that, I say." Guy stepped back as Cuthbert
sprang into the driver's seat and slapped the reins against
the patient horse's rump. As the cart rolled away, something tugged the loose sleeve of Guy's robe. Turning, he
nearly stumbled over the enchantress of the raven locks.

"Pardon, good Father," she began, each syllable falling like drops of heady French wine. "But I do not understand English very well. What did you say about my
aunt?" Her eyes, if anything, appeared to grow larger,
burning deeper into his soul.

"Broken leg," Guy muttered brusquely, trying to avoid
her stare. Why did she have to look at him as if he were the
fabled unicorn? "Best that you mount up and ride quickly
to the priory. You do ride, do you not, my lady? You will
catch a chill and fever if you stand here. You are wet
through."

Before he realized what he was doing, his gaze slid down
from her face to her slender white throat, and from there
to her soaked bodice. The wet burgundy velvet molded her
high breasts, boldly outlining the delicious promise that lay
scarcely hidden there. Another fiery bolt impaled him. He
nearly groaned with the painful pleasure. A mere night on
the chapel floor would not suffice. He vowed a full day of
penance, as well.

"I thank you for your concern, Father," she murmured in a low, slightly husky voice that reminded Guy of
hickory smoke—and hot passion between fresh sheets.

God forgive him for the unholy thoughts that whirled
about his fevered brain. He would wear a hair shirt when
he did his self-imposed vigil in the chapel.

An impish smile curled the corners of her full cherry
mouth. "And I do ride quite well—like the wind. Not very

ladylike, they tell me." As she turned toward the horses, the back of her hand brushed against his. He jumped as if he had been caressed by a burning brand.

"Oh!" Turning her wide eyes upon him once more, she lifted her hand to her mouth, as if she, too, had felt the fire.

Their glances locked for an eternal instant. Guy felt himself plummeting into an abyss. Her gaze spoke unvoiced poetry to his heart. He could not tear himself from her power until she blinked; then he turned quickly away.

A hair shirt, and twenty-four hours on the hard flagstones—and fasting. Yes, he must fast, as well, Guy decided as he watched the grizzled old retainer lift the girl into the saddle of her palfrey. Hitching up the trailing hem of his oversize robe, Guy followed after her down the road. Tonight, he would pray that she would ride out of his safely ordered life as quickly as possible.

As he watched her back sway rhythmically in the saddle, his mind wandered from his holy intent. "Lissa," the aunt had called her. What sort of name was that?

Chapter Two

" "'Tis not often we have the opportunity to entertain such charming company as yourself, Lady Celeste." Father Jocelyn Pollock, prior of Saint Hugh's, wiped his fingers free of chicken grease on his rough linen napkin. Nor was it often that he dined so richly, and he wondered if his digestion would pay the price for this indulgence in the middle of the night. Nevertheless, he enjoyed the opportunity to exercise his French. Brother Giles, acting as servitor, poured more wine into a simple pottery cup, which he offered to the lady.

"*Merci,*" she murmured, her long, dark lashes fluttering like a butterfly on a midsummer's day.

Father Jocelyn noted how the lady's eyes sparkled in the candlelight, and he made a mental note to keep his novices and younger monks out of her sight. On second thought, he should keep most of his charges within the confines of the cloister, lest they be beguiled by this extraordinary creature. Already, in the space of an hour at supper, Lady Celeste had transformed solemn Brother Giles into a blushing, stammering schoolboy. Praise be to the entire heavenly host that the young woman had no idea of the power of her charms. Father Jocelyn sighed into his napkin. She would learn soon enough.

" 'Tis most unfortunate that your aunt has suffered a fractured hip, as well as a broken leg," Father Jocelyn continued. His unexpected guests presented him with a number of problems, the least of which was Lady Marguerite's injuries.

"But she will recover, *oui?*" Placing her eating knife across her trencher, Lady Celeste raised her eyes in supplication.

The prior nodded. "Aye, my lady. She will be made whole again under the care of our gifted Brother Cuthbert." Frowning slightly, he swirled the dregs of the wine in his cup. "However, 'tis out of the question for her to travel anywhere before Christmastide. At which time, it would be advisable for her to return to your home in France, where the weather is kinder to knitting bones."

For a moment, Lady Celeste did not speak. Then she sighed. "I suspected as much, good Father. Indeed, I am hardly surprised. 'Tis merely one more misadventure we have suffered since . . . we left L'Étoile."

Father Jocelyn crumbled the crust of his trencher between his thumb and forefinger. "There have been other accidents, my child?"

"Accidents?" Her dark brows arched to a point. Her lips curled into a half smile. "This entire journey has been one long accident, Father."

The prior snapped his fingers to attract the attention of Brother Giles, who looked as if he had been kicked in the head by Daisy, the monastery's infamous donkey. Coloring, the brother began to clear the board. Yes, Father Jocelyn decided, watching Brother Giles trip over the hem of his robe, he definitely must send the Lady Celeste on her way as soon as possible.

The prior cleared his throat. "Traveling is always difficult. I am surprised to find you accompanied by so few retainers, and so late in the year."

The lady dabbed the corners of her lips with her napkin before answering. "It was not so in the beginning. We left my home in late August. My father provided me with my aunt as chaperon. I also had good Gaston, a dozen men-at-arms, my maid, Suzette..." Here, she faltered and bowed her head for a moment. Father Jocelyn had the distinct impression that the lady's tale was not a pleasant one.

"There were also two wagons, and the drivers," she continued in a soft throaty voice.

Father Jocelyn cocked one eyebrow. "Two wagons? Pray, go on, my lady."

"All went well—in France."

"Ah, 'twas the crossing of the Channel?" The prior had done that once himself, when he visited Italy in his youth. He had vowed if God would let him live through the experience, he would never leave England again.

"*Oui!*" Her eyes flashed. "We were all sick, even the poor horses. In truth, good Father, I prayed for death over and over as our ship pitched and dived among the waves. Is that not wicked of me?"

Father Jocelyn shook his head. "Understandable, given the circumstances."

"It was over a week before we landed safely in a place called Bristol. I must confess that I fell to my knees and kissed the ground."

"Also understandable." Father Jocelyn had done the same thing upon his return to England.

"Pah! Had I known what was in store for us here, I would have turned right around and ordered that miserable boat back to France!"

Brother Giles tittered. The prior flashed him a scorching look. Father Jocelyn wished he could send the younger man back to the kitchen; however, the lady's reputation, as well as the prior's, required that a third party be present at all times. Who would have expected that soberminded Giles would be reduced to a quivering mass of suet pudding by a smoky voice and a pair of violet eyes?

"Once our stomachs returned to their rightful places, we set out, going north toward Chester, I believe. I fear I am not acquainted with the English countryside."

"No one would expect you to be," interjected Brother Giles with feeling. Father Jocelyn glared at him.

"*Oui!* You have grasped the very kernel of the truth. Our party wandered over hill and dale, because it amused the common folk to misguide us—even when we paid them for their directions. I am sure we looked a fool's progress as we turned in circles at their whim. Indeed, at one point we discovered we were headed in the opposite direction, when we found a milepost pointing back toward Bristol!"

"Surely there must have been some honest folk you met on your way?"

Lady Celeste shrugged her shoulders slightly. "*Oui,* though it took us nearly a month to find one. When at last we were headed north again, the skies turned against us, and it rained for days on end."

"I fear our weather is one of the crosses we must bear," the prior remarked gently.

"It rained so much that all the little brooks became rushing rivers. We lost a wagon while fording one. If it were not for Pierre's quick thinking, we would have lost the horses, as well. He leapt on the back of the lead mare as she thrashed in the water. At peril of his own life, he cut the traces. Our Pierre is only sixteen, but he is very brave, no?'' Her eyes sparkled as she recounted the harrowing incident.

He's probably suffering the loss of his wits. The prior kept that observation to himself. The girl warmed to her tale, despite its gravity. Father Jocelyn found himself wondering if she secretly relished the adventure. How unsuitable for a young lady of gentle breeding!

"We were able to save some of the furnishings my mother sent with me for my new home, but the wagon? Fah! Firewood!" She sipped her wine. "Gaston sent the first driver and his team back to Bristol." She sighed. "They are most likely at home by now."

Father Jocelyn suspected the young lady wished she was back in L'Étoile, as well. He couldn't blame her. When he saw a small frown knot itself between her delicate eyebrows, he asked, "There is more?"

Lady Celeste sighed again. "*Oui,* though I wish there were not. I believe we ate some poorly cooked food in an inn outside of..." She struggled to think of the name. "Outside of Hereford. Many of my men came down with stomach cramps. It was most piteous to hear them moan. At one point, I feared for their lives. My dear little maid, Suzette—she was so very sick. We stayed in that miserable town for almost two weeks. At last, everyone recovered, but they were very weak. Suzette lost so much weight, I could not bear the thought of making her continue the journey. She is only fourteen, Father. When she was well enough, I sent her back to Bristol with three of the men."

The prior shook his head. The lady sitting opposite him didn't look much older than her maid, yet she seemed to have been made stronger by the series of setbacks. "And now your aunt. It seems God has sorely tested your mettle, *ma petite.*"

Her eyes flashed with an inner fire. "You have spoken truly, Father, yet I must go on. My father gave his word that I would wed Walter Ormond, and the word of the chevalier of Fauconbourg is golden. Even if I arrive at Snape Castle in only my shift, I must go on. The honor of my family is at stake."

The bridegroom's name jangled a faint bell within Father Jocelyn's memory. He had heard something about a branch of the Ormond family that was not altogether savory. "Walter Ormond? Would his father be Sir Roger Ormond?"

For the first time that evening, she truly smiled. The effect nearly shattered Brother's Giles's fragile composure. "*Oui,* the very same!" She clapped her hands with delight. "Do you know him, good Father?"

The prior wet his lips before answering. He had half a mind to tell her to flee back to France immediately, but he suspected she would face death before disgracing the family name. "The Ormonds live on the northern outskirts of civilization. I fear they are a rough and uncultured lot. Tell me, my child. How is it such a well-bred lady as yourself happened to become betrothed to the heir of such a far-flung estate?"

Lady Celeste swallowed at his words, though her gaze never wavered. "My father came to know Sir Roger and his son eight years ago, when your King Henry met with our king, François, at a beautiful city of tents outside of Calais, which people now call the Field of Cloth of Gold." Her violet eyes gleamed as she recalled that near-legendary event.

"My father was a member of Francois's court, and he entertained Sir Roger often during that fortnight. Oh, Father Jocelyn! I was there for a few days with my mother and sisters. It was truly the most magnificent sight!"

The old prior nodded. He had heard of the sumptuous feasts, the splendid tournaments and the brilliance of the two glittering courts, each vain monarch trying to outshine the other. He could well imagine how such a magnificent sight would have impressed the imagination of a young girl. "How many sisters have you, *ma petite?*"

"I have the honor of being the fifth and youngest daughter of Roland de Montcalm." Her chin tilted up a notch.

"Five daughters! And brothers?"

"Only one survived. Philippe is the baby of the family." She looked wistful as she spoke of her little brother. "We spoil him terribly."

"Are your sisters married?" Father Jocelyn wondered if they were as striking as the lady opposite him.

"*Oui,* that is why my father allowed all of us to come to the Field of Cloth of Gold—to find good husbands. I am the last—and the only one who was betrothed to an Englishman." She sighed softly, then flushed and glanced at the prior. "Pardon my manners, Father. It is not that I do not like the English, it's just..." She groped for the right words.

"It's just that you would have rather stayed in France, near your family?" he suggested in a gentle voice.

Lady Celeste rewarded him with a smile that lit up the small, Spartan guest room. Brother Giles hiccuped with suppressed pleasure.

"You are very wise, Father, to know my mind." She cocked her head to one side. "Perhaps you can tell me what I am to do now that my aunt is sore injured and my only wagon is broken. I am most needful of good counsel. I must go on. I cannot return to L'Étoile. It would disgrace my father's name, and...and..." She bit her lip.

"Yes, *ma petite?*" Father Jocelyn resisted the urge to lay his hand on her bowed head.

"It is my only offer of marriage, Father," she confessed in a near whisper. "After settling dowries on my four older sisters, there was very little left for me. Sir Roger is kind enough to accept me when I bring his son so little to the marriage settlement." She gave her slim shoulders a shake, then stared into the candle's flame. "But I will bring him my honor, my virtue, and…and I will try to love him, as well."

"Then Walter Ormond will be a rich man indeed," murmured the prior, though a wing tip of apprehension brushed against his soul.

The morning air smelled fresh and clean when Guy emerged from the darkness of the chapel, where he had spent a cold, dank night lying facedown on the flagstones. The sun's rays fell with welcome warmth on his chilled skin and robe, still damp from the rain of the day before. Guy moved stiffly across the cloister toward a low gate. A day spent tending the monastery's herb garden would be good for both his sore body and his troubled mind. He wished Father Jocelyn had let him wear a hair shirt while he prayed on the chapel floor. Its rough discomfort might have banished the visions of deep violet eyes and flowing black hair that had danced through Guy's meditations during his nocturnal penance. He hoped the troubling lady was gone by now—on her way to wherever it was. Anywhere but here at Saint Hugh's.

Silver, rippling laughter brought Guy to an abrupt halt. His heart skipped its normal rhythm and strained against the confines of his chest. No member of Saint Hugh's Priory laughed with such crystal sweetness, not even the youngest choirboy. Stepping back into the shade of a pillared archway, Guy peered over Brother Timothy's prized rosebushes. Seated on a stone bench not ten feet away, the temptress who had plagued his prayers now toyed with Jeremiah, the kitchen's ill-tempered cat.

"La, puss-puss," the lady crooned, stroking the sensitive whiskers of the black-and-white mouser with a long piece of straw. "What a fine, handsome fellow you are!"

The cat's docile behavior surprised Guy. He sucked in his breath when he saw the lady lean over and pick up the overfed creature. Guy tensed, expecting Jeremiah to lash out with his claws bared.

"Truly, you would make an admirable knight, if cats could wear armor," she continued, settling him on her lap. "You are such an elegant puss-puss," she continued in admiring tones, her fingers moving through Jeremiah's thick fur in long, even strokes.

Guy shivered as he watched her graceful hands. Should he warn her of the cat's irascible nature? Yet that would mean he would have to speak to her again, to look into those beguiling eyes once more. The short encounter of yesterday had been enough to send his thin defenses crashing down.

Perhaps it would be best for the sake of Guy's troubled soul if the cat did scratch the girl. Then she would go away, or at least leave the cloister rose garden. Only a little scratch would do—the merest swipe. Not enough to draw blood, nor to injure her creamy skin. Just a suggestion of a scratch. Perhaps only the sight of a half-open talon. Guy bit back his alarm as the lady, heedless of the risk she took, swung Jeremiah over her shoulder and draped him around her neck like a fur collar.

"See, *mon chat?*" The lady picked up a small book, bound in dark blue leather, that had been lying on the bench beside her. "You would look most magnificent, I think, if you were dressed as the Knight of the Loyal Heart." Absently, she rubbed Jeremiah behind his ears. "See this picture? You would wear the helm of the winged heart most nobly, *oui?*"

Closing his eyes, the cat nudged his head against the palm of her hand. Guy could almost hear the creature purring. Perhaps Jeremiah was befuddled by her French. Maybe he had never been this close to a woman before. In any event, he wasn't acting normally. In fact, the cat looked as if he had found paradise within the dark tresses that peeped from under the lady's sheer veil. Guy trembled with indignation, though he could not tear his gaze away from the simple domestic scene in front of him. That woman—nay, that chit of a girl—was the devil's handmaiden, brought here to seduce the souls of this community of celibates. She even wove her witchcraft on the bellicose Jeremiah!

"La, dearest cat, you would save the poor damsel, Sweet Grace, from the evil power of the awful sorceress Denial, wouldn't you?" The lady rubbed her cheek against the cat's fur, as she turned to another page in her book and held it up for Jeremiah's inspection. Even at a distance, Guy could see the exquisite detail of the illustration, rendered in jewel colors and bright gilding.

A book of romance and troubadour songs. Strange devotions for a well-bred young girl to read, especially within the walls of a holy monastery. Guy knew he should turn away in disgust. Every moment that he lingered in the shadows of the archway only heightened the danger to his vows.

Her hands fluttered over the cat like two butterflies in the sun. A sudden breeze threatened to lift the velvet French coif from her head. Guy caught himself wishing it would. He swore under his breath, then, aghast at what he had just said, whispered a hurried prayer after his oath.

By the Holy Grail, what was happening to him? Who was this creature but yet another one of those empty-headed females whom he sought to escape once and for all time behind these gray stone walls? He had had enough of women in all shapes, sizes, social orders and states of undress in the past twelve years to convince himself that not one of them was worth a groat.

Ever since Anne Boleyn had caught the king's roving eye, Great Harry's lust had doomed to extinction whatever shreds of honor and virtue still lingered in the corners of Westminster Palace. Guy counted himself well out of it. Now, when he least expected it, temptation played in the October sunshine. And his body—not to mention his very soul—responded like a starving man at a feast. Angrily he stalked toward the herb garden, taking care that he made no noise to attract the attention of those fascinating violet eyes.

Not even the bewitched Jeremiah looked up.

"What?" Guy sputtered, breaking into a sweat, though the evening air was cool. He cast a sidelong glance at Brother Cuthbert, who stood behind the prior's chair. No trace of humor glinted in the older man's gray eyes. Guy considered throwing himself to his knees, but thought the gesture might seem too dramatic within the confines of the prior's office. "I pray you, Father, do not lay this burden on me!"

Father Jocelyn barely hid his smile. "How now? A burden? I should think you would welcome a chance to get out and enjoy the countryside. Mother Nature has trimmed herself in her best finery before cruel winter's onslaught. 'Twould only be for a few weeks."

"But why me?" Guy raked his fingers through the fringes of his thick blond hair. "I am only a novice. Perhaps it would be better for someone who has already taken his vows to go—someone who has been here a long time and would like a short holiday." He glanced over to Brother Cuthbert.

Father Jocelyn coughed behind his hand. "Perhaps, but I think you are the best choice, Brother Guy. You understand French, and you know the lay of the land well. Northumberland is your home, is it not?"

Guy swallowed with difficulty. "Aye, Father, but..."

The prior held up his hand for silence. Guy bowed his head, though he could feel his heart thumping uncomfortably under his robe.

"Lady Celeste has already experienced a most difficult journey. In faith, I am tempted to return her to her home, but the lady won't hear of it."

Guy looked up, raising one brow in question. Obviously, the girl hadn't a sensible bone in her body.

"She tells me that her family's honor demands that she go on, come rack or ruin—which I fear may happen at the rate she is proceeding."

"But, Father..."

The prior continued as if he hadn't heard Guy's disrespectful interruption. "Now that her aunt must stay behind, Lady Celeste needs some sort of chaperon, and that, Brother Guy, you will provide. No one will think it amiss if they see her traveling in the company of a priest."

"Priest!" Guy erupted. He had never intended to take holy orders. He wasn't worthy—not after the hell-bent life he had led. "Father, I am the furthest thing from the priesthood."

Father Jocelyn gently shook his head in silent reproof. "It matters not what you truly are, so long as you are what you seem to be. To the world you are a man of God, and therefore above reproach.''

"And the lady—?'' Guy tried not to think of her voice, like exotic incense, and her hair, the color of silken midnight.

"Lady Celeste will be none the wiser.'' The prior's lips curled at the corners. "Your virtue will be safe with her.''

Safe? Those liquid violet eyes and those lush lips, like satin rosebuds, promised scant safety to any mortal man. The prior had no idea what he was asking. Guy dropped to his knees. "Do not make me bear this cross, Father.'' Hearing his own words, Guy realized he sounded a little overblown, but perhaps the prior would be moved by his biblical plea.

Father Jocelyn stood and slid his hands into the wide folds of his sleeves. "When you joined our community six months ago, Brother Guy, you promised obedience in all things.''

"Aye, Father.'' Guy bowed his head and shut his eyes, trying to blot out what he knew was coming.

"Now I am commanding you to escort the Lady Celeste de Montcalm and her men safely to Sir Roger Ormond of Snape Castle, near Morpeth, in Northumberland. There she will wed Sir Roger's son, Walter. After the ceremony, you will return here. Do I make myself clear in this matter, Brother Guy?''

"You do, Father.'' Guy tried to control the tremor that shivered down his spine. Walter Ormond of Snape? Sweet Jesu! Nay! 'Twould be flinging a gentle dove into the talons of a hawk.

"Excellent!'' Father Jocelyn nodded in satisfaction. Brother Cuthbert merely sucked in his breath.

Guy wet his lips. "But, Father, I fear for my soul to travel in the company of such a...such a lady as that." He bit back the urge to bellow at his superior.

The prior chuckled. "I admit she is a most beauteous lady, Brother Guy. I am glad to see you have not lost your keen perception. As to your soul, I will lay on you one further commandment." He paused as he glanced at Brother Cuthbert.

Guy waited tensely. The uneven flagstones bit deeper into his knees. He again licked his dry lips. He had a feeling he wasn't going to like whatever the prior had in mind.

"At vespers tonight, you will make a solemn vow of silence. Henceforth, you will not speak, nor utter a sound, until Lady Celeste's wedding day," Father Jocelyn pronounced over him. A note of humor softened the tone of his voice.

Guy lifted his chin with firm resolve. "Aye, I will, Father Jocelyn." If he couldn't speak to her, there was a chance he could evade her wiles and snares. "And tonight, for my penance—"

"What penance do you think you need now, my son?" A warm twinkle danced in the prior's eyes. "You were up all last night at prayer. You need your rest tonight, for you will depart with the lady at first light. Her wagon is repaired, and time is of the essence. The good weather will not hold for long."

"Perhaps I could wear a hair shirt?" Guy suggested. Pain. He needed pain to keep his thoughts from wandering down the path of sweet perdition.

"That is hardly necessary, Brother Guy. I think riding astride Daisy for several weeks will be penance enough for even the worst of sins." Before Guy could make a further suggestion, Father Jocelyn traced the sign of the cross over him. "Go in peace, my son."

Guy rose, bowed to both the prior and his assistant, then let himself out the door. A myriad of thoughts tumbled through him as he fled for the silence of the chapel. By the rood! How was he going to survive the next month? Though the words of his prayers poured from his lips, he saw in his mind the beguiling beauty of Lady Celeste de Montcalm—and the well-remembered sneer of Walter Ormond.

From the side door of the chapel, the two Franciscans watched their newest novice wrestle with himself.

"Do you truly think it wise to send young Guy off with the lady?" Cuthbert murmured in an undertone.

Father Jocelyn nodded slowly, his eyes never leaving the kneeling form praying before the sanctuary. "Aye, Brother, I do. 'Tis for the best."

Brother Cuthbert raised one eyebrow so high, it nearly lost itself in the mouse-gray fringe encircling his head. "How so?"

The prior tapped his finger against his nose. "Let us say that I have my suspicions concerning the sincerity of young Cavendish's vocation."

"But surely the lad is sincere. In the garden, in the chapel—he is constantly on his knees!" Cuthbert blustered in a whisper.

"Peace, good Brother. Time will tell." The prior smiled at his old friend. They had entered the monastery together as boys, nearly thirty-five years ago. "When you and I took our final vows, we did so with great joy—running to our Lord. I suspect Brother Guy is running away from himself."

Chapter Three

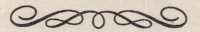

"**Y**ou sent for me, Aunt Marguerite?" Celeste peered around the heavy wooden door of the guest infirmary.

Propped against several thick muslin-covered pillows, the older woman smiled and held out her hand to her niece.

"Come in quickly, Lissa, and shut that door tight behind you. Fah! This damp weather will kill me long before any horse and wagon." A chuckle softened her words.

Celeste did as she was told, then drew up a small three-legged stool beside her aunt's bed. Marguerite's skin had regained a healthier color, and Celeste could tell by the brightness of her eyes that her aunt's tart humor had returned to its full strength. The older woman held her niece's hand as she regarded her by the light of the tallow candle on the bedside table. Celeste glanced at the clay pitcher and cup there.

"Would you like me to pour you some water?" she offered, making a move to do so. Marguerite merely tightened her grip on Celeste's fingers.

"Water? Do I look like a fish? *Non,* but that know-it-all Brother Cuthbert thinks I am!" She sniffed loudly. "He means to drown me at the first opportunity. But never fear, Lissa. He has met his match!"

Celeste hid the smile that plucked at the corners of her lips. The unsuspecting brother had indeed encountered a formidable opponent, she feared, and she wished him all the courage he could muster. She suspected that Aunt Marguerite would sorely try the man's patience, not to mention his sanctity, in the coming months, while she recovered from her injuries.

"I shall miss you, *ma petite*," Marguerite said with surprising gentleness.

Celeste swallowed back a tremor of sadness at these words. All afternoon she had tried to push away the idea of continuing on her journey alone. Now, in the depths of the night shadows, the reality of the situation had to be confronted, just as she had faced her fears of ghosts lurking in the dark corners of her home in the Loire valley. Celeste leaned forward and kissed her aunt on the cheek. Her skin felt cool and dry to the touch.

"And I shall miss your chiding tongue, your scolding frowns and your many instructions concerning my deportment. La! I never thought I would say those words, dear Aunt, but they are true. You are a dear part of me."

Celeste banished a small sob that hovered in the back of her throat. She wouldn't show weakness now. She had many miles to travel, alone in this inhospitable country, and she couldn't let her aunt know how very frightened she was at that prospect.

Marguerite squeezed her hand again. "Humph! You spin a pretty tale by the firelight—almost as farfetched as those romantic ballads you love so much." Her voice caught. "I believe I will have a sip of that marsh water, after all," she said, brusquely waving at the pitcher.

Celeste poured half a cup and held it out.

The patient took it and sipped in silence. Celeste fidgeted with one of the embroidered roses on her yellow satin skirt. The candle sputtered, a thin wisp of smoke curling back onto itself as it rose toward the low plastered ceiling. After a strained silence, Marguerite handed back the cup.

"Surely they must have wine in this place. I shall speak to that Brother Cuthbert about it. He shall know my mind on the subject by the terce bell tomorrow, I assure you!" Marguerite nodded to her niece.

"I pray you have mercy on the poor man," Celeste replied, pitying Brother Cuthbert even more.

"Mercy?" Her aunt looked surprised at the very idea. "Lissa, am I not always the soul of understanding, tact and mercy?"

Celeste cleared her throat. "So you have often told my sisters and me," she countered as diplomatically as possible.

"And so I shall be." Another uneasy silence draped itself over them. Celeste made a move to leave, thinking her aunt needed to sleep, but the older woman's grip remained firm around Celeste's hand. "Sit still, child, for I have much to tell you, and there is so little time."

Puzzled, Celeste leaned forward. "*Oui*, Aunt? I am listening."

Marguerite patted her cheek. "You were always such a good girl. It is a pity that my brother was too pigheaded not to see it."

Celeste shifted uncomfortably on the hard stool. All her life she had tried to please her formidable father, to win his love with her cheerful banter and her singing, which everyone else said was sweet as a meadowlark's on a May morning. Though it had never been spoken aloud, Celeste knew that she was far from the chevalier's favorite daughter. "Papa has a great many things to attend to," she murmured in his defense.

"Bah! Let it be said plainly now, for I do not know when we shall meet again on this earth. Your father wished for a son, and when you, the fifth daughter, arrived, he was angered like a small boy who has been denied a promised sweetmeat. It is a scandal the way he has treated you—sending you off to this godforsaken place to be wed to a stranger who probably can't even speak passable French!"

Celeste stared into the candle's flame, trying to conjure up the face of this unknown bridegroom. The picture of Lancelot in a book in her father's library swam into her imagination.

"The Ormonds are a noble family," Celeste whispered to the flickering point of light. "Walter will possess the qualities of a fine lord, I am sure."

"Quit your woolgathering!" Marguerite's voice echoed around the tiny room. "This bridegroom of yours is not some pretty picture. He is a real man—and that is the nut and core of what I must tell you!"

Celeste widened her eyes. She was not sure she wanted to hear whatever caused her aunt's distress.

"Do not alarm yourself so, dearest Aunt," she murmured, though her own heart beat faster.

"Ah, *ma petite,* I had thought there would be more time to speak of this later—before your wedding day. I promised your dear mama..." She ran her tongue across her lips.

"More water?" Celeste offered, a flutter of panic tickling her throat. What on earth could it be that curbed her aunt's usually tart tongue and sent such shivers of fright through Celeste?

"*Non,* more words. Tell me truly, has anyone spoken to you of what passes between a man and his wife after they are married?"

Celeste blinked at the surprising question. "Why, love passes between the two. With God's blessing, it grows as the years go by."

Marguerite passed her free hand across her forehead, as if to wipe away the thought. "Sweet little fool! You have filled your mind with too many troubadours' posies. Nay, I speak of the wedding night, when a man and woman lie together in bed. Have any of your sisters spoken of it to you?" Her voice held a note of hope.

"*Non.* Why should they?"

Marguerite blew out a long sigh. "I was afraid of this. It is no good to cosset young girls under glass, like delicate damask roses, then pluck them rudely out of their loving homes and expect them to enjoy it!"

"Aunt Marguerite? What are you trying to tell me?"

The lady squared her shoulders and seemed to grow larger against the pillows. "'Tis this and none other, child. On your wedding night, your husband will strip the clothes from your back, examine you as one does a horse for sale, then he will . . . he will . . ."

Never had Celeste known her aunt to falter in the telling of anything. "He will what?"

"He will unlace his tights, open his codpiece, and thrust his man-root between your legs, into the most private part of your body!"

"Oh!" Celeste gasped as a hot flush rose into her cheeks. The scene painted by her aunt sounded appalling. "Surely this is a rude jest, Aunt. It is cruel of you to tease me so!"

Marguerite's lips trembled. "It is not a jest, but the plain truth. And you must let him do it, for that is his husbandly right. And I must warn you further." Now that she had breached her initial embarrassment, there was no stopping the torrent of words that poured from her mouth as if from a rainspout. "You will experience pain and blood."

Celeste shuddered, and gripped Marguerite's hand. "Must this thing happen? Could we not merely kiss and whisper sweet loving words, and hold each other in the night? I thought that was what happened betwixt a husband and wife. I've seen such behavior with my parents."

Marguerite's lips drew back into a sliver of a smile. "*Oui*, if you are fortunate with your husband. And these kisses and cooings and such like are the honey of the marriage bed, but this other, this coupling—*that* is the meat and drink."

"Why?" None of the beautiful books in her father's library showed such a thing. Lovers kissed in flower gardens, held hands, entwined their arms about each other and slept together like the best of friends. No one had ever seen Celeste naked except her maid—certainly no man, not even her little brother, Philippe. "It is not natural!"

The older woman gave a dry cackle. "It is the most natural thing in the world. And the why of it? For the begetting of children! How did you suppose they get a start? Do not look so moon-faced, Lissa. In time you will grow to crave it—if your husband is a skilled lover. Of course, he *is* English, and I have heard it said they are not the wisest in this matter. Fah! Your father! You should have been married to a Frenchman, rather then sent off to the arms of a barbarian! There now, I've said my piece."

"Good Aunt, what am I to do?" Celeste bit her knuckles.

Marguerite snorted. "Close your eyes, lie still...and think of sweet, fat babies."

Celeste spent a restless night, tossing on the narrow, straw-filled mattress. Finally, she fell into a dreamless sleep. When the lauds bell woke her to the sight of a misty dawn creeping through her narrow window, the frightening conversation of the night before seemed merely a fragment of a nightmare. Only the images evoked by the words *naked, pain* and *blood* remained sharp in her mind.

Perhaps Aunt Marguerite's long-dead husband had been something of a beast, Celeste concluded as she hastily dressed herself in her burgundy travel gown. Besides, this day promised to be a fine sunny one, and her unknown bridegroom was miles away, in deepest Northumberland. She would confront the problem of the wedding night when the moment—and the man—were at hand. In the meantime, she had more pressing problems—such as learning to tie up her laces by herself, learning to wrap her tongue around the harsh sounds of the English language and, most of all, learning a good deal more about her new travel companion, Brother Guy.

For the few days she had been a guest at Saint Hugh's, Celeste had spotted the brother with the celestial face only for brief moments. He always seemed to be rushing somewhere. Once she had tried to speak with him—to thank him for his help on the day of the accident—and he had literally picked up the hem of his robe and run into the dark chapel. His beautiful face had had the most amusing expression on it as he fled.

Another time, while practicing her lute in the cloister garden, she had thought she saw his tall figure hovering behind one of the pillars. When she looked up again, no one had been there. At least the adorable Jeremiah liked her music and had taken to sunning himself on the bench beside her while she played. She would miss the cat's company when she left the priory.

Her final leave-taking of her beloved aunt was brief, and full of the usual admonishments.

"Watch your funds carefully, Lissa, and don't let these peasants cheat you."

"No, dearest Aunt."

"Remember you are a lady at all times. And practice your English, as well as your singing."

"*Oui.*"

"Do not drive poor Gaston to distraction. He has his hands full enough with those clod-brained men of his."

Celeste suppressed a smile. She suspected Gaston was secretly relieved not be to traveling with "Madame Wasp-Tongue," as she knew he called her aunt behind her back.

"Be sure to brush your hair a hundred strokes before bedtime every night—no skimping, mind you. Keep your teeth clean, chew mint leaves before entering company, and you must promise me to attend your prayers. No day-dreaming about knights in shining armor."

Celeste chuckled. "How can I avoid praying, dearest Marguerite? I will be watched over by a priest. No doubt he will have me saying my paternosters all the way to Snape Castle!"

Marguerite slapped her hand playfully. "Do not tease the good brother. I understand he is sworn to a vow of silence, so do not plague him with endless chatter. He has no defense against you."

Celeste cocked her head. "Such an odd vow! How am I supposed to practice my English with a silent Englishman for company? La! I swear, I'll take no such vow to accompany him! I will talk for the both of us."

"Lissa! Mind what I said—"

Brother Cuthbert's arrival cut short all further instructions. The monk reported that Gaston and his men waited for the Lady Celeste by the lych-gate.

"I shall pray daily for your speedy recovery, dearest Aunt." Celeste took her aunt's hands in both of hers. The

moment of parting had arrived, and she felt woefully un-
prepared for it. She wanted to say something memorable,
something loving, but the words hung back like shy choir-
boys.

"*Adieu,* my heart." Marguerite lifted her face for a last
kiss. "I shall hold you in my thoughts, and pray they keep
you safe in this miserable country." She returned Celeste's kisses on both cheeks, then gave herself a little
shake. "You, Brother Cuthbert! I have a bone or two to
pick with you. First, let us discuss your wine cellar."

Celeste grinned as she slipped out the door, leaving the
poor monk to his own defenses. At least Aunt Marguerite
had not again mentioned that awful idea of the wedding
night. Perhaps it had merely been rambling talk brought
on by one of Brother Cuthbert's potions for pain. After
receiving a blessing from Father Jocelyn and giving Jeremiah a final hug and a kiss, Celeste skipped out to the lych-
gate where Gaston waited to hand her up onto her dap-
pled gray palfrey.

An unabashed giggle bubbled up from her throat when
she caught sight of Brother Guy. His loose brown robe
hiked up to his thighs, he sat astride a meek-looking little
donkey. His long bare legs dangled on either side, almost
touching the ground. A thunderous expression clouded the
brother's angelic face. When he heard her inadvertent
laughter, he stared up at the blue-washed skies and appeared to be already deep in prayer.

Celeste rolled her eyes in silent exasperation at Gaston.
Oh, la, la! This adventure would not turn into a somber,
psalm-singing journey—not if she could help it.

Chapter Four

How long had it been since he had last ridden beyond the walls of Saint Hugh's? As the little party crested the hill, Guy looked back over his shoulder at the squat priory buildings. Bluebells had dotted the fields with splashes of spring color when he first came down this road, going in the opposite direction. He recalled that his heart had been as light as the April breezes that ruffled his hair. Now a cold north wind blew across the bare patch of his novice's tonsure. He had not expected to leave Saint Hugh's until that distant day when God called him to his final rest and his fellow monks carried his shrouded body out the lych-gate for burial.

A small, traitorous emotion fluttered within his breast as he inhaled the autumn's earthy smells and the scent of a peasant's woodsmoke. With a pang of guilt, Guy shook off the sudden pleasure he took in savoring the crisp air, the clean open sky, the harvested fields rolling to the horizon—and the disturbing company of the young lady who insisted upon riding beside him.

He cast Lady Celeste a surreptitious glance out of the corner of his eye and discovered with a sharp jolt that she examined him with an equal keenness.

"Bonjour, mon frère!" she sang in a lilting voice. Her deep purple eyes sparkled as amethyst crystals in a sunbeam. "I mean..." She paused for a moment, her delicate dark brows furrowed with some inner struggle. "Goo morrning, Broozer Guy." She drew out the English syllables, then cocked her head, reminding him of a clever robin waiting for a bounty of bread crumbs. "Well? Did I not say it correctly?" she asked in French.

Guy blinked. Was she expecting him to give her English lessons? By the look on that lovely young face, he realized that she did. Hadn't anyone told her about his vow?

She sighed with an uniquely French eloquence. "La, Brother Guy! You need only nod or to shake your head at my pronunciation. Is that too hard for you? It is a little nod, like this." She demonstrated, with a sly grin turning up the corners of her full mouth. "Or a mere shake, like so." She moved her head slowly from side to side, her gaze never leaving his face. "Goo morrning, Broozer Guy," she repeated.

He blew out his cheeks. They were scarcely a mile from the haven of Saint Hugh's, and already the little witch tempted him. Guy considered the long road ahead of them. Three hundred miles to Snape Castle, by his reckoning. He groaned inwardly.

"Hey-ho, Broozer Guy!" Her words, like warm raindrops, pattered through his musings.

No peace! He shot her his haughtiest look and shook his head. Her smile disappeared, and he was instantly sorry for its loss. She looked as if he had just struck her. Lesson one: Lady Celeste did not take criticism well.

"Was it the good-morning or your name that was not well-done?" she asked in French, with a toss of her head. The accompanying breeze lifted her veil, revealing the wealth of blue-black hair beneath.

Guy sighed again. Her prattle would drive him witless before Shrewsbury. At least her voice was pleasant on the ear.

"Goo morning," she repeated with a determined glare.

Guy inclined his head slightly. Perhaps she would take her small victory and reward him with blessed silence.

"*Bon!*" Celeste clapped her hands. "Broozer Guy?" she continued.

Guy shuddered and shook his head. Unhooking his slate from his belt, he let go of Daisy's reins long enough to print out *Brother* on it, underlining the *th*. He held out the slate for her perusal.

"Bro—" The pink tip of her tongue appeared enticingly between her white teeth.

Guy looked away quickly, though he could still see its wetness in his mind's eye as he listened to her draw out the *th* for an eternity.

"Bro-*th*-er, *oui?*" She finally released the poor word from her mouth.

Guy nodded, then nudged Daisy's belly with his bare knee. Perhaps the English lesson, which showed every promise of lasting until hell froze over, would be terminated if she saw only his back. He squared his shoulders as he moved ahead of her. Better this way. He didn't have to look at her, to see those mysterious purple eyes full of secrets, the blush of a midsummer's rose on her cheeks, or the curve of those luscious, full lips, which—

Guy ground his teeth together. Great Jove! From where had those secular thoughts sprung? He must not permit them to intrude again. He had renounced all cravings of his body six months ago.

A small sound behind him pricked his attention: a pent-up burst of air, followed by several others in quick succession. Was she crying? Had he offended her by riding ahead so abruptly? Churl! He glanced over his shoulder to apologize and saw that Celeste had covered her mouth with one gloved hand. Hearing her suppressed giggles, he realized that he was the source of her mirth. At that moment, a throaty laugh escaped her.

"Your pardon, Brother Guy, but it is too amusing!" She laughed again. Some of the men-at-arms nearby grinned at the contagious sound. "Your poor, poor little donkey! It is very hard to tell if she has four legs—or six! In truth, good Brother, you could walk all the way to Northumberland and still be sitting astride!" Full-blown gales of laughter punctuated this last remark. The escort joined in her mirth.

Guy scowled. Had the chit no respect for a man of the church, that she would laugh at his humble means of transportation? He looked down at Daisy's neck, with its rough ridge of a mane. Memories of Moonglow, his gray war-horse, rose in his mind. If this minx of a girl had but seen him astride that noble steed, she would never have laughed at him. Nay, she would have been frightened half to death. Smiling at the thought, he kneed Daisy into a faster walk. The donkey, a devil despite her meek facade, blew a loud, wet snort of protest through her nostrils.

"Oh, la, la! I have offended you, Bro-*ther* Guy?" The lady hurled the *th* sound after him. "Did they cut out your sense of humor when they shaved your tonsure?"

Guy chose to ignore her. He was bound to escort her to Snape Castle; he was not obliged to like her. In fact, a little mutual aversion might be healthier for the sake of his soul. Gaston, riding ahead of Guy, grinned over his shoulder at him before returning his attention to the meandering roadway ahead.

How wise Father Jocelyn had been to invoke this vow of silence! Had he not been so constrained, Guy knew, he would have broken a number of the holy Commandments by now. His long frame rattling with each plodding step the donkey took, Guy rode in stoic silence. They said the Blessed Mother had ridden a donkey all the way from Nazareth to Bethlehem when she was nine months pregnant with the Holy Infant. How on earth had she stood it?

Behind him, Lady Celeste maintained a surprising silence. Guy relaxed his shoulders. Perhaps she felt some remorse for her laughter and would maintain her own silence until eventide. Guy fervently hoped so.

A fly tickled his ankle. He shook his leg, then squinted against the sun at the milepost ahead. How many miles was it to the next town? The fly returned, this time landing on the back of his calf. Repressing the urge to swat at it, he shook his leg again. Saint Francis of Assisi, patron of his order, enjoined that the monks should respect the natural world and all its creatures, one of which was "Brother Fly."

I'm being tested, Guy thought as the annoying Brother Fly moved up to roam at the open nape of his neck. He waved his hand at it. *Respect all God's creatures, great and small.* The fly hovered at the sensitive skin behind his ear. Guy waggled his head to and fro. Why didn't Brother Fly pester Lady Chattering Magpie instead? Again he shook his head at the persistent insect. His conscience pricked him. It was wrong of him to wish ill upon the lady—or upon the poor fly, for that matter. *She* probably would have no compunctions about killing it. The fly landed on the bald patch of his tonsure. Guy brushed his fingers over it. Why couldn't the creature bother Daisy? Weren't flies supposed to be drawn to horses and their kin? They deserved each other. The persistent insect tickled his tonsure again.

One of the rear men-at-arms guffawed. Guy heard the other two shush him, though there was an odd tenor to their hissing. Suspicion formed in the back of Guy's mind. More noises, sounding for all the world like a number of fools' wind bladders, confirmed his theory. When next Brother Fly touched his ear, Guy whirled in his saddle.

Celeste froze, her eyes wide with surprise. In her hand, she held a long stalk of roadside grass, its downy tip inches from Guy's shoulder. He opened his mouth, remembered his vow in time, then pressed his lips tightly together.

"Poor Brother Guy!" Celeste murmured, recovering her composure. She held up the offending grass as if it were a queen's scepter. "What? Nary a smile? Not even the barest movement of your lips? Pah!" She sighed as she tossed the grass away. "Surely a smile is not breaking your vow of silence, good Brother? A smile is very quiet."

Her eyes sparkled with merry mischief, and her bowed mouth curled upward before it broke into a beguiling grin. Sweet Lord! How could any man resist such a charming aspect—even if she was just a mere girl!

"I ask you this, Brother Guy," she continued, as her smile increased in warmth. "If the good God above did not want us to laugh, why did he make it so pleasant to do so? *Oui*, it is easier by far to laugh than to frown, *n'est-ce pas?*" Cocking her head again, she regarded him through her long dark lashes.

Guy stared at her without moving a facial muscle, though his lips quivered to return her smile with one of his own. By the rood! Celeste had played a goodly trick on him with her piece of grass. In an earlier time, he would have— Nay! He could not give in to her teasing. Their journey together had just begun. He must maintain a firm upper hand. *Pride goeth before the fall,* a little voice whispered in the back of his mind.

* * *

The travelers picnicked in the forenoon by a clear spring that bubbled out of a cleft in the rocks before it continued on its rushing way to the sea, sixty miles to the southwest. The October breeze held the last warmth of the year, and wanton puffs of wind occasionally lifted the light veil covering the lady's hair. A few stray tendrils of black silk had worked their way loose from the confines of her French hood, and these tantalizing bits of beauty kissed her cheeks as the breezes did what Guy's fingers longed to do. Catching his wandering thoughts before they continued to their natural conclusion, Guy withdrew from the lady and her men. Seated on a grassy knoll beside the spring, Guy looked heavenward and began to say the office for the sext hour.

Behind him, he heard the low murmur of French, punctuated by male laughter. Daisy and the horses champed on the clumps of grass with noisy satisfaction. Above him, a flock of wild geese winged southward, to the warmer climes of Spain, honking their progress as they flew. An idyllic day. Just the sort of day Guy used to go a-hawking. In his mind's eye, he saw his favorite female peregrine soar from his wrist into the polished blue overhead, then pause at the zenith of her ascent. She could hang in the air, as if frozen in place—a black dot against the canopy of the sky. Then, folding her wings, she would drop at tremendous speed, snatching a dove in flight, before the gentle bird ever realized her fate.

Guy closed his eyes against the beauty of the day, trying to shut out images of bygone pleasures—pleasures he had happily renounced only a few months ago.

"Bro*ther* Guy?" Her husky voice swooped upon his thoughts as surely as his hawk had attacked the dove. Slowly, he opened his eyes.

"Does your vow also mean you do not eat?" Lady Celeste proffered a fine linen napkin on which she had arranged a tempting choice of bread, baked that morning in the priory's kitchen, wedges of apple, a soft white cheese and a half breast of cold roasted chicken. "If you grow faint with hunger and fall off that most ridiculous animal of yours, none of us will be able to lift you up again. You are far too...large."

Her gaze roved unashamedly over him, pausing at his shoulders, then moving down across his chest. Though she stood more than three feet away, he swore he could feel a searing heat wherever she looked. The lady blinked, then glanced away, instead of pursuing her assessment below his rough hemp belt. "In truth, you are quite the tallest of our company," she concluded with a delicate shrug of her shoulders, a careless movement that Guy found too enchanting.

"Your wretched beast has my deepest sympathies." Celeste thrust the food at him. "Eat, good Brother. Here is wine—good French wine." She held out a small clay cup, brimming with a ruby liquid. The sweet wines of France had been one of his earliest downfalls, when he first encountered them years ago, while attending King Henry at the fabulous Field of Cloth of Gold. Guy's taste buds quivered treacherously.

Shaking his head, he gently pushed the cup away, pointing to the spring. Her black-winged brows rose high across her forehead. "You drink water? Fah!" She wrinkled her face in disgust as she regarded the sparkling stream gushing a fat jet from the rocks. "The water of England is not drinkable," she pronounced in clear tones of authority. "And even if it were, this damp climate would not encourage the drinking of it. Here, Brother Hardhead."

She placed her food and wine on the grass beside him, then turned away with a wide sweep of her burgundy skirts. "Eat, and give thanks." She tossed the words over her shoulder as she picked her way back through the grass. "Or starve and so go to the devil!"

Guy struggled to repress his grin. What a little spitfire she was! Good! The lady would need every spark of spirit, if she was to survive the gloom of Snape Castle and the hands of her betrothed, Walter Ormond. The sweet taste of her apple turned sour in Guy's mouth as he remembered the last time he had seen Walter.

Ormond had been near twenty then, though his behavior had suggested five or six years younger. His father's eldest son, Walter had fancied he cut a fine figure amid Great Harry's sumptuous court, when, in truth, the nobles had laughed at him behind his back. Their humor had turned to mocking soon enough, and from there to animosity, except for Walter's small group of preening hangers-on. In a self-indulgent court where the royal pleasure commanded dancing, cardplaying, masques and hearty good times, Walter's gambling debts, overindulgence in expensive wines and obnoxious behavior had soon drawn disgust within the highest circles.

As to women, the servants had gossiped that young Ormond mounted them like a shameless dog—here, there and everywhere. Such behavior had made a deep impression—and one not long tolerated. Within two short years, Walter had managed to get himself banished not only from court, but from London, as well.

That had been four years ago, and if the rumors wafting around the gaming tables and the tiltyard were to be-lieved, "Ormond's Spawn" had not yet learned his lesson, but, instead, continued his wastrel ways in the north.

There, far from the refinements of the courtly life, Walter had sunk into coarser pursuits.

Guy could barely swallow the crusty bread as he considered the odious embrace into which he led the lady. How long would it take Ormond to curb her saucy humor? When would those twinkling purple eyes be filled with perpetual tears? How soon would the bloom in her cheeks turn to ashen gray and dark circles settle themselves under her eyes? And how many years would it be before the little French bird would give up her light spirit within Snape's cold stone walls?

Unthinking, Guy snatched the cup from the grass and downed its contents in one ferocious gulp. The Bordeaux's unaccustomed tang smarted, making his eyes water. By Saint George, he hadn't meant to drink her wine! Nor to eat her good cheese and sweet fruit. He had promised himself to dine only on bread and water, in penance for his wandering thoughts. He caught himself before he dashed the cup against the rocks. What injury had the cup done him? Nay, 'twas the little temptress's spell that wove itself about him. A trill of her laughter brought him back to the present. With a quick prayer, asking for strength and forgiveness, Guy rose and ambled back to the group.

"Eh bien!" Gaston grinned at the sight of the empty cup in Guy's hand. "It is good you eat and drink well. Forgive my bluntness, Brother Guy, but from the looks of those shoulders, you would have made a better knight for your king than for the good Lord. Those hands were made to draw a bow, hold a sword or stroke a—" Gaston broke off with an abrupt fit of coughing that left his countenance even ruddier than before.

Maintaining his composure, Guy stared over the sergeant's shoulder, as if he had no idea what the remainder of Gaston's observation might have been. The lady, either unmindful of the implied remark or choosing to ignore it, stood and brushed a few crumbs from her gown.

"Do not tease the good brother so, Gaston," she remarked mildly, attacking the *th* sound with a sharp thrust of her tongue. "His shoulders must be wide enough to carry the weight of all our sins with him when he prays for us. *N'est-ce pas,* Brother Guy?" A flutter of mirth danced on her lips.

Inside the long sleeves of his robe, Guy clenched his fists, digging his nails into his palms. His heart hammered against his chest. *How long, O Lord, will I be able to resist her?* When his breathing became more steady, he pointed to the sky, then to the horses.

"*Oui,* he is right, my lady." Gaston gave her his arm. "The sun does not wait for us. We must hurry on, if we are to reach a decent inn before dark."

"I hope the days to come are as pleasant as this one," the lady remarked as Gaston helped her into the saddle. She arched one eyebrow at Guy when he settled himself once more on Daisy's bony back. "I do enjoy such gladsome company. And so we shall make merry all the way to Snape Castle." She urged her horse into a walk.

I should be escorting you to my home, Lissa, and not into the maw of the Ormonds.

That thought from nowhere seared his mind like a flaming arrow. Its sharpness and heat so amazed him, Guy reined Daisy to a halt and found himself sneezing in the dust of the mended wagon as the lady and her luggage ambled past him along the king's post road.

By the holy Book, was he fast losing his wits?

Chapter Five

"For shame, Brother Guy!" Celeste clucked her tongue at him. "Why must you frown on such a pretty afternoon? God saw fit to give you a..." She paused as she surveyed him intently. "A passable face, but you mar it with a sour look."

Guy could only grimace his frustration. Couldn't she leave him alone? Why didn't she talk to Gaston, or one of the other men? Guy squinted into the sun. Two more hours of good light before they would have to start looking for lodging. Surely she could do something else in that time besides concentrating her entire attention upon him. Where were her manners? Hadn't anyone ever told her she shouldn't make personal remarks, especially to men she barely knew?

"Poor Brother Guy," Celeste continued ignoring his unsociability. "Perhaps the wine at noon did not agree with his digestion. What think you, Starlight?" Leaning over her horse's neck, she spoke into its pricked ear. All the while, her eyes twinkled with lavender amusement.

What in the name of all the saints was a mere man supposed to do? She knew he wasn't allowed to speak. Guy ducked to avoid her pretty eyes. A girl like that shouldn't possess such winsome weapons. In truth, Guy could not recall another pair of eyes that had glowed with such a joy of life. One glance from her and a man could declare himself drunk from the experience. Her eyes were beautiful, so full of fire, so full of passion, so full of the promise of—

God forgive him! What was he doing meditating on the eyes of a little black-haired temptress? No doubt his thoughts wandered because he had not been near a woman for over six months. In truth, women bored him, didn't they? What was more, not one of his former dalliances possessed an ounce of virtue or honor. Nor did this lady, who was not only female—but French! Guy kicked Daisy in the flanks, much harder than he intended.

The donkey snorted at the sudden command for more speed. Uttering an offensive sound not fit for polite company, Daisy lowered her head and dug her hooves into the dirt of the road. Before Guy realized her intent, she kicked out with her back legs, tossing her rider over her ears. Guy landed headfirst in a ditch. For almost a full minute, his ears rang with the chiming of a hundred cathedral bells and he saw swirling stars instead of the blue sky.

As the clanging subsided and the heavens regained their correct color, Guy realized that his loose gown had fallen around his ears. The cold air blowing across his bare backside told him that a very private part of his anatomy had made an unexpected appearance. A rich peal of feminine laughter confirmed his worst suspicions.

Rolling over, he struggled to sit up, despite the fact that the landscape tended to tilt sideways.

"Magnifique!" Celeste laughed with unabashed humor. Gaston and the men-at-arms joined her. "Forsooth, Brother Guy, I have never seen such...such... " Another fit of merriment overcame her.

A string of dormant oaths crowded behind Guy's lips as he pulled himself into a standing position. He clamped his teeth tightly together to keep back the tide of his righteous anger.

"Such a beautiful moon in the middle of the day!" The chit managed to complete her sentence before erupting into another gale of laughter.

The tips of Guy's ears burned as a hot flush spread itself up from his neck. Perdition take the girl! For a farthing, he would haul the little vixen off her horse, turn her over his knee and soundly administer a well-deserved chastisement to her backside. How dare she laugh at him!

Guy clambered out of the ditch. His fingers shook with suppressed rage as he snatched up the reins of the innocent-looking donkey. Turning his back to her, he slowly remounted the creature. Surely Father Jocelyn could not have foreseen this situation when he placed the novice under his vow of silence. Guy itched to let loose a torrent of words that would truly shock the brazen minx.

"Peace, my lady," Gaston hissed at her. "See? You have offended the good brother. What would your aunt say to this behavior?"

Celeste managed to stifle her laughter in a series of hiccups before answering. "Gaston! You know very well what she would do. While she scolded me with her tongue, her eyes would have enjoyed the same view as much as mine. Perhaps even more so. In truth, I have never seen . . ."

Gaston cleared his throat loudly, then glared at the other men, who were still sniggering at the memory of the monk's naked show. "You crawling vermin!" he shouted. "Are you paid to idle about? Be off with you!"

He punctuated his order with several blistering oaths. Just listening to their richness and variety made Guy feel better. It pleased him even more to see how Celeste blushed at Gaston's curses. Good! If the girl was going to act like a common serving wench, she deserved to have her sensitivities shocked in return.

Holding his head high and squaring his shoulders, Guy nudged the now-placid Daisy into a walk. Laugh at his backside? No woman of his considerable experience had ever found his nakedness a rude jest! They had complimented his goodly proportions and firmness in all areas. They had squealed and giggled with delight upon personal inspection of his nether regions. Most particularly, their supple fingers had given pleasurable approval to his hindquarters. Not once had any woman, high-born or low-born, *laughed* at the sight of his most sensitive area—until now.

What a sweep of vanity!

A niggling little voice whispered its rebuke. True, vanity was sin, and he should pay the price for it. But must her amusement be his penance? Guy swallowed the bile that lurked in the base of his throat. Perhaps he should say a few prayers to calm his soul's turmoil. Upon reflection, he amended that thought. He needed to storm heaven's gate with a quiver full of litanies begging forgiveness for his unseemly thoughts and beseeching patience to deal with his charge.

"Good Brother Guy." Celeste's husky voice spoke close behind his shoulder. Gone was her comic pronunciation of his name. Did he detect a new note in her tone?

"Good Brother, please forgive me," she continued. Her lilting accent made the language sing. Guy glanced in her direction.

If anything, Celeste's eyes looked even more enormous—twin pools of crushed violets, watered by a sheen of tears that he could see hovering about her thick lashes. The shameless jade of a moment ago had now changed into a fairy creature. Her pale skin, those teary eyes and her rosy mouth, trembling with her contrition, made Celeste appear like the virgin in a tapestry who lured the unsuspecting unicorn to her side. A mixture of emotions played havoc with Guy's body. In some places he hardened and burned, while in others he melted into the folds of his woolen gown. His vocal cords begged to murmur sweet nothings in her ear. He swallowed again.

"Frère Guy," she entreated, leaning across her horse to him. He stared straight ahead. "Bless me, good Brother, for I have sinned most grievously. Forgive my laughter at your misfortune, and my disgraceful conduct afterward."

Out of the corner of his eye, he saw her mouth twitch at the remembrance of that very behavior for which she now sought forgiveness. Licking her lips with that enticing pink tongue, she wiped away the suggestion of an uncontrite giggle.

"I am heartily sorry for having offended you, particularly as you are a man of God. Please forgive me, Brother Guy, and give me a penance, that I may show you my true sorrow for the transgression."

Penance? Sweet Saint Anne! She was not merely asking for forgiveness, but for the full sacramental rite. Cold beads of perspiration popped out on his forehead. Did Celeste think him to be a priest, and so felt her laughter a true sin of disrespect, perhaps even sacrilege? Guy's momentary shock melted into something entirely different— a smug anticipation of revenge.

Gravely he nodded at Celeste, then made the sign of the cross over her bowed head. *Wicked!* the little voice twittered in Guy's conscience. Not so. He told himself he was merely giving her what she craved, absolution, as well as what she needed—a lesson in humility.

"Merci, bon frère. And for my penance?"

How could he possibly deny her request? Taking out his slate and chalk, he quickly wrote on it, then handed it over to her.

"*Ma foi!* Fifty Ave Marias?"

Guy tried not to smile at her appalled expression.

"That will take me hours to say!"

He fervently hoped so—perhaps even until suppertime.

Celeste lost count somewhere past the thirty-seventh Ave. Fah! The late afternoon was too lovely to spend with one's head bowed over the neck of a horse. Rolling her shoulders back to ease the tension in her muscles, Celeste shifted in her saddle and gazed at the road in front of her— and at a pair of wide shoulders clothed in a coarse brown woolen habit.

How very big Brother Guy was! Celeste grinned as she enjoyed the sight of his well-proportioned calves, which gripped the donkey's sides. She wondered if the monk could run very fast, especially in that cumbersome robe. What would he think if she challenged him to a race? At L'Étoile, Celeste had always beaten her sisters whenever they managed to avoid the disapproving eye of Aunt Marguerite and ran down the long, grassy *allée* in the garden. Her gaze traveled up his back and rested on the tan bald patch of his tonsure. What would Brother Guy look like if all his hair grew back in? Such a golden color! She sighed.

Was his hair soft or rough to the touch? It looked soft as a baby's, but his body proclaimed him a man. She shook herself and said another Ave Maria quickly. She wondered if it was wrong to stare at a monk's body that way.

Such broad shoulders! Did his mother have to make his shirts extrawide, so that the sleeves would not rip out when he practiced with his sword? Surely he must have used a

sword at some time in his life—before he became a man of
God. His accent and his noble bearing suggested that he
came from a good family, and it was no sin to know how
to use arms. Saint Michael was a warrior, as well as an angel. What would Brother Guy look like in a suit of armor
such as the one worn by the hero of her dreams, the Knight
of the Loyal Heart? Celeste could easily imagine Brother
Guy wearing the winged heart on his helm.

Thinking of her favorite book reminded Celeste of the
troubadour songs. It seemed like a month of Sundays since
she had last heard those sweet tunes. She caught herself
saying the next prayer while humming "The True Heart's
Lament." How well the Latin words fit with the simple
melody! She hummed another Ave, slightly louder.

Over his shoulder, Brother Guy scowled at her.

Zut alors! Didn't that man ever smile? Such a pity! He
had such a handsome face. Perhaps he was out of practice. Maybe smiling was forbidden in the monastery. No
matter. They would be together on the road for many days
to come. Celeste knew she could get him to smile at her
eventually. People always did. She cocked her head and
grinned at him as she continued to hum.

The monk put a long finger to his lips.

Celeste resisted the urge to stick her tongue out at him.
What a sobersides!

"I am saying my penance," she told him in an innocent
tone of voice.

Frowning, Brother Guy shook his head. He put his finger to his lips again.

"Bah! You did not say anything about the method of my
prayers, Brother Guy." She deliberately blew the difficult
th sound out of her mouth. "Do you not chant your own
prayers—that is, when you are permitted to speak?"

Guy's finely arched eyebrows rose slowly up his wide forehead.

"Just so," Celeste continued, sensing she had made a point. "You chant and I hum. Now, I have not heard the quality of your voice, so I do not know if your chanting offends the ear of the Divine or not, but—"

He scowled again. Celeste wondered if that was a good or bad sign. She plunged on with her logic.

"But I have been told on excellent authority that I possess a sweet singing voice. I would not say this of myself, you understand, but only because others—"

The monk waved his hand at her, signaling the end of his attention. Gathering that she had been granted permission to continue her unusual mode of prayer, Celeste cleared her throat.

"*Ave Maria, gratia plena,*" she sang, to the tune of "Lancelot and Guinevere." As Guy turned away, Celeste thought she spied the hint of a grin hover around his lips and a softer look steal into his blue eyes.

"*Sancta Maria.*" She let her voice lift to the heavens, her spirit in tune with the sweet melody.

I shall capture your elusive smile yet, Brother Guy! Just watch me!

Chapter Six

The slanting rays of the setting sun softened the red sandstone walls of the massive castle above the town of Ludlow as Guy led the weary bridal party across the Ludford Bridge. Halfway up the steep slope of Broad Street, he turned Daisy into the yard of one of the town's more reputable inns, the Feathers. The fresh-painted sign proudly displayed a trio of white plumes, the badge of the Prince of Wales, in honor of the last Plantagenet heir to the throne, the ill-fated King Edward V, who had lived in Ludlow before returning to London, where he had met his mysterious end in the Tower.

Now the Tudors ruled England, after a century of civil unrest. Guy wondered if the news of King Henry's obsessive infatuation with Anne Boleyn had reached the ears of this hamlet, so far from the intrigues of Westminster. How would this landlord react if he knew that Henry's lawful queen, Catherine, was ignored and virtually banished from the court? Being a prudent man with an obviously thriving hostelry, the innkeeper would probably only shrug.

After stepping off Daisy's back, Guy turned toward Celeste to help her down from her saddle, but slowed his steps before he reached her. That service was Gaston's by right. He watched Gaston place both hands around Celeste's slim waist and lift her easily from her palfrey. Sweet Saint Anne! The girl must weigh less than thistledown. A green worm of envy wriggled through Guy. He pushed away the insidious emotion, reminding himself that she was merely his charge. He had already dedicated his heart to a higher calling.

"Thank the guardian angels the monk knew of a good rest house," muttered Gaston, handing Celeste her saddlebag. His gaze swept around the washed-down cobbled yard. "This is the best lodging I've seen in a fortnight."

Celeste studied the wide half-timbered facade, with its many gabled windows jutting out from under the slate roof. *"Oui."* She chewed her lower lip. "But who will speak to the innkeeper, now that Aunt Marguerite is no longer with us?"

She broke into a smile when she spotted Guy, standing by Starlight's head. "Ah, Brother Guy! Will you use your slate and tell the innkeeper what we require for the night?" She looked relieved at the idea.

In answer, Guy took out his slate and quickly wrote upon it. He passed his message to Celeste.

Probably can't read, spelled the blurry chalk letters.

Her eyes darkened into twin purple storm clouds. "But if the innkeeper is unlettered, who will speak to him?"

She looked adorable, standing in the middle of the bustling yard, clutching her worn leather bag with such a perplexed look on her upturned face. Guy almost smiled at her, but caught himself in time. Hardening his features, he gravely pointed to her.

"Moi?" she squeaked, her eyes widening at the prospect. "But my English is so...so barbaric."

Guy wiped the slate with his sleeve, then wrote *Good practice for you.*

"Fah!" she snorted. Guy remained unmoved. "Well, if it is to be, then let us confront this English lion in his den. At least, it looks to be a clean den." Turning on her heel, she marched smartly to the door of the taproom, with Guy and Gaston following close behind.

"Such fire, that little one!" Gaston chuckled. "Let us hope her new husband is not a milksop, or she will reduce him to pudding."

Guy gnashed his teeth at the thought. Walter Ormond was no whey-faced boy. Nor would he be ruled by anyone—certainly not a sweet maid with a poor command of the English language. Guy reminded himself once again that her future married life was none of his concern. Why not? that annoying little voice asked him as he pushed his way through the door of the boisterous Feathers.

Unerringly, Celeste singled out the master of the establishment. *"Pardon, monsieur."* Taking a deep breath before continuing, she ran her tongue over her lips, which immediately gained her the innkeeper's appreciative attention.

"We want room for the night, yes?" Celeste smiled coquettishly at the ruddy-faced man and fluttered her lashes.

Hooding his eyes, Guy observed her. The little vixen might be young, but she knew enough tricks to befuddle a man's wits.

The innkeeper appraised her with a shrewd glance. "Frenchies, by the look of ye."

Celeste drew herself up to her full height, which put her at chin level with the man. *"Oui,* but we pay in the English silver." She flashed him a brilliant smile, then nodded toward Guy. "And the goood bro*ther* 'ere is English and understands all you say."

Stepping forward at this introduction, Guy loomed over the host. Taking in the monk's height and shoulder width, the innkeeper stepped back a pace.

"Begging yer pardon, Friar, but we had a wee bit o' trouble with the frogs afore, and a man can't be too trust in' with any o' that lot."

Before Guy could react, Celeste erupted with a sputter of French, followed by an equal torrent of English. "Frog? *Mon Dieu!* 'E says I am the frog?" A delightful blush of pink crept into her cheeks. "Bah! *Imbécile!* Am I green? Do I 'ave the face of the frog? Look you!"

Lifting the hem of her gown, she displayed a slim ankle and the lower portion of a shapely calf, encased in a bright yellow silk stocking. "Is this the leg of a frog?"

The landlord whistled through his gapped teeth at the unexpected sight, while the nearby patrons of the taproom craned their necks for a better view. Glowering, Gaston tugged at her hand.

"Lady Celeste! Drop your skirt!," he muttered in rapid French. "What do you want these pigs to think you are—a woman of no reputation? Marguerite de la Columbiaire would have my brains served for a dog's breakfast if she knew what you were doing."

"My aunt will never know, Gaston," Celeste whispered back to him, though she immediately let go of the velvet burgundy skirts.

Guy stepped closer to her and sent a scorching look at the jostling assembly. Jesu! This was only the first night! He would be lucky to get her to Snape Castle in one piece, at this rate. And why did she have to possess such a fine leg? He promised himself he would sleep without bedding tonight in penance for the pleasure he took in the revelation of that dainty part of her.

Celeste smoothed her skirts, then cocked her head at the innkeeper. "Now, *monsieur*, do I 'ave the room?" Smiling, she fluttered her lashes again. "The best in the 'ouse, *oui?*"

"My pleasure, m'lady," he all but slobbered.

"I also 'ave men, 'orses, and the wagon?" Her smile became broader.

"The stable lad will see to them. 'Tis a shilling a horse."

Celeste looked to Guy for approval.

Glaring at the landlord, the monk shook his head. The man was nothing less than a highway brigand. Guy held up four fingers, then all ten.

"Ah, the good Brother Guy say three shillings for all our 'orses, and my men-at-arms—weeth supper, oui? 'E is a man of God, *monsieur*, and is *très 'onest*."

Repressing a smile at her bargaining skills, Guy nodded in agreement. The landlord glanced at the giant monk, then to the grim-faced sergeant, and finally to the dimpled lady. He threw up his hands in resignation.

"I'll be a-standing in line at the dole hatch yet, and no mistake, but seein' that ye've men-at-arms, I trust ye to be a lady of—" He flushed and glanced at the hem of her gown, which now primly concealed the yellow silken leg. "Of quality. 'Tis me best room, at your service. Second floor, at the end of the hall."

Celeste produced a groat from her reticule, which hung from her waist. Taking the landlord's beefy hand in both of hers, she pressed the coin into his palm. "*Merci, monsieur*. And there will be 'ot water and a fire and supper, all in an instant, *oui?*"

"*Oui*," the man gasped, not even noticing the size of the tip he grasped. Several of the onlookers thumped their wooden cups on the oaken table with noisy good humor.

"Lady Celeste, a wise soldier knows when it is time to withdraw. That time is now." Gaston looked to Guy, who nodded his agreement.

Good for you, Gaston! Get her out of sight before she stirs up too much unwelcome interest. Slipping his hand under Celeste's elbow, Guy guided her firmly toward the stairs. As they ascended, her smothered giggles surprised him.

"I did well, *non?*"

Guy looked straight ahead, though he curled his fingers tighter around her arm. He strove to ignore what his practiced touch told him lay inside the velvet sleeve. She felt warm and soft, yet a current of wildfire coursed through her being—a promise of passion that would set a man's soul blazing. Jesu! He must kneel half the night in solemn prayer for harboring such tempting sweet thoughts.

The room proved to be surprisingly well appointed. Firewood lay stacked on the hearthstone, waiting to be laid. A tinderbox promised relief from the chill night air. A stout table and two plain chairs sat before the fireplace. Celeste gave a small chirp of pleasure when she spied the large canopied bed in one corner.

"*C'est bon!*" she pronounced as she prodded the coverlet. "Clean linen, and the mattress feels as if it has been newly stuffed." Leaning over, she investigated the underside. "New roping, and the chamber pot is clean. This landlord keeps a good inn."

Without further ado, she began to push the saddlebag under a corner of the mattress. Guy glanced at Gaston, his brows raised in surprised query.

"Lady Celeste's dowry, good Brother." Gaston knelt at the fireplace and began to lay several of the split logs on the iron dogs.

A thick piece of ice felt lodged in the back of Guy's throat. By all the devils in hell, was the silly creature carrying a large bag of gold as if it were a change of stockings? What could her father have been thinking, to send her off with only a few men and such a fortune? And why wasn't Gaston more concerned? Guy shot a fierce look at the sergeant's back.

Celeste's honeyed laughter rippled over him. "Oh, la, la, Gaston! If you could see what a fearful face our good Brother Guy just made!"

His glare at her only provoked more laughter.

"Hey-ho, *mon frère!* Now what have I done to so displease you? In truth, I have said all my penance, and I do not laugh at your... that is, at you again."

Guy pointed at the saddlebag, which poked out from under the covering. Celeste arched one sable brow.

"My dowry? But surely you expected that I would have it with me." Her lips pursed together into a delectable pout, though her eyes twinkled.

Such kissable lips! Guy caught himself wondering if any young nobleman of France had savored the sweetness of those lips. Frowning more to himself than to Celeste, he snapped his fingers, then pointed to the bag.

"You wish to see my dowry?" Celeste cocked her head. Gaston regarded Guy with a thoughtful expression.

"Let him see what you carry, my lady," the old soldier suggested softly. "Since we have been given into his charge, he should know all. As you said, he is a man of God, and honest." Gaston unsheathed his dagger, studying its keen edge as if he had never seen it before.

Celeste shrugged, then pulled the bag out from under the mattress. "*D'accord.* I agree." She plopped it on the table, then slid it toward Guy. "I fear it is not the treasure of the Eastern kings.'' While Guy fumbled with the buckle, she strolled to the window.

After opening the flap, Guy withdrew a blue leather box; neither its flatness nor its light weight denoted a chest of coins. Lifting the lid, he frowned at the contents with some confusion.

''*Oui,* good Brother,'' Gaston remarked, in the same soft tone, though Guy detected a note of danger beneath it. ''You see before you the worth my master has placed upon his youngest daughter.'' The sergeant spat into the fire, causing it to hiss as if a small serpent lurked within the flames.

Though her back was to him, Guy saw Celeste stiffen.

Nestled on a bed of ivory satin were twelve silver apostle spoons, the tiny figures of the saints on the handles shining with a thin gilt wash. Picking up one, Guy recognized Saint James the Greater by the minute pilgrim's staff clutched in his right hand. A pilgrim's hat hung down his back, and a tiny dove, no bigger than a pin's head, sat on the saint's halo. From the nicks and scratches in the bowl of the spoon, Guy deduced that the set was not only old, but well-used. Though the silver appeared of good quality, he knew the collection was not an appropriate dowry for a French noblewoman. Holding out the spoon to Gaston, he questioned the old soldier with a lift of his brows.

''A christening present, I heard.'' Gaston's lip curled down. ''And an old one, at that.''

Guy shoved his hand deeper into the saddlebag. Surely there must be something else besides this. A deed to a French estate, perhaps? Gaston chuckled without mirth.

''By the beard of Beelzebub, that's the whole of it.'' He spat again into the fire.

With her back still to him, Celeste spoke from her position by the window. ''I have four older sisters, Brother

Guy. They..." Her voice wavered for a split second. She cleared her throat, then continued in a stronger tone. "They made brilliant matches with some of the finest families in all of France. Their marriage contracts cost my father much more than anticipated. Then, when it seemed almost too late, my little brother, Philippe, was born. After that..." She turned around, her deep purple eyes piercing the distance between them.

"My father wished to protect the rest of the estate for his only heir. It is understandable. But I was still unspoken for. Then your King Henry came to Calais to meet with our King François at the Field of Cloth of Gold."

Guy heard the note of awe in her voice. He, too, remembered that fortnight—or, at least, some of it. He had been a reckless twenty-year-old then, and eager to win his spurs in the tournaments. His angelic good looks, as well as his prowess with lance, sword and bow, had won him many prizes and far too much acclaim. The adulation had gone to his head as quickly as the good burgundy wines that flowed from the many fountains set up amid the colorful silken tents.

The ladies of both camps had made much of the tall young courtier from England. He had passed every night in the giggling company of the fair sex, who offered their own prizes in a much more intimate sport. Maids and matrons alike—not one of them had resisted when he wooed. Not one of them had pleaded honor, virtue or fidelity as he untied the laces of their shifts. Guy blinked to erase his lusty youth from his memory. That was behind him now— worth less than the trampled grass of that French meadow where kings had once played and strutted like peacocks.

Celeste stared into the fire, and its glow sparkled in the depths of her eyes. "Such a sight it was, Brother Guy! The world has never seen the like of that fairy-tale city of tents.

By the time we returned home, I was betrothed to Walter Ormond, the son of an English lord.''

"English!" Gaston spat out the word like a curse.

"This midsummer, I passed my eighteenth birthday and, as agreed between my father and Sir Roger Ormond, I have journeyed here to wed my English lord. But..." She cast a long look at the spoon, which Guy still held between his fingers. "My father could not spare much for my dowry. There is Philippe, you see...."

She plucked another spoon from its satin nest and twirled it in the firelight. Guy saw that it was Saint Mark, with his open book and a small lion crouched at his feet. "They are quite pretty, *n'est-ce pas?* And the workmanship is fine." She carefully replaced it among its fellows. "When Sir Roger meets me and sees what a good wife I will make his son, he will not mind too much if my dowry is small, do you think?" She looked at Guy, with hope coloring her expression.

His heart slammed against his chest. Sir Roger would have to be blind not to see what a pearl of great price the chevalier of Fauconbourg had thrown at the Englishman's feet. But Guy knew the senior Ormond well enough. Clarity of sight was not one of the old man's stronger points. The lord would be livid when Celeste finally arrived at Snape Castle and presented this paltry box to him. And was Walter counting on French golden ecus to buy him back into King Henry's good graces? Would he take out his disappointment on the flesh of this sweet angel?

"While I do not have a wealth of gold in my bag, good Brother, I count my virtue, my loyalty and my honor as precious as jewels. Sir Roger is a good man, I am sure. Were I to arrive at his threshold in only my shift, with my spoons, he would still greet me as a worthy bride for his son. I know it, for is he not a knight, and so bound by the laws of chivalry?''

Guy tore his gaze from the depths of her eyes, his mouth working in silent protest. Your father is a bastard! he wanted to cry out to the sooty beams above their heads. And Sir Roger was no gentle knight of a romantic tale, but a grasping, thieving, murdering half savage who lived by his sword in the wilds of Northumberland.

No, sweet Lissa, Roger Ormond and his wastrel son will melt your little spoons for the few coins they will make and, after Walter has finished using your soft body for his perverted pleasures, he will toss you and your fine ideals into the mud with the slops.

Chapter Seven

The cold wind from the North Sea whined around the stone corners and through the chinks of Snape Castle's dank chapel. His face as chill and unmoving as the walls surrounding him, Sir Roger Ormond watched the flames of thick beeswax candles flicker above the casket of his second wife as an age-bent priest muttered through the poetic sequence passages of the mass of the dead.

"Liber scriptus proferetur, in quo totum continetur, unde mundus judicetur," he intoned in a reedy, nasal voice. *Then shall written book be brought, showing every deed and thought; from which judgment will be sought.*

Roger's lip twitched. His one good eye stared at the rough-hewn wood that concealed the body of his wife. What thoughts had ever lingered in Edith's goosedown brain? he wondered. The woman had barely ever whispered more than two sentences together. When she stood before the throne of God, what judgment could he render to such a coney rabbit as her? What deeds had she done, either good or bad, during the three-and-twenty years she had lived upon this earth, except to hover in the shadows and whimper when Roger visited her bed? Aye, the wench had been a ghost long before she died.

But the children ... His eye moved from the larger coffin to the two smaller ones next to it. Somewhere deep inside him, a stinging pain thumped against his heart, as if a lute string, too tightly wound, had snapped, recoiling painfully upon the musician's fingers. Edward, nearly five, and his sister, little Edith. Their mother accompanied her children in death. Roger sighed softly. Was it only two days ago they had clambered upon his knee, begging for the spiced wine-dipped sops from his trencher? How like little birdlings they had been, so rosy and bright, as they gobbled the dripping treats from his fingers!

Then had come the headaches: first the boy, then little Edith, and afterward, in the gloaming, their mother had pressed her temple against the cold stone of the stairwell and sworn she could not climb the curving steps. The children had cried that the hall spun about them like a whirligig, and Roger had seen their eyes grow too bright by the devil-dancing fire on the hearth. Roger had ordered them carried up to bed, the three tucked in together. In less than an hour, their bodies had poured forth a stinking sweat. Little Edith had raved that she saw a small boy, all clothed in gold, standing by the door, beckoning to her. Edward had moaned that his head was bursting. Their mother had said nothing, merely whispered the name "Jesu."

Then, at the turn of the hourglass, the three had breathed as one and then were gone. The nurse, a superstitious old fool from the Border country, swore she had seen their spirits arise from the soaking bed and fly out the high arched window—the baby in her mother's arms and Edward laughing and skipping before them.

Riders from York had warned Roger that the dread sweating sickness had stalked the cobbled streets of that fair city since late August, but he had ignored them. Even when he heard that the king's paramour, Anne Boleyn, had been taken ill, Roger had shrugged off the news as only a tidbit of court gossip. There had never been an outbreak of that strange illness at Snape Castle, not even the year before, when so many in the southern shires had died. Suddenly, within the space of a week, Roger had lost a number of peasants who tilled the home fields, then some of the household in the laundry and pantry, then a groom, a gardener, and, last of all, death had reached out his bony hand and dared to take Roger's own.

So merry at dinner the children had been; so very dead by that evening's doleful supper.

"Judex ergo, cum sedebit, quidquid latet, apparebit..." The priest droned on. *Before the Judge enthroned, shall each hidden sin be owned.*

Roger shifted slightly, then glared at Edith's coffin again. *She* had no sins, hidden or otherwise—of that much Roger was sure. She hadn't had the wit to commit them. He, on the other hand... Zounds! Time enough for thinking of that later—when these same words were uttered over his own wooden box.

A snigger from his blind side distracted Roger's morbid meditations. He shifted his position so that his son's profile came within his line of sight. Of late, Walter had taken to staying on his father's right hand, even though he had known from early childhood this annoyed Roger. Though his left eye was still as keen as a swooping hawk's, Roger's loss of the right bored deeply into his vanity. Where once a silver-gray eye had regarded the world in unison with its mate, now a jagged white scar pressed the lid shut, covering the empty socket. A Border cattle raid thirty-two years ago, during Roger's youthful days, when both his judgment and his fighting skills were green, had left him half-blind and twice as wise.

With Edward and little Edith gone, his eldest son, Walter, remained the lone survivor of eight children—the result of Roger's two misadventures in the marriage market. Women did not seem to last long here in the cold, wet north. Even as the funeral mass was being chanted, another woman—some chit from France—was on her way to Roger's door. He wondered if Walter's bride-to-be had put any meat on her bones since the last time he saw her, eight years ago. He remembered her as a scrawny pullet of nine or ten—all legs and arms, with large dark eyes and a high-pitched giggle. She had better be more filled out by now, or the winter would claim her before she got half a chance to breed Walter a son.

Walter chuckled again, trying to muffle the sound in the folds of his thick woolen cloak. Roger frowned at his son's disrespect. Walter had never taken to his stepmother, but he should at least show the proper manners at her funeral. As Roger turned to glare at him, Walter lowered his head, drawing deeper into his clothing, like a tortoise into his shell.

Roger glared at the tall man next to him. Something was not quite right. He noted the pallor in Walter's complexion, and the angry inflammation around his eyes. Sweet Christ! Not his only son! Feeling his father's gaze upon him, Walter turned away. As he did so, the neck of his cloak slipped, revealing a small ulcerated lesion under his jawbone.

Roger clenched his teeth as he spied another sore behind Walter's ear and a third creeping into his hairline. As for the hair itself, Roger noticed for the first time that it looked more like an old, moth-eaten fur than the healthy brown locks Walter took such care to comb and perfume. God's teeth! The boy was riddled with the pox!

The bitter iron taste of bile rose in Roger's throat. All his life he had devoted himself to one goal—to advance the Ormond family from that of the petty landless knight his father had been to one of England's finest families, like that of his overlord, Sir Thomas Cavendish, earl of Thornbury. By the good fortune of riding on the victorious shirttails of Henry Tudor at Bosworth field, Roger's father had been granted Snape Castle, a poor holding on the windswept northern moors. Through two advantageous marriages, as well as a number of savage raids on his weaker neighbors and across the Scottish border, Roger Ormond had managed to expand his father's lands and increase the family fortune. Only fear of the powerful earl of Thornbury, whose vast domain now lay directly to the west of Snape Castle, kept the rapacity of the ambitious Ormonds at bay.

When Walter first arrived at Henry VIII's court six years ago, all the world, it seemed, had eagerly spread out their costly cloaks at the feet of the handsome young man. Roger winced inwardly at the memory. How proud he had been to see his son and heir feted and fawned over by the great of the land! That pride had turned to gall all too soon. Roger could not remember a time when his anger had so choked him as when Walter came crawling back to Snape, whining of his ill-treatment at the hands of the king himself.

Roger had hoped the disgrace would straighten out the headstrong boy. Perhaps in time, and with gold, the damage to the family's ambitions might be repaired. Instead, Walter had slunk into lower company and absented himself often from Roger's watchful gaze. Now the ghastly piper demanded to be paid his dire reckoning. And the price? God's nightshirt! What an ignoble end to such a promising beginning!

The priest had barely uttered the final *Pax Domine* when Walter turned on his heel to leave.

"Nay!" Roger's hand clamped around his son's wrist. "Whither away so quickly?"

"To ease my bladder, Father." Walter's thick cloak muffled the sting of his sneering reply. "Surely I do not need your permission to do that?"

"Then be quick about it. I will see you in my closet immediately after," Roger growled, tightening his grip.

"I have an appointment elsewhere." Walter broke his father's grasp, then edged backward into the deeper shadows of the emptying chapel.

"Attend to it later. I will see you first." Gathering his own cloak more tightly about him, Roger strode past the younger man. "Mark me, boy, or there will be the very devil to pay."

Roger did not wait for a further reply, but stalked through the doorway.

In the chill outer corridor, Roger spoke to one of his retainers. "Wait upon my son, Grapper," he instructed the burly man. "Make sure he is in my presence within a quarter of this hour."

"Aye, master." The servant touched his forelock.

"And if you must truss him like a bandy cock, then do so. I care not in what state he arrives, only that he comes."

The retainer grinned, revealing a few yellowed teeth rooted in blackened gums. "'Tis my pleasure, sir." With that, he hurried after Walter's retreating figure.

"Your man laid hands upon me!" Walter's fury choked his words.

Roger turned from the low fire where he had been warming himself after the cold of the burial service. "'Tis no surprise, since you were apprehended saddling your horse in the stable.''

Walter's eyes blazed from the shadows cast by his low hood. ''My appointment will not wait,'' he rasped. A cloud from his breath hung in the damp air before him.

Roger slammed his fist down on the thick oaken table-top, rattling the account ledgers stacked there. ''Your doxy can wait until doomsday! Indeed, she is better off without your attentions.''

Walter's shoulders shook with suppressed rage. ''My business is mine own. I take it ill that you should question me. I am of age, and I do as I please.'' He put his hand to the door latch of the tiny counting room.

Roger picked up a heavy clay inkpot and hurled it at his son. Walter swore a loud oath as the vessel missed his head by inches. Striking the door, the pot shattered; the ink splattered against the wood leaving a large black stain. Walter swore again when he saw that a number of thick drops had splashed onto his cloak.

''By the devil and his dam, you will not move until I give you leave!'' Planting his palms on the table, Roger leaned across it toward his son. The distance between them rippled with his hot wrath. ''Remove your cloak, knave!''

Walter backed away, nearly falling over a low three-legged stool. ''The room is cold. I prefer to keep it on.''

''Your cloak, sluggard, or shall I have Grapper cut it from your back?''

Walter opened his mouth to make some retort, then thought better of it. Unbuckling the clasp, he swung the heavy cloth from his shoulders with a flourish. Holding it at arm's length, he opened his hand, allowing the material to fall to the floor in a woolen puddle. He followed up with an elaborate bow, his right leg extended.

"Now take off your hat," his father ordered in a low dangerous voice.

Walter's eyes widened a moment before he assumed a cynical air. "Does my bonnet displease you, sir? Has my hatter been remiss? The color does not suit? I am most amazed."

Roger drew himself up to his full height. At six feet three inches, he enjoyed his reputation as a giant among men. Over the years, he had found that his mere presence could intimidate his adversaries, and he often made it a point to use his height and bulk to his advantage. "Your hat, Walter. I shall not ask again."

Backing against the wall, Walter snatched the black velvet bonnet from his head. He tossed it on top of his cloak. As he glared at his father, his eyes gleamed like twin daggers of heated Spanish steel.

Roger struck a flint to his tinderbox, and lighted the double-branched candlestick on his desk. Then he lit the candles on each side of the stone mantelpiece. The round tower room glowed with golden light.

Walter stared into the flames like a mesmerized moth. His tongue ran across his lips. "Are we celebrating the fair Edith's death?"

Roger replaced the tinderbox precisely next to his sealing wax. "How dare you!" he whispered, staring at his son. To his surprise, Roger found himself enjoying this little scene. He couldn't remember the last time Walter had looked so uncomfortable in his presence. "Have you no respect for the dead?"

"Only when you have respect for the living," Walter snarled in reply.

Roger crossed around to the front of the table, like a cat stalking a mouse in the dairy. Walter slid along the wall, putting as much distance between them as the room allowed. "Remove your doublet," Roger commanded in the same menacing whisper. "Be quick about it, knave. My quiver of patience is already spent this day."

"Is this some jest, Father?" Walter's gaze flickered across the closed door. "Is it your pleasure to freeze me to death?"

"If you were not my heir, I might be tempted to try it." Roger drew his dagger from his belt and ran his finger lightly along the blade. "The hour runs apace. Take off your doublet, and your shirt, as well."

Walter backed toward the fireplace. "Has your mind snapped in twain? I must give Edith more credit than I thought. I did not know you harbored so deep an affection for her that your brain has become sickly at her death."

With a roar, Roger vaulted over the stool. Shoving one arm against the younger man's throat, he pinioned his son against the wall. Ignoring Walter's struggles, Roger slashed through the padded green velvet and the cinnamon-colored satin lining of Walter's jacket. Within a minute, the expensive clothing hung in tatters from the young man's shoulders. This violent action reduced Walter to frozen shock.

Grabbing his son by the scruff of his neck, Roger pulled him into the center of the light cast by the four candles. When he saw the profusion of open sores dotting Walter's chest and disappearing below the drawstrings of his trunk hose, Roger nearly gagged. He pulled Walter's head closer to the flames. His stomach turned sour at the sight of the bald patches shining through Walter's close-cropped hair. A red mist rose up before Roger's eyes, and a deep ringing filled his ears.

"You pernicious piece of a dungheap!" Roger followed up these words by slamming Walter once more against the coarse stone wall.

"What mean you?" Walter gasped, attempting to pry Roger's finger's from around his throat.

Roger suddenly released his son, who staggered to the stool and flung himself down upon it. The sting of scalding tears pricked at the older man's eyelids, before he dashed them away. "How long have you had the pox?"

Walter picked up his cloak and drew it around his shivering shoulders.

Roger drew back one thick-booted foot and kicked the stool out from under his son. The wood splintered as Walter fell to the stone floor. "Where did you collect this souvenir of pleasure?" Roger growled. "At court? In the stews of London? Under a hayrack?"

Hugging the cloak, Walter scrambled away from the stamping feet.

"Answer me!" Roger roared. A vein at his right temple began to throb. By nightfall, he knew, he could expect another one of his vicious headaches. He ignored the warning. "When did you know you carried this . . . this filth?"

"'Tis but a rash." Pulling himself to a standing position, Walter stared his father in the eye. "I have been scratching overmuch. 'Tis nothing but lice."

A small part of Roger's mind applauded his son's impudence, though the fury of hellfire still burned through him. "Lice? Aye, that and more, from between a drab's legs! Mince no words with me, hedgepig! I've seen enough of the world to know the pox. Have you sought treatment?"

Walter paused before answering, surprised at the turn of questioning. "A physician in York gave me mercury, though I think he sought to kill me, not to cure me."

Roger turned toward the fire and stared into the glowing embers. "Too bad 'twas young Edward who died. 'Twould have been better if it had been you," he said very softly, not caring whether Walter heard him or not. All his hopes and ambitions for the Ormonds had disappeared like the feeble smoke curling up the chimney.

"You *are* mad!" Walter gasped behind him.

Roger whirled. "Nay!" he growled. "Not yet, but by all that is in heaven and hell, I may become so!"

Walter jutted out his chin. "Then do so, dearest Papa, so that I may come into my birthright all the sooner." He snatched up his hat from the floor. "It seems we are stuck with each other—you and I—like two flies in a web." He fluffed the white feather pinned to the headband. "Like it or not, I am your heir, and I will be served, even with the pox. I am all you have." With a sneer, he set the cap on his balding head at a jaunty angle.

Watching him, Roger shuddered at the grotesque sight. Like a flash of summer lightning on the moors, a sudden idea leapt into his mind.

"Not quite, my son." The more he considered this new possibility, the more certain Roger became. God had not totally abandoned him.

Walter's hand dropped from the latch. Slowly he faced his father. "What mean you? Have you some bastard hidden away? No court in the land will honor a bastard's claim. Not even our good King Henry can manage that, or he would have proclaimed the young duke of Richmond as his heir long before this."

Roger shook his head. "No bastard, but a wife. I shall marry the wench that comes here soon, and upon her I shall get another son—a healthy son. Mayhap two boys, God willing." He smiled at the prospect. He was not that old, and perchance his third attempt at marriage might prove the charm.

A dark red flush stained Walter's pallor. His features, once so handsome, contorted into a mask of mottled anger. "Bastard!" he screamed at his father. "You are the only bastard in this house!"

Now that he had made up his mind, Roger found Walter's anger amusing. He perched on the edge of his counting table and chuckled. "Then stand up for bastards, say I."

"The French girl is mine. You signed the agreement years ago."

"'Tis true. I do recall putting my name to the paper. Mark you, 'twas *my* name I signed."

Walter's face drew in like a pig's, all snout and small eyes. Roger laughed at the sight, which angered Walter even more. "But you signed for me!" the younger man sputtered. "I am to wed, not you. You are past your prime, old man."

"And you'll not live long enough to enjoy yours." Roger stared at his firstborn with something close to loathing. Once he would have given his very life for his son, but not for this piece of carrion. "Nay, not so, but I fear you'll beget no more children on any woman who is still willing to lie with you." He held up his hand to still the rage he saw hovering on Walter's thin lips. "Hear me, Walter. I need a son—a healthy son—who will take our family into the next generation. I have labored too long and sacrificed too much." His hand touched the place where his eye once had been. "I will not dash it all at the feet of a poxy jackanapes who is already on the path to perdition."

"I'll not—" Walter began.

"You have spoken truly. You will not do anything. Your time is flying toward the twilight. Enjoy what is left of it. As for me, I shall wed Fauconbourg's young daughter within the hour of her arrival here."

Walter yanked open the door, revealing Grapper, who had been kneeling at the keyhole. "I wish you joy in your new marriage, Father." Walter smiled, with venom lurking in the corners of his lips. "But first, your bride must come. May I point out, she is not here yet?" With that, he strode out, pausing to give Grapper a sharp kick.

"Rot in hell!" Roger bellowed after him.

"In due time," Walter's answer echoed back.

A finger of ice traced a furrow down Roger's spine.

Chapter Eight

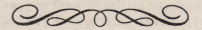

Celeste awoke with a start. For a brief moment, she could not remember where she was. The drawn bed curtains made the darkness around her even thicker. Sitting up against the two pillows, she yawned. An inn, she recalled, in some hilly little town.

She drew her knees up to her chest and wrapped her arms around them. For the first time in her eighteen years, she felt truly alone. Marguerite lay in a comfortable infirmary miles away, while her lively maid, Suzette, was probably back in the Loire valley by now.

Celeste bit her lip to stifle the wave of homesickness. At L'Étoile, she would have been sharing her bed with one of her cousins, each keeping the other warm in body and safe from the unseen fears of the dark. Only last night, she had slipped from her narrow bed in the priory's guest house and sought out her beloved aunt, who lay a few comfortable steps down the corridor.

Celeste drew back the drapes. The pale light of a half moon shining through her small window lit up the slate gables of the house across the way. She noticed that the neighboring brick chimney pot canted a bit to the left. Idly she wondered if it would fall over sometime during the winter months ahead. For the sake of the people who dwelled within, she hoped not.

Celeste swung her legs over the edge of the bed, then searched with her toes for the pair of soft sheepskin slippers she had positioned before retiring. Sweet Mary! The floor was like ice to the touch. Finding the shoes, she slipped into them, then pulled her tawny silken *robe de chambre* over her shoulders; its brown fur trim brushed comfortingly against her ankles.

Feeling her way with her hands, she located the curtains that separated her alcove from the room beyond. Quietly she pulled them apart. Gaston's soft snore told her that the old soldier occupied the bed nearest hers. She smiled in the darkness at the sleeping form. *Thank you, Gaston. You are my father's best gift to me.* She knew she would miss him dreadfully once he left her at Snape Castle and returned to France. She shook her head. Mustn't think of that now. Weeks would come and go before that final parting.

The moon's watery beams revealed that the other bed was empty. Apprehension prickled the back of her neck. Had the tall monk abandoned them and returned to his safe little priory? Not that Celeste would blame him in the least. She had sorely tried his patience today. Still—

A muffled sound from the hearthside caught her attention. Creeping closer, Celeste saw Guy stretched out on the hard bricks, his arm pillowing his head, which faced the dying embers. Barely daring to breath, she leaned closer to study him by the silver moonlight.

How very long he was! Did he have a cot especially made for him at the priory? she wondered. And why was he sleeping on the cold floor, without so much as a blanket for warmth? Hearing a freshening wind rattle the wooden shutters, Celeste shivered. Glancing at Guy's empty bed, she furrowed her brows. There was no need for him to get chilled, when there were several blankets nearby. Perhaps he had fallen asleep while praying.

Moving slowly, lest she disturb the sleepers, Celeste tiptoed over to the empty bed, grabbed two blankets and a pillow, then returned to his side. She paused before laying one of the blankets over his bare feet.

How cold his toes looked! Did monks wear only sandals, even when the snows came? She shivered again at the thought. Fah! Certainly God did not require his servants to catch their death of cold. Celeste wrinkled her nose. Brother Guy must stay healthy until they reached Snape Castle, since he was the only one who claimed to know where this mysterious place lay. She did not think the good Lord would mind if she wrapped up Guy's feet for the night. In fact, it would be an act of Christian charity to do so.

Gently she lifted his ankles, slipped the blanket under them, then set them down again. She had half a mind to run her finger along one of his insteps to see what would happen, but the voice of prudence cautioned her against the idea. She already knew well enough that Brother Guy would not find her trick amusing. Besides, the poor man needed his rest. But he did have such a lovely high arch!

Sighing softly, she laid the rest of the blanket over him, up to his waist. Taking the second blanket, she placed it over the first, draping it from his knees to his neck. She would have liked to tuck the ends around him, to keep out the drafts that whispered under the hem of her night shift, but she feared that her touch would waken him.

The pillow posed another problem. How could she slip it under his head without disturbing him? Was Brother Guy a sound sleeper? And what was he like when he first awakened? Celeste's father was always a cranky bear in the mornings, until after he had broken his fast. Gaston was the same, only he roared instead of muttered. Perhaps all men were difficult in the mornings. Considering Brother Guy's great size, he would probably act like a fire-breathing dragon.

The embers cast a reddish glow on his crown of golden hair. Celeste wet her lips as she gazed at its silken fineness. Was it as soft as it looked? Would he mind if she touched it? *Imbécile!* she chided herself. Of course he would mind—if he knew. But asleep? Ah, that was another thing altogether, *n'est-ce pas?*

Holding her breath, she reached out and stroked an errant curl that lay invitingly across the neck of his robe. *Mon Dieu!* It was like the down of a new chick. Celeste twined the curl through her fingers. She knew she didn't have much experience in these matters, but shouldn't a man's hair be rough? Thoughtfully she combed her fingers through several more curls, being careful to avoid touching the bare patch of his tonsure. The temptation to nuzzle her cheek against the softness of his hair almost overwhelmed her.

Ma foi! Why was she sitting on a cold floor in the middle of the night playing with a strange man's hair—and he a man of God, no less? Her mother and father would be deeply shamed by her brazen behavior, if they knew. She could almost feel the sting of the birch twigs on her bare backside. *And Marguerite! She would skin me alive, using only her tongue!*

Celeste pulled her fingers away from Guy's locks as if they were a nest of garden snakes. Better to put the pillow next to his head and be done with it. Perhaps he'd sense it was there and roll onto it. Standing, Celeste looked down at him again. At least now Brother Guy looked a little more comfortable. She cocked her head. What did his face look like when he slept? Surely he could not maintain that stern mien all the time. One little peek wouldn't hurt—just to satisfy her curiosity. Raising herself up on her toes, Celeste leaned far out over his body, twisting to get a glimpse of his expression.

Brilliant, unblinking sapphire eyes met her gaze, and one thick brow slowly rose.

With a small shriek of surprise, Celeste lost her precarious balance and toppled over Guy, toward the fireplace. His hands caught her before her head hit the hearthstone, and his body cushioned the impact of her fall.

A rasp of drawn steel rang out in the darkness. "By the cock of the devil, unhand her, you cur!" Gaston bellowed as he leapt from the bed. The moonlight glimmered on the naked blade of his sword.

Guy's hands tightened around Celeste's arms for a moment as he stared deeply into her eyes. Then, rolling over, he pushed her away from him.

Celeste caught her breath at the intensity of the blue flame that had blazed momentarily in his eyes. Only Gaston's string of thunderous oaths shook her from the spell of his gaze. "Peace, Gaston!" She held out her hand to the angry sergeant. "I pray you, all is well. Good Brother Guy did no wrong."

"I'll cleave him in half!" Gaston bristled, his bare legs dancing in a frenzy as he circled the couple on the floor. "Move away, my lady, or you'll get blood on your clothes."

In one swift move, Guy rose, his blankets falling away from him like brown leaves off an elm tree in autumn. Before Gaston and Celeste could gather their wits, Guy chopped his hands down across the old soldier's wrist. The sword clanged against the hearthstone. Cursing in pain, Gaston cradled his injured arm.

Bunching up the voluminous material of her gown and robe, Celeste pulled herself up between the two men. "Peace, I say! I am the one at fault. Oh, Gaston, are you sorely hurt?"

"Nothing's broken, no thanks to that…Englishman!" Gaston spat out the word as he glared at Guy.

Celeste looked from one to the other. Guy's hair stood out on all sides, like an angered lion's. Gaston's silvered strands bristled from the top of his head, as if they were the flames on a candlewick. Celeste put her hand over her mouth, but could not stop the flow of her giggles. The more she tried to control herself, the harder she laughed.

"Oh, la, la!" she gasped between bouts of mirth. "If you two could but see yourselves!" Another wave caught her. "In faith, two bantam cocks! *Oui!*" She nodded as both men glared at her.

"Lady Celeste!" Gaston threw his shoulders back with tattered dignity. "I've been charged upon my life to see you safely to your husband, and I'll thank you not to make me into your jester for doing so!"

He looked so injured, Celeste immediately sobered. What on earth had gotten into her? In the meantime, Guy tossed another log on the fire. A shower of sparks flew up the chimney. The room grew brighter, illuminating the monk's face. If Celeste had thought him stern before, now Guy looked exactly what she imagined an avenging angel would be on the final day of judgment, when he turned his eye upon the damned. Biting her lip, she looked down at her fingers which were clasped tightly together.

"*Pardonnez-moi,*" she begged the two men in a soft, husky voice. "I have wronged you both." She cast a sidelong glance at Gaston, who still glowered at Guy with a bloodthirsty look. "Pardon my laughter, good Gaston. I am deeply indebted for your swift protection of my life and honor.''

She tried to avoid looking at his bare legs, which were exposed from the thigh down. How very hairy they were, and how comical! She bit the inside of her cheek before continuing. She couldn't laugh again, not at this precise moment, anyway.

''And, good Brother Guy...''

His face flushed, from either the heat of the fire or his anger. The ruddy color heightened his wrathful expression. She swallowed. ''Forgive me for disturbing your rest. I only meant to make you more comfortable.''

Gaston exploded. ''What?''

Celeste gasped as she realized the implication of her words. ''*Non,* Gaston, it is not what you think. Brother Guy was asleep on the floor without covering, and the night is cold. I was only trying to...'' She left off her explanation before she said anything that would further anger the sergeant.

''I suppose my folly requires another penance, Brother Guy?'' She didn't dare look directly at him.

Through her lashes, she saw him slowly nod.

''Do you not think my lady has done enough penance?'' Reining his horse beside Guy, who was again mounted on Daisy, Gaston looked back over his shoulder at his silent mistress. ''*Pauvre petite!* Never have I known her to be so silent.''

Guy swallowed. Perhaps he had been a trifle harsh last night, when he inflicted his punishment on Celeste. After all, she had no idea what she had done to him in those few moments when her hands so gently stroked his hair.

His instincts had awakened him the minute Celeste crawled out of her bed. Years of combat in the service of

Henry VIII had honed Guy's reflexes to a razor edge. As he lay on the uneven bricks of the hearth, enduring his self-imposed retribution for his tempting secular thoughts, he had been aware of her every movement. The nearer she crept to him, the louder his heart had pounded. Surely she must have heard it. He had known, without turning, when she stopped and he swore he could feel the heat of her gaze as it traveled over him. It had taken every ounce of his self-control to feign sleep, when in fact his treacherous body ached for her.

Guy had not needed the blankets she so gently placed around him. He had grown hotter with each passing moment. He had almost leapt into the fireplace when Celeste first touched his hair. He recalled the cold droplets of sweat that had beaded his brow as she threaded her slim fingers through his hated curls. Delicious chills, which he had not experienced in a long time, had coursed down his back. His own fingers had tingled to take her into his arms and return the sweet torture she inflicted upon him.

When Celeste finally stood, he had thought himself saved, until he realized that she was leaning over him. In a heartbeat, she had fallen into his arms—just as he had fantasized. Her startled expression and sleep-tousled hair had enchanted him. He had wanted to clasp her to his chest and murmur sweet nonsense in her ear. Thank heavens Gaston had interceded when he did! Guy did not want to contemplate what might have happened if he had not been there.

I would have made love with her there and then, and let the devil take the hindmost. Sweet merciful Lord, help me!

"Have you taken a vow of deafness, as well as silence, monk?" Gaston prodded him with the handle of his riding crop. "Lady Celeste has held her silence all morning.

I have never known her to keep so still for so long, and I have known her all her life.''

Guy stared straight ahead at the rutted road. He tried to tell himself that Celeste's enforced silence was to teach her a much-needed lesson, but his conscience knew otherwise. The very sound of her smoky voice, her bell-like laughter and, most of all, her sweet singing made his blood race through him with unholy desire. Her punishment was not for her, but for him.

"Fah! You are a man of stone, I see," Gaston snorted. "Much like my lady's father."

At this, Guy finally turned toward Gaston. He raised one brow in a silent query.

"*Oui,* my master, the old chevalier. He is a man like any other. He wanted a son. What does the good Lord give him? Four daughters! Lovely creatures, like so many roses in a garden. Then Lady Eugénie is pregnant again. An old soothsayer predicts a boy—'one who will o'ertop the rest,' were her exact words. The chevalier became transported with joy. Gave the old witch much gold, and the hag departed, never to be seen again. It was a good thing that she did so, for when Lady Celeste was born..." Gaston shook his head at the remembrance.

Guy snapped his fingers, encouraging the old soldier to continue.

"The walls of L'Étoile shook with my lord's anger and disappointment. Wouldn't even look at the babe, nor give her his blessing. And such a sweet thing she was! In my humble opinion, the prettiest of the lot. And such a cunning little mind, that one!"

Glancing over his shoulder, Gaston grinned at the subject of his story. "All sunshine and quicksilver. The other girls? Beautiful, like their mama, but I tell you true, good Brother, there is not a thimble full of good sense among the lot of them. Not so with my little lady." He chuckled with affection.

"She made her father notice her, *oui!* We all noticed her clever jests, her merry spirits, and her many little pranks, for which she was often switched."

Guy's eyes widened. Lissa beaten? He would have flayed alive anyone who marked such a delicate skin.

"She did not seem to mind, and went on her merry way as before. But her singing voice!" Gaston sighed with rapture. "You have never heard her truly sing, Brother Guy. She shames the larks in the meadow—yes, even the angels in heaven." The old soldier leaned over in his saddle and spoke in a lower tone. "My men miss the sound of her singing, good Brother. Especially Pierre." He nodded toward the young wagon driver, who lazily waved the whip over his two charges, warding off invisible flies.

Like a spun-sugar castle crumbling at the end of a feast held in an overheated room, Guy's resolve disintegrated. He was nothing like Lissa's cold father. He had no wish to snuff out her lively spirits. That would happen soon enough at Snape Castle. Guy gritted his teeth at the thought of the forbidding Ormond stronghold.

He nodded to Gaston, then took out his slate and scribbled a few words on it. Halting Daisy's bone-jolting stride, Guy waited for Celeste.

Celeste's lips twitched in a tentative smile as she drew abreast of Guy. Maintaining his stern composure, he thrust the slate at her.

You may sing, she read. A brilliant smile wreathed her face, and she clapped her hands. "*Merci,* Bro*ther* Guy! I am now forgiven, yes?" Joy-filled laughter rippled from her.

Each delightful sound struck Guy like a stinging dart, **assail**ing his senses, opening the floodgates he had dammed up so long ago. Gripping the slate until its sharp corner bit into the soft part of his palm, he shook his head and pointed to the word *sing*.

Celeste cocked her head, allowing the yellow feather in her bonnet to sweep against her shoulder. "Only sing, good Brother?"

Guy nodded sternly.

"And no talking?"

He nodded again.

"Not even one or two words of pleasant conversation, such as one would while away the hour—?" The fierce knotting of his brows cut off her further remarks.

She looked up at the sky for a moment, wrinkled her nose, then proceeded with the first verse of a slightly bawdy tavern song about a maid and a hunter. Guy opened his mouth to object, remembered his vow and gritted his teeth. Celeste continued into the chorus, with a gleam of pure deviltry in her dark eyes. Kneeing her horse, she trotted past him, singing her very heart out.

"My good thanks to you, Brother Guy." Gaston gave him a friendly whack between the shoulder blades. The sergeant might be a little long in the tooth, but he still had a strong right arm, Guy thought, arching his back.

"I agree that my lady's choice of ballads may not be proper for a young girl to sing," Gaston continued, his warm brown eyes shining with pleasure, "but she sings it well, *non?*"

Guy gave him a weak smile in agreement. Then his eyes narrowed as he regarded Celeste's slim body, swaying slightly with her music.

You little minx! You know exactly what you are doing, don't you? Well, Lady Lissa, there's two who can play that game, and you've just met your match!

Chapter Nine

By unspoken, even unacknowledged mutual consent, Celeste and Guy maintained a polite distance over the next few days. For his part, Guy found this stalemate oddly annoying. Of course, he should have been relieved that Celeste didn't fall into his arms again, or even brush against him in passing up the stairwells of the various country inns where the party lodged at night.

Yet, wrapped in the cloak of midnight, Guy found himself lying awake. He remembered her silken hair, the slimness of her waist in his hand, and the moment when her firm little backside had nestled in his lap before he thrust her away. Neither prayers, nor fasting, nor cold dousing under a pump at dawn, could erase the hot ache of desire that had taken up a permanent abode within him.

Not that Lissa completely ignored him. If she had, it would have eased Guy's torment. Daily she bubbled with a never-ending stream of witty observations of the countryside, snatches of poetry—mostly from the romantic tales of chivalry—bright, one-sided conversation and glorious singing. Gaston was right. The lass did possess the voice of an angel. Even so, Guy's defenses could have withstood all of this. It was her attempts at speaking English, coupled with her ceaseless campaign to make him smile, that threatened to beat down the protective bulwark with which Guy had enclosed his heart.

"Hey-ho, Brother Guy!" she chirruped behind him as the party rode out of the village of Leebottwood two days later. "The landlord of that house is a knavish raw-beet sucker, *non?*"

The surprise of Celeste's pronunciation, and her new vocabulary, nearly caused Guy to fall off Daisy's increasingly uncomfortable back. Rabbit sucker! Where in the devil's name had Lissa picked up that phrase? Suppressing his initial urge to grin, he glowered at her over his shoulder. The little witch dimpled prettily in return.

"Do not frown at me that way. I am merely trying to speak peench-'potted English. And that man—he asked too much money. 'E is what I say 'e is." She grinned mischievously. "A peench-'potted raw-beet sucker!" She rolled the words around her mouth with the relish of a matron eating a dish of sweetmeats.

Guy bit down on his tongue so hard the pain watered his eyes. He would not laugh, or even permit the merest flicker of a smile past his lips. He would not give her that power over him. For the precarious sake of his tortured soul, he must maintain his facade of aloofness and disapproval. On the other hand, he wholeheartedly agreed with her opinion. Their innkeeper of the night before had cheated them shamefully. Had he been allowed to speak, Guy would have blistered the ears of that grasping scullion with a fine display of noble temper. That was the only thing most of these common folk understood—brute strength and bellowing. Lissa was right: the Churl was indeed a pinchspotted rabbit sucker.

Still, Guy couldn't let her think these words were appropriate for a young lady. What if she blurted them out in good company? Jesu! What if she said them to her husband? The mere thought of that weasely Walter Ormond putting his hands on Lissa was enough to deepen Guy's frown.

"Ma foi!" Celeste had lapsed back into French. "And what have I done now to displease you, Brother Grumpy? Bah! I must learn this horrible language, since I am to be an English lady, and you are the only one who can help me." She rolled her violet eyes to the cloud-laden skies. "And what help is that? Nothing but frowns and sour looks. Upon my soul, Brother Guy, I think I would rather converse with your donkey!"

Guy wrote on his slate, then held it out to her. She leaned over in her saddle and read his latest dictum.

"Where did I learn those words?" Her eyes widened with amethyst innocence. "At supper last night. I overheard two men talking, and they said those words over and over. I think they sounded very fine. Raw-beet..."

Guy shook his head so vehemently the wreath of his blond curls lashed his face. If she said that one more time, he didn't think he could restrain himself—from either bursting out into laughter or dragging her off her horse and stopping her mouth with a kiss. God's teeth! Where had that wanton idea come from?

Guy wiped the slate clean with the back of his sleeve, then wrote again.

"'Ladies do not say rabbit sucker or pinch-spotted, or anything else they may hear at an inn,'" she read aloud. Celeste digested this instruction for a moment, then smiled beatifically at him. *"Très bien,* Brother Guy. You can write in complete sentences."

Flicking her crop, she spurred her horse ahead of him. Her low golden laughter drifted back over her shoulder.

That evening they crossed a stone bridge that arched over the Severn River and entered the bustling town of

Shrewsbury. Within the protective city walls, the majestic stone spire belonging to Saint Mary's Church, built in the twelfth century, attempted to pierce the gathering gloom, made darker by the heavy gray clouds that had accompanied the bridal party all day. Their horses' hooves echoed down the cobbles of Grope Lane, where high black-and-white half-timbered houses leaned companionably over the street toward each other, like whispering gossips around a cider bowl.

The weary travelers gratefully accepted the hospitality of the convent that sat hard by Saint Mary's walls. *At least Celeste won't pick up any more foul language here.* Guy allowed himself a small smile of satisfaction as he rubbed Daisy down before offering her a bucket of oats.

Instead, the tall abbess had a great many words to say to Guy in the privacy of her spare office.

"I am thunderstruck!" She rattled the thick rosary beads that hung from her waist. "A scandal, to be sure! What could have the chevalier of Fauconbourg been thinking, to let such a beautiful young daughter go off to England without a proper chaperon?"

Her aunt was injured in an accident, Guy wrote on his slate.

The abbess crossed herself in a prayerful attitude before continuing. "Still, that is no excuse!" she snapped.

Guy swallowed his anger. *I am in charge of the lady's honor.* Pressing down too hard on his chalk, he accidentally broke it into two pieces. The old she-dragon!

The abbess pursed her lips as she appraised the tall monk. "You are far too young for such a duty," she continued waspishly. "And too handsome for your own good, as well. I trust you remember your vows. Poverty, obedience—and *chastity.*" She practically spat out the last word at him.

Guy drew himself up to his fullest height. No wonder this woman was in a convent! She would have made a merry hell for any man witless enough to wed her.

I must attend to my prayers, he scribbled across the slate.

The abbess rattled her beads again, coughed, then blew her nose before answering. "Aye, a wise idea. And I shall pray for the Lady Celeste, that she may not fall among wolves 'ere she reach her waiting husband."

With a curt nod, Guy turned to go.

"Your blessing, Father?"

Even as she knelt at his feet, the abbess's chin jutted out in silent disapproval. Guy wondered if her request was purely pious or an unvoiced challenge to his authority. After quickly tracing the sign of the cross in the air in front of her, he sought sanctuary within the dim church.

Jesu! What if the abbess asked him to say mass on the morrow? He would have to explain that he was not ordained. Then what? Would she permit Celeste to continue in his company? Or would she lock Lissa inside the convent and send him back to Saint Hugh's with a large flea in his ear? The abbess looked exactly the type of shrew who would do just that. Faced with this possibility, Guy realized how very much he wanted to see this journey to its conclusion.

'Tis my charge on my honor. Guy prayed before the tabernacle on the altar, as its rich gilding reflected the light from a solitary candle. *Lissa is safer in my care than with all the chaperons in the world. I would protect her with my life.* It took a moment for him to realize he was shaking.

"Gaston, have you seen Brother Guy?"

Celeste looked down the table in the convent guest

house. The men had almost finished their meal of roasted capons, fresh-baked bread and dairy butter, rabbit stewed with onions, sharp cheddar and baked apples in a pastry cover. Both ale and a middling red wine rounded out the meal. Though the convent's food was plain, it filled everyone to satisfaction.

Gaston scraped the last morsel of baked apple from the bowl, then wiped his mouth on his sleeve, before answering. "I saw him in conversation with the mother abbess. Then he went into the church."

Celeste regarded a wedge of the savory cheese that Gaston politely placed on her wooden plate. She wondered if she ought to wrap up some of the food for the missing monk before the dishes were cleared from the board.

"Again he does not eat!" she sputtered. "And when he does, it is only a crust of bread, a cup of water or a piece of uncooked fruit."

"He is a man of God," Gaston observed mildly. "And this is one of God's houses. He is doing what he supposed to do—he prays." He took a deep swallow of his ale.

"Fah!" Celeste stabbed the inoffensive cheese with her small eating knife. "He is *not* doing what he is supposed to do at all."

"Oh?" Gaston cocked one bushy brow at her. "Then permit me to ask what he should be doing?"

Celeste played with a gold ring on her finger. "He should be here with us, eating this good supper. He needs his strength."

"*D'accord,*" Gaston murmured into the depths of his tankard. "I agree, but what does one do? Do I tie him up and feed him like an invalid?" He shrugged the thought away. "I do not think the good brother would like that. And I do not think I am the man to try it."

"He will be sick if he does not eat. *Ma foi!* He is such a big man. He needs a lot of food." Pulling off her napkin as she spoke, Celeste laid the cloth out on the table and began to pile bread, cheese and the remains of a capon in the middle of it.

"A midnight supper, my lady?" Gaston jested.

"Oui." She tied the ends together. "For one who keeps too many late hours as it is."

Gaston caught her wrist as she turned to go. "Remember, my lady—Brother Guy has dedicated his life to the church."

Celeste did not like the sergeant's stern look, or what his words implied. She tossed her head back proudly. "And I do not forget that I am all but married, either."

She slammed the door behind her.

Across the garden, she could make out the side door leading into Saint Mary's. Clutching her bag of food, Celeste glided down the stone corridor of the cloister.

The large interior of the church reminded Celeste of the pictures of a cave that she had seen in one of her father's books. Tall stone pillars receded into darkness as they stretched toward the arched roof. The chill air held a faint scent of candle wax, dust, mold and lingering incense. Celeste waited a moment while her eyes adjusted to the darkness. She spied Brother Guy's spear-straight form in front of the rood screen. Even when kneeling, he looked tall.

Celeste quickly traversed the aisle, then dropped down beside him. The uneven stone paving bit into her knees through her many layers of petticoats and gowns. She glanced at him out of the corner of her eye.

If he knew she was beside him, Guy gave no indication, but merely continued to stare at the altar as if mesmerized by its flickering candle. Celeste bowed her head, though not in prayer. She hated to disturb Guy when he was so obviously deep in his devotions. Yet, what was she to do with her gift of food, especially since its various contents emitted a pleasing, though strong, odor? Hesitantly she put it on the floor in front of her, then made the sign of the cross.

Memorized prayers sprang to her lips without prompting, though her eyes were anywhere but on the altar. She shifted on the uncomfortable flooring, landing directly on a particularly sharp stone. She muffled her gasp of pain, then cast Guy another sidelong look.

He neither moved nor blinked.

Celeste considered pretending a faint, just to see what he would do, but she could almost hear Aunt Marguerite's voice telling her not to act like such a silly goose. A pale white spider caught her eye. Fascinated, she watched it walk up Guy's gown, its legs moving one at a time. When it reached the end of his sleeve, it wavered for a moment, then disappeared inside.

Holding her breath, Celeste waited for Guy to come alive and shake the thing out. Nothing happened.

Growing more alarmed, Celeste stared directly at him. Was he in a trance? Would he fall to the floor in convulsions any minute? Should she run for help?

"Brother Guy?" she whispered, tentatively touching his robe.

Without shifting his gaze from the altar, he slowly raised one hand and put his finger to his lips. Then he returned to the attitude of prayer.

Celeste blinked. How could he concentrate like that? Never had she seen anyone so single-minded in his devotions. At L'Étoile, a perpetual hum of twitching, scratching, coughing, sneezing and whispering accompanied the daily mass. Even Père Jean-Baptiste made unholy noises at inappropriate times, and she knew for a fact that the old man couldn't stay on his knees for more than five minutes.

Celeste stared down at her hands, twined her fingers together and tried to meditate on matters spiritual.

Impossible! Though both the air and the stones under her knees were cold, Guy seemed to radiate his own heat, which spilled over onto her. His striking hair formed a golden halo about his head, giving him the appearance of a divine creature not of this world. His hands, with those long fingers, were folded in peaceful prayer. By the dim light, Celeste noted their strength. She recalled his touch from the other night. How easily he had lifted her from the floor of the bedroom. How gently he had held her, and how disappointed she had been when he set her aside.

Celeste squeezed her eyes shut. *Mon Dieu, forgive me! He is yours—not mine.*

Gathering her skirts, she pulled herself to her feet. Her knees stung where they had borne her weight. She tugged at Guy's sleeve.

"Supper!" she hissed. Turning on her heel, she marched stiffly down the aisle. She deliberately let the side door bang loudly behind her.

Lifting her skirts scandalously above her ankles, Celeste raced down the cloister walkway until she reached the solitude of the tiny room assigned to her for the night. There she pressed the single pillow to her mouth, not caring that the small cushion was stuffed full of straw. It muffled the sobs that rose unbidden from her throat.

Guy released a long breath and flexed his shoulder muscles. Then he shook the wandering insect from the depths of his clothing. If Lissa had said anything else, or stayed next to him for one more minute... He let the thought pass unfinished. He felt exhausted from the labor of controlling his temptations. Glancing down at the bundle on the paving stones, he felt his empty stomach rumble with anticipation. He smiled in the dark.

Surely the good Lord didn't want this particular offering left on his doorstep. Nor did Guy seriously think the Divine Master would object if his servant disposed of it in an appropriate manner. After all, Guy reasoned as he picked up the bulging packet, one should never reject an act of charity, and wastefulness was indeed a sin.

After a final "Amen," Guy let himself out the side door. As he spread his feast on a stone bench in the cloister garden, he could have sworn he heard Father Jocelyn whispering, "God works in strange and mysterious ways, my son."

Chapter Ten

After hearing mass said by the resident priest—which relieved Guy's midnight anxieties—the travelers left Shrewsbury as a wet gray dawn rose over the walls of the castle. The abbess had said nothing more to Guy about Celeste's escort, and he was glad to see the town sink into miniature behind them.

"Achoo!"

Hearing Celeste sneeze for the twelfth time, Guy tugged on Daisy's reins, finally bringing the stubborn animal to a halt. He waited for the girl to draw alongside of him.

"*Ma foi!*" She said by way of greeting, shaking out her handkerchief. "This wretched cold and damp! I think you will not sing at my wedding, Brother Guy, but at my funeral." She dimpled at the thought. "But I forget, you will not sing at all, Brother Guy, will you? You will stand silently by like a great stone angel with your wings folded and your head bowed. *Quel dommage!* Though in truth, I have never seen an angel quite so tall as you. Then again, I have never seen an angel at all." Another loud sneeze cut off any further observations.

Guy frowned at the sound. Lissa's eyes looked as red and runny as her nose. Yet she made no complaint of her ill health. God's teeth! Every other woman he had known, including his own mother, took to her bed at the slightest sign of indisposition—or even the pretext of one. Yet this delicate French flower, unused to the harsher English weather, continued on, when it was evident she was unwell.

How fare you? he wrote on his slate, then held it out for her to read. The light rain that had accompanied them since they left the convent softened the chalk letters into a smudge.

Celeste waved her handkerchief like a lace-and-linen flag. "It is naught but a stuffiness in my head." She leaned forward and confided to Guy, "In truth, it is a blessing, for my men are in much need of a change of clothing, and now I do not have to smell them, *oui?*" She sneezed again.

Guy's frown deepened. Lissa might jest about her funeral, but its possibility was all too real in his mind's eye. They had to stop somewhere for a few days, to give her a chance to recover her health. The weather would grow worse as they went farther north.

"Ah, Bro*ther* Guy! Do not frown so! My aunt Marguerite used to tell my little brother that if he made wicked faces God would make them permanent. You might try a little smile, *oui?*"

Guy bit the inside of his cheek, to keep from complying with her request. He was in no mood to banter. He must find shelter, and soon. He kicked Daisy into a jarring trot. Celeste's next sneeze followed behind him.

"*D'accord.*" Gaston nodded when he read Guy's slate. "I agree we must stop for my lady's sake, but where?"

Guy stared at the large black stallion Gaston rode. Dared he ask to borrow the animal for an hour?

When Gaston read Guy's request, he threw back his head and laughed loudly, which startled several of the men riding nearby. "That is a good jest, Brother Guy! Do you know the name of this beauty here?" He stroked the horse's neck fondly as he spoke. "Black Devil. A churchman riding the Devil? *Oui,* this I would like to see. But, my friend, be forewarned. He is well named, for he is very strong and swift. Can you handle such a mount?" Gaston cast a baleful look at Daisy.

Guy permitted a small smile to curl the corners of his mouth. Gaston did indeed have a fine horse, but it couldn't hold a candle to his own gray charger, Moonglow. In his memory, Guy could still hear his proud steed's hooves as they pounded down the lists at Hampton Court, leaving his opponents lying in the dust of King Henry's tiltyard.

Guy slid off Daisy's back and held out the reins to Gaston. Behind them, Émile smothered a chuckle. Gaston threw the man a savage look. Ahead of them, Celeste sneezed again, her cloaked shoulders shaking with the effort. Spurred by the sound, Gaston dismounted and snatched up Daisy's reins.

"Try not to break your neck, Brother, for I have enough worries as it is with my lady. And you." He shot another stern glance at the grinning men behind him. "If I hear but one word out of any of you malt-worms, I will skewer your livers for my supper, mark me well." With that, he threw his leg over Daisy's back.

Daisy flattened her ears at the unaccustomed weight and bawled a protest. Guy tried to hide his excitement as he leapt into Gaston's plain but serviceable saddle. How long had it been since he last felt a real horse between his legs? His muscles remembered exactly what to do. Guy's heart exulted at the feeling. Then, a moment later, he regretted his vanity.

Forgive me, Lord, but 'tis for the lady's sake that I do this. Aye, he thought as he wheeled the great horse and shot down the road ahead, but you should not take such earthly pleasure in it. Leaving Gaston's final admonition hanging in the misty air, he overtook Celeste. A small burst of manly pride tickled him as he noted her stunned look when he sped past her.

I promise to do a midnight vigil as my penance. Lord, why did you make such magnificent animals if we weren't expected to enjoy riding them? After this heady experience, Guy knew that returning to Daisy would be the hardest penance of all.

Two hours later, Celeste found herself tucked up in a high four-poster bed, with clean sheets, and a hot brick wrapped in red flannel at her feet. Guy's search for a shelter had been more than fruitful. Burke Crest, home of Sir James Foxmore and his lady wife, Eleanor, had lain less than three miles down the road. Celeste didn't bother to wonder how Guy had made himself understood by these good people. It did not matter now. Her hair and feet were dry, the room was warm, and Lady Eleanor was goodness itself. Best of all, the lady spoke a pleasant French.

"La, *ma petite!*" Lady Eleanor clucked to her guest as she held out a posset of warmed milk, honey and wine. "What do those men of yours know about women, I ask you? Just because *they* like to ride all day in the rain, that doesn't mean that you must!"

Celeste sipped from the steaming mug, allowing the delicious concoction to flow down her scratchy throat. "*Non,* Lady Eleanor, it is not Gaston's fault, but mine. I have been too long on your country roads, and I am sure by now my betrothed must think I have run away from my father's agreement—and taken my dowry with me." She smiled ruefully when she thought of the pittance she carried. "And we must arrive in the north country before the snows, I am told."

Lady Eleanor crossed her arms over her rounded middle—she was expecting her fifth child early in the New Year—and slipped her hands into her wide oversleeves. "What you say about the snow is true, but if you do not get rid of that cold, you will not have to worry about going anywhere at all."

"You are most kind to take such good care of me." Celeste wiggled her toes against the hot flannel. So much better than her damp, muddy boots! "I do not wish to intrude upon your hospitality."

Lady Eleanor waved off Celeste's further objections. "Fie, child! Your visit comes in good time. Since I have been unable to ride, I have not seen a new face to speak to in a month of Sundays, at the very least. I am perishing for want of company. You are an answer to a prayer."

Celeste hid a yawn behind her hand. "As to that, you will have to thank Brother Guy. He is the one in charge of our prayers. Indeed, he does nothing *but* pray."

Lady Eleanor smiled, her brown eyes twinkling with secret merriment. "Aye, perhaps he has much to answer for, and is making amends for his past life."

Celeste detected a story behind that remark, and the smile that accompanied it. Her fatigue momentarily forgotten, she sat up against the bolster and regarded her hostess.

"You have met Brother Guy before?"

Still smiling, Lady Eleanor nodded her head, then settled herself on the bed beside Celeste. "We saw him at court not a year ago, and he was a much different young man then."

"*Mon Dieu!* I did not know that he had ever been to court. I suppose he was the chaplain for one of the queen's ladies?" Celeste did not like that idea. She much preferred to consider Brother Guy as hers alone. *Sweet Jesu!*

Why am I acting like a jealous maiden? She bit her lower lip in shame, though she leaned closer as Lady Eleanor continued her tale.

"Chaplain?" The lady rocked the mattress with her laughter. "Aye, there were many ladies who sought his ministrations, but not, I fear, of the spiritual kind."

"What mean you?" Saints above! Was Brother Guy some manner of rogue priest, who had been banished to that priory in the middle of nowhere because of his ungodly behavior? Celeste couldn't believe that.

Lady Eleanor started to say something, then laughed again and patted Celeste's hand. "Nay, it is nothing to concern you. Your Brother Guy is a fine and honorable man, and you are well protected in his company. Aye, my child, you are as safe with him as with Saint Michael himself. Lie back now, for I see that sleep plays about your eyelids." She stood and smoothed the coverlet over Celeste. "When you are feeling better, we shall talk again."

Though Lady Eleanor's remarks danced through her mind as maids about a flowered maypole, Celeste found she could not stay awake. Without quite realizing when it happened, she slipped into the first sound sleep she had enjoyed since leaving her aunt at Saint Hugh's Priory. A tall knight in silver armor galloped through her dreams, astride Gaston's Black Devil. A pair of golden wings sprouted between his shoulder blades, and his lance was a long tongue of blazing fire. When he paused upon a green hilltop and removed his helm, Celeste saw the unmistakable golden curls and brilliant blue eyes of Brother Guy.

"Will you take some cider? 'Tis fresh-pressed, and very sweet to a dry throat." Sir James held out a brown jug to Guy. When the monk shook his head, his host only nodded and smiled. "So, I see you *have* taken your new vocation seriously. There were a great many at court who wagered that you would not last a month in the bosom of the church. Not when there were so many other bosoms..."

A warm flush stole over Guy's face, and he turned away so that Sir James would not notice his embarrassment. It was most fortunate, for Lissa's sake, that Burke Crest had been near at hand. At the same time, the old family friendship with Sir James put Guy in the awkward position of having his past resurrected before his eyes.

"Sit down, Guy, and take your ease." Sir James waved at a cushioned bench opposite him. " 'Tis good to see you again, though by my troth, I think you have lost some weight since you've taken the cowl. Don't they feed you at Saint Hugh's, or have you renounced food, as well as women?"

Guy settled himself on the bench. When he glanced at the knight's eyes, he saw them twinkling with good humor. He answered Sir James's remark with a wry smile.

"Aye, that's more like it!" Sir James poured himself another cup of cider, then pushed the jug invitingly toward Guy. "You look more like your fair mother now, though that good lady would be much distraught if she had as bald a patch as you. Is she well?"

Guy swallowed, then nodded. How could he tell this kindly gentleman how surprised she had been when he announced his intention of becoming a monk? Nor could he forget the anger of his father, who had ranted and raved about Wolf Hall that the king's best knight was also the king's biggest lackwit. Since entering the Franciscan order, Guy had received only one message from his family—a note of greeting from his mother on his twenty-eighth birthday.

Sir James chuckled. "I knew who you were the moment I clapped mine eyes on you. By the Book! The sight of you riding into my courtyard on that great horse, with your robes hitched up around your hips— Why, my scullery maids will not forget that sight for a season!"

Guy stared down at his sandals. This embarrassment was his just punishment for taking such pleasure in that glorious hell-for-leather ride over the countryside. He promised to offer up his prayers, as well as Sir James's good dinner, for the soul of any maid who might have been tempted to wanton thoughts by the unseemly display of his bare legs and his other manly parts.

Sir James cleared his throat, attracting Guy's attention. "Speaking of maids, that is a fair young lady whom you escort, and you did right well to bring her to us. From the looks of her, I'd say you have been driving her as hard as you drive yourself. That old soldier of hers told me part of the story, but his accent is difficult for me to comprehend. Do I understand she is destined to marry that Ormond spawn?"

Guy's eyes narrowed at the sudden harshness in Sir James's tone. Taking his chalk, he quickly scribbled on his slate.

"What news of the Ormonds?" Sir James repeated Guy's question with a lift of his thick black eyebrows. "Ha! Only bad news follows the Ormond spawn, as you yourself well know. God's teeth! Is that poor child in my best bed truly betrothed to Sir Roger's whelp?"

Guy ground his teeth as Sir James gave full voice to the outrage in his own heart. He nodded again.

"By all that's holy, man! Take her back to her father and be done with it. 'Tis a match made in hell."

She's from a proud family, Guy wrote on his slate.

"Proud, eh? Well, two weeks with that churlish scantling will cure her of that. Walter Ormond will beat all her pride, and everything else, out of the lass. Have you truly lost your wits?" Sir James put his elbows on the oaken table and leaned across to Guy. "Have you so renounced the fairer sex that you now throw them away to ravenous dogs?"

Guy flinched at the rebuke. Everything Sir James said was exactly what he had been asking himself since this mad journey began, almost a fortnight ago.

She cannot return to France, he wrote. He underlined *cannot.* Guy stared into the crackling fire in the hearth while Sir James pondered his words.

The older man stroked his short beard, a new fashion of King Henry's, much copied by his courtiers. "The word from the north is that the Ormond spawn suffers from the pox." Sir James nodded slowly as Guy gaped at him. "Aye, 'tis true. They say the knave carries all the marks, and will not live out another twelvemonth. That will be cold comfort to your lady. By the time he's in his grave, she will be riddled with the pox herself. What say you to that, churchman?"

A roar of anger filled Guy's lungs. He wanted to shout down the new chimney pots into a heap of brick and rubble, then ride to Snape Castle and strangle Walter Ormond with his bare hands. Instead, Guy choked back the black fury churning his blood and dug his nails into the palms of his hands. He knew he should ask God's forgiveness for harboring such violent thoughts, but what was God thinking, to allow so sweet an angel as Celeste to be mated with a poxed devil? How could Guy bow his head and pray, "Thy will be done" when it was his own will he wanted?

I am bound to obey, he scrawled furiously across the slate, his hand shaking with the effort.

Sir James reached over and brushed a hot tear from Guy's cheek. "I'm glad to see you have not yet turned into stone, my boy. Take care of the lady as best you can—and pray for a miracle."

Chapter Eleven

Nature cooperated during the next week in helping drive away Celeste's cold. The rain stopped the day after she arrived at Burke Crest, and a warm October sun sent its healing rays through Sir James's new diamond-paned windows. Thanks to Lady Eleanor's careful nursing and herbal remedies, as well as the infectious good spirits that pervaded the household, Celeste felt more fit in body and soul than she had since leaving France.

Everyone took special pains to make her welcome, especially the Foxmore children—four delightful scamps who strove with varying degrees of success to speak French to their new guest. Celeste, in turn, added to her store of English, which eleven-year-old James and eight-year-old Amanda made a game of teaching her. The other two children, Nell, aged five, and young Harry, a sturdy lad of three, did their best to entertain Celeste, bringing her flowers yanked by the roots from the gardens, birds' feathers, several kittens from a recent litter and assorted sweetmeats cadged from the kitchens.

Once Lady Eleanor allowed her patient out of bed, Celeste enjoyed strolling around the newly built manor house, of which Sir James was inordinately proud. She politely listened to her host's rambling discourses on the cistern in the attic, which allowed the collected rainwater to flow down tile pipes to the kitchens, the size and width of the new fireplaces and the large number of ornate chimney pots, the latest fashion in windows, using a great deal of glass, the artful linen-fold paneling in the private rooms and the wide carved staircase descending to the great hall.

Gaston reported to her that the men and horses relished their respite from the journey. Sir James's servants treated them kindly, even though their knowledge of French was next to nothing. Warm smiles and shared pots of ale—better brewed than most—went a long way toward ensuring good Anglo-French relations. Celeste suspected that the serving maids of the household found her men very interesting, especially now that they had taken proper baths in the nearby river, shaved the stubble off their good honest faces and washed their clothing with lye soap.

As for the young driver, Pierre, Celeste had spied him shyly courting Harry's nursemaid in the garden, singing to her in his fine tenor voice. When the lad tried to steal a kiss, Celeste had made ample noise to warn him away from such forward behavior.

Only Brother Guy appeared to grow more dour and morose as the pleasant days skimmed by. He rarely came to the midday dinner, and almost never to supper. As had happened at the priory, the tall monk disappeared if Celeste came upon his solitary meditations, and his eyes flashed blue fire whenever she caught him staring at her. Celeste couldn't understand his behavior. His brooding appearance alarmed her, though she knew it was pointless to chide him about it—as if he would linger long enough for her to speak more than two words to him.

One particularly sunny afternoon, toward the end of the week, Celeste sought out her favorite bench in the garden. A few late-blooming roses offered their heady perfume to her as she arranged her green brocade skirts. The sun's rays fell warmly on her back as she bent over her favorite book. Dear Mama had given her this exquisite copy of old King René's Book of Love. Celeste cherished the blue leather-bound volume, not only because it was her mother's parting gift, but also because its beautiful tale of the Knight of the Loyal Heart's quest to win the love of the Lady Sweet Grace was Celeste's favorite romance.

Opening the book at random, she soon lost herself in the music of the French poetry and the magic of the full-color illumination that showed the valiant knight arming himself to do battle against the black-clad Knight of Sorrow. The sunlight gleamed on the gold leaf of the True Knight's winged helm, and the page decorations of blue forget-me-nots and red gillyflowers sparkled with their fresh jewel colors. The lavish illustrations reminded Celeste of that long-ago time in her childhood when her father had allowed her to visit him at the legendary Field of Cloth of Gold.

What enchantments that tented city had held for a wide-eyed girl of eleven! What wondrous food and drink! For once, no one had scolded her for eating like a pig. She happily stuffed herself with baked turbot and salmon, pears smothered in cinnamon and cream, roasted peacocks served in their own feathers, and a strange new delicacy called asparagus, which looked like thick stalks of grass but tasted glorious, especially when served in a light lemon cream sauce.

She remembered the spice breads, buns stuck full of raisins, and those thin, sweet wafer biscuits, which tasted especially good with a glass of wine. And the wines! The very fountains standing amid the bright-painted tents had literally flowed with the sweet wines of Burgundy. Celeste licked her lips in remembrance. In truth, she had visited those fountains a bit too often for her own good. Thank the stars no one but an interested dog or two had seen her get sick behind the stables.

The tournaments had left the deepest impression upon her memory. Bright-colored flags above the flower-bedecked pavilions had snapped in the fresh breezes blowing off the Channel, and the teasing June sun had played hide-and-go-seek over the huge tiltyard. Hundreds of knights had participated in the jousts, which began in the early mornings and continued through the long summer afternoons. Celeste had sighed over the handsome knights encased in their armor, burnished to a silver sheen, and their colorful coats of arms emblazoned on their flowing saddlecloths, their shields and their silken surcoats. Long ostrich plumes dyed purple, red, yellow and white had hung from their helms, fanning in the breeze. The young Celeste could hardly contain herself, with all the excitement around her and she had almost been sent back to her father's tent when she snatched the blue veil from her head and held it out to one of the knights as a favor. Alas, the magnificent hero, on his huge charcoal-gray charger, had never even noticed her tiny fluttering scrape of silk.

Lost in the romantic daydreams of her very own Knight of the Loyal Heart, Celeste failed to hear approaching footsteps until a long, dark shadow fell across her page.

"Brother Guy! You startled me!" Celeste snapped the book shut and tried to cover its title with the folds of her skirt. She didn't think the stern-faced archangel in the plain brown robe would approve of her reading material.

She smiled at him, the curves of her mouth deepening with added pleasure when he seated himself beside her on the bench. In fact, she could not remember if they had ever sat next to each other in this way before. At dinner this past week, she had always sat on Sir James's right, while Brother Guy, if he bothered to appear for the meal, took a place down at the lower end of the table, with Gaston and her men-at-arms. Observing him now through the fringe of her lashes, she again noted how very tall he was—even when sitting down. He literally loomed over her, encompassing her in his shadow. A sweet, warm rush filled her body as she raised her eyes to his.

Brother Guy held out his hand, palm open.

"What is it you desire?" she asked lightly. Why was her heart beginning to pound so loudly? "You wish my hand? Do you intend to tell my fortune? La, for shame, good Monk!"

If anything, Guy's expression grew sterner. He shook his head, pointed to the corner of her book, which peeked out from under her green velvet skirts. Then he held out his hand again.

Zut alors! He wanted to see her book. How shocked he would be when he discovered it was not a book of hours, the approved reading matter for gently bred ladies! Not daring to look directly into those blue eyes that seared her soul, Celeste drew the book from its hiding place and dropped it into his hand. Long ago, when her many pranks had threatened the retribution of a hickory switch, she had learned that the best defense was an immediate offense.

"Oh, la, la, Brother Guy! What would your good Father Jocelyn say if he spied you reading a book of romance? I think he would be very shocked, and he might even question the sincerity of your vocation."

Brother Guy said nothing, but merely turned the pages slowly, giving each picture his complete attention. Celeste noticed a small muscle twitching along his jawline. Why did he have to look like such an avenging angel all the time, when he would be so much more pleasing if he just smiled?

"Does the poetry amuse you, Brother Guy?" She twisted the material of her skirts with her fingers when he did not acknowledge her question. "I am sure you will agree that the illustrations are most beautiful, *n'est-ce pas?* I cannot help but wonder what the poor monk who worked so long on them must have thought, especially when he painted the lady's breast in such a warm, living color." Celeste could tell by the way the handsome monk at her side suddenly stiffened that she had scored one direct hit.

"Do you think he had to run to his confessor after he put down his brush, Brother Guy?"

The monk raised his golden head and impaled her with the brilliance of his eyes. Celeste caught her breath, then covered her gasp with quick laughter. "Hey-ho, Brother Guy! I do but jest with you. Don't tell me you have never been teased by a lady before!"

Guy willed his fevered blood to cool. He should have never given in to the temptation to sit beside this bewitching minx. Only his guilty conscience had prompted him to approach her. She had looked so hurt when he deliberately avoided her gaze at supper, or when he passed her in the hall, or at prayers in the chapel. Now he merely wanted to let her know that he was not angry with her. In fact, he found he missed her endless stream of merry chatter, the music of her low laughter and the twinkle of her violet eyes.

Only his self-loathing had kept him away from her rose-scented presence. He ached to join her when he saw her skip down the autumn-strewn garden paths with the little Foxmores. Each time he heard her sweet voice lifted in song, now blessedly clear of the hoarseness of her cold, another sharp pain stabbed his heart. Too soon, he must deliver Lissa up to the poxy Ormond who claimed her for his bride. Too soon he would be the instrument who sucked her dew-fresh beauty from her cheeks when he abandoned her behind the walls of Snape Castle. Guy hated himself for what he had sworn on his honor to do.

"Ma foi!" Celeste murmured next to him, her voice filled with mirth. "If you pull your face any longer, Brother Guy, your chin will drag upon the ground. Why so sad on such a lovely day? Are you angry that God has not sent you a storm to fit your black mood? Pray you, be of good cheer."

Guy wanted to smile for her. His lips quivered at the thought. He wanted to laugh and weep at the same time, then clasp Lissa to his chest, smooth the downy skin between her raven-winged brows with his thumb and tell her she would be safe with him always. He wanted to part her lips with his, delve his tongue into the honey of her mouth, and—

God forgive me! What devil had crept into his thoughts just now and pried opened the locked box of his worldly desires? Tonight he must do more penance, facedown on the dank stones of the chapel floor. Guy wished he had a scourge to chastise himself with, but Father Jocelyn frowned on such practices, calling them "barbaric." Guy craved pain to banish the pleasure that engulfed his senses as he sat on the bench beside Celeste.

Pulling himself together, he pointed to one of the knights who dominated the illustrations in her book.

Celeste sighed, the color of her eyes changing to a lavender mist. *"Oui,* he *is* very handsome. That is the Knight of the Loyal Heart. He is the true and noble knight who seeks to be worthy of the Lady Sweet Grace. You can see his device upon his helm, the winged heart, which shows that a true heart is light and speeds his love to the lady. Upon his shield are three forget-me-nots, to show that he always remembers his lady and the love he bears for her, no matter what adversities he may meet. And he meets many, many evil ones, *oui.*''

Guy cast Celeste a brief sideways glance. *She speaks of this knight as if he were real!* He marveled at the softness of her voice and the faraway expression in her face.

Looking up from her book into his eyes, Celeste stopped abruptly. A becoming pink blush tinted her cheeks. ''You must think me moonstruck, *n'est-ce pas?* Do not shake your head, Brother Guy, for I can read it in your eyes. You have not offended me. I have heard that remark often enough. My good aunt said I lived with my head in the clouds—and my feet everywhere else.''

Guy's lips twitched with his yearning to smile. Lissa could make a gargoyle grin, if she put her formidable wit to it. Nay! Guy must restrain himself. He could not lower the drawbridge to his heart—not even for so charming a lady as Lissa. Especially not for Lissa!

A sigh like a single golden leaf floating on a pale autumn breeze escaped her lips. Then Celeste smiled brightly at him—too brightly, he thought.

''Perhaps my father-in-law-to-be will have a tournament in honor of my wedding to his son. Do you think that is possible?''

Knowing both the Ormonds and their greed, I highly doubt it. Guy shrugged his silent answer—glad he couldn't voice the truth.

Much to Guy's inner distress, Celeste waxed warmer on the subject. ''It would be such a marvelous thing, with all the flags flying and the trumpets announcing the combatants and my husband riding into the lists as my true champion.''

Green bile rose in Guy's throat. Walter Ormond was no one's knight, true or otherwise. His behavior at court had banished him long before he could earn his spurs. And fighting for a lady's honor would be the very last thing Ormond desired on his wedding day. Rutting in the middle of the marriage feast would be his idea of combat.

"La, I would so like to reign over a tournament as the Queen of Truth and Beauty. Just once." Her slim finger lightly touched the illustration of the Knight of the Loyal Heart. "I saw a tourney in France, when I was eleven. It was at the Field of Cloth of Gold when our two kings met and entertained each other. There was the most splendid knight there—taller than all the rest, and he wore the device of a fearsome wolf, teeth all snarling and a long red tongue hanging out."

Guy went very still. A dormant ember of pride burst into flame in a secret place of his heart. By the rood, Lissa had seen him joust in his early days at King Henry's court! The wolf emblem belonged to his branch of the Cavendish family, and while both he and his brother Brandon had broken many lances on the field of honor, there was no confusion about which brother was which. Though Brandon was a year older, Guy was the taller by a head. And Lissa had seen him joust!

Celeste shook her head with a sad, sweet smile. "He was such a tall knight, he didn't notice me. I was quite small then, you understand, even shorter than I am now. When the Knight of the Wolf rode to the wall and filled his lance with the ribbons and favors of the ladies—many ladies, I may add—well..." She lifted her shoulders in an eloquent shrug. "He did not see me standing there. Do you know I have kept that little blue veil I tried to give him? A silly thing to do, you may think. Perhaps, but it is also very romantic."

A shy smile fluttered across her lips. "I must confess a secret to you, Brother Guy, for I know you will not betray

my confidence. You see, I have always been secretly in love
with my brave Knight of the Wolf, even though I never saw
his face. My sisters teased me for years, calling him my
dream lover. It is true, for he has often been found haunt-
ing my pillow at midnight."

Celeste tossed her head, as if to wipe away her last
words. "Of course, now I must put away such childish
fancies, for soon I will have a real knight by my side—my
husband. Perhaps I shall wear the little blue veil on my
wedding day for luck."

Guy felt as if the icy fingers of the Northumberland
winter held him fast in their grip. Down through the years,
Lissa had loved him. Nay, his conscience reminded him,
she loved the faceless knight with a wolf's device. She
never knew *you,* therefore she did not love you. Besides,
what does it matter now? You are for the church, and she
is for... Guy squeezed his eyes shut to blot out the grotesque image of Walter Ormond that pranced through his
mind.

"*Pardonnez-moi,* Brother Guy!" Lissa's sweet voice
instantly banished the sickening sight. "I have been remiss. I see you suffer a headache, *oui?* And all my prattling has made it worse. Forgive my stupidity."

With that, she leapt up from the bench, snatched her
book and, lifting her thick skirts, which revealed her slim
ankles, dashed down the gravel walk. The pale green veil
attached to her coif caught on an outstretched branch of a
yew as she rounded the hedge, but she quickly disengaged
it and disappeared.

Guy sat very still on the hard stone bench and wondered when he had last yearned so much for the touch of
a woman.

Chapter Twelve

Leaving Burke Crest after early mass the next morning proved to be very difficult for both the Foxmores and Celeste's party. Little Harry bawled loudly to see Pierre, his newfound playmate, leap into the driver's seat of the wagon. Harry's pretty nursemaid looked equally bereft. Lady Eleanor managed to rescue Nell's secret gift of a new kitten, who yowled in piteous tones for its mother inside a canvas sack amid the baggage. With many thanks for the Foxmores' generous hospitality and many more promises to keep in touch with her new friends, Celeste mounted her palfrey.

"It is too bad that the young James is not old enough to be your husband," Gaston muttered as he adjusted her saddle girth. "I would approve of that marriage."

Celeste leaned over so that only Gaston could hear her. "You mean you approve of his father's ample larder and their even more generous cook, *oui?*"

Gaston puffed out his cheeks and knotted his thick brows. "The devil take you, my lady, for spying on a man's private affairs."

"Oh, my good Gaston, I did no spying myself, but the children! *Ma foi!* What can one do with four pairs of bright eyes watching every move?"

"Bah! Little foxes they are!" Gaston glanced over his shoulder at the four forlorn faces watching from the top of the stairs. "I will remember your sins in my prayers!" he shouted to them in French, with a huge grin of forgiveness.

Young James swept him a courtly bow. "*Merci beaucoup,* brave soldier," he answered.

"The young jackanapes has picked up a fair speech in just a week. *Mon Dieu!* What I could do in a month with a boy that quick!" Gaston muttered with an approving gleam in his eye.

Celeste laughed, in spite of her sorrow at leaving. "My mind is not wide enough to contemplate that possibility, Gaston."

Guy left last, detained by Sir James, who engaged him in a private conference. Neither man looked happy upon parting.

"Remember what I said, churchman!" Sir James called after Guy as the party wended its way out the gates of Burke Crest. " 'Twill be upon your soul!"

Guy said nothing, of course, but his face looked thunderous.

Celeste spent the rest of the cool, misty morning wondering what her kind host had meant by his strange admonition. She knew it was pointless to ask Guy. Sitting as straight as a poker on his beast, he acted as if he were going to his execution. Perhaps he was beginning to miss the priory, and longed to be back within its safe confines. On the other hand, perhaps Brother Guy just hated being astride balky old Daisy again. After listening to Gaston's complaints about the donkey's sharp bones and sharper disposition, Celeste couldn't blame the monk, though he bore his discomfort with his customary stoic forbearance.

* * *

The fierce wind from the North Sea spewed winter on its breath, turning the bare trees on the moorlands of Northumberland into glistening frosty sculptures. Nightly, ice formed a thin cover in the wells and horse troughs. Even the washing water in the master bedroom froze before morning. Walter Ormond drew his cloak tighter around his shivering body and damned the arrival of an early snow.

Only today a weary messenger had brought the discouraging word to Snape Castle that the promised bride—*his* bride—had delayed her journey once again, this time on the pretext of some sort of indisposition.

"When the wench is mine, I'll see to it that she moves right smartly," he growled to Scullion, one of the few minions who still enjoyed Walter's company—or Walter's purse. It mattered not. Scullion would sell his own mother for a farthing.

"Aye," Scullion nodded, then drained his pot of hot ale. "Ye make all the lasses skip to yer tune, m'lord." He wiped both his mouth and his runny nose with the back of his hand.

"That I do," Walter agreed without humor. He splashed more ale into his cup from the large brown jug that warmed on the hob. "So where are these good men you promised me?"

"They come, by an' by," replied his coarse companion.

"When it suits them," Walter snarled. "If they want to be paid, they'd best learn to hop when it suits me." He drained his ale without pleasure.

"'Doin' the devil's own work is ticklish business, m'lord," Scullion pointed out in a mild tone. "Dark deeds need dark hours. They will come anon."

Walter slammed his empty cup on the table. "Taking a wife is no dark deed."

Scullion answered with a sharp laugh followed by a hiccup. "Aye, but takin' another man's wife, now that be right murky."

"The wench is mine by law." Walter stifled the impulse to push his fist into Scullion's greasy face. The dim voice of prudence reminded him that friends, even those bought with silver, were getting sparser for him.

Walter knew that people called him Ormond's spawn, and probably a good deal worse. Few wenches would lie with him any more, unless they were toothless hags, or even more pox-ridden than he. Every time he thought of the fresh young French bride coming to him, he salivated. The devil and his dam take his father! The girl—and her needed gold—were Walter's.

It seemed to Guy that since he'd wanted to delay the journey as much as possible, the bridal party had made even better time than before. By late afternoon, they arrived at the outskirts of Chester. From here, they would cross over the spine of the country and head north for York, the largest city outside of London. Guy found lodging at a small but reputable inn he knew, under the sign of the Blue Boar. Despite the building's slightly shabby facade, Guy knew the innkeeper to be an honest, cheerful man. And one blessed with too good a memory, as Guy discovered when the travelers entered the taproom.

"Welcome back, my lord!" A tiny, spare man, almost lost in the folds of his apron, bounced out from behind the counter. "Or is it Brother Monk now? Aye, by the look of you, I'd say it is. So you *did* go for the church, just as you told me you would last March—or was that April when you passed through here?"

Barely pausing for reply or a breath, the innkeeper turned his hospitable charm on Celeste. "And I see you bring glad company to brighten my establishment. Welcome, welcome!"

Celeste drew herself up as tall as possible and smiled prettily at the host of the Blue Boar. "Good evening, good man," she began slowly in English. Her better pronunciation surprised Guy. Since she preferred to speak French to him, he had not heard how well her English had progressed thanks to the young Foxmores' tutelage. Catching sight of his surprise, Celeste shot him a quick grin of triumph. "We 'ave much need of a room for the night."

The innkeeper made a small bow. "Right you are, my lady! And you've come to the finest hostelry in Chester. I am honored." He looked around to Gaston and the other men, nodding and smiling all the while.

No doubt our friendly landlord is sizing up the wealth of his customers. Taking out his slate, Guy questioned the fee. He hoped it hadn't been raised since his last visit, on his way south to join the monastery. The innkeeper glanced quizzically at the slate.

"Your pardon for asking, my lord, but has the cat got your tongue?" The little man chuckled at his own joke.

"'E is without speech," Celeste informed him.

"Aye." The innkeeper nodded as if that explained everything. "With your beauty, my lady, I can see why."

Celeste dimpled in reply and fluttered her lashes a bit. Guy wanted to shake her before she got too carried away by the man's compliments. He wrote, *Four shillings for all, dinner included?* The price was more than fair, yet not ruinous to Celeste's dwindling purse.

The innkeeper nodded again. "Aye, and there you have it, my lord monk, my lady." He ushered them toward the timeworn stairs ascending to the first-floor gallery. "I have the finest hostelry in Chester,'' he bragged. ''Table linens changed daily, and every traveler who lays his head upon my pillows is assured right well of clean sheets and no bedbugs.'' He puffed himself up very proudly.

''For the lady,'' he intoned, opening the door to a small side room. The fading light through the dormer window revealed a plain bed, a table with pitcher and bowl, and a stool. ''And your men can sleep in here.'' He waved to the common room at the end of the hall, which held four cots, as well a larger table and stools before a small fireplace.

The innkeeper glanced at Guy, then scratched his head. ''Would Your Lordship prefer—'' he began, but Guy cut him off with a quick hand motion.

The monk had renounced the trappings of nobility when he donned the simple brown robe of the Franciscan order, and the innkeeper's babbling about ''Your Lordship'' embarrassed him. Also, it would be better if Lissa thought that Guy was a poor man, and not the son of a Border lord. Guy pointed to the floor of the hallway just outside Celeste's door.

The host of the Blue Boar shook his head, a puzzled knot wrinkling his brow. ''Aye, you may sleep there, if that is your pleasure, my lord.''

'Tis not my pleasure but my pain. I dare not name the place wherein I would rather sleep this night. Guy's mouth went very dry, and he longed for a cooling draft of ale.

The innkeeper turned again to Celeste, who stared, mouth agape, at the monk. Guy could see a question forming on those full pink lips of hers, and he didn't want to answer it. Fortunately, the innkeeper rattled on, diverting her attention.

''Now, my lady, twill be but a tick of the clock and I'll have a fire for your comfort in yon room and a bite of supper. I'll warrant you are famished. Hungry?'' he added in a louder tone, speaking to her as if she were deaf. "What say you to a bit of beef, and new-laid eggs fried in sweet butter and garnished with parsley?"

Smiling, Celeste nodded, which encouraged the landlord to greater heights of description.

"Bread, both brown and white, so please you, my lady, and an apple tart, fresh-baked this morning by my good wife. You like apples?" He raised his voice again and spoke slowly.

Celeste didn't flinch under his well-meaning onslaught. "*Oui,* good man. I am ver-rey..." She paused, struggling for the correct word. "I like apples ver-rey much. *Merci.*" she concluded, flushed with her latest triumph over the foreign English.

"Good, good." The landlord stood nodding and smiling at the pretty young woman. Guy finally gave him a little push and pointed down the stairs. "Aye, my lord monk, to be sure." The little man backed up, teetering on the top step. "A fire and supper and water for washing. At once, and again, welcome to the Blue Boar." With that, the innkeeper all but fell down the narrow staircase in his haste to serve them.

"By the petticoat of Saint Catherine!" Gaston snorted as the clatter of the landlord's thick shoes died away. "I pray that fellow is as long on his drafts of ale as he is on his talk. If we are fortunate, we shall have supper sometime before midnight." He handed Celeste the worn saddlebag containing the apostle spoons. "I think I will go down and hurry him along a bit, for I swear by the stars, I could eat a horse. Aye, even a horse roasted by an English cook."

Gaston, with Émile, Paul and René in tow, descended to the taproom, leaving Guy and Celeste alone together. Guy shifted his feet nervously. The narrow hallway seemed to close in about them.

Celeste cocked her head, and a soft, sensual smile wreathed her lips. "Thinking of flying away again? So where will you run to now, my *lord* priest?" she asked, reverting to French in her rich brown-velvet voice. "It is most strange, I think, that you never want to be in my company." Her violet eyes darkened to a deep purple. "Is it because my breath is sour? *Non,* I think not, for I chew mint leaves every day."

Guy turned to go. With her standing so close to him, the musk of her rose scent invaded his defenses. He tried not to think how tempting her sweet mouth looked, or how the stray locks of her midnight hair beckoned his fingers to roam therein.

Celeste blocked his exit down the stairs. "Oh, la, la! Have I suddenly turned into a dragon, Brother Guy? Do I frighten you? Boo!" She folded her arms over the saddlebag and stood her ground.

Aye, Lissa, you scare up the very devil in me.

Fixing a deep frown on his features, Guy pointed down the stairs. If he wanted to, he could sweep her off her feet as easily as he could a kitten, but he knew that once he held her slim waist in his hands, he would be loath to put her down again. He tried to shoulder his way around her, though he feared she might fall down the stairs.

"I will let you go—for now." Celeste grinned, a wicked look in her eye. "But only if you give me your solemn word of honor that I shall have the pleasure of your company after supper."

Guy's eyes widened. What mischief did this minx have in mind? Her invitation echoed many others he had received when he played cupid's fool at court. Surely she could not think of seducing him! And yet, for all her wit and professed honor, Celeste was still only a weak woman, and he, God help him, was losing his last shred of fortitude against her wiles. A cold wash at the well, that was what Guy needed this minute. That, and several hours on his knees, in deep meditation on his sins.

She tapped her foot lightly on the scarred floor. "I am waiting for your promise, Brother Guy. I think the time has come for the reckoning due me."

What was Lissa talking about? What did he owe her but his sworn duty to deliver her into the hands of a fiend? That day of reckoning would come soon enough.

"Your promise to meet me in the great room after supper, my lord monk, or you will have to push me down the stairs."

Don't tempt me, fair Lissa.

"*Ma foi!* You would think I have asked you to strip off your robe and dance naked under the moon!" Her eyes glowed.

Haven't you, sweet temptress?

"Well, Brother Guy?"

Clenching his teeth, Guy nodded his assent.

"*Très bien!* I shall expect you then." She stepped aside.

As Guy brushed past her, she grabbed hold of his sleeve. "And do not think you can hide in the jakes all night. I have no shame, and that is the very first place I shall look for you." She released his sleeve. "Best be warned, Sir Monk. I always get what I go after."

Guy took the rest of the stairs three at a time. Her smoky laughter followed after him.

Chapter Thirteen

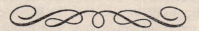

True to his unspoken word, Guy appeared at the doorway of the common room shortly after the delicious supper promised and provided by the cheerful little host of the Blue Boar. Guy looked like a forbidding wraith, except for that bright golden halo of curls about his head. Pretending she hadn't noticed him, Celeste fiddled with the skirts of her crimson velvet gown, its furred hem falling warmly over her thin house slippers. Crimson was her favorite color, and Celeste hoped her choice of gown would put Guy into an amenable frame of mind.

Though Celeste tried to convince herself that she was doing the right thing, her fingers trembled a little as she pulled the small table closer to her and rearranged the items upon it—a candlestick with a new taper, a small jug of the landlord's best wine, two cups and a fresh deck of cards. Celeste picked up the cards and began to shuffle them. The familiar feel of the smooth pasteboard sliding through her fingers put her a little more at ease. She loved card games. At home in L'Étoile, she was considered the family champion. Now she would see if she could use her skill to relax her glowering—and challenging—escort.

It is only an innocent game or two of cards, not an assignation, she reasoned with herself. Then why was her heart skipping so erratically, and why had her breathing become more difficult the minute he stood at the door? *It must be the stays of my bodice. I pulled them too tight when I dressed.*

Celeste smiled up at him with all the charm she could muster, despite the flock of butterflies fluttering in the pit of her stomach. "Good evening, Brother Guy. Please come in and sit down." She indicated the stool opposite her. "Oh, la, la!" she continued lightly when she saw him hesitate. "Do you think I have asked you to hear my confession?"

An expression of pure horror etched Guy's face. Celeste suppressed her inclination to giggle. Instantly she decided that Brother Guy was not the one to hear her whispered transgressions.

"But no, good monk. I have no great sin to confess—at least, not yet," she couldn't help but add with a mischievous tilt of her head. Poor Brother Guy was really such fun to tease. She reminded herself to be careful not to wound his vanity again, the way she had done when Guy took that unfortunate spill off Daisy's back. She suspected that under his shapeless robe there beat the heart of a very proud man.

"Please sit down. I promise not to bite." She ruffled the cards again. Through her lowered lashes she watched him silently pad across the floor between them, like a wary kit fox who must be coaxed from its den with patience and food. Guy lowered his large frame onto the stool and eyed Celeste intently.

Good. We have crossed the first bridge, she thought.

Celeste continued to shuffle the deck. "I thought we might pass a pleasant evening together playing cards. I think you pray too much. The good Lord made us to play, as well as to pray, *non?*"

Guy eyed the cards in her hand, and his frown deepened.

"*Ma foi!* Such a face! Come now, Brother Guy, surely there is no harm in a game of cards? I know you have no money, so we will not gamble."

Guy's eyes narrowed to icy slits as he looked from the cards to the wine. He made a move as if to rise.

Celeste quickly placed her hand over his. The touch of his warm skin under her fingers sent her butterflies into full flight, knocking against the sides of her breast. When he turned his startled eyes upon her, she snatched back her hand as if it had been burned.

"Please!" she murmured. "Stay with me a little while."

Celeste swallowed, trying to regain her composure and to erase the raw loneliness in her voice. She couldn't let him know how much she craved company—his company—or he'd bolt like a hare and never come near her again.

Guy wavered; his eyes, like a blue sky full of shifting clouds, mirrored a quick succession of emotions she couldn't read.

Celeste sat back, squared her shoulders and flashed him a winning smile—at least, she hoped he'd find it winning. It always worked on her mother. "What is a game of cards? Pah! Nothing but a chance to while away the tedious hours between supper and sleep. What am I to do? The light is too poor for reading or sewing." She leaned forward and lowered her voice. "And to tell the truth—and as you are a man of God, I must tell you the truth—I sew very badly. I hope my new husband will not mind."

Guy looked away from her. Celeste had the feeling she was losing ground. "I cannot go to the taproom and sing songs and make jests, as Gaston and my men do. That would be unseemly for a lady. So, good Brother Guy, tell me. What am I to do?"

Having fired her last arrow, Celeste held her breath. Very slowly, Guy turned his beautiful face toward her again. The ice in his eyes had melted, and they gazed at her with the color of a new-washed May morning. He pointed to the cards and nodded.

Relief flooded Celeste. She had no idea how important this little game of cards had become until this moment. "*Merci,* Brother Guy. Consider this an act of sweet charity on your part. Besides, I do not recall that you took a vow *not* to play cards. Wine? The landlord has assured me it is a French vintage—but I think he would tell me anything I wanted to hear."

Guy's lips twitched. Grasping the jug, he poured the ruby liquid into the cups.

Celeste shuffled the deck again, though she knew it needed no further mixing. "Do you know the game of piquet? I believe the English call it cent, though *why* they call it that I do not know. I find that the English take great pleasure in turning our beautiful French language into something horrible and not French at all. Have you ever heard how they pronounce the fine name of Beauchamps?" She made a wry face. "Beech-hem! *Sacre!* It is enough to make the stones weep—good *French* stones, that is!"

Guy's lips twitched again. He drank some of the wine.

"So we play cent, *oui?*"

Guy nodded. His eyes seem to blaze blue sparks in the candlelight. Celeste wondered if her imaginary butterflies would suddenly fly out of her mouth.

She took a tentative sip of her wine and was pleasantly surprised to find it good. "Since you cannot speak out your points, let us keep score on your slate, *oui?*"

In answer, Guy set his slate and a bit of chalk on the table.

Celeste leaned across to him. "Now, good Brother, what shall we wager?"

Guy frowned. Celeste quickly hurried on. Here was the nut and core of her plan—the main reason for the card game in the first place.

"I speak of simple things, not money. For instance, if you win, what shall I have to do? Sing a song? Tell a story?"

Guy shook his head. He folded his hands together, palm to palm.

"Pray?" Celeste sighed. Of course he'd think of that! Wasn't prayer his favorite occupation?

The corner of Guy's mouth wiggled. He shook his head. Holding out his folded hands, he slowly opened them, then pretended to read what was written on his palms.

"Ah! I am to read you a story! *Ma foi!* I do not think my book of love is to your taste, Brother Guy."

He shook his head again. Then he continued to pantomime reading, even wetting his finger and turning an invisible page. At the end, he blessed himself.

Celeste should have guessed his wager from the first. "You wish me to read from my book of hours?"

Guy nodded, his face a mask.

Celeste blew through her nose. She knew every prayer by heart in her book of devotions, and their routine repetition tended to lull her to sleep. She wondered if the good Lord got very tired of hearing everybody saying the same words to him over and over again. When she prayed, Celeste much preferred an informal chat with the Almighty.

"I agree, you crafty man. In the unlikely event that I lose, I promise to read my book of hours—for one full day."

Guy's brows rose inquiringly.

Celeste smiled. "In all honesty, good Brother, I cannot promise more. One day for me is like a month for everyone else. Do you accept this forfeit?"

Guy nodded, then took another drink. Celeste was pleased to see him enjoying her wine. She wasn't sure if he had sworn off food and drink except for his customary bread and water, but a little wine strengthened the blood. Everyone knew that—except the English, who insisted that their ale was a healthy drink. Fah! Disgusting!

"And if I should win this game, Brother Guy, you will have to pay the forfeit of..." She cocked her head and enjoyed his shifting discomfort. Did he think she would demand the usual kiss? What a tempting thought! But, no, Celeste must always remember that the archangel seated across from her was first and foremost a man of the church. "A smile, Brother Guy. I wager you for a smile."

He nodded his agreement.

"*Très bien,* and so we begin our game." With that, Celeste dealt out the cards, twelve each.

She quickly discovered that she had underestimated Guy's skill. By the tenth trick of the first game, she began to fear that not only would she be nosedown in her book of hours all day tomorrow, but worse, she would never see him smile. She glanced at him over the top of the few remaining cards in her hand. Guy's face could have been carved in stone—beautiful, expressionless and cold. The only alive thing about him was his eyes, which occasionally seemed to twinkle at her, though she discounted that as a trick of the flickering candlelight.

After miserably losing the first game, Celeste concentrated harder on the second. Though she did not lose as many tricks this time, her score was still very low. The image of that wretched book full of saints and angels floated in her imagination. She must win that smile! She knew that once he smiled for her, the ice would be broken and he would act much more friendly toward her in the future.

By the fourth game, Celeste had managed to narrow the gap in the score. Though Guy's expression remained impassive, little indications, such as the way he slapped his cards on the table, told her that he was not happy with his losses. *Bon!* It was high time this glowering giant learned a lesson or two in humility. Good for his soul, Celeste told herself.

At the end of the sixth game, Guy tallied the marks. He stared at the slate for a moment, then poured out the last of the wine for himself and tossed it back in a single gulp.

Celeste bit back a smile. "May I see the score, *s'il vous plaît?*"

Not looking at her, Guy pushed the slate across the tabletop. Its passage made a grating sound. Celeste saw at a glance that she had won by a mere six points, but she pretended to linger over the marks as if she could not add them up. She waited to see if he would confess his defeat.

After a minute or two, he suddenly reached out and snatched back the slate. He rubbed out the marks, then scribbled something across its cleaned surface. *You won.*

"Ah, Bro*ther* Guy, I thank you for your honesty. And now, my forfeit, if you please?"

Folding her hands on the table, Celeste waited. Guy lifted his eyes to meet hers. For a long, heart-stopping moment, they stared at each other across the narrow width of the table. His ice-blue eyes changed to an indigo. Celeste felt herself drowning in their depths, and she prayed that he could not read the most unmaidenly thoughts that tumbled about in her mind like whirligigs in a high wind.

His lips twitched, then slowly pulled back into a grimace that showed a great deal of teeth and nothing else.

Celeste shook her head. "*Non,* Bro*ther* Guy. That is not a smile. That is a look of a horse who does not like the taste of the bit in his mouth. My wager was a smile—a real smile. Not with your teeth, but with your eyes, as well. Not with your lips, but with your heart."

She held her breath. Would he do it? Guy blinked once, and then his lips twitched in that now-familiar way. The corners of his mouth began to curl upward. As his smile deepened, his eyes took on a softer hue—an azure lake on a misty day. Celeste trembled as she watched an amazing change sweep over him. Gone was the stern, unapproachable statue of an angel. Now, before her, appeared Saint Gabriel in the flesh. She could almost imagine blinding rays of light emanating from his halo of curls. Had she thought Guy handsome before? That had been nothing but a murky shadow of the true man. His sheer beauty transfixed her. If she never saw another smile from him, Celeste knew, she would never forget this spectacular one. Its warmth seared through every fiber of her being; its fire left an indelible imprint on her heart.

"*Magnifique!*" she breathed.

The sound of her voice extinguished the blaze in his eyes. As a candle snuffed out his smile disappeared, leaving only Guy's customary chiseled expression. Abruptly he stood. Turning on his heel, he strode out of the room. Several of the cards fluttered in his wake, landing in a dejected heap on the floor. His swiftly retreating footsteps thundered down the stairs.

Celeste stared at his vacant place for a long time, trying to understand what had happened. When she finally rose and carried the candle into her own room, she felt a black emptiness within her. The butterflies had died.

Guy pressed his forehead against the cold stone of the stable's outer wall and inhaled a deep breath of the brisk night air. Though he had managed to walk through the crowded taproom without attracting unusual notice, his heart hammered as if he had run five miles in full armor. Squeezing his eyes shut, he prayed for help and guidance.

Lord, forgive my weakness! He should have never agreed to meet Celeste alone. Once there, he should not have let her talk him into that card game or drunk her wine. She caught him off guard with her remark about hearing her confession. God's teeth! One of these days she might very well ask him to do just that, and expect him to give her absolution.

Nay, what sins could such an innocent have committed thus far? Except the sin of stealing the heart of a weak-willed, struggling Franciscan novice who should have been made of sterner stuff. Ah, but that last hour with her had been sweet!

In Great Harry's court, Guy had enjoyed the reputation of a skilled gamester, not only with women but with cards. Many a night he had filled his purse with princely winnings from the games of cent, primero and hazard, only to spend it all the following day on some idle fancy for his latest ladylove. Never in his life had he played at cards for so trifling a stake as a smile. Never had his loss been so expensive, for what was money compared to the price he placed upon his soul?

I wanted to leave that life behind me, and now it follows me in a guise more desirable than I have ever known. The lady is a devil!

While his mind fumbled through the first part of his nightly office, his memory conjured up her sweet face. The more Guy strove to banish thoughts of Lissa from his prayers, the more she intruded into them.

Never again would he allow her to breach his weak defenses. Never again would he trust himself to be alone with her. Lissa was all grace and beauty, fire and rose petals. Like the proverbial pearl of great price, this most stunning woman would shortly be cast at the feet of the greatest swine that had ever mucked through England's bogs, and he—Sir Guy Cavendish, a knight sworn to the code of chivalry and a man of God sworn to obey—by his right arm he would hurl sweet Lissa to her undeserved fate. Afterward, Guy knew, he would damn himself to the grave for his part in such a foul deed, while he prayed to the silent God above for forgiveness.

She is nothing to me but a temptress—and someone else's bride. I must only do my duty by her, then begone. She has no hold on me, nor I on her.

A mocking laughter echoed in the dark recesses of his brain. A truth colored by wine.

Fearing to return to the scant comfort afforded by a pallet on the floor of the upstairs hall—the floor just outside Celeste's door—Guy bedded down in the stable, drawing a thick covering of clean straw over him for warmth. But the sleep he craved did not lie down with him. Eyes open or shut, he could not blot Lissa out of his racing thoughts. Nor could he forget the look of anguish she had given him when he bolted from her and ran. Never had he deliberately hurt a woman—until now. As surely as if he had shot her with an arrow, he had wounded the one woman who deserved only kindness from him.

In an early hour of the morning, when all the world slept shrouded in thick darkness, Guy rose, shook the straw from his robe and crept back inside the Blue Boar. The boy who played the night watchman was startled awake, but he grinned in a lopsided manner when he recognized the tall monk. Guy blessed the lad, then made his silent way up the stairs.

Looking like a large wolfhound, Gaston lay across Celeste's closed threshold, snoring loudly. As Guy stepped past him, Gaston snapped awake and drew his dagger from under his blanket.

"Say one last prayer, you shag-eared ruffian, before I skewer your liver." Whispering his threat in French, Gaston pressed his blade against Guy's side.

Reacting instinctively, Guy wrapped one hand around Gaston's knife-wielding wrist, while the other closed around the old soldier's throat. Gaston struggled, then suddenly relaxed in Guy's grip.

Jesu! I could have killed the man so easily! Guy released his hold. Gaston sputtered and choked, muffling the noise in his blanket.

"By the devil's cock, man, you have a damnable strong hand for a puling milksop of a monk," Gaston gasped, when he could finally get breath enough to speak. "What do you mean to sneak up here this way, instead of keeping good Christian hours?"

In the dark hallway, Guy could do nothing to answer Gaston's question.

"If it had not been for that robe you wear, I wouldn't have recognized you, and you would have been greeting Saint Peter at heaven's gate by now." Gaston sheathed his dagger, then massaged his neck. "*Oui*, you think your strength bested me, Brother Guy?" He blew out a blast of ale fumes. "Fah! There's not a man I've yet met who has fully tested my mettle. Now I'm for my bed, and you are welcome to this reeky pallet."

Gaston lumbered into the large communal room, leaving Guy holding his thin blanket. A squeak of the knotted bed ropes told Guy that Gaston had found his resting place. In less than five minutes, Guy heard the old soldier's heavy, even breathing. So, his earlier snores had been just a ruse, Guy thought with increased respect for Celeste's aging watchdog.

As he stared at her door, Guy's hand hovered over the handle. Perhaps his scuffle with Gaston had awakened her, and now she cowered under the covers, too frightened to see what had happened.

Gently he lifted the latch, and pushed open the door. By the light of the waning moon, he saw her form in the middle of the bed. His ear barely detected her soft, steady breathing. Telling himself that he merely wanted to be sure she was safely asleep, he crossed to her bedside like a night-prowling cat.

A cascade of black hair fanned across the pillow. By the Book! She was more beautiful than he recalled from that last memorable time he had seen her in her nightgown. The heat he had spent so many hours quenching rose again in his blood. As he looked closer at her face, a sharp knife of guilt twisted in his heart. Down her cheeks, the moonlight revealed the traces of dried tears—tears shed, no doubt, as a result of his churlish behavior.

Forgive me, dearest Lissa, because I cannot forgive myself. He caught himself before he stroked her forehead. *If I could, I would ride into your life on my gray charger and whisk you away from all tears and pain. I would give you only joy for your bread and laughter for your drink. I would...*

He backed away from the bed, appalled at himself for his unholy thoughts. Hating himself for all that he yearned to have and knew he couldn't possess, Guy huddled under the blanket outside Lissa's door.

Sweet Jesu, what are you doing to me?

Chapter Fourteen

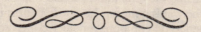

Over the next few days, Celeste and her retinue pushed northeast, through the villages of Helsby and Daresbury. Though Brother Guy politely acknowledged her presence whenever Celeste rode close to him, she realized that he had entrenched himself more firmly behind his aloof barrier. Her clever plan to make him more friendly toward her had failed miserably. Perhaps it was for the best. In the secret recesses of her heart, she admitted she was growing too fond of him. Celeste tried to put him—and that memorable, shattering smile—out of her mind, and to turn a cheerful face to her companions.

A day out of Manchester, the weather changed for the worse. Rain, whipped by a stiff wind, howled down upon the travelers and turned the already soft road into a quagmire. Despite Pierre's best efforts to guide the horses, the lumbering cart carrying all of Celeste's worldly possessions constantly bogged down in enormous water-filled ruts.

"God's nightshirt!" Gaston bellowed as the men struggled with the wagon for the fourth time that afternoon. "This is too impossible in this weather. Put your weak-hinged backs into it, or by the beard of my father—" He cut off his threat when the cart squeaked and groaned out of the hole. "Load it up quickly again, before we lose daylight altogether. A pox on it! Does it do nothing but rain in this cursed place?"

Celeste, mounted on her palfrey, huddled deeper in her cloak under the scant protection of a leafless tree and tried not to think how long she had endured this trip. It seemed they had been traveling these unfriendly roads all her life. Only thoughts of the warm hearths of Snape Castle and the handsome face of her waiting bridegroom kept up her waterlogged spirits. She dared not tell Gaston that her throat felt raw again. As soon as they found shelter for the night, she would dose herself up with hot spiced wine and honey, and go to bed immediately. A good night's sleep would clear up the light-headedness she experienced. She must not allow another bout of ill health to prolong this wretched journey any further.

"Good Lady, are you ready to go on?" Gaston reined his huge black steed in front of her. When she looked up at him to give her assent, he swore a very shocking oath.

"The devil take it! You are not well!"

Celeste shook her head. "*Non*, good Gaston. I am merely wet. Let us be gone from this place."

Gaston put his hand on her bridle. "You may hood-wink half the world, young lady, but I've known you since you were in leading strings, and you cannot fool me. Brother Guy!" he roared over his shoulder.

"Do not disturb the monk, Gaston. We have tried his patience sore enough as it is." Celeste didn't want Brother Guy to think her a weakling. He obviously found her a trial enough as it was.

"*Sacre!*" snorted the old soldier, the fire of determination blazing in his brown eyes. "I will disturb him, all right. I will blast him off that waggish, rump-fed flea-house of his. Brother Guy!"

Guy appeared, ghostlike, out of the curtain of rain. Celeste pulled her hood lower over her face and hunched into her cloak. Even without looking, she knew when Guy turned his piercing blue eyes upon her. His gaze scorched through her thin defenses.

"You know this country, monk, and I pity you for that. My lady has a fever again, and I'll not have her die here on the road. Not for the king of this hag-ridden land himself! We need a goodly house for shelter." Leaning over in his saddle, Gaston nearly shouted his last words into the stony face of the angel on the ill-tempered donkey.

Celeste squeezed her eyes shut with embarrassment. If she didn't feel so giddy, she'd chastise Gaston for his rudeness. As it was, she knew his diagnosis was correct.

For the first time since that evening at the Blue Boar, Guy touched her. Caught by surprise, Celeste nearly fell out of her saddle when he took her wrist in his hand. He pressed his fingers against her pulse point and appeared to be listening to her heartbeat through the skin. By the stars! Could he tell how fast her pulse raced because he was so near?

Dropping her hand, Guy reached up and felt her forehead. The hard planes of his features changed and became almost tender—or was it her hopeful imagination that made Celeste think so? She quickly glanced down at her hands, which clutched the leather reins.

"I am well, just fatigued, Brother Guy. Let us be off, or it will be the horses who will catch a cough," she murmured.

Shielding his slate with his body from the downpour, Guy quickly wrote, *Lend me your horse,* and thrust it under Gaston's nose.

"Oui." Gaston quickly dismounted, and Guy leapt into the saddle with ease, despite the heavy soaked robe that wrapped itself around his body.

Guy pointed to Celeste, then to the place in front of him. Nodding again, Gaston reached up to help Celeste down.

"What is this?" She clutched Gaston's cape. Were they going to abandon her here on the road?

"Be still, my lady. The good brother will carry you to safety, and you will get there faster on Black Devil than on your own dainty horse. Pierre, come here!" Ignoring Celeste's weak protests, Gaston handed her up to Guy.

The monk easily lifted her, then settled her on the saddle in front of him. Guy gathered her close against his broad chest with one arm. Celeste had the feeling that she weighed nothing in his hands. Though they were both wet to the skin, the heat from his body warmed her. His shoulders curved over her as if he had sprouted golden wings with which to enfold her. Her head felt very heavy, and she let it fall back against him. Celeste's ear pressed so closely to his chest, she could easily hear the beating of his heart through the single layer of woolen fabric. Its steady, strong rhythm soothed her.

When Pierre dashed up, Gaston pointed to Celeste's mount. "Ride my lady's horse and follow close to the monk. When you find out where they are going, come back and lead us there."

Pierre made a wry face. "On that? It's a saddle for a woman."

With a muttered oath, Gaston ripped open the cinch and pulled off the offending sidesaddle, leaving a bit of damp blanket. "Now it is fit for a dog-hearted whipster. Get on."

Pierre nearly flew onto Starlight's back. If Celeste didn't feel so giddy, she would have laughed at the sight. As it was, the desire to sleep stole over her. She snuggled deeper into her cloak. Guy's arm tightened about her. *Mon Dieu! I am in the arms of Saint Michael himself.* In her half-wakeful state, she wondered if Black Devil would suddenly take to the air and they would fly up to heaven.

"Be off with you, Brother Guy, and take care you don't drop her." Gaston whacked his hand against Devil's glistening rump, and the horse sprang into a canter.

Guy cushioned Celeste against the sudden acceleration. She opened her eyes, squinting into the wind and rain that slapped her face. The brown-and-orange landscape blurred in her vision. Lowering her head again, she closed her eyes and concentrated on maintaining her balance. Somewhere close beside them, she heard Pierre's enthusiastic shouts. That boy would laugh all the way through the gates of hell.

Celeste had no idea how long or how far they rode. She might have dozed off, though afterward she could not recall sleeping. The great stallion seemed to fly over rocks and hillocks. Then Black Devil drew to a halt, and many hands reached up to help her down. Voices, all speaking at once, babbled around her. She could make out Pierre's above the rest, for he alone spoke French, but she couldn't quite understand what he said. Then a soft blackness enveloped her, and she was, at long last, warm—very warm.

When Celeste next opened her eyes, she thought for a moment she was back with the Foxmores. The room looked similar, though not as lavishly furnished. As she shook the sleep from her mind, she saw through an opening in the bed curtains that the walls of this room were made of a gray stone covered with large, bright tapestries. She remembered that Burke Crest's walls were paneled in carved wood.

Celeste pulled herself into a sitting position. The room tilted at a sickening angle. She thought for a moment that she might faint, but slowly everything settled into its rightful place and her vision sharpened. A bright fire danced in the stone hearth. Candles burned both on the chimneypiece and on the table by her bed. Looking about her, Celeste wondered where the people were. Dimly she heard noises from beyond the closed door, but she herself was alone.

"Hey-ho!" she called out, though not very loudly. Her throat scratched like a rusted nail in a doorframe. Celeste sank back against the pillows and stared up at the canopy overhead. A pleasant scene of silver stars and golden suns danced across an expanse of dark blue velvet.

Perhaps this is Snape Castle. The thought did not bring her the comfort it should. Celeste drew the coverlet under her chin as she awaited an answer to her summons. She frowned at herself. She should be glad if her journey was over, and yet...

What if Brother Guy had already left and was on his way back south, to Saint Hugh's? Not that she would blame him. The trip had not been to his liking, and no doubt he wished to return to the priory before winter caught him.

What if I never see him again? A sob threatened. Pah! What was the matter with her? Brother Guy was a monk, and not the least bit interested in young brides-to-be. Speaking of brides-to-be, if this was indeed Snape, then her bridegroom must be nearby.

Celeste clutched the covers. *Silly goose,* she scolded herself. *There is nothing to be afraid of. Walter Ormond is your loving husband—or will be soon. He will protect you now. Won't he?* Her aunt's horrible description of the wedding night returned to her. Then the half memory of Guy's embrace pushed that frightening thought aside.

Such a broad, strong chest Guy had! How tightly he had held her, his arm just under her breasts. Beneath the covers, Celeste's nipples tightened as she recalled how very close his arm had been to them. And his thighs! *For shame! It is indecent to think of a man's thighs, especially those of a monk!*

But what strong firm thighs he had! Celeste remembered quite distinctly how her legs had rested atop of his as they rode. *Ma foi!* With his robe hitched high, his legs had been naked, while her skirts had been pulled up past her knees. Sweet Saint Anne! Aunt Marguerite would have whipped Celeste soundly if she knew ... Knew what?

A flush, not fever-induced, spread across her cheeks. *I have never been that close to a man—any man—in all my life.* The feeling, she had to admit, had been wonderful— what she remembered of it. And now Brother Guy was gone? Without a goodbye and a Godspeed?

"Hey-ho!" she called again, forcing a louder sound out of her raspy throat. Why didn't someone heed her? Could she be a prisoner in an ivy-covered tower?

Celeste recalled the illustration in her book of the Lady Sweet Grace looking out the narrow window of a high tower guarded by the evil personage of Denial. How sad the lady seemed as she waited for her Knight of the Loyal Heart to rescue her!

Celeste struggled upright and again waited for her giddiness to subside. If she was a prisoner, then Brother Guy and poor Pierre must be, as well. She must escape from this room and set them free. No doubt they would lock Guy in a deep dungeon, because of his imposing strength and size. Celeste paused in her imaginings as she again recalled his strong arms around her. A flutter deep within her responded.

The door latch rattled, then opened. Celeste drew back against the pillows. Best not to let her captors know she was awake.

A cheerful woman of middling age, with a huge headdress and a red, cheery face bustled in, followed by a serving girl, who carried a wooden tray full of crockery.

"Awake, my pet?" the woman prattled in English. "Here now, Nan, put the tray on yon chest. Aye, there's a poppet!"

The woman approached the bedside, flung wide the curtains and smiled down at Celeste. "Aye," she announced with satisfaction. "Awake, and hungry like a newborn kitten, I'll warrant."

Celeste understood most of what the woman said. She bided her time before speaking.

The woman took a steaming cup from the girl and offered it to Celeste. "Drink this, my dearie-duck, and you'll feel right as rain in no time."

Celeste took the cup and sniffed the steam. A comforting mixture of cinnamon and clove scents greeted her. The woman chuckled. "Bless you and keep you, child. 'Tis no witch's brew, I vow, but a goodly posset. Drink it up."

Celeste glanced with a wary eye over the rim of the cup. "Where is Pierre?" she finally asked. If the women looked guilty, then Celeste would not drink her poison.

"Pierre, Nan?" the older woman questioned the girl by the fire.

"The French boy who came with Lady Celeste, Mistress Kate." Nan grinned widely.

Mistress Kate chuckled. "Oh, him! Rest you easy, my lady. That lad of yours is no doubt lolling by the kitchen fire and charming all my scullery maids. Aye, he has a fair tongue to him." She glanced meaningfully at Nan, who giggled and turned back to tending the fire. "Or so I have been told."

"And Brother Guy?" Celeste held her breath. Pray God he was still here.

"In the chapel, my lady, where he stays most of the time. He has been on his knees night and day since he brought you here. Now, no more questions. Drink up the posset, afore it cools and loses its strength."

Relieved more than she cared to admit, Celeste did as she was told. The drink slid down her throat with healing goodness.

"Nan, run to Lady Mary and tell her our guest is awake and feeling better. Lackaday, my lady! You gave all of us a good fright." Mistress Kate took the cup, then settled herself on the edge of the bed with a bowl and spoon in hand.

"Oxtail soup," she said in answer to Celeste's look of silent query. "We had best enjoy our meat now, seeing that Advent is coming nigh. I tell you, my lady, every time I turn around 'tis some sort of fast day or other. Makes a body wonder how the bishop stays so fat. Open wide, so please you." She held out the wooden spoon, brimming with rich broth and tempting chunks of meat and vegetables. With a contented sigh, Celeste drank it down.

"Gaston and the men?" she asked between mouthfuls. Considering that it came from an English kitchen, the soup tasted better than expected.

Mistress Kate laughed and almost spilled the next portion on the coverlet. "By all the saints, my lady. That man of yours, Gaston—he is a piece of work, and no mistake."

Celeste opened her mouth to ask what Mistress Kate meant by that, but got another spoonful instead.

"What a merry band they are! Like Robin Hood's men of old. And you be Maid Marian, I trow." She laughed at her jest, though Celeste did not see the humor of it. Were Gaston and the rest misbehaving with the castle's servants? How could they dishonor the name of de Montcalm?

"Frown not, my lady." Mistress Kate sopped a piece of crusty bread in the bottom of the bowl and held out a morsel to Celeste. "Your lads mean no harm, and none is taken." She chuckled again. Celeste obediently swallowed the dripping bread.

"Is here Znape Castle?" Celeste asked, after the bowl and spoon had disappeared.

Mistress Kate's brows soared up toward her preposterous white headdress. "Bless you, my lady, no. I know not Snape Castle, save that I ken that is where you journey. Nay, you are here at Cranston Hall, home of Sir Martin and Lady Mary Washburne. Sir Martin has been at court these past four months waiting upon His Majesty, but my Lady Mary is here and craves your company. She has grown weary of our faces, and her nephew refuses to talk with her."

"'Er nev-few? 'E is ill?"

Mistress Kate's mirth threatened to tumble off her headdress. "Nay, not so, unless it be in his head. You ken more of that than I. Bless you, my pet. Lady Mary's nephew is Sir Guy Cavendish—him that brought you here."

The ceaseless rain and chill wind put Walter Ormond even more out of temper with his minions than their odious personal habits. If it weren't for the threat of becoming the laughingstock of Snape's lowest society, Walter would have abandoned this idiotic quest for his elusive bride four days ago, when the rains began. It appeared that the girl had completely vanished.

In the beginning, when Walter inquired at the sign of the Red Lion, outside of Manchester, easy victory had danced within his grasp. The innkeeper had remembered a French lady traveling with baggage and an assortment of men. She had even had her own confessor with her. Just what Walter needed—a wife who prayed a lot. Never mind. He'd give her plenty of reason to fall on her knees when he finally found her. Or—better yet—to fall on her back. His cracked lips twisted into a smirk. The innkeeper had said the wench was a beauty. All the more reason she should be his bride and not wed the burnt-out man his father had become.

Raindrops spattered down the chimney of the Lion and Child in Huddersfield, causing the embers to sizzle. Walter stretched out his legs toward its feeble warmth. He shivered all the time in this hell-sent weather. He drained the ale in his mug. On the other side of the chamber, his hirelings slept; their snores grated against Walter's taut nerves. The devil take the lot of them, and be welcome! They stank enough to make one retch. And that Deighton! Walter shuddered.

Walter had known his share of lowlifes in the stews of London, but Deighton would make even those ruffians quake in their boots. *He plans to slit my throat.* A gladsome thought on such a foul night. Walter presumed the ham-fisted lout was biding his time, waiting until the Frenchie and her dowry were in hand. No doubt, Deighton would then kill the lot of them, with or without the others' help. Afterward, he'd make for the borders with his ill-gotten gains.

I'll serve him in his own stew first. Walter placed his mug quietly on the floor. He didn't want to risk waking the dogs that necessity forced him to lie down with. A hot coal of anger burned in his gut. God's teeth! Where had the wench and her gold flown to now?

Chapter Fifteen

Though she understood only a smattering of French, Lady Mary Washburne found her new houseguest utterly charming. She couldn't have been more surprised when Guy, outlandishly dressed in a monk's habit, appeared at the door of Cranston Hall, carrying, the unconscious girl in his arms. It didn't take Lady Mary long to discover how very ill Celeste was. For five days, the girl had tossed in a feverish sleep, babbling in French. The entire household had breathed a sigh of relief when Celeste finally regained her senses and began to eat.

Like a restless spirit petitioning at heaven's gate, Guy haunted the chapel. Her nephew looked in a shocking state himself. Where once he would have devoured half a roasted ox in one sitting, now Guy turned away from every dainty dish the housekeeper, Mistress Kate, could devise. The boy had dwindled to a long, lanky bundle of skin and bones. And this ridiculous vow of silence! Guy should be allowed to speak to his own aunt. Lady Mary never had quite understood what possessed her nephew, always a merry, robust lad, to renounce his birthright and bury himself in some cold little monastery. Just look what that folly had done to him!

"I am glad to see you strong enough to dress and join me," Lady Mary said to her guest when Celeste entered the warm, well-lighted gallery just off the master bedroom.

Though frost cloaked the tiny diamond-shaped panes of window glass, a cheerful fire, crackling in the grate, kept the early winter's cold at bay. Sitting in a high-backed settle facing the warmth, Lady Mary was embroidering a design of ivy leaves on the collar of one of her husband's shirts. She patted the cushioned seat beside her.

"Sit here, my dear, lest you get chilled again. We don't want that to happen, do we?"

Celeste smiled wryly as she took the place next to her hostess. "*Non,* I do not like the sicknezz."

Lady Mary draped a furred lap robe over Celeste's knees. "I should think not. 'Tis a foul time of the year to have the ague. You must not think of traveling until you are completely well." Lady Mary put up her hand to stop the protest she saw forming on Celeste's lips. "Nay, I insist. 'Twill do you no good to chase off after your bridegroom in this weather. The man has waited all this time for you, he can wait another few weeks. I shall send him a message this very day."

"Weeks?" Celeste looked stricken. "Oh, no, good lady, I must leave before the snow."

Lady Mary merely shook her head. "Then you are already too late, my dear. We had a light covering on the Feast of All Saints, when the fever still held you."

"*Sacre!*" Celeste murmured under her breath.

"Aye, 'tis melted now, but the roads are still frozen. You are more than welcome to stay here as long as you like. Why not pass the Christmas season with us? My husband, Sir Martin, will have returned from his duties at Westminster, and he would be right glad to meet you."

"*Merci,* you are ver-rey kind, but I must go soon." Celeste chewed her lower lip.

Lady Mary made another neat stitch in her embroidery. The girl was moonstruck, or perhaps she didn't understand the severity of the English weather. That must be it. Before she could say anything else to Celeste, the door at the end of the room opened and Guy slipped inside.

Both women by the fire looked up at him and smiled as he approached them. Leaning over the back of the settle, Guy kissed his father's sister on the cheek. Then he nodded to Celeste, hoping his profound joy at her recovery wasn't too apparent on his face. It would not be right if she knew how much he had worried and prayed for her good health. He wanted to kiss the faint pink roses that bloomed under her skin and brush his lips over each of those velvet-violet eyes. The urge to pick Celeste up and swing her around the room was so great, Guy had to stuff his hands deep inside his wide sleeves to keep from grabbing her around the waist.

Lady Mary patted Guy's shoulder with all the warmth of her affectionate heart. Then she looked from one to the other of her visitors, with an undisguised twinkle of excitement in her blue eyes. "Now, what am I to do with the two of you? You, Guy, are as skinny as that foolish donkey of yours. And, Lady Celeste, you are almost as thin."

Guy caught Celeste's gaze. He winked at her before he realized what he had done. She blinked with surprise, then, when Lady Mary wasn't looking, winked back. Guy suppressed a natural chuckle. The minx was too adorable by half. Fortunately, his aunt had not noticed the exchange, and she continued pursuing her line of thought. Guy knew from experience that Lady Mary would worry her subject to death like a badger.

"I have instructed Mistress Kate to see that the kitchen does its best for you. You must eat, both of you. Advent is only a few weeks away, and you need the strength of good meat before the season of fasting. Guy, I am surprised. I have never known you to refuse one of my dinners." She turned to Celeste. "Both he and his brother Brandon were always hearty trenchermen. Many a time they have stopped here on their way to or from the court and proceeded to eat us out of house and home."

"Oh, la, la!" Celeste cocked her head at Guy, her eyes wide open with apparent innocence.

He sat down by the hearth and tossed another log on the fire, then busied himself with the poker. Though she hid it well, Guy detected Celeste's mounting interest in his past life—the life he had sworn away forever. If it had not been for the seriousness of her illness, he would have bypassed Cranston Hall without either his aunt or Celeste being the wiser. He stabbed the poker deep into the glowing coals.

Every time he recalled that hellish ride to the safety of his aunt's home, he shivered. Thank the good Lord, Gaston's horse possessed a great heart. After the first five miles, Guy had left Pierre trailing far behind him. Twenty-three miles through the rain and later sleet, Black Devil's hooves had pounded the rocky ground. All that time, Celeste had lain still in his arms, like one dead. By the time they finally arrived at Cranston Hall, Guy had feared he had killed her. No penance on earth would have soothed his soul for that. Guy struck the log so hard with the poker, a shower of sparks rose up the flue.

"Guy, stop your woolgathering. I pray you, give me your attention. We must devise ways to entertain Lady Celeste while she is my guest. And mark me, nephew, I shall not have you forever on your knees in my chapel."

Lady Mary arched one brow at him. "You were never loath to be entertained before."

Guy stared down at his red, chapped toes, still primly shod in his worn sandals. When he first donned the simple garments of the Franciscans, the weather had been warm, with spring breezes followed by the summer's sun. Guy had forgotten how very chill and raw the winters could be. He realized now that he must learn to ignore the numbing cold. Discomfort was part of the life he had chosen. On the other hand, this fire did feel uncommonly good on his bare, near-frozen feet.

"So, I pray you, tell me, what shall we do to while away the hours?" Lady Mary had finally finished her soliloquy. The Cavendish family height, and her finely chiseled features, belied Lady Mary's high spirits and love of play, which bubbled just beneath her serene exterior.

"I like to play cards ver-rey much," Celeste suggested.

Guy glanced quickly up at her. By the rood, Celeste would win every last farthing of his aunt's housekeeping money! Celeste saw his look. A smile hovered at the corners of her lips, and then she flashed him another wink. Guy got up from his place on the floor and crossed behind the settle—away from the little temptress. He really should return to the chapel—the frigid chapel—and pray for the safety of his vocation.

One of the pages knocked on the door and announced dinner.

"In good time!" Lady Mary nodded with approval. She held out her hand for Guy to assist her to her feet. "And I shall seat you both, one on each side of me, and watch you like a mother hawk to make sure you fledglings eat every morsel. Or there shall be no tansy cake for your sweet tooth, Guy." Lady Mary whisked the lap robe off Celeste, then confided to her guest in a low, teasing voice,

"Guy dotes upon tansy cake, especially with peppermint cream on top."

"*Mais oui?* Then I must have this cake, too." Celeste held out her hand as Guy attempted to sweep past her. "Brother Guy, will you escort me?"

Trapped! And the slyboots knew it. Guy touched her hand. Her long, slim fingers closed around his, sending jolting shocks, like summer lightning, coursing up his arm.

"And perhaps the peppermint cream will make you smile again for me, *n'est-ce pas?*" she murmured in French as they went out the door behind Lady Mary.

Like a fish caught in a weir net, Guy ceased his inner struggle. He wondered how long Aunt Mary planned to keep them in too-comfortable Cranston Hall. The aroma of roasted venison filled the air as they descended the broad stairs. Guy's stomach rumbled with anticipation. Whatever the length of their stay, he knew it was going to be too long for the good of his vocation—and too short for the growing love in his heart.

As Guy had known she would, Aunt Mary filled the following fortnight with a variety of pastimes, games of chance, music, dancing and food. As Celeste grew stronger, she willingly joined in the merriment and bloomed under his aunt's care. Gaston and the men-at-arms spent their days hunting in the estate's forests and their nights singing, dicing, and amusing the maids of the household. Despite his best intentions to the contrary, Guy found himself enjoying Aunt Mary's milder pursuits, such as the nightly game of cards after supper. He told himself he played only to keep Celeste from bagging all the silver plate, but the truth, when he admitted it to himself in the cold darkness of the chapel, was that he looked forward to his hours in Celeste's company.

Because she was forced to speak English to Aunt Mary, Celeste's knowledge of the language grew. At least she was no longer calling anyone a "peench-'potted raw-beet sucker." Guy discovered that he missed hearing her say that particular phrase. As the perfect guest, Celeste happily fell in with whatever plan Aunt Mary suggested, be it learning the steps to a new galliard or devising a masque with the village children.

This last project, entitled *The Wedding of the King and Queen of the Faeries*, kept the entire household, including a reluctant and still-silent Guy, busy for several days, as everyone made costumes and practiced the little ones in their parts. When the six-year-old lad portraying King Oberon balked at kissing his five-year-old Queen Mab, Lady Mary immediately enlisted Guy's aid.

"By my troth, Guy, don't behave like such a lackwit!" chided Aunt Mary while Celeste, several serving maids and most of the village children looked on with amused interest. "I am sure young Ned here will do it right well, if you would just show him how easily 'tis done. 'Tis not as if you've never kissed a maid or two yourself, you know."

Guy felt the beginnings of a blush, but there wasn't much he could do about it, since shouting down the rafters was forbidden to him.

"*Oui,* Brother Guy, show us how this kissing is done," added Celeste with a devilish gleam in the depths of her amethyst eyes.

Aye, you raven-haired witch, I'd teach you all you'd ever need to know about kissing.

Appalled at his unexpected lustful thought, Guy sank to his knees in front of the winsome blond faerie queen and quickly kissed her cheek. The rest of the children shrieked with laughter, while Ned tried to dig his toe into the wooden floor of the hall.

"See, Ned? 'Tis as easy as falling off a log," Aunt Mary cooed encouragingly.

Ned shook his head and kept digging with his toe.

Aunt Mary continued to reason with the embarrassed faerie king. "But, sweet poppet, the groom always kisses his bride."

Guy couldn't help feeling extremely sorry for the lad. He could remember a time when he hadn't liked to kiss girls, either.

Celeste challenged him in a slightly mocking tone. "If you are a champion at kissing, Brother Guy, per'aps you show Ned again?"

Guy groaned inwardly. He didn't need to look over his shoulder to see Celeste grinning at his discomfort. Ned cast a beseeching look at him, that reminded the monk-to-be of a cornered rabbit. On the other hand, Guy knew that once his aunt set her mind to something, nothing short of an earthquake could dislodge her.

Guy took the little girl by the hand, swept a courtly bow and kissed it. He arched his eyebrow at the boy. The faerie queen fidgeted. Ned stopped digging his toe into the floor. Guy took the boy's hand and placed the girl's in it. The other children erupted with mirth.

"Ma foi!" Celeste rounded on the rest of the cast with a colorful blend of French and English. "You little black beetles! One day ver-rey soon, you will not be able to stop the kissing of each other, *oui?* Then who will have the last laugh, eh? I tell you—*moi!"*

Not a child moved or twittered as Celeste trained her attention upon the wilting groom. "And you! You are the king, *n'est-ce pas?* And the king is ver-rey brave. He is not afraid of the kiss, *non!* He is the best kisser in all of faerieland. So now, you kiss the queen, and then we all have the sweetmeats to eat. *C'est bon, n'est-ce pas?"*

Ned considered his options, and then, like a hawk swooping on the wing, he pecked the queen's cheek. "There, so please you!" the lad chirped.

"Bravo!" Celeste hugged both children, while Lady Mary beamed her pleasure. Over Ned's curly locks, Celeste winked at Guy.

Why do you have to learn so quickly that which makes you all the more desirable, Lissa? Guy trembled as if caught by a fever.

While Celeste and his aunt conducted the children to the kitchen for the promised treats, Guy fled to the chapel. There he spent several hours freezing while he tried to sort out the confusing turmoil within his heart. When Guy emerged, stiff from kneeling on the stone floor, the solution to his dilemma still eluded him.

The masque, held in the hall on the following Sunday afternoon for the entertainment of the household and the surrounding community, proved an overwhelming success. Young Ned kissed his bride with a resounding smack, which elicited a burst of applause. The little choir sang with sweet enchantment, the dancers did not trip over their flowing costumes. The refreshment tables, presided over by Mistress Kate, were quickly cleared of their bounty. Gaston and the other Frenchmen enjoyed the attentions of the maids and the wine Lady Mary brought up from the cellars. Everyone deemed the day a success—except Celeste.

Just after the wedding scene, Guy saw her face crumple. Hiding behind her handkerchief, Celeste slipped out of the hall. Fearing that she might be ill again, Guy followed and found her crying softly in the upstairs gallery. Quietly shutting the door behind him, he crossed to where she sat huddled on the window seat. Celeste looked up just as he knelt beside her.

"*Pardonnez-moi*, Brother Guy, I didn't mean to break the good cheer." She dabbed her eyes with a corner of the handkerchief.

Are you ill? Guy wrote on the slate.

Celeste shook her head. "*Non. Oui*—I do not know. Pray excuse me. It will pass."

She didn't look well, Guy thought as Celeste chewed her trembling lower lip. She looked as if she had seen a demon. Knowing he shouldn't, he took her hand in his. As if she were drowning, she gripped his fingers tightly.

"Forgive me," she said in answer to the surprise in his eyes. "I am acting like a silly goose."

Guy took her chin between his forefinger and thumb, forcing her to look at him. Sweet Saint Anne, how he wanted to kiss her tears away!

"It is nothing—only a child's play—and yet . . ."

Guy waited as patiently as he could. He realized that she was deathly afraid of something, which surprised him. Not once during their time together had Lissa shown anything but good humor and courage in the face of all her adversities. What had the masquing done to frighten her so? Did Lissa really believe in the faerie folk?

"I will tell you, Brother Guy, but you must promise, on your honor as a man of God, to keep my secret." Her eyes sought his and held them in her thrall.

Guy wanted to bolt from the room. He couldn't hear Lissa's confession. It would be a sacrilege. Yet she needed comfort and had turned to him. What was he supposed to do? He bowed his head over her hand, which still gripped his.

"The play reminded me of my duty—of my marriage to Walter Ormond," she began, speaking as if from a far distance. "And I must confess to you, Brother Guy, I am sore afraid of this wedding."

Guy glanced up at her. Had she heard of Ormond's pox?

"That is..." She ran her tongue across her lips. "Of the wedding night. Just before we left the priory, Aunt Marguerite told me that I must submit to my husband in all things—even my body."

Guy began to understand. The old woman must have terrified Lissa with some sort of old wives' tale. Considering Ormond's case, no villainy could be underestimated. Guy squeezed her hand.

"She said that he... he would strip me n-naked." Tears began to gather in her eyes, though Celeste fought them back.

"And that he would... that..."

Guy knew all too well what came next, and he gave her what silent comfort he could. She presumed that he was a priest and was used to hearing people confess all manner of evil things. Thank God he wasn't! How could anyone bear listening to the sorrow and pain of others day after day?

Celeste leaned against the frosted window. "She said he would hurt me. That there would be pain and blood." She swallowed hard at the thought. "Aunt Marguerite said that wives must accept this punishment by their husbands. Am I so very wrong not to want this thing? How can I deny my husband his rights over me? Oh, Brother Guy, I am so very, very frightened of this marriage!"

Guy reached to take her in his arms, then dropped his hand to his side and clenched his fist. God's teeth! He would have liked to strangle that old woman before she had the chance to scare the wits out of Lissa. Dried-up, bitter crones shouldn't be allowed near marriageable virgins. It was a wonder there were any children in the world at all, if this was how a girl was prepared for the most important day in her life. Guy wished he dared to enfold her in his arms and, with his kisses, banish her fears. Instead he merely took her hand in his. Celeste gazed into the depths of his eyes and read his anguish there.

"Please, do not feel sorry for me. I will be a good wife. I do promise that." She gave him a brave little smile, then slid off the window seat and smoothed down her skirts. "Come, let us return to the feast, or we shall disappoint your good aunt."

Guy rose, as if in a dream, and followed her out of the gallery.

Lissa, I would teach you joy, not fear, I swear. But even as he made that promise, Guy knew he could not keep it.

Chapter Sixteen

Two days later, the sun reappeared, shedding its feeble rays for the first time in several weeks. Celeste announced to her startled hostess that she must leave. Though she had much enjoyed her stay at Cranston Hall, Celeste felt guilty for lingering the extra days once her health had returned. By now, her parents must think her well wedded, and perhaps even expecting her first child. How angry and ashamed they would be if they knew she still kept her noble bridegroom waiting!

Again the travelers turned northward, crossing the rugged Pennines, where they spent a full day pushing the wagon through the snowdrifts that covered the higher passes. They were relieved when they descended to the valley and encountered the gentler landscape of heather, peat and brown grass. Wearied by the days of travel over the frozen, rutted roads, the party ate ravenously every night and went to bed early in the various hostelries that Guy found for them. Celeste's singing and cheerful banter had disappeared since her illness. She used all her strength to stay warm and upright in her saddle as they plodded northward.

How could Guy stand the bitter cold? she wondered as another storm lashed them with needling sleet. He wore no cloak over his one shabby robe, and the cold had turned his feet bright red. He had gained back some weight under his aunt's prodding, but Celeste feared he would soon return to his former gaunt appearance. At least he covered his bare head with his hood, and she noted with a secret pleasure that a new growth of his golden hair had finally obliterated his funny little tonsure.

Ma foi! How handsome he was! Celeste agreed with Lady Mary's observation that Guy's holy vocation was a waste of a fine man. She closed her eyes against the sting of the wind and tried to imagine what Guy looked like dressed in fine velvets and particolored hose. She already knew what strong legs he had. Indeed, she had seen considerably more of those extremities than most people, save Guy's former squire. She sighed and pulled her hood lower over her face. She hoped her betrothed looked just as handsome.

Late one afternoon, they came upon a lone boy, crawling in the roadway that led out of Leeds. The lad, whose only name was Pip, had badly twisted his ankle from falling through the ice crust of a deep, rock-laced pothole.

"Pauvre petit!" Celeste crooned over him as Gaston lifted the boy into the baggage cart.

"Little vermin!" Gaston growled, watching Celeste bind Pip's ankle. "The boy is crawling with lice and fleas, my lady. Do not touch him. You'll become infested yourself."

"Peace, Gaston, you are frightening the child." Celeste tucked the end of the bandage under the wrappings. "Have we any brandywine? He is near frozen."

Pip, who didn't understand a word of French, lay very still. His stark fear glittered from under his half-closed eyes.

"I canna pay," he protested when Celeste offered him the wineskin.

"Drink," she urged in English. She smiled, hoping to calm his anxiety. "Is good. You need not pay. Rest now, *oui?*" She brushed the shaggy red hair out of his eyes.

Pip glanced at the glowering old soldier beside her. He ran his tongue over his lips, but he made no move to take the bag.

"I think he is afraid of you, Gaston," Celeste murmured to her sergeant.

"And well he should be!" Gaston grumbled in return. He pointed to the wineskin. "Drink!" he barked in English.

Pip's eyes widened. He glanced from the woman to the men around the cart. Finally his gaze rested on Guy. The solemn monk pointed to the bag and nodded slowly. Then his face relaxed into a broad smile.

At the surprising sight, Celeste almost let the winesack slip from her fingers. She had not seen the full force of Guy's beatific smile since that night at the Blue Boar. By now she had given up hope of ever seeing it again. *Ma foi!* An angel had come down from the overcast skies above, even if he did wear a ragged robe and ride a skinny donkey.

"Much thanks, my lady." Pip grabbed the wineskin, and drank down a large gulp of the fiery liquid before Gaston could stop him. Immediately the lad coughed and tears ran down his cheeks. The men-at-arms laughed good-naturedly as Gaston thumped him on the back.

"Take leetle," Gaston growled, retrieving the sack.

"Is better?" Celeste stroked Pip's forehead.

The boy gulped, wiped his nose on his sleeve, then nodded. "'Tis a right fine drink," he agreed. "There's a fire a-running all through me."

Guy's smile widened, and Celeste thought for a brief moment that a laugh might escape his lips. Catching her gaze, Guy sobered again. He pulled out his slate from his pocket.

Ask Pip if we are near an inn, he wrote.

"Show him your slate," Celeste replied, shaking out a spare blanket and covering the boy with it.

Guy scribbled, *He can't read.*

"Pah!" Celeste tossed her head, then returned her attention to Pip, who had watched the proceeding with open interest.

"Did he get his tongue cut out?" he asked her, staring with awe at the tall man.

Celeste laughed. "*Non,* he does not talk to anyone except God. He is a ver-rey holy man."

At that, Guy abruptly turned his back on them and remounted Daisy.

"He asked is there an inn soon?" Celeste continued. What was the matter with Brother Guy? One minute he was warm and friendly, the next cold and withdrawn.

Grinning, Pip pointed down the road ahead of them. "Yonder, lady. The Hawk and Hound. I am a stable boy there."

"*C'est bon!* Then we take you home, eh? You will be good with Pierre." Celeste introduced the good-natured young driver. "Pierre is ver-rey clever with horses and little boys."

Pip jutted out his chin. "I be nae so little, neither!"

Celeste bit her tongue to keep from laughing at his youthful pride. Pip reminded her of her brother, Philippe. "*Pardonnez-moi,* Master Peep. I am but French, and do not know too many English. I wonder, are you hungry, eh?"

Pip nodded. "Always, lady."

Celeste tapped the side of her nose. "Ah! Just so!" She spoke to Pierre in French. "Give the boy some bread, and whatever else you have with you. But make sure he does not sample the brandywine again. I think he has had enough of that."

"D'accord!" Pierre agreed. He pulled a bag out from under the seat and passed to Pip a chunk of Mistress Kate's finest white bread.

Pip's eyes widened. "Oh, aye, lady! I ne're tasted the like of this!" He fell upon it like a wolf cub. "My thanks," he mumbled through a mouthful.

"If you are finished playing Lady Charity, let us begone," Gaston rumbled in her ear. "The light is fading, and we'll never make this inn if we stand here in the mud."

Celeste allowed Gaston to help her back into her saddle. "You have a caring heart," she teased him.

"I'll have a pack of fleas by supper," he growled as he returned to his patient horse.

Without looking behind him, Guy kicked Daisy into a protesting trot, and the party headed down the road to the Hawk and Hound.

The promised inn proved to be one of the fouler establishments they had encountered. If snow had not begun to fall just as they arrived at its sagging door, Guy would have urged the party onward. Unfortunately, he knew there was little chance of a better place between here and York. As they led their horses into the run-down stable, Guy plucked at Gaston's sleeve.

Set a guard, he wrote on his slate.

"Oui, my friend." Gaston's brown eyes blazed in the semidarkness of the dank stable. "I smell danger, as well as a bad privy. Stay close to my lady."

I would have her as close as my heart.

Pip stopped Celeste and Guy before they crossed the yard to the taproom. "My master is John Coldshanks, and he's nae used to fine company. Take care, good lady. He cheats."

Celeste placed her hand on the boy's shoulder. "Thank you for your good advice, Master Peep." She gave him a shilling, and before he could stammer his thanks, she kissed him on the cheek, which left him speechless.

Guy offered her his arm. Celeste held it tightly, clutching the saddlebag that held her precious dowry in the other. They picked their way across the dung-spattered yard to the taproom. Gaston, Émile and René followed close behind, leaving the others to stay with the horses and baggage.

The taproom stank of unwashed bodies, fried onions and a poorly drawn fire. The minute Celeste entered the room, all talking ceased. Bellowing in French when his English failed him, Gaston made short work of expressing their needs to the innkeeper, Coldshanks.

Without moving his head, Guy scanned the room with his eyes. A rough-and-tumble lot with light fingers, he judged, but none who looked to be an out-and-out cutthroat. For the first time since hanging up his sword and lance, the monk wished he had a weapon at his belt. He draped his arm protectively around Celeste's shoulders as their skulking host conducted them to a room at the end of the upstairs hall. Celeste said nothing, but held her head high until after Guy closed the door.

"By the warts on the devil's nose, what a way-stop to hell this is!" Gaston knelt by the cold fire grate and tossed a few rotted logs onto it. "It's that knavish waterfly's fault we are here, my lady. I've a good mind to thrash the boy soundly." He struck a spark with his tinderbox, then tried to coax a reluctant blaze.

Celeste flung open the window and drew in a deep breath of the snow-filled air. "*Non*, Gaston. He meant only to help us, I am sure."

"He's a coney-catcher, and I intend to sleep with both eyes open this night." A weak flame licked at the logs.

"I fear this was the only inn on the road. Is that not so, Brother Guy?"

Turning from the window, Celeste gazed up at him. Her midnight hair, released from her furred cap, blew about in the wind, framing her delicate features.

Guy nodded. How beautiful Celeste looked—and how tired! The day's journey had been particularly difficult. Guy wished they could dispense with the deuced wagon altogether. He flashed her a brief smile of encouragement. She responded with a ripple of low, smoky laughter. Guy pretended to inspect the mattress and bed ropes. He must be careful not to encourage Celeste. Already they had become much too familiar for their own good. Nightly he wrestled with the demons of his desire for her. Daily they grew stronger.

Supper in here, Guy wrote on his slate. The others in the room agreed. He rubbed out the first message, then scribbled, *Gaston take first watch, René in three hours, I the mid-three, Émile till morn.*

Celeste put her hands on her hips. "*Et moi?*"

You sleep, Guy printed in large letters, not daring to meet the fire in her eyes.

"*Sacrebleu!* I am as good a watchman as the rest of you. *Non*, I am better. I do not drink as much wine."

If the situation were not so ominous, Guy would have been tempted to take up her challenge and give her the midnight shift. He gestured to Gaston to reason with her.

"When we left the priory, your good aunt made me swear to keep you safe. And you promised to follow my orders."

"But..."

"But no." Gaston folded his arms across his chest and glared down at her in the way he probably had been doing all her life. "You go to sleep directly after supper. We will leave this pesthole by first light."

The old soldier and maid glowered at each other for a full minute. Guy wondered what Celeste had been like as a child. By the Book, she must have been a hellion in petticoats—she still was. Again he regretted not noticing her at the tournament eight years ago, when she had tried to give him her blue veil. Guy shook himself from the memory. It did not matter where she had been as a child, it was where she must go now that plagued Guy. Lissa would need every shred of her spirit to survive living with the Ormonds.

"Ha!" Celeste snapped her fingers under Gaston's large nose. "I shall go to bed. But, I promise you, my dear Gaston, I shall not sleep a wink. I shall be kept awake all night by your loud snores. Fah! So you may as well give me something to do."

"By the devil's—" The old soldier checked his language in time. "Be mindful, my lady. You are not too old for a spanking, and I am still strong of arm." Without giving her a chance to retort, he flung himself out the door, growling at the two smirking men-at-arms to follow.

Celeste moved over to the fire and stretched out her hands toward its weak flames. Guy shut the window, then stood in the gathering shadows, watching her wrestle with her determination.

"Is it as dangerous as Gaston thinks, Brother Guy?" she finally asked, a note of nervousness creeping into her voice.

Guy crossed to her side, knelt down and took both her hands in his. Her fingers were chilled. He blew on them and rubbed them vigorously while he tried to think how to answer her question.

"Tell me the truth, Brother Guy. Will someone try to harm us?"

Guy raised his eyes to hers, and quelled the desire to cover her anxious face with his kisses. He nodded his head quickly, then held up his hand and balled it into a fist. He smacked his fist against his open palm.

Celeste covered his curled fingers with her feather-light touch. She swallowed hard, lifted her chin and boldly met his gaze. "Then I shall sleep well, for I know I am in good hands."

Their gazes interlocked and held. A silent understanding passed between their souls; as light as a sigh on the wind, as strong as a sword of Spanish steel.

The taproom had emptied by ten that night. Folk did not like to stay out late in this part of the country, especially as the snow continued to fall. Exhausted from his adventures of the day and sore from the beating Coldshanks had given him for coming back late, Pip curled in the far corner of the inglenook and fell into a pleasant state of half sleep, dreaming of the most beautiful lady he had ever met, even if she did call him "Peep."

Suddenly the front door banged open, nearly causing Pip to fall into the fire. Four of the most unsavory men he had ever seen stamped in, shaking the snow from their cloaks and bawling for the innkeeper. Pip knew instinctively he wanted nothing to do with this lot. Furtively he edged himself deeper into the darkest corner.

"Hellfire and damnation! Landlord, stir yer stumps!" The largest man banged on the wooden counter. The three others huddled around the fire, jostling for the warmest position. Pip made himself as small as possible.

"Who calls at this infernal hour?" Coldshanks bustled in from his room in the back, rubbing his eyes. Pip could tell that the rude awakening had put his master in a mean mood.

"Yer betters, knave!" the oaf roared. "A jug o' yer best beer and some supper, man. My master's near perished for want of food." He waved toward a fifth person who stood deep in the shadows near the entrance.

Coldshanks sneered at the loud one. "My better, eh? In a stained jerkin and holes in his knees? Be gone!"

Pip stifled his gasp as the loud man's knife flashed in the firelight. The others paid no mind to the proceedings, but Coldshanks cowered at the sight.

"Know ye, scullion, my master is the son o' Sir Roger Ormond of Snape Castle. 'E's a noble gentleman. So look sharp, or this blade will find its home in yer gut."

Coldshanks broke into a round of twitches and blubbering the like of which Pip had never before witnessed. "At your pleasure, sir. Pray seat yourself, sir. Supper in a moment, sir."

The one with the knife shoved the innkeeper aside. "Aye, 'tis more like it. Now, move your plagued bones!"

"Wait!" The one in the shadows stepped forward into the firelight.

Looking at him, Pip wanted to gag. Raw open sores covered the fifth man. A pair of red eyes glared out of his thin, pasty face. Though he kept his cap on, Pip suspected him to be bald. The man looked the very image of a walking corpse. Pip surreptitiously made the sign against the evil eye.

"Do you know of a lady—a French lady of great beauty—who is traveling this road?" the face of death asked.

A sly smile flitted about Coldshanks's lips. "Perchance I might."

The burly one lifted the innkeeper by the collar. "Then ye best spill yer words in my master's ear, afore I spill yer guts on the floor."

"Peace, Deighton!" The apparition called Ormond waved his hand. "A bit of silver will tell me far more than your bit of blade." He grinned horribly, revealing red, bleeding gums. "What say you, innkeeper?"

"Aye, my lord. The lady you seek is..." Coldshanks lowered his voice to a hoarse whisper. "Upstairs as we speak, all tucked up with her father confessor. And a cozy little lot they is, too, if you get my meaning, sir."

Five pairs of evil eyes gleamed at one another. Ormond threw his leg over a bench and sat down. "Asleep, say you? Good. First we shall dine, and then, perchance, we'll invite the lady downstairs to dance." The others guffawed at this ominous remark.

With more bowing and scraping, Coldshanks scampered about—drawing beer, setting crockery and cups on the table, racing for the cold kitchen to wake the cook.

Pip ached inside. He must warn the good lady, but how could he move without being seen? The stairs to the first floor were near enough, but he must bide his time and hope the men would bide theirs. Pip hadn't been inside a church since Easter, but he now prayed for all he was worth and hoped that the Lord above wasn't too angry at him for his past omissions.

"Help the lady, good Lord, for she is a sweet lady."

The night grew later and colder, though Pip felt nothing but terror in his corner. The men ate and drank heavily—especially drank. Coldshanks usually watered his beer. The brew was a strong one, and no one hereabouts noticed or minded the dilution. But considering the tenor of his customers, the innkeeper must have served it full-strength. Within two hours, the men were nodding over their cups and their speech had slurred into sleep—all except the sickening lord. Though he held his cup and lifted it often to his lips, Pip noticed that he drank sparingly. All the while, the lord kept a sharp eye on the big one, Deighton.

When Ormond stepped outside to relieve himself by the doorframe, Pip drew in a deep breath, uncoiled himself from his corner and crept out of the inglenook. He begged his guardian angel to give his injured ankle strength, just for a little while. Then he sprinted to the stairs, climbing them two at a time. Each step on his left foot shot daggers of pain up his leg, but he paid it no mind. Only the beautiful lady mattered now.

Chapter Seventeen

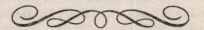

Sitting on a stool in the shadowed corner of the upstairs room, Guy listened to the snores of Gaston and the other two who slept in cots near the fire. Lissa made no sound from behind the curtain they had hung in front of her bed. Guy hoped she slept. The dark smudges under her eyes worried him, and he feared a recurrence of her fever. While he kept watch, he tried to pray his office, but thoughts of Lissa, and the fate to which he was forced to lead her, rose up in his mind. Why had Father Jocelyn given him this task in the first place? Yet Guy realized that there had been no other in the priory whom the abbot could entrust with the safety of such a precious flower. If he had not renounced his worldly life for the church, Guy would take Lissa for himself and . . .

A gentle scrape outside the door interrupted Guy's secular musings. The hairs on the back of his neck stiffened. The old familiar rush that he used to experience just before entering the tiltyard flooded his body. God's teeth! What he would give for a sword in his hand! *But you are a man of peace now.*

The latch rattled, then slowly lifted. Guy slipped behind the door, ready to spring. By the low light of the fire's embers, he saw Gaston curl into a crouch. That old fox must have a second pair of ears! The door opened slowly inward. Guy drew his breath. A slim figure crept in. Guy lunged forward, clamping one hand over the intruder's mouth while grabbing him around the waist with the other.

The only sound in the ensuing struggle was a rasp of steel as Gaston pulled his dagger from its sheath. Guy knew he held a squirming boy in his grasp—Pip? Gaston lit the low tallow candle. Guy whispered, "Shush!" to Pip before realizing that he had uttered a sound. The horror of that indiscretion almost made him lose his grasp on the boy.

"It's that rascally varlet we helped earlier today," Gaston whispered, holding the candle up to Pip's face. "See? The scantling has come to rob us in our sleep!" He waved his dagger in front of the wide-eyed boy and spoke slowly in English. "Do not make a move or I will kill you."

Shivering, Pip nodded. Guy slowly relaxed his hold on the boy's mouth.

"There's five men below," Pip gasped. "Ruffians, by their look, and they asked after the lady."

Hellfire! Who would know of Celeste? Someone from the last inn, who had followed them, thinking that she carried money? Perhaps the landlord had sent word to a band of local brigands, hoping to share in their spoils.

"Five?" Gaston repeated, then glanced at Guy. "We are only three and you, Brother. The others— *Mon Dieu!* What if they have killed them in the stables already?" His face contorted with anger.

Not comprehending Gaston's speech, but understanding the rage in the man's face, Pip sent a beseeching look to Guy. "The men are besotted with drink—all except one. Aye, he looks the very devil. You must escape now."

Guy slowly released Pip. The boy's suggestion made sense. As much as he hated to turn tail and run, Guy knew that was their wisest option. At all costs, Celeste must be kept safe. He crossed to the window. Without the moon's light, a black void swallowed up the view. Guy turned to Pip and pointed out the window.

The boy nodded his understanding. "The inn yard is to the right side below. The storehouse roof to the left," he told them in a whisper. "At the far corner of the storehouse is the stable."

Guy opened the window. A frigid blast of wind, mixed with a few snowflakes, swirled in, causing the candle flame to flicker. Celeste and the two men-at-arms could get through the window. The opening would be a tighter squeeze for Gaston and himself. Guy pointed toward the door, then down.

Pip shook his head. "Nay, the only way out is through the taproom."

Guy stuck his head out the window and assessed this dark avenue of escape. Meanwhile, Gaston quietly woke Émile and René. Mercifully, Celeste had not stirred. Despite her declaration that she would stay awake all night, her fatigue had bested her. Good! Too soon, she would need all her strength and spirit.

" 'Tis not far to the storehouse roof," Pip said, coming to his side. "I could jump to it with ease—if'n my ankle did nae hurt so."

Guy stepped back and motioned for Gaston to look out. The old soldier withdrew his head from the window, muttering several profane curses, for which he did not apologize to Guy.

"It is a dog's hole out there. One could call it a leap of faith, eh? René, have you a great deal of faith?" Gaston pointed out the window.

Crossing himself, René peered out, then threw both legs over the sill. Pip pointed slightly to the left. René nodded, then hunched forward and pushed himself off the ledge. Guy heard him land just below him. René hooted softly, mimicking an owl on the hunt.

"Bon!" Gaston licked his lips with satisfaction. "We will cross the storehouse roof to the stables. From there, we will walk the horses out of the yard, then ride like the wind. Thanks be to God for sending the snow to muffle our sounds."

As Émile prepared to follow René, Guy pulled back the makeshift curtain to waken Celeste. He found her crouched in the middle of the bed, clutching her small eating knife. Her dark eyes glowed like a cat's in the darkness. When she saw him, her shoulders sagged with relief.

"I heard a noise, Brother Guy," she whispered.

Pip looked around the open curtains. "Evil men downstairs, lady. We are going to escape out the window." His voice shook with the excitement of the adventure.

"Ç'est vrai!" she breathed. "It is true, then. I thought I was dreaming." Gathering up the folds of her night shift, she climbed out of bed and began to don her petticoats.

Shaking his head, Guy stopped her. She couldn't waste valuable time dressing in all those clothes. Instead, he handed her the fur-lined cloak and her shoes. Celeste opened her mouth to protest, but stopped when she read the serious expression on his face. Without a word, she flung the cloak about her, then wiggled her feet into her stiff riding boots.

"Come, my lady." Gaston motioned to her from his place by the window. "It is as easy as jumping out of the pear tree at home."

"Wait! My spoons!" Celeste rushed back to the bed and pulled the saddlebag from under the mattress.

Guy took the bag from her, then guided her toward the window. Celeste leaned out. For a split second, Guy expected her to balk at the prospect of jumping into the darkness.

"'Tis only a little way down, lady," Pip assured her. "Easy as cream for a cat."

Celeste smiled at him, then nodded. Gaston lifted her over the sill. "Look to the lady," he whispered to the men waiting below.

Just before she let go of the window frame, she glanced over her shoulder to Guy, her huge eyes seeking his assurance.

I love you, Lissa. Lord forgive me, but I do. He smiled at her, willing his love to give her his strength. She returned his smile, then jumped.

As Gaston made ready to follow her, Pip tugged at his sleeve. "Take me with you, sir. They'll kill me sure if'n I stay here."

Gaston stared at the boy, then plucked him up and dropped him out the window. With a great deal of grunting and whispered curses, Gaston wedged himself through the opening. Guy heard his solid landing.

Silently crossing the room, Guy pressed his ear against the door to the hallway. Muted snatches of a tavern ballad, sung off-key wafted up from the taproom. Good! No one had heard their escape. Taking a small piece of wood, he jammed it between the door and the frame. That would hold the kidnappers for a few extra minutes. Then he moved swiftly to the window.

"*Sacrebleu!*" Gaston growled just below him. "Do not tarry, Monk!"

Knowing his shoulders were the widest part of him, Guy angled his head through the opening. A protruding nail head in the wooden frame tore at his shoulder as he forced himself through the window. Though he disliked the thought of going headfirst, Guy saw no other way. As the rest of his body followed, he twisted so that his hands clutched the sill—in effect, somersaulting out the window. Once he hung upright, he let go, and was surprised when he dropped only a foot onto the flat roof of the store house. The snow on the roof lapped over his bare toes. He drew in his breath at the icy sting.

In the yard below, light spilled from the taproom's only window. Gaston pointed to the far end of the roof. Guy could just make out René waiting for them. Nearby, Celeste huddled next to Pip. Guy swept her up into his arms. The tightness around his lips relaxed into a slow smile as he looked down into her startled expression. He excused his vigilance over his tightly reined emotions, citing to himself the danger of the moment. When she returned his smile, a warm triumphant sensation filled him.

"Allons," Gaston whispered, tossing Pip over his shoulder like a sack of grain. "Let us go!"

Crouching low, they ran along the roof. At the far end, they found their way made easier by a small shed that leaned against the storehouse. They leapt from one roof to the second and then to the ground, as if they were descending giant stepping-stones.

By the time Guy reached the safety of the barn with his precious burden, the men-at-arms had already bound and gagged the ostler and were busy saddling the restless horses. Reluctantly Guy put Celeste back on her feet. His arm lingered around her for a moment longer than necessary before he turned his full attention to the problem at hand.

Seeing Pierre about to hitch the horse to the wagon, Guy stopped him.

"But my lady's clothes! Her goods!" Pierre protested.

Guy shook his head.

Celeste put her hand on the driver's arm. "We must leave the wagon, Pierre. Too noisy, *n'est-ce pas*, Brother Guy?"

Surprised by the quickness of her mind and the absence of wailing over the imminent loss of her worldly possessions, Guy nodded to Pierre. Then Guy lifted a canvas bag that he knew held some of Celeste's clothing. He motioned to Pierre to load up Daisy with the lesser bundles.

"But what will you ride, Brother?" Pierre asked as he worked quickly, transferring the bags onto the donkey's back. Daisy showed her supreme dissatisfaction at this midnight disturbance by flattening her ears and baring her teeth at Pierre.

Guy pointed to one of the horses. The little chestnut mare would do much better than the skittish Daisy. Without another word, Celeste sifted through her belongings for what she could easily carry. As Guy turned away to search for a bridle for his new mount, he saw Celeste stuff her Book of Love into her saddlebag, alongside the apostle spoons. He couldn't help but smile in the darkness. Her dreams meant more to Lissa than her damask tablecloth and napkins.

In less than five minutes, the party were ready to make their escape from the inn. Holding Black Devil's nose to keep him quiet, Gaston surveyed his little troop as if he were one of the famous French generals at the battle of Tournai.

"*Bon*, my friends. We leave in single file, and we walk the horses across the yard. Understand? Brother Guy, you lead with my lady behind you. Pierre, you hold the reins of that miserable donkey, and if she so much as farts..."

His teeth flashing in the dark, Pierre grinned his understanding.

"You, Peep, go with Pierre on 'ees 'orse." Gaston did not bother to ask Pip if he knew how to ride; nor did the boy enlighten him. Guy saw Pip cast a dubious look at the mount he would share with Pierre. The boy swallowed hard.

"Jean, Paul, Dom and René, you follow after, and each take one of our enemies' horses." Gaston chuckled. "They will not go far without them. Flipot and Émile, what do you say we start a little fire in the storehouse after the others are safely away, eh? We make everyone nice and warm this night!"

Guy shook his head quickly. He didn't want the local officers of the king's justice to be after them. Gaston narrowed his eyes.

"Pah, Brother Guy! What is a bit of horse-stealing and a small bonfire to me? I have very little soul left to save. *Non,* let me have my fun, eh? As for those bunch-backed nags of theirs, we can turn them loose in a mile or two. If they have wit enough, they will find their way back to their oats. Now, enough! Begone!"

As he helped Celeste into her saddle, Guy said a quick prayer for Gaston's nefarious enterprise. Leaning over, Celeste whispered, "Do not think poorly of Gaston, Brother Guy. I have not seen him so happy since we left France."

Guy leapt onto the mare's broad back and gently kneed her into a slow walk. After the animal warmth of the stable, the cold night air greeted him with a shock. The trickiest part of this enterprise lay in maintaining silence as they passed by the taproom door. Guy again thanked the good Lord for a dark night and the muffling cover of snow.

Glancing into the taproom as he passed, he saw the shapes of several men slumped over the table in front of the low-burning fire. Just then, another man stood. A spear of apprehension stabbed Guy's chest. He watched as the cloaked figure crossed and stood in front of the fire, his back, mercifully, to the window. Guy signaled to the others, behind him, to hug the stable wall.

As soon as they were safely out of the confines of the Hawk and Hound, Guy broke into an easy canter, hoping to put enough distance between themselves and their would-be pursuers before Gaston's arson aroused the neighborhood. He hoped the old soldier, Émile and Flipot would be able to follow their tracks. Though the snow had stopped for the moment, Guy prayed for another snowfall before morning, or else there would be a hue and cry over the countryside for them. The landlord of the Hawk and Hound struck Guy as the type who would ride into hell to revenge a slight.

Celeste urged her palfrey abreast of Guy. When he glanced her way, the corners of her mouth lifted a fraction in a mute salutation. Before he could respond in kind, he heard rapid hoofbeats thudding behind them. The men turned and drew their short swords. Leaning across to Celeste, Guy took her reins, ready to put their mounts to flight.

"It's Gaston!" announced Paul, speaking aloud for the first time since being awakened in the stable.

Black Devil came to a skidding halt in front of Guy and Celeste. His rider threw back his head, and roared with laughter. "If you sniff the air, my lady, you will soon smell smoke. The storehouse was full of grain—very dry grain!" He jumped off his horse with an agility that far belied his years.

The sound of Celeste's laughter, like a bubbling brook on a summer's day, caught Guy by surprise. He realized he had not heard her laugh like that for some time.

"Oh, la, la, Brother Guy, I think we must find Gaston some more barns to burn, if it will keep him in such good temper." She covered a yawn behind her hand.

Gaston held out his reins to Guy. "Take my beauty—both of them, Brother. Lady Stubborn will not admit it, but I have eyes. I see her even now swaying in her saddle. My horse will hold you both again while I will ride your mare. At least, I will ride her until I find a sweeter one anon. *Sacrebleu!* Your pardon, my lady!" he finished with an unrepentant grin as he helped Celeste off her horse.

What a lion Gaston must have been in his prime! Guy mutely applauded him.

"Be quick, sluggard Monk," the older man admonished. "My lady is half-asleep, and we must ride like the wind."

Guy shook himself, then slid off the mare's back. He hated to admit that riding Black Devil again would be a great pleasure, and to ride with Celeste in his arms... He dared not contemplate that.

Gaston hurled himself onto the mare, then waved to his men. "Scatter those shag-eared brutes and let us begone, my friends! By the beard of Beelzebub, it is a fine night to raise the devil. Let us quit this place!"

Celeste nestled within the crook of Guy's strong arm. He tucked the cloak tightly about her, drawing the hood over her free-flowing hair. *Ma foi!* Was he scandalized to see her without a ladylike coif? Guy's fingers lifted the wind-whipped strands of hair out of her eyes and smoothed them under the hood. When his knuckles gently brushed against her cheek, Celeste shivered with a new sensation. Though the biting wind chilled her, her skin burned where Guy had touched it.

As Guy urged the huge black stallion into a mile-eating canter, Celeste relaxed against his broad chest, sinking into his cushioning embrace. In response, Guy's arm tightened around her waist, holding her more secure. Guy's heartbeat, which kept time with Devil's plunging stride, imparted the calm assurance Celeste craved after the frightening events of the past hour.

Celeste had never experienced such fear—not even on the horrible boat trip between Calais and Bristol. As the danger receded, fatigue descended upon her. Closing her eyes against the stinging wind, she burrowed deeper within the furs of her cloak and said a quick prayer of thanksgiving for Gaston's audacity and Guy's steadfastness. Lulled by the rhythm of the great stallion's hooves and secure in the protection of her guardian angel, she fell into a dreamless sleep.

From her relaxed weight against him and her even breathing, Guy realized that Celeste slept. Good. The ride to York would be long, especially when snow covered the ruts in the post road. At least they didn't have to worry about the deuced wagon. Guy supported her slumbering head against his shoulder.

Celeste's hood slipped back, allowing Guy to explore her face in a manner he had not dared before. He marveled at how her black lashes fanned out over her silken cheeks. He took pleasure in admiring the high, exotic cheekbones in her delicate face. Her short, cold-tipped nose begged to be kissed. Guy gritted his teeth as a warm stirring grew within him. His gaze wandered down to the beckoning moistness of her full lush mouth.

Guy ran his tongue across his lips. His throat constricted, making breathing difficult. His blood pounded in his veins, turning to liquid fire. His hand caressed the softly rounded curve of her hip. Her warm body, cradled in his palm, gave promise of sweet pleasures. His loins ached. Black Devil's hooves beat a cadence through his fevered brain.

Remember your vow.

I am silent.

Remember who you are.

I am first a man.

Remember what you have renounced.

I am in agony.

Remember you are a monk.

Not yet.

Celeste's rose-petal lips, parted in sleep, turned upward to him. Without thinking, Guy dipped his head and, like a whisper in a lover's ear, his lips softly brushed against hers.

Celeste murmured in her sleep, then snuggled closer against him, turning her face toward his chest—where his heart raced like a whirligig in a storm. Guy snapped himself upright in the saddle, his lips burning as if a blazing ember had branded them. *Great Jove! What have I done?*

He lifted his eyes to the starless heavens and thanked whatever saints might have seen his disgraceful behavior that Celeste had not awakened at that wonderful and awful moment of his weakness—and that she was not now aware of the throbbing hardness between his legs.

Remember where you are going.

I am in heaven and in hell.

In the snow-filled gray of dawn, the exhausted, numbed and bedraggled party spied the soaring towers of York Minster ahead. Bowing his head over Celeste's sleeping form, Guy promised strict penance for his wanton transgression. Despite his good intentions, he savored the sweetness he held in his embrace.

Chapter Eighteen

For the next few days, inclement weather forced the bridal party to remain in their pleasant accommodations at the Rose and Crown, a large inn located near the Micklegate of York. After the frightening experience of their narrow escape from brigands at the Hawk and Hound, Celeste and her men were more than happy to enjoy the hospitality of the landlord and to view the sights of the beautiful old city.

Pip proved himself worthy of the new set of clothes that Celeste bought him by acting as her interpreter on shopping excursions whenever her growing English vocabulary failed her. The boy had a quick ear and an even quicker tongue. Within several days, Pip had learned to speak in short conversational French phrases. Gaston and the other men took a great deal of pleasure schooling Pip in the more colorful swear words—a skill the boy understandably did not practice in front of either his new mistress or Guy.

Once the travelers had settled into their lodgings, the novice monk quickly removed himself to the great cathedral of York Minster. Pausing to eat only when his body felt faint, Guy spent the succeeding days before the high altar, praying and pondering what he should do.

Guy knew that Snape Castle lay less than seventy miles to the north. Given a break in the weather and decent roads, they could be there in four or five days. Within a fortnight of her arrival, Lissa would be wedded to Walter Ormond. A sickening taste rose in his throat every time Guy recalled the journey's goal.

He tried to tell himself that his attraction to Celeste was merely lust, made more tantalizing by the fact that he hadn't been near a woman for months. He reasoned that Lissa was no more beautiful, or charming, or seductive, than many other women of his experience, but that falsehood stuck in his craw.

For months Lissa had struggled to get this far—traveling with a meager dowry, in a strange country whose language she barely spoke, to a cold, wet castle where she did not know a soul. There, with only a precious few in attendance and without any member of her family to comfort her, she was to be wed to a man she knew nothing about— thank God. Guy winced when he imagined her first meeting with Walter Ormond.

Though the money her father had given her for the trip was nearing its end, Lissa made sure all her men ate and slept as well as she. Given all the trials she had endured thus far, any other woman would have run for home. Not once had Celeste considered turning back. Time and again she had told Guy her family's honor was at stake. To Lissa, honor was everything.

Rising from where he had knelt for the past several hours, Guy stretched out the kinks in his calves. Then he slowly began to stroll around the side aisles, his head bowed in his meditations.

"Brother!" intruded a mildly annoyed voice at his side. Startled, Guy looked up.

A Grayfriar, slightly older than himself, fell into step with him. "You must have a great problem upon your mind, Brother, for I have been speaking to you for the last few minutes."

Guy lowered his gaze in a mute apology.

"You are the silent Franciscan who travels with the French lady, are you not?" When Guy flashed him a surprised look, the Grayfriar chuckled softly. "York is a very small pond filled with large-mouthed fish. Here, news travels as fast as the plague. Rumor flies even faster."

The two men crossed the nave, genuflected together in front of the high altar, then continued their walk down the far aisle.

"They say your lady is betrothed to the son of Sir Roger Ormond of Snape Castle. Is that true?"

Guy's lips tightened into a thin line. He nodded. It pained him to hear Lissa's fate spoken aloud, especially by one who did not know her.

The Grayfriar paused and placed a hand on Guy's sleeve. Concern colored his open countenance.

"Did you know that Sir Roger's wife died of the sweating sickness a month ago?"

Guy shook his head and made the sign of the cross for the soul of the late Lady Ormond. The Grayfriar followed suit.

"Sir Roger suffered a greater loss. His second son, as well as his only daughter, died within hours of their mother." The Grayfriar moved closer to Guy and continued in a low whisper. "Furthermore, they say Walter Ormond—your lady's intended—is riddled with the pox. They say he will not last out the year."

Guy nodded brusquely. He did not need to be reminded of that unsavory fact. If it were not a sin, he would have spent this past month praying for Walter's early demise. In unguarded moments, he had caught himself wishing it had already happened.

"Sir Roger wants an heir to carry on the family name. He knows that Walter cannot do it, even if he were married to the most . . . ah . . . fertile woman on earth."

Guy glared at the shorter monk. How dare he discuss Lissa's intimate duties in such a public manner?

The Grayfriar merely smiled at Guy's frown. "Nay, hear me out, good Brother. They say Sir Roger means to marry your lady himself, and get another son upon her."

Guy's head snapped back as if he had been struck. A mass of conflicting emotions clashed within his soul. Relief—that Lissa would not be bedded with a pox-ridden husband. Fear, accompanied by sorrow—that a marriage to an Ormond would indeed take place now, no matter what happened to Walter. Anger—at himself, for wishing to prevent it. Confusion—wondering what he should do about his dedication to the church once he returned to the priory. Loss—that Lissa would be gone from him forever.

The Grayfriar cocked his head, with an understanding look. "Aye, the father is old, and not much to look upon, I warrant, but 'tis a better match for the lady."

Poor Lissa, with her dreams of her handsome Knight of the Loyal Heart! Guy ached for her. He had never felt so powerless in his life.

"Be warned, Brother. The son, Walter Ormond, rides the king's highways seeking his bride. If the rumor is even half-true, he means to wed her as soon as he can lay hands on her."

Guy exhaled a breath that formed a misty cloud in the cold dampness of the church's stone interior. With a sinking sensation, he guessed who had sought them at the Hawk and Hound. God's teeth! What could they do now? Flee to sanctuary within the church? Lissa would never

consider it. She was betrothed to the very man who sought
so desperately to wed her.

Observing Guy's expression, the Grayfriar nodded.
"Forewarned is forearmed. I shall light a candle for you
and your lady, and remember your cause in my prayers.
Peace be with you, Brother."

With that, the friar continued on his way. In stunned
silence, Guy leaned against the sarcophagus of a long-dead
crusader.

Sweet Jesu! Ignoring his need for food and water, Guy
sank to his knees again. Covering his face with his hands,
he prayed for guidance—this time, not for his own weakness, but for the future of his beloved lady.

*Free her from her bond to the Ormonds, and I will do
whatever you ask of me, Lord. I will lock myself away
from her forever. I would give my life for her.*

An hour later, when Guy rose, light-headed, from his
knees, a fierce smile wreathed his lips. Though no complete plan had formed in his mind, at least he knew how to
buy some time for Lissa. And time was God's most precious gift to his earthly children.

Celeste shuffled her cards as a shower of sleet drummed
against the windowpanes of her sitting room at the Rose
and Crown. She should be thankful that here she was
warm, dry and safe. A cheerful fire crackled in the grate,
and several lit candles expelled the gloom of an early twilight. At the other end of the room, Dom and Flipot taught
Pip the intricacies of dicing, in robust French. Downstairs, she knew, Gaston and the other men enjoyed the
landlord's hot cider, while keeping a watchful ear and eye
for news of their recent adventure.

Sighing, Celeste laid out a hand of patience on a small
table. Would this horrible journey never end? Had her fa-

ther had any idea how far away Snape Castle was when he sent his daughter to England with only dear Aunt Marguerite and a set of silver spoons? She gave herself a little shake. Who was she to question her parent's decision? She reminded herself how lucky she was that Sir Roger had agreed to have her for his son.

Celeste glanced at the card in her hand. *Le valet de coeur*—the jack of hearts. What was he like, her husband-to-be? This jack of her heart? The colored figure on the pasteboard card seemed to wink mischievously at her. Would Walter smile in such a roguish way? Did he have a sense of humor? She hoped so! Would he like to sing, to dance, to play card games, to tell amusing stories?

Celeste closed her eyes and tried once again to imagine their first meeting. Her Walter would ride out on his white horse from his banner-bedecked castle. The golden rays of the sun would reflect off his burnished silver armor as he came toward her. And when he reined in his horse before her... Oh, yes, the horse would stop so suddenly it would rear on its hind legs. Then, when Walter had the animal under his firm control, he would raise his helm and she would see...

Guy's beautiful face floated into her musings. His golden hair framed his features, and his smile bedazzled the sun so much that it hid its face in a cloud for shame at the beauty of her betrothed lord—Sir Guy Cavendish.

Celeste swept the pack of cards to the floor. *Non!* Not Guy—in his brown Franciscan's robe. Never Brother Guy—who was God's man, not hers. It was Walter whom she was to marry very soon. Walter Ormond. She must never forget that.

Kneeling amid the cinders, Celeste gathered up her cards. When she wiped a speck of soot off the face of the jack of hearts, it smudged the picture. Hastily she buried the blackened image deep in the pack. The last card she retrieved was the ace of spades—the dark card, and the one worth the most points. Was it her imagination or did the bit of pasteboard seem to glow in her hand? *Silly goose!* She shuffled it into the deck and scolded herself for her superstition.

The weather finally improved several days later. Gaston hurried the men to load the new cart he had purchased. Celeste stood beside her horse, rubbing its nose. *Ma foi!* Her baggage had grown considerably smaller since she had left France, nearly three months ago. She had sailed across the dreadful Channel with trunks full of gowns, shifts, undergowns, petticoats, laces, ribbons, stockings, veils, cloaks, coifs and slippers. She sighed.

"It is my slippers that I think I miss the most, Starlight," she confided to her horse as she fed him pieces of a carrot Pip had produced from some place best not known. "A whole box full of them, washed away in a wretched river. And then, my favorite red ones . . . you remember them, eh? The ones with the golden stitching? I wondered if they burned up at that peench-'potted inn?"

Something touched her arm. When she looked around, she saw Guy standing by her side. She drew in her breath at the sight of him. He had been absent from her company ever since she had awakened at the Rose and Crown after a long twelve-hour sleep between clean sheets. As he gazed down at her, he looked as gaunt as he had before their stay at Cranston Hall, but now his face was different. In the past, he had frowned when he looked at her. This time, something else lay hidden in the mysterious depths of his blue eyes. Celeste didn't know what it was, but she approved of the change.

His stone facade had fallen away. The face of her own special guardian angel had finally come alive.

Again slowed down by a cart, the bridal party plodded their way up the York-to-Edinburgh post road. Guy hoped they would reach the village of Thirsk before early evening overtook them. Twenty miles a day was the best they could manage, considering that the roads through the Vale of Yorkshire were not as well maintained by the crown as those farther south. Though cold, at least the weather was clear, and everyone bloomed with good spirits, even the obnoxious Daisy.

Bringing up the rear, Guy kept to his own thoughts for company, though periodically he would look up when he heard Celeste's laughter. She passed the time in alternately teaching French and teasing the smitten Pip. Under the shadow of his hood, Guy smiled to himself when he heard her jests and quips carried back to him on the cold, bright air. He thanked the saints that he was not the source of her amusement this time.

Lost in his contemplation of the future, particularly Lissa's future, Guy did not hear hoofbeats behind him until Paul, who rode nearby, turned in his saddle, then called out, "Riders approach!"

Up ahead, Gaston wheeled Black Devil around and drew alongside Celeste. Pierre pulled the cart off the road to allow the approaching party room to pass. Guy yanked Daisy to a halt, then looked over his shoulder.

Five men thundered down the road from the direction of York, the hooves of their horses tearing up great clods of mud as they came. All of them were armed with longbows and daggers. Their leader carried a double-bladed broadsword at his belt—a knight's weapon. A knot of apprehension twisted in the pit of Guy's stomach. Scanning the empty road ahead of them, he cursed inwardly. A perfect spot to waylay travelers! His fingers itched for a sword to hold.

"Who comes?" Paul asked out of the side of his mouth. His hand rested on the hilt of his short sword.

Guy squinted in the fading light. The lead horse wore a saddlecloth emblazoned with a coat of arms. As they drew nearer, Guy choked on his sudden anger. The three black crows on a golden shield proclaimed the Ormond crest. Walter Ormond had come a-wooing at last.

In the cart, Pip let out a small yelp, then jumped out of the seat and ran back to Guy.

"'Tis the very knaves I told you about, Brother Guy!" The boy's eyes widened with fear. "The same as at the Hawk and Hound."

Sweet Jesu! Guy's heart raced in double time. His anger threatened to burst from the confines of his control. Lissa should have been greeted with music and flowers, not by a band of cutthroats.

Guy pointed to Gaston. Pip turned on his heel and sped back down the road, where he relayed his message to the venerable soldier. Guy pulled the edge of his hood low over his face, hoping Walter would not recognize him from his days at court.

As Walter rode closer, Guy seethed with his impotent anger. The Ormond spawn visibly crawled with the hideous scourge of the pox. Guy could barely look at the man's face without retching. *Sweet Saint Anne, protect Lissa from this . . . this . . .*

"Do you know them, Brother Guy?" Celeste drew up beside him.

He didn't want to answer, yet he must. She would know the truth all too soon. On his slate he wrote, *Walter Ormond.*

"My betrothed?" she whispered in her low, husky voice. She gave a weak, desperate laugh—challenging Guy to retract his words.

Sick at heart, he nodded.

"What is wrong with his face?" she gasped.

Pox, Guy wrote, then rubbed out the word, wishing he could erase Walter with equal ease.

"Mon Dieu!" A glazed look of despair spread across her features.

Guy wanted to seize her in his arms and run. He wanted to cast off his robe of peace and don his armor. He wanted to grind what was left of the miserable Ormond into the mud. Instead, he could do nothing but sit in silence upon a paltry donkey and pray Walter did not recognize him.

"By the devil's bulging cock!" Gaston reined in his stallion beside Celeste. "The boy tells me those are the very dogs we left behind us. God's teeth! We should have kept their horses. We shall fight them now."

"Non." Celeste shook her head, all the color drained from her cheeks. "We cannot. You see, dear Gaston, that is Walter Ormond—my husband-to-be."

Guy tensed, waiting for Gaston to erupt in righteous anger. Instead, the man went white, then spoke to Celeste in a terse undertone. "Give me your leave, my lady, and I will make you a widow within the hour."

Celeste shook her head. *"Merci,* Gaston, but I must see this...thing to the end, for the honor of my family." Squaring her shoulders, she sat up straighter in the saddle as she watched the riders circle them.

Chapter Nineteen

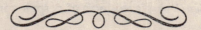

" 'Tis the wench, I'll warrant, m'lord!" Deighton's unshaven face split into a leer. "An' by the look o'her, she'll fiddle a merry tune to your joints!"

After several weeks in Deighton's gross company, Walter could hardly wait to be rid of him—with eight inches of good steel betwixt his ribs. Ignoring the foulmouthed knave, Ormond regarded his stiff little bride, who sat so primly in her saddle. She'd be pretty if she smiled. Walter clamped his jaws tighter. What woman had cast him a welcoming smile in the past six months?

"Celeste de Montcalm?" Walter shouted. Of course it must be she, but he'd best confirm it.

The wench inclined her head slightly. Was she afraid her headdress might fall off?

"Oui," she answered crisply.

Damn the chit! She wouldn't even look directly at him! Walter vowed to remedy that in short order. "You've taken long enough to get here, woman." He rode directly up to her side, pushing by a fuming old man. "I am Walter Ormond, son of Sir Roger Ormond, lord of Snape Castle. Have you no kiss of greeting for your husband?"

Celeste shot him a quick glance out of the corner of her eye, then stared ahead as before. "I am not married to you yet, my lord," she replied in French.

"Hell and damnation, wench! Answer me in plain English. I'll brook none of your foreign ways." Walter sat back in his saddle, satisfied to see a stricken look flit across her face. Important to let her know who was the master now.

"I have no husband," Celeste replied slowly in English. "And I give no kiss to you." She stuck her little nose up in the air.

A dull headache throbbed in Walter's temples. For a farthing, he'd haul the minx off her horse and whip her naked in front of them all. Only a shred of prudence stayed his hand. Once he had wed her, he could discipline her at his leisure. Beating that proud look off her face might prove highly entertaining.

"Understand this then, mistress mine. You will have a husband before the next hour has run its course."

Her startled expression gave Walter immense satisfaction.

"But this is not possible!" She sent a pleading glance to the old man.

"You take us to Snape!" the graybeard bellowed.

Walter would send this meddlesome old bastard packing back to France as soon as possible—tonight, preferably. He shook his finger at the old man. "You do not give the orders here. I do!" Walter glared at the wench's party, taking stock of each in turn. One old man, a half-dozen striplings, a boy and a lanky priest.

"We burn daylight!" Deighton growled behind him. "Get on with it, my lord, for I itch to settle a thing or two with these scum. They gave us the slip the other night, an' I will have me own back on them. Aye!"

Walter clenched his fist tighter around his reins. Very soon he would serve Deighton his own justice. Until then, Walter knew, he must be patient. He dismounted and strode up to the girl.

"Then we shall tarry no longer." He clamped his hand around Celeste's wrist and yanked her out of her saddle. Light as a feather—easy to handle.

The pack of Frenchies started to draw their weapons, but Walter's men acted faster. Excellent! Perhaps he would give the varlets a good feed before he killed them.

"What is this?" The girl tried to escape from his grip.

Spirited little thing! Walter concluded he'd have to tie her to the bedpost, before he whipped her. He liked that idea.

"'Tis our wedding, sweetheart. I have waited long enough."

"*Non!*" She tried to slap him with her free hand, but Walter fetched her a blow across her face. The girl staggered, her dark eyes enormous. Her men swore, but they had been rendered powerless.

Walter tensed, waiting for her scream, but none came from her white throat. He had hit her hard enough; he could see the imprint of his hand on her cheek. No matter. Later on, he would make her shout the tower room down.

"Is not a good place for a wedding." She practically spat the words in Walter's face.

Ormond chuckled at her growing anger. Angry wenches excited him in bed, and Walter knew he needed all the encouragement he could get since the pox had taken over his body.

"Have you not heard of the old English custom of being married under a bush? Nay? 'Tis no matter. I say 'twill be done." He pointed to the brown-robed priest, who sat still on an undersize donkey. "And here's the very man who will do us the service. 'Twas most provident of you to bring your own confessor. You, priest! Get down and come here!" he shouted. Probably this clod didn't speak a wit of English.

Holding both his boiling anger and his voice in tenuous check, Guy slid off Daisy. When the knave struck Lissa, Guy had very nearly gone for Walter's scrawny throat. If he had followed his inclination, Guy knew, he would now be lying dead in the frozen mud. Patience, he counseled himself. Keeping his head bowed so that Walter could not see his face, he stood close to Celeste. He felt, more than saw, that she trembled under her cloak.

Don't let this scum know your fear, sweet Lissa. He will feast upon it.

"Do you understand my speech, priest?" Ormond shouted. "I want you to join us as man and wife."

Guy nodded, then pointed toward a small rise away from the road.

"Damn you to the devil's own broth, treacherous monk!" Gaston spat at him as they passed by him. Guy did not acknowledge the understandable insult. He prayed Gaston would react quickly when the time came.

Walter followed, pulling Celeste behind him. Everyone else stayed mounted, each side watching the little procession wend its way up the hillock. Guy drew to a halt on the other side of a lone tree, out of sight of the road. Fortunately, Walter had not noticed how far he was from his guard. Facing them, Guy tensed, waiting to catch Ormond off guard. Fortunately, Celeste stumbled on the trailing hem of her gown.

"Get up, damn you—"

The instant Walter diverted his attention, Guy sprang, throwing his bulk against the lighter man. Both of them hit the ground with a solid crash, Guy on top. Without pausing, the novice monk cocked his arm, then slammed his knotted fist into Walter's putrid face. The cartilage of Ormond's nose crumpled under the impact with a sickening crunch. Blood poured down Walter's face.

"By the—"

Guy cut off further speech by drawing Walter's sword and pricking his neck. The coward quaked underneath Guy, though red pinpoints of fury shone in his eyes. "What manner of priest are you?"

"A good one," Celeste answered with a grim smile of defiance.

Guy, marveling at her coolness under the circumstances, nodded his head toward Walter's belt. Celeste understood, and whisked his dagger out of its sheath before the stunned and bleeding suitor could gather his wits. Hauling Walter to his feet, and holding him securely with one arm pinioned behind, Guy led them back to the road. Celeste brought up the rear, humming and skipping as if she were just returning from a pleasant walk.

"*Bravo, mes enfants terribles!*" Gaston stood in his stirrups and waved his cap. Then he drew his own sword and pointed it at Deighton. "You see your master? You see he will die if you do not drop your...your..." He motioned at the notched bows the ruffians held.

"Weapons!" Pip prompted in a loud, cheerful voice.

"*Oui!* Do it!"

"Do as he says!" Ormond shouted, struggling against Guy's grip. "Or this whoreson will kill me—and you'll not be paid," he added, hastily.

With oaths and grumbling, Ormond's guards threw down their weapons. Gaston dismounted, shouting rapid orders to his men. He strode up to the shivering Ormond and berated him in blistering French.

"I do not bother to speak in your language—you have no brains to understand anything! Pah!" Gaston spat contemptuously at Walter's boots. "But there is one thing I must do for the honor of the family de Montcalm."

Before Guy could stop him, Gaston hit Walter as hard as he could. The force of the blow rendered the odious lord completely unconscious. Guy laid the man down, surprised at both the power and the vehemence of Gaston's anger.

"That scurvy slug will never forget this day, I think. And I hope he will never forget me and this important lesson." Gaston gathered Celeste in his thick arms. "*Pauvre petite!* Does your sweet face hurt still? Maybe I should kill him, eh?"

Guy shook his head. Gaston probably did not realize the severe penalty for attacking a member of the English nobility. Strictly speaking, a court of law would find Walter's treatment of his betrothed to be his right—especially since Celeste was French and therefore suspect of almost anything in the eyes of the average Englishman. Guy didn't want to compound the problem any further. As much as he would like to strangle Walter, Guy, a sworn man of God, could not. The Bible said that justice was the Lord's province, and Guy sincerely hoped that was true.

"This time we will take their horses with us, eh?" Gaston's brown eyes twinkled. "We could leave them Daisy."

Guy shook his head again. Though he disliked the beast, he couldn't subject her to the mercies of an Ormond with a broken face and outraged dignity.

The men-at-arms bound the foul-swearing Englishmen, using pieces of their own reins. Under Gaston's direction, they removed the knaves' boots and stockings, ignoring the howls and dire threats of their prisoners. Tossing the weapons and footwear into the cart, they gagged the brigands with the reeking stockings and dragged them over the hillock, where they would not be discovered soon by any late-wandering travelers.

The early twilight descended. Guy knew that once Ormond and his men were found, there would be a hue and cry out for the French. The leisurely trip he had envisioned in the peace of the cathedral must now become a dash to safety—but which way?

Do you wish to return to France? he wrote on his slate, then held it out to Celeste.

She stared at the chalked letters for a long moment. A sheen of tears filmed over her eyes, turning them to a deep amethyst.

"I cannot," she whispered. "I must honor my father's bond to Sir Roger."

Guy pointed over the hillock where Walter lay and wrote, *With that?*

Celeste lifted her face to him, her lower lip quivering. "I must meet with Sir Roger, Brother Guy. Only he can release me from my father's contract." She tried to smile. "Perhaps he is a kind and just man."

Guy couldn't look her in the eye. If the Grayfriar's rumor proved true, Celeste might be walking into a dragon's nest. As Guy contemplated their best course of action, she shivered in the rising evening wind and drew the cloak about her.

"*Sacrebleu!* Let us be gone," Gaston rumbled. "The men are hungry, and so am I. Where do you want us to go?"

He looked from Celeste to Guy and back again.

"To Snape Castle," she replied firmly.

Growling an oath, Gaston threw up his hands in disgust. Celeste laid a slim hand on his arm. "You know I cannot return to L'Étoile, Gaston. You know my father will not take me back."

The old soldier covered her hand with his. "*Oui*, little one. I know him too well, and what you say is true." To Guy he explained, "Better a child's death than dishonor to her family—that is what Roland de Montcalm would say. We shall proceed to Snape Castle and lay your grievance at Sir Roger's feet. Pray, God the father is not like his whelp."

Amen to that! Guy quickly wrote to Gaston, *Loan me your horse. I will take Celeste on a faster route over the moors.*

Gaston narrowed his eyes and pursed his lips. "I do not like this plan. Why separate? Where do you intend to take my lady?"

To Snape Castle, Guy wrote.

"With night coming on?" Gaston reminded Guy of an old bear with one precious cub.

Guy nodded. Speed and safety for Celeste. He wanted to get her far from Walter Ormond and his band of felons, as quickly as possible.

Gaston stroked his chin, then asked Celeste, "You wish to go with him?"

"Do you know the way in the dark?" she questioned Guy in turn.

I belong to this land. His white letters stood out like ghost writing in the creeping night gloom.

Celeste turned to Gaston. "Then I will put myself in his hands." While she mounted her horse, Gaston grabbed Guy by the arm. "And your hands best behave themselves, master monk!"

Guy swallowed his guilty thoughts and attempted to look surprised at Gaston's thinly veiled warning.

"*Oui*, Brother Guy, I am not so addlepated as some young ladies think I am. I have eyes that have seen much in my fifty-odd years. I see the looks you give her. Remember, you are a man of the spirit—not of the flesh. If you forget this, I will remind you—in blood. Do you understand my meaning?"

Guy looked directly into the old soldier's eyes and nodded. Though he gave his oath silently, he considered himself honor-bound by it.

"*Bon!*" Gaston handed Black Devil's reins to Guy. "We will stay on the main road. When you get to this Snape place, send someone out to find us."

Nodding again, Guy firmly gripped Gaston's arm in his for a moment.

"Do we ride or do we dance a pavane, gentlemen?" Celeste cocked her head, a grin on her face.

"Go with God," Gaston replied in a strangely husky voice.

"Oh, la, la! I go with the next best thing, good Gaston. I ride with one of his archangels."

Chapter Twenty

A frosty full moon rose over the rolling moorland as Guy led Celeste across its wild, near-barren terrain. Sometimes they walked their horses around boggy or rocky areas, other times they spurred Black Devil and Starlight into loping canters. Despite the unfamiliar ground and growing fatigue as the night wore on, Celeste's little mare kept up with Guy's huge stallion.

Guy allowed only two short rest stops. When Celeste ventured to speak to him, he brusquely acknowledged her presence. Most of the time, he stared at the horizon. Guy's moody distance confused her. After his magnificent bravery this afternoon, Celeste had thought that he would be much more open with her—even if he didn't talk.

Had her decision to go on to Snape Castle angered him? If that was the case, he should have left them this afternoon. She would not begrudge him his understandable desire to return south before worse weather set in.

Celeste dipped her handkerchief into the chill water of the tiny rill beside which they rested. She patted the soaking cloth against her flushed cheeks, hoping that the cold water would sharpen her senses. Despite the excitement and novelty of this midnight ride, she had trouble keeping her eyes open.

Guy sat apart. The moonlight illuminated the beauty of his face with its unearthly glow. Celeste took a secret pleasure in studying his handsome profile. When she told Gaston she rode with one of God's angels, she had jested. Now she wondered anew if Brother Guy were truly a heavenly visitor come down to earth in disguise. If she hadn't met his delightful aunt Mary, Celeste might have been tempted to fantasize Guy's mysterious past. She realized she knew very little about this fascinating man whom she accompanied across an unknown stretch of landscape in the middle of the night.

She covered another huge yawn with her hand and hoped Brother Guy had not noticed the first two. She didn't want him to be held back because of her weakness.

Guy suddenly rose, and helped her to her feet. Though the night had turned quite cold, his hand felt warm as it closed around her near-frozen fingers. He took her other hand and rubbed both of them to warm them. Celeste sighed aloud with pleasure.

"*Merci,* Brother Guy." His callused fingers sent tingly showers of sensation on her soft skin. The glow he generated intoxicated her. "I do not feel the night's discomfort, with you to keep me warm."

Guy dropped her hands as if they burned him. He frowned, then pointed to her horse.

Taken off guard once again, Celeste straightened her shoulders and tried to shake away the smothering fatigue that closed in upon her. She mutely agreed it was wiser for them to remount their horses and be on their way. If he had continued to hold her hands, Celeste feared, she might have fallen asleep standing up. Guy grasped her around her waist and lightly placed her on her sidesaddle. For a brief moment, their gazes locked and held. His blue eyes reflected the moon's glimmering beams of crystal light. In their depths, she saw a message that she did not understand but that caused her breath to come in short gasps and her cheeks to flush with a fiery heat. Hearing her gasp, he quickly lowered his lids, then turned to his own horse.

More than a little shaken by their silent encounter, Celeste clutched the reins firmly in her hands and fought off another yawn. She reminded herself that soon she would be at her journey's end and could at last have a bath and a safe night's sleep. Through the fringe of her lowered lashes, she watched Guy mount Black Devil in a single fluid movement. She couldn't help admiring the way he controlled the temperamental horse. What a perfect knight Brother Guy would have made! Celeste chewed her lower lip. Once she had dreamed of Walter as her champion, but now that she had met him... No, she wouldn't think about that now. Out here in the middle of nowhere was not the place to mourn the shattering of one's childish fancy. She kicked Starlight into a trot and followed after Guy.

It seemed only a few minutes later when he signaled her to stop. After dismounting, he tied Devil's reins to a low bush beside a cluster of rocks. Celeste blinked. Had she fallen asleep in the saddle and traveled farther than she thought? Guy walked around to her near side and held up his hands to her.

"Are we lost?" Celeste scanned the countryside. It looked the same in all directions.

Guy's lips twitched, and then he shook his head.

Celeste allowed herself to be lifted off her horse. She would never have admitted it but her backside was numb and her every muscle ached.

"Why have we stopped so soon?"

In answer, Brother Guy opened his mouth in an enormous, jaw-breaking yawn. Then he stretched his arms out to each side, the movement accompanied by a faint cracking of his joints. He concluded this performance with another yawn, and a fierce rubbing of his eyes, followed by a shrug. Celeste did her best not to laugh, but failed miserably.

"You are tired, *n'est-ce pas?*" Guy had never once admitted either hunger or fatigue during the past two months.

He nodded and laid his head on his folded palms, miming a pillow.

Celeste put her hands to her hips. "Sleep? But where?"

Nearly folding himself in half, Guy crept under the rock outcropping. He beckoned to her to follow. Lifting her skirts from her ankles, Celeste picked her way over the gently sloping boulder until she was inside.

"*Ma foi!*" Celeste gazed at her escort with wonderment. "You must have the eyes of a cat, to find this small cave in such a wild country. Either that, or an angel sits on your shoulder and showed you the way, eh?"

Guy arched his brow, then patted his shoulder. In the darkness, the moon lit up his white teeth as he grinned at her. He brushed away the loose dirt and pebbles, then pointed to the cleared spot. Did he expect her to sleep here? Outdoors, on the bare earth?

Before she could voice her objections, Guy ducked outside and tended to their horses. Celeste sat gingerly, wrapping her cloak about her. She hoped no spiders or mice lurked about. Admittedly, the tiny cave provided a windbreak and a little warmth. The earthy smell of moss and peat filled her nostrils. She found the scent oddly comforting.

Guy crawled back inside, carrying both their saddles. He spread out one of the horse blankets and motioned for Celeste to lie down on it. He placed her dowry bag under her head. Without warning, he pulled off her boots, then tucked her stocking feet securely under the second blanket.

"But where do you sleep, Brother Guy?"

Surely he didn't intend to lie on the cold ground—or, worse, stay awake all night. He pointed to the mouth of the cave.

"*C'est impossible!* You will freeze in only that poor robe of yours. No, you must have one of the blankets. I have my cloak to cover me." When he started to shake his head, Celeste narrowed her eyes and glared at him. "You should have listened more closely to Gaston when he told you that I can be a very stubborn woman. You will take this blanket, or I will stay awake all night."

Guy studied her thoughtfully for a moment; then he bowed his head and accepted her offer. Taking his place at the mouth of the cave, he rolled up in the worn blanket, which smelled strongly of Black Devil.

Having gotten her way, Celeste laid her head on the lumpy leather saddlebag and burrowed under her cloak. For the first time since meeting Walter Ormond, she allowed her thoughts to wander over the events that had brought her to this hard, cold bed.

Sweet Saint Anne! What would happen on the morrow, when they finally arrived at Snape Castle and met Sir Roger? Celeste tried to remember what the man looked like, but she had only a dim recollection from eight years ago. At age eleven, she had been much more interested in gazing at the handsome knights of the French and English courts, sampling the various sweetmeats and shopping with her sisters for such gaudy trifles as pretty songbirds in wicker cages. All she could remember of Sir Roger was his loud voice and a grizzled beard.

Celeste rolled over in an effort to get more comfortable, then returned to her train of thought. Sir Roger must

be halfway civilized, or else Papa would never have allowed her to marry his son. Celeste shuddered as Walter's
hideous face rose in her mind's eye. How could Sir Roger
let her come all this way, knowing his son's disease? Perhaps he was not so civilized as Papa thought.

*Ma foi! He lives at the end of the world! Good Lord,
give Sir Roger a cup overflowing with compassion and
have him free me from this contract, for I swear I will die
before I marry with his odious son.*

Something rustled in the bracken near the cave's entrance. Celeste sat up with a start. Guy didn't move. Being a man—and a monk—he naturally was used to sleeping
in uncomfortable places with unknown creatures roaming
under his very nose. They probably had mice in his priory.

Celeste hugged her knees. She vowed not to wake him
with her fears. He needed sleep more than she did. And she
did not want him to think she was a coward.

When she was a little girl, she used to beg her nurse to
let her sleep in the garden on the nights when the moon
rose fully round. People said the faerie folk always danced
on such nights, and Celeste had passionately wanted to see
them. Now, huddled in a dirty cave in the middle of a savage land, Celeste rued her youthful wish.

She heard the flap of wings as some night bird swooped
low. Bird? Or bat? Celeste grimaced in the darkness. Aunt
Marguerite had once told her that bats liked to roost in a
maiden's long hair. Celeste flung herself back down on her
makeshift pillow and pulled her cloak over her head. *In a
month I shall laugh at this adventure.* She squeezed her
eyes shut. A month seemed so very far away.

Guy lay still and watched Celeste through slitted eyes.
Poor thing! This was probably the first time she had ever

slept on the ground. He hid his grin when she jumped at an owl's soft hoot. Any moment he expected her to call to him. He couldn't go to her side unless she invited him. And he desperately wanted to lie as close to her as he could. He squeezed his eyes shut.

Guy imagined himself lying on a four-poster bed, with a feather mattress and a velvet coverlet, and making long, sweet love to a very naked Celeste. He could almost feel the silky curtain of her raven hair cascading over his chest. He ran his tongue over his lips as he imagined the taste of her kisses. He grew hot and hard with a deep, aching desire.

Guy inhaled the cold air and tried to banish the tormenting image. Once he delivered her to Snape Castle, he would fast for a week—and wear a hair shirt, if he could find one. Most of all, he would pray—pray without ceasing for forgiveness for the weakness of his flesh.

Less than three feet away, he heard her shiver, despite her furred cape. Surely she would ask him to come warm her. *No! You must not wish for that!* his conscience chided him. He had renounced the pleasures of a woman's soft body molding against his while her fingers gently teased him into sweet agony.

Guy dug his nails into his palms. *I am in agony now, and there is no sweetness about it.*

As he wrestled with his demons in the darkness, Guy became aware that Celeste had grown quiet. He cocked his ear, but could not hear her breathing. Jesu! Had she been bitten by some poisonous thing, and died within the reach of his arm? Goaded by this terrifying thought, Guy threw off his blanket, and crept over to where she lay.

Only when he put his ear close to her mouth did he hear her soft, even breathing. In spite of her fears, and the uncomfortable bed, she had fallen into a deep, healing sleep. Touching her cheek with his knuckle, Guy found her skin cold. 'Twas a Christian duty to give comfort to the weak, he reasoned as he pulled his blanket over both of them. Celeste did not stir. Guy carefully edged his long body next to hers, silently offering his warmth to her. Like a flower seeking the sun, Celeste relaxed against him, her face resting a heartbeat away.

Guy's body burned with a familiar fire. If he stole a kiss from those tempting lips, no one would know—no one except himself and God. What was a little kiss? He had tasted her lips once already, and a bolt of lightning had not thundered down from the sky. One gentle kiss—a brotherly kiss of affection—to comfort her.

Guy moistened his lips. *To steal an unsuspected kiss from her while she slept is a sin,* his conscience told him, stinging like a horsefly in June. *To take is not to give. Remember, she is in your protection.*

The horsefly stung him again. *Would your flaming desire allow you to stop at one "brotherly" kiss? Where is the honor you are so proud of, Cavendish? Remember why you left the court in the first place? Or have you now decided to follow your king's current fashion and make a mistress of a virgin you cannot wed?*

Guy stared up at the low, rocky ceiling and whispered every prayer he knew. He didn't remember falling asleep.

Gray clouds welcomed the chill mist of the morning. Guy woke, and wondered for a moment why he felt so stiff. Then he recalled the day before, and the long night that had followed. He gazed at the lady nestled in the crook of his arm. Celeste's sleep-softened face made her look much younger than her eighteen years. During the night, her gray-velvet coif had fallen off, and her hair spilled over his arm. Thicker than he expected, it reminded him of a skein of costly silk from the mysterious East.

Gently, so as not to awaken her, Guy eased his arm out from under her. He needed a brisk walk. He needed confession and absolution. He needed to drown himself in a peat bog.

Outside, Black Devil and Starlight cropped the brown grasses which poked through the thin cover of snow. Overhead, a hawk wheeled against the pewter canopy of the sky. Guy stretched and gulped down deep drafts of the clean, sharp air. Home! He could taste it. Just a few leagues over the horizon, and yet the gates of Wolf Hall were no longer open to him. His father had made that perfectly clear the day Guy bade his parents goodbye and headed south to join the Franciscans.

"Brother Guy?" Celeste poked her tousled head out from the tumble of blankets. Blinking away the sleep from her eyes, she reminded him of a young vixen, snug in her burrow. He dropped down on the damp grass beside the opening.

She yawned behind her hand. "Did we really sleep all night in this place?"

Stifling the urge to grin, Guy nodded.

"Gaston would never believe it." She opened her pack and pulled out her ivory comb. She began to work it through the tangles of her hair. "In fact, I think it might be wiser if we didn't mention it to him at all, eh? Gaston would not approve of your sleeping arrangements for me." A delightful dimple appeared by the corner of her mouth. "He is very old-fashioned."

Guy couldn't bear to watch her groom her hair. He yearned to take the comb from her hand and do the service himself. Instead, he snatched up the blankets, shook them out, then threw them over the horses' backs.

Celeste crawled out from the shallow cave and stood unsteadily, massaging her shoulders. "*Zut alors!* I am like a stiff old lady all dressed in widow's weeds. Ah! I even have the weeds to prove it!" She pulled a piece of prickly gorse out of her bodice, and laughed as she flung it to the wind.

Saddling the palfrey, Guy ignored her until she hiked up her skirts and pulled on her boots. Great Jove! What a shapely leg she had!

"I don't suppose there is anything to eat?" Celeste asked, with a hopeful look in her violet eyes.

Guy shook his head and pretended to be very busy adjusting Devil's girth strap. Why didn't she pull her skirts back down, like a proper lady?

"No friendly rabbit to hippity-hop by and join us for breakfast?" She sighed as she stood again. "Have you ever eaten a jugged hare—all dripping with butter, wine sauce and parsley?" She closed her eyes and swayed a little, caught up in the imagined delights of rabbit stew.

Guy walked around to the far side of Black Devil, where he leaned his forehead against the saddle as Celeste continued to enumerate and describe a feast found only in heaven. Guy's empty stomach rumbled in protest.

"Finis," she announced, finally coming to the end of her menu. "There, did you not enjoy that sumptuous repast? *Ma foi,* I confess I am so full I could not eat another bite. You will have to finish the baked custard tarts by yourself, Brother Guy."

Guy looked over Black Devil's back and wondered if yesterday's events had unhinged her mind.

Celeste burst into a waterfall of laughter when she saw his expression. "Oh, la, la! Have you never played pretend, Brother Guy? I am so sorry for you! It does wonders to make you feel better. At home in L'Étoile, I used to do it all the time, whenever I was locked in my room without supper and . . ."

Guy barely heard the rest. Sweet Saint Anne! What sort of an upbringing had this poor girl had? Locked up and starved on a regular basis? He gripped the stirrup to keep himself from gathering her into his embrace. At the very first opportunity, he would find her something to eat. He would heap the bounty of earth, sea and sky on her trencher, if he could.

Celeste clapped her coif on her head, then straightened the filmy gray veil over her hair. "So? Do we stand here on this very wet ground and look at each other, or do we ride, Brother Guy?"

To the ends of the earth.

Chapter Twenty-One

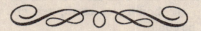

"**Y**our pardon, my lord, but the French lady has come," announced Talbott.

Sir Roger Ormond looked up from his accounts ledger and squinted in the dimness of the gray afternoon. In an effort to save his precious store of candles for the dark winter months ahead, Sir Roger worked as much as possible by the natural light that cast its feeble rays through the narrow lancet window of his estate office.

"The French lady?" he repeated, racking his brains for whoever it was his steward meant.

"Lady Celeste de Montcalm." Talbott enunciated slowly. "The lady who is betrothed to Master Walter."

Sir Roger laid down his quill pen, and rubbed his hands together. By Jupiter and his court! So the lass had finally arrived. He had received so many messages in the past three months detailing her accidents, illnesses and loss of baggage that Roger had all but given her up.

"They wait upon you in the hall, my lord," his steward continued.

"Tell me, Talbott. Is she fair?"

Talbott shifted from one foot to the other. "She is young, my lord."

A plague on the man! "But is she comely? Out with it!"

Talbott licked his lips like a dog eyeing a bone. "She is of less than middling stature, my lord. Of her looks, they are dark, and silky, and she has well-marked eyebrows."

"Dark?" Sir Roger stroked his chin and realized he had not shaved for the past two days. A dark wench might prove a shrew—'twas a well-known fact. "But her face? Her figure? Do not waste my time in tittle-tattle, jolt-head. Is the lady a beauty?"

"Of her bosom..." Talbott shrugged. "'Tis not much raised, nor do I think she is trussed up, as is the fashion in the south. She has an elegant long neck, like ivory. Her hair? From what I could see of it, 'tis as black as midnight. And her eyes..." A stupid, sheeplike expression stole over Talbott's face.

Sir Roger resisted the impulse to hurl the pot of ink at the stretch-mouthed rascal. "Is she squint-eyed? Is there a cast to them? What about her eyes?"

"'Pon my very soul, they are purple in color, my lord. I have ne'er seen the like, and she uses them with great effect."

Sir Roger slammed the palm of his hand down on the table, which caused the quills to shiver in their holder. "Lackwit! Answer my first question! Do you find the lady pleasing?"

Talbott pushed his straggling red hair out of his face before replying. "This lady is a most beautiful maid—in my humble opinion, my lord."

Sir Roger sat back in his plain wooden chair. This was a fair piece of news. Talbott's eye for women was legendary below stairs. Sir Roger permitted a slow smile to crease his face. A young, comely wife to warm his old bones—not a bad way to greet the coming Christmas season, even if she was a foreigner.

"And her attendants? How many accompany her?" How many did he have to feed, and how soon could he send them packing back to France?

"That is the nut and core of it, my lord. There is but one, her confessor."

Sir Roger's bushy gray eyebrows shot up toward his hairline. "No baggage? No outriders? I was given to understand she came with half of France." Had she lost everything in her numerous ill-fated adventures. Pray, God, not her dowry!

Talbott shrugged again. "I know not, save her confessor is very odd. He does not speak."

"Ha! A former felon, gone for the church! No doubt his tongue was cut out for some early transgression. No matter. There are enough prattling priests in this world as it is."

"And the lady does not speak English very well," Talbott added.

"Of course not, you tedious fool. She's French! Aye, but we shall instruct her soon enough."

I shall instruct her in the English manner of lovemaking within this very week, Sir Roger thought to himself, with a growing heat in his loins. Cupid have mercy! He felt like a green youth a-wooing his first maid. It had been far too long since he last had a woman—and a pretty one at that! Poor Eleanor had been a whey-faced creature who did nothing but sigh and cry—a perpetual red nose and a long, skinny body, God rest her soul.

"In the hall, you say? Come, let us view this dainty morsel." Sir Roger breathed a quick prayer of thanks that Walter had gone boar-hunting.

Celeste paced back and forth in front of the massive fireplace in the soot-blackened hall. The few logs on the grate barely emitted enough heat to warm her toes, and she hesitated to draw too near it, for fear of awakening the large, scruffy-looking wolfhound who lay on the hearth-stones.

When they rode over the last rise and Guy pointed out Snape Castle, Celeste had wanted nothing more than to bolt back across the uninviting moors. Rising starkly out of the barren countryside, Snape's thick stone walls and thin windows bespoke centuries of defense against marauders from the north, but it had none of the softer influences of the south. Her new home was a solid, unforgiving fortress, without a flower garden, an orchard or even window glass to enhance it.

She wished she was back home in L'Étoile! It was a blessing that dear Aunt Marguerite had not come all this way to behold this rock heap—or its putrefying heir! If her aunt had, perhaps she would have ordered Celeste to return immediately to France.

Celeste tossed her head. *Non!* Her father had given her to the Ormonds, and she must honor that contract. *Please, dear Lord, let Sir Roger take pity upon me and tear up the agreement. I do so want to go home!*

She cast a quick glance at her silent companion. Earlier this morning, as they paused at a fork in the track, Guy had looked longingly down the left road. Ever since then, he had withdrawn from her, lost in his own thoughts. Celeste wondered if it had something to do with his family. She recalled that Father Jocelyn had said Guy came from these parts. Squaring his shoulders, Guy kicked Black Devil into a trot, and he rode toward the castle's yawning portcullis without looking back at her.

The inside of the stronghold appeared worse than its outside. If ever a woman had put a feminine touch here, cobwebs, dirt and neglect had rubbed it out. A dank, cold air exhaled from its stony walls, and the spare furnishings appeared in various shades of gray. Neither candle nor torch burned away the gloom. Only the fitful fire in the hall gave any warmth and color.

The servants they encountered shuffled about with their eyes downcast, or they stared at her with an open boldness. All of them needed baths, haircuts and fresh clothing. Celeste glanced down at her own gown. After sleeping on the moor last night, she looked as beggarly as the inhabitants of Snape.

"Welcome to my home!" a deep voice growled in French from out of the depths of the far stair. The dog on the hearth leapt to his feet and wagged his tail.

Celeste managed to drop a curtsy as a huge man, his pewter-gray hair standing straight out from his head at all angles, strode across the rush-strewn flagstones toward them. Under her skirts, her knees quaked. Guy extended his hand to help her rise. Before letting go, he gave her fingers a warm little squeeze. Then he drew his hood lower over his face, folded his arms inside his loose sleeves and stepped back into the shadows. Celeste took a deep breath, then lifted her eyes to face the man who held her fate.

"I am honored to be here, Sir Roger," Celeste murmured. For once, her witty tongue eluded her.

"Wine!" the master of the castle bellowed, sending his redheaded servant scurrying away. Celeste hoped the wine would be a decent vintage, and not the vinegar the English liked to drink.

"You have traveled a far piece," Sir Roger observed, in a slightly gentler tone. His accent was atrocious, but at least he spoke French.

Celeste twitched under his one-eyed scrutiny. His other eye was hidden by a dark patch of cloth, from under which a jagged white scar streaked down his face. Celeste tried not to stare at it.

"*Oui,* I think God sent every trial in his book to test my fortitude. But, as you can see, I have arrived," she ended lamely. She wished he wouldn't scrutinize her in such a direct manner. He acted as if he were planning a purchase at the butcher's.

"And how do you find England, my lady?" Sir Roger circled her slowly, in a manner that irritated Celeste.

"In truth, I find your country a rainy little island on the far edge of the civilized world," she retorted without thinking.

Sir Roger gaped. "Zounds, mistress! You do not blunt your arrows. Well aimed. I like a woman with spirit—though not too much, mind you."

"Does your son also like spirited women?" she asked, watching his face intently. *Let us see if he changes color.*

Sir Roger frowned. "My son is away at the moment, hunting the wild boar. We need not speak of him."

"*Mais oui,* I fear we must, my lord." She could not let this falsehood slip by. Walter would make his way back to Snape soon enough. "Walter is not hunting boar, but brides—*moi.*"

"The devil take it!" Sir Roger shouted so loudly the swords which hung on the chimneypiece rattled in their scabbards.

"I agree, my lord. The devil can take him anywhere he pleases. I met Walter Ormond yesterday afternoon, on the road betwixt here and York. He proposed to marry me under a bush, he said."

"How now? What jest is this?" Sir Roger was growing very ruddy in the face.

"No jest, my lord," Celeste responded evenly. "Unless being dragged off my horse and threatened with lewd hints and rough handling be your idea of a jest."

"Is this true?" Sir Roger glanced at the tall hooded figure. "Did you see this, Brother monk?"

Keeping his face half-covered, Guy nodded. Then he stepped beside Celeste and gently drew back the sleeve of her gown. Even in the dim light of the hall, the dark bruises left by Walter's cruel fingers showed plainly on the pale skin of her wrist. Guy took her chin between his thumb and forefinger and lifted her face so that the appalled father could see the mark of his son's hand on her cheek. Guy's thumb lightly brushed over the tender swollen area under one eye. Then he released her and stepped back once again into the shadows.

"God's death! My son did this to you?"

"*Oui*. He said I had made him wait too long for wedding and bedding, and that he would not wait an hour longer." Celeste covered her wrist from the outraged father's stare. "If it were not for Brother Guy's swiftness, even now I would be married to... to..." Celeste bit her lower lip. She dared not tell Sir Roger what she really thought of his loutish son.

"Oh, foulmouthed and calumnious knave!" Sir Roger hurled his anguished bellow to the gloomy vaulting of the hall. A number of curious servants peeked around corners. "This shame derives itself from unknown loins—not mine, I warrant you. My temper grows hot! Where is the molting jackdaw now?"

Celeste shrugged. "At this very moment, I know not. As of yesterday, we last saw him and his wretched minions tied to a tree, with their shoes and stockings off."

Sir Roger's anger turned to a sudden burst of harsh laughter. "Aye? How did such a slip as you and one long-shanked priest accomplish this feat?"

"My men, under the command of Sergeant Gaston Domaine, did that. They are traveling on the main road, and will be here anon. Brother Guy and I rode overland. We thought it best to come as quickly as possible." Celeste passed her hand across her forehead. With little sleep and no food since dinner yesterday, she felt faint.

Guy came up behind her and helped Celeste to a bench. At this moment, the redheaded servant reappeared with a tarnished silver tray that held several brimming goblets. Guy snatched one before the drinks were even offered to Sir Roger and held it up to Celeste's lips.

"The devil!" their host growled in surprise.

"Pray, forgive Brother Guy's manners, Sir Roger." Celeste sipped the ruby liquid. A little raw of taste, but very restoring. "We have not eaten for nearly a day. We rode through the night, as well." She took a deeper drink.

"Sprites and fires! My son may keep his own grace, but he is run out of mine, I can assure you, my lady." The raging father lifted his great head and shouted down the hall. "Grapper! Where is your poxed carcass?"

Celeste gripped the goblet. What manner of madhouse had she entered? Did Sir Roger never speak but to shout, bluster and yell? At least he seemed to believe her. The strong, unwatered wine began to work its potency upon her. If Sir Roger didn't show her to a room very soon, Celeste feared she would fall asleep on the bench.

Guy stood closer behind her. As Sir Roger stalked about the flagstones, working himself up into a frenzy, Guy placed his hand on Celeste's shoulder and squeezed it gently. She leaned back against his comforting form. She wondered if he could feel her trembling. Mustn't close my eyes, she told herself. Meanwhile, Sir Roger fell into a loud discussion with another servant—one who looked almost as evil as Walter's knaves. *Mon Dieu!* Did the Ormonds employ highwaymen and murderers?

"Go to it, Grapper!" Sir Roger concluded. "And bring him back here immediately—tied to a hurdle, if necessary."

"A pleasure, my lord!" The brigand bowed to him, then smiled at Celeste. Two of his front teeth were missing. "Welcome to Snape Castle, my lady."

"Tell me I am dreaming and that this is merely a nightmare, Brother Guy," she murmured for his ear alone.

In answer, Guy squeezed her shoulder again, his long fingers gently caressing her tired, aching muscles.

Please don't abandon me now, dear guardian angel! Despite her best intentions to stay awake, the room began to spin and dissolve, and a sweet blackness descended upon her.

Guy lifted his eyes to the small sanctuary candle flickering in its red glass globe. The cold wind off the moor whistled through the chinks in the chapel's wall. Alone in the heart of night, Guy permitted himself the luxury of shivering in his single robe.

'Tis my penance, sweet Celeste, for having brought you to this pesthole.

At least she now lay safely tucked up in the late mistress's bed. Guy himself had carried her unconscious form up the winding stairs to the bedroom, and made sure that his gentle charge would be well treated by the housekeeper, Mistress Conroy. The woman had a good face, he judged, and Celeste would come to no harm in her care.

Guy bowed his head again and prayed for guidance. In good faith, his duty was discharged. He had conducted the little bride to Snape Castle with both her dowry and her virtue intact. He could leave tomorrow morning with a clear conscience.

And abandon Celeste in this filthy den of howling wolves? Great Jove! When had the rushes last been swept? It would not surprise Guy one whit to spy a team of rats playing at ball under the high table. He had known Snape Castle would be grim, but not like this. How soon would these depressing surroundings quench Celeste's fire and spirit?

Besides, Guy couldn't leave her until Gaston and the others arrived. Then what? He dug his thumbs into the corners of his eyes and rubbed away the fatigue lurking there. He couldn't possibly return south until the matter of Celeste's marriage contract had been resolved. Marriage to whom?

Not to Walter, judging by the tenor of his father's fury. Guy wondered if the York Grayfriar was right, and Sir Roger wanted Celeste for himself. Guy must stay by her side. Celeste needed his counsel.

Nay! If truth be told—and where else should truth live, but in God's house?—Guy needed Celeste. Against all reason, and all vows made in solemn splendor and blessed with good intentions, Guy realized that he needed Celeste as a man needed air to breathe, water to drink, food for strength, fire for warmth—and a wife to love.

He sat back on his ankles and stared at the veiled tabernacle. When had he ever considered marriage? In his former life, lovemaking had held his interest, but never the irrevocable step of marriage. Guy had sworn not to be caught in those perfidious chains. Few women honored their vows to their husbands. He had proved that truth time and again at court. Few lords in the king's circle escaped wearing the horns of a cuckold. The ladies had thrown themselves in Guy's path at every opportunity.

Look at Great Harry himself! It might be treason to speak aloud against the latest whims of the king's most accommodating conscience, but here in God's silent company, in the furthermost reaches of the realm, Guy could ponder the king's "great matter" in the safety of a cold chapel.

For over twenty years, good Queen Catherine had been the king's most beloved and esteemed wife. Despite her Spanish background and accent, people high and low loved her. Then had come the dark-haired witch Anne Boleyn. Over night, it seemed, the finest prince in Christendom had turned into a cruel stranger as he danced attendance upon Mistress Anne while the poor queen pined away in her apartments. Though Guy boasted himself as no champion of virtue, he could not bear to see the court turn from the good queen, like a weathercock in a tempest. Finally, the king's mad affair and the excesses of the fickle court had driven Guy into the monastery.

Now came his own black-haired witch to make him forget all his fine resolves and to think of—marriage? Nay! No matter who Celeste married, it could not be to Guy Cavendish—Brother Guy, who would soon take his final vows in the order of the Franciscans. Marriage was not an option for Guy.

Celeste is as true as fire, a little inner voice murmured to him, *and she has come through fire to prove it.*

Guy lifted his eyes once again to the flickering light above the altar. *I am at a loss, Lord. What do you want me to do?*

Chapter Twenty-Two

When Celeste awoke, she discovered that she had slept nearly a full day. During that time, Gaston, her men and even her few pieces of baggage had arrived at Snape Castle. After a hot bath, supplied by a grumbling Mistress Conroy, and a change into fresher clothing, Celeste ate a hearty meal of oat porridge, brown bread with butter and honey, baked salmon, baked pears and wedges of sharp cheddar. Thus fortified, she felt ready to face Sir Roger and the problem of her betrothal to his son.

Before descending to the hall, where she had been told he awaited her, Celeste opened the blue leather box containing her dowry. Despite the many mishaps she had endured to get to this lonesome, windy castle, the twelve apostle spoons still gleamed in their satin bed. Celeste ran her fingers lovingly over them for the last time. She plucked Saint Mark out of his place, breathed on the bowl of the spoon, then rubbed it with the trailing end of her oversleeve. She had always liked Mark's little lion, crouched at the saint's feet. The creature had such a soulful look, as if waiting for Mark to finish reading his book, so that they could go on a long walk through the fields.

With a small sigh, she replaced the spoon with its brothers. After pinching her cheeks to give herself a bit of color, she tucked the box under her arm and walked out the door.

Sir Roger slouched in an armchair in front of the central fireplace, which crackled and danced with a well-tended blaze. The master of the castle had drawn up a second chair opposite him. An open casket filled with parchments sat on a stout oak table between the chairs. Beside the casket, a dull silver wine pitcher with two goblets awaited the pleasure of Sir Roger. When Celeste made her appearance, Ormond rose and pointed to the empty seat. Though he had shaved and combed his hair, she noticed that he still wore the hose and doublet in which she had last seen him. As she drew nearer to her host, she could also detect an odor of grease, sweat and wet dog about him. Celeste applied her perfumed handkerchief to her nose and pretended to sneeze when he bowed to her.

A slight movement in the shadows of the inglenook caught her attention. She smiled with a mixture of pleasure and relief when Brother Guy stepped into the light and bowed to her. She wondered why he still pulled his cowl so low over his head, since she knew his tonsure had grown back long ago—unless, of course he had shaved it again, which she hoped he had not. Brother Guy looked much more handsome without that incongruous bald patch.

Celeste bit the inside of her cheek to remind herself that Brother Guy's personal appearance should mean nothing to her, especially now that she had come face-to-face with her prospective father-in-law. She could not allow her mind to dwell on the obvious, painful differences between the beauty of Brother Guy's face and heart and those of Walter Ormond.

"Good evening, Lady Celeste," Sir Roger softly growled as he returned to his seat. "I trust you slept well?"

"Very well, with my thanks, Sir Roger. The bed is most comfortable." Sitting, Celeste spread out her blue brocade skirts and placed the leather box on her lap.

"Wine?" he growled again.

Celeste nodded. *"Merci."* She came to the conclusion that Sir Roger must have damaged his voice from years of shouting and bellowing, and that this strange growl of his—like a dog who has cornered something unknown—was Sir Roger's idea of gentle speech.

Guy stepped forward and filled two goblets. Celeste noticed he poured none for himself. *He must be fasting again.* Indeed, Brother Guy looked a little drawn and white about the mouth, which was the only part of his face she could see distinctly. The monk handed a goblet to Sir Roger, then one to Celeste. As she accepted the cup, his fingers caressed hers in passing. The tender sensation nearly caused her to spill the wine on her dress.

Sir Roger drank deeply, then set the goblet on the table. "I am a bluff man, my lady, and not one to spend half a day on courtly courtesies. Let us get down to cases."

Celeste swallowed more wine than she had intended. She coughed into her handkerchief. "Pray, proceed," she said when she could speak.

Sir Roger fixed her with a single piercing stare that reminded her of her father's favorite peregrine. "You've met my son, Walter, and for his behavior, I apologize. Though it pains me to confess it, from his youth my son has been malicious, willful and hard-hearted. Of late, the corruption of both his nature and his body has so overcome whatever good points he may once have possessed that, like a wild horse which no bridle can hold, he runs headlong into disaster. No fear, shame, punishment, nor anything that I have devised, has prevailed upon him to pull him back from his fall into perdition. The long and short of it, my lady, is that he is not fit to wed you.''

Celeste relaxed against the high back of her chair. Thank the angels and saints above! She could go home now with a clear conscience. ''I give you much thanks for your understanding, Sir Roger.'' Celeste took another sip of wine.

''Aye.'' Standing abruptly, Sir Roger poked at the fire for a moment before he cleared his voice, rumbling like distant thunder. ''You may not know, but I have recently lost my second wife and two younger children.''

Celeste set her goblet down and leaned forward. ''No, my lord, I did not. It grieves me to hear of it.''

''For your sympathy, much thanks, but that does not settle my problem.''

The slight shift of the tone in his voice set off a little warning bell inside Celeste's head. The wind was up, but she didn't know which way it blew. She had a feeling that it boded no good for her. ''Your problem, my lord?'' she echoed.

Silently moving like the wraith he looked, Guy took a position directly behind Celeste's chair. If she had wanted to, she could have touched his sleeve merely by extending her hand.

Sir Roger replaced the heavy poker against the brick of the fireplace, then faced her. Behind him, the flames leapt higher, as if they had sprung from hell. ''My problem is this. I have worked all my life to amass a goodly estate and to build up our family's reputation. I am in need of an heir—a healthy heir—who will live after me and inherit all that I have gained. My son Walter is not worthy of my title and, given the opportunity, he would beggar my fortune within a year—should he live so long.''

A cold breath of fear wrapped itself around Celeste. Did he mean to wed her himself? Please, dear God, she prayed, do not let this happen to me. She pressed her spine against the unyielding chairback.

"The nut and core is this—you have come to marry into the Ormond family. I am in need of a wife to give me another heir. Therefore, Lady Celeste, I will marry you as soon as the banns are published."

Celeste wanted to scream, "No!" but knew she could not. Admittedly, the father was a better match than his worm-eaten son. On the other hand, Sir Roger was a far cry from her dreams of the glorious Knight of the Loyal Heart, riding out on his beautiful white charger to claim her. Sir Roger was too old, too war-torn, for her taste. Rough in manners, as well as in voice, he frightened her. She had come all this way to find love and protection. Instead, a grizzled old bear and a scaly, half-grown serpent greeted her. She clutched her box of spoons, while her mind spun in a whirlwind of fearful emotions.

Without giving her a chance to speak, Sir Roger took another fierce gulp of his wine, then pawed through the casket until he found the paper he desired. "'Tis the marriage contract signed by your father and me eight years ago in France. Perchance you remember?"

Dully Celeste nodded. "May I see it?" she asked in a weak voice.

Sir Roger blinked his good eye. "You can read?"

Celeste lifted her chin. "Both Latin and French."

"I don't hold with educating women," he muttered, though he relinquished the parchment into her hands.

Celeste quickly scanned the simple Latin phrasing of the contract. In very straightforward terms, it stated that Roland de Montcalm, chevalier of Fauconbourg, gave his fifth daughter, Celeste Marie, in marriage to Walter, son of Sir Roger Ormond of Snape Castle, upon her eighteenth birthday. The dowry agreed upon was more vague—

divers goods of silver and gold. Celeste closed her eyes for a moment. *Oh, Papa, what a cunning mind you have!* Both men had signed the parchment and affixed their seals to it. The red wax had darkened with age, but there was no mistaking its authenticity.

Sir Roger took back the contract, as if he were afraid she would throw it into the fire. "About the dowry," he growled. "I presume you brought it with you?"

Mutely Celeste handed him the box of spoons. While Sir Roger put it on the table and lighted a candle to better examine the contents, Celeste cast a troubled look at Guy. In answer, he took her hand and held it. For a wild, brief moment, she wished he could clasp her to himself in the same way he clasped her hand in his. Of all the men she had known in her short life, Brother Guy was the closest to her ideal knight, though he wore only a simple brown robe and scuffed sandals.

"Such beauties!" Sir Roger took out each spoon and held it up to the candle's flame. "We have little chance to see such fine workmanship this far to the north."

Celeste hid her amazement. She knew her poor little spoons were not half so fine or as large as those given to her elder sisters. The saints be praised that Sir Roger didn't know the difference!

"I look forward to seeing the rest of your dowry, if all your other pieces are as well made as these."

The dreaded moment had arrived. A dull pain formed at Celeste's temples. Guy squeezed her hand tighter. She might as well get it over with. Perhaps Sir Roger would reject her if the dowry did not please him.

Celeste assumed her haughtiest look. "That *is* my dowry, Sir Roger. Every jot and tittle of it. The apostle spoons are indeed 'divers goods of gold and silver,' according to the marriage contract." She leveled her gaze at him, though inside she quaked. He wouldn't dare strike her, would he?

"What?" Sir Roger slammed the spoons onto the table. Several apostles fell to the floor with a clatter that startled the dozing wolfhound. "The devil take it!"

The master of the castle drew himself up, swelling in size like a bullfrog. Celeste tensed, waiting for his explosion. Guy stepped around the chair, shielding her with his body.

"I have been poorly used!" Sir Roger bellowed. "Your father has cheated me of the fortune he promised me! I should have known not to trust that malmsey-nosed French knave!"

A mixture of burning anger and cold shame choked Celeste. She opened her mouth to defend her family's honor, but the strong pressure of Guy's thumb on the back of her hand stopped her. He shook his head when she glanced up at him.

Sir Roger splashed more wine into his goblet, then drank it down in one gulp. "Did you know of this perfidy?" he asked, staring at Celeste, his one eye glowering in the firelight.

She took a deep breath before answering. "Eight years ago, my father signed that contract in good faith, my lord. I was his youngest child then, and so he expected to endow me with all the requisite goods. Since that time, my four older sisters married—each with a dowry larger than anticipated. Then my little brother was born. Now that my father has an heir, naturally he wants to preserve the bulk of his estate for Philippe."

Without giving Sir Roger a chance to renew his diatribe, Celeste rose, with all the dignity she could muster. "If my dowry displeases you, you may send me packing at any time. If this is your intention, please inform me soon, so that my men and I may return to France before your foul English weather locks us here in your...home until spring. I bid you good night, my lord." Still clutching Guy's strong hand, Celeste made a dignified exit.

Her fortitude carried her as far as the top of the stairs, where her knees gave out under her. If Guy had not been at her side, she would have tumbled backward, down the stone spiral steps. Guy lifted her in his arms and carried her into her room, where he laid her on the bed.

"What will become of me now, Brother Guy?" she asked, though she did not expect an answer from the silent monk. "I am a pawn in old men's follies. I cannot stay here. I cannot return home a rejected spinster. Perhaps I should enter a convent, but I do not think I was born to be a nun." She hugged one of the thick bolsters and gazed into the low fire in the grate.

Folding back his cowl, Guy revealed the sad expression in the depths of his sapphire eyes. Kneeling by the bedside, he took both her cold hands in his and brushed his lips across her fingers. The shock of his intimate touch sent her jangled emotions into exciting unexplored territory. Celeste gasped as a liquid fire coursed through her. A low moan escaped her lips.

Instantly Guy dropped her hands and stood, turning his broad back to her.

"*Pardonnez-moi,* Brother Guy. I am at sixes and sevens and know not what to do. Please do not turn away from me now. I feel so friendless in this cold place. My sorrow is such that I have cause to eat my bread with ashes." Celeste lay back on the bed and stared, unseeing, at the shabby canopy above her.

Guy crossed to the fireplace and tossed a few more logs onto the flames. Soon a brighter fire blazed merrily in the room. Then he returned to Celeste's side and flashed her a brief, heaven-kissed smile, that lightened her mood. At least, Brother Guy would remain faithful to her—as a true knight should.

He wrote on his slate, *Sir Roger loves his wealth better than a wife.*

Celeste's lips quirked in a rueful smile. "*Now* you tell me this? Fah! So play the prophet, good Brother. What am I to do?"

Guy folded his hands and stared thoughtfully at the floor.

If he suggests I pray for the answer, I shall box his handsome ears! Celeste sat quietly, though her stomach churned inside her. How ghastly the meeting had been. Far worse than she had imagined it. *Sacrebleu!* What if Sir Roger decided to wed her to Walter after all, just to spite her? She balled her hands into fists. If he tried that, she would run away across the moors. Death would make a better bridegroom for her!

Feeling a sob well up in her throat, she bit her knuckles until the pain banished her self-pity. Turning at her muffled sounds, Guy frowned when he saw her chewing on her fingers. He took them from her mouth, and gently rubbed the reddened joints. Celeste longed to lay her head against his shoulder and cry out her heart's sorrow. Only propriety and her sense of family honor held her back.

The troubadours had sung of the de Montcalms' courage in battle for the past three hundred years. Though she was only a woman, Celeste knew she had the blood of those brave warriors in her veins. Besides, what would her mother, not to mention Aunt Marguerite, say if they saw her in the arms of a cleric—a young, breathtakingly handsome monk?

Guy finished his ministrations far too soon. Then he took out his slate.

Delay, he wrote.

Confused by his single word of advice, Celeste plucked at the threadbare patches on the woolen bedcover. "I do not understand, Brother Guy. Delay what?"

Your marriage, he wrote under the first word.

She cocked one eyebrow at him. "You think he will have me either for himself or his son? Pah!"

He needs an heir. The chalk words burned into her brain.

"And I am merely the means, *oui?*"

Guy hooded his eyes, and the room seemed somehow darker. He slowly nodded. Then he pointed to the word, *Delay.*

"I would gladly do that until doomsday, Brother Guy. But how? Why?"

Guy rubbed out the first message, then wrote, *Advent starts at midnight day after tomorrow.*

Celeste studied the message carefully. Advent was the church's time of fasting and penance before the solemn feast of Christmas. Four weeks during which no songs were sung, there was no dancing in the hall, no red meats were eaten—and no marriages were performed. An invisible weight slid off her shoulders.

"What can happen in four weeks?" she ask softly.

A miracle, he wrote, then added, *Pray.*

Guy slipped into the drafty hall after bidding Celeste good-night. He knew he left her with a lighter heart, for she had tried to entice him into playing a game of piquet. For the safety of his shaky vows, he declined.

It was all well and good that Celeste felt better, but what of himself? The delaying tactic, which he had first conceived in the peace of York Minster, would work temporarily, but what miracle could he hope for on Christmas morning? He didn't know the answer, only that he felt strongly in need of the extra time.

Deep within his soul, Guy knew that he must stay at Snape until the resolution of Celeste's dilemma. Father Jocelyn must have foreseen this. Hadn't he placed Guy's vow of silence upon him until Celeste's wedding day? On that fateful day, Guy would speak to Celeste in his own voice—and when he did, he would *not* congratulate her on her marriage to an Ormond.

As Guy crossed the upper gallery, he heard angry voices below in the hall. The stone walls of the castle echoed and reechoed with the turbulent meeting between father and son. Drawing his cowl low over his face, Guy stole down the stairs to listen and observe.

"The wench is rightfully mine, by all that's holy," snarled Walter. He paced in front of the fireplace. Guy noted that the younger Ormond limped slightly. Perhaps he had tried to walk home barefoot.

"Do not speak of what's right and what's holy—at least not in the same breath, you changeling!" Sir Roger slopped more wine into his goblet. Guy wondered how much the elder Ormond had drunk since Celeste had left him.

"The bitch used me poorly, and I mean to return her the compliment—either as her husband or as her stepson. Mark my words, I shall be revenged upon her and that mangy cur of a priest." The firelight outlined Walter's ghastly sores with a hellish paintbrush. He looked like one of the damned in an illuminated manuscript.

Sir Roger leaned over his son, his bulk dwarfing the emaciated man. "And you mark me, dissembling villain, you will not touch a hair of the lass's head, or I'll spare you any further suffering of your...illness. She'll get me a fine son in your place—aye, two or three, by the look of her hips. As for her confessor, 'tis a mortal sin to strike down a priest.''

"And you're afraid for my soul?" Walter sneered.

"I care not a fig for it—but you shall soon, when you roast on the devil's coals. Be gone! I'll hear no more of your puling. The lady will be my bride, and you can go hang yourself. Aye! And take those unhallowed slaves of yours with you. You will be in fine company then!" Shattering the goblet against the side of the fireplace, Sir Roger stomped from the hall.

Walter stared into the dying fire for a long time, while Guy watched from the bottom of the steps. Then, with a terrible oath, Walter limped away in the opposite direction.

Guy pressed his back against the clammy wall and sent a heartfelt prayer to heaven. *Give me a lance, a sword and my charger for one hour, Lord, and I will praise your name forevermore.*

Chapter Twenty-Three

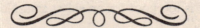

"**G**ood Morrow, my lady! I have goodly news for you."
Sir Roger's voice boomed across the hall and echoed down
the soot-encrusted rafters as Celeste entered at the far end
of the room.

Her heart thumped against her ribs, and a thick knot
formed in her throat. Though she had not known her host
for long, Celeste already realized that a cheerful tone was
not Sir Roger's usual one. Biting her lower lip to keep it
from quivering, she cast quick glances up and down the
sides of the huge hall, hoping to spy a familiar face there,
either one of her men's or Brother Guy's—especially
Guy's.

Save for Sir Roger, the redheaded steward and that huge
sleeping hound, the hall was empty. As Celeste approached Sir Roger's chair, he waved the steward away.

"Good news is always welcome, my lord," she replied
evenly as she sat in the chair he offered her.

"I have given the matter of your marriage contract
much thought, mistress. Though your perfidious father
tricked me in the matter of your dowry, I shall not hold
that against you." He folded his arms across his chest and
beamed down at her.

Celeste ran her tongue across her teeth. Brother Guy was right. Sir Roger did mean to wed her, no matter what. Under the loose folds of her dress, she knotted her fingers together. *Sweet Saint Anne, give me courage!*

"I am glad to hear of it, my lord." Where was Brother Guy?

"As for Walter, even if I were disposed for him to wed, your dowry is too poor for an eldest son. No one would dispute that."

"Of course not." Celeste lowered her lashes, though she continued to study Sir Roger through her half-closed eyes. Obviously she was not the only one who had sat up half the night considering her plight.

"But, as my third wife, a large dowry is not so necessary, especially considering your youth, your beauty and your good health."

Particularly my good health for childbearing. I wonder if he will examine my teeth as he would a brood mare's?

"Therefore I have decided to overlook the letter of the agreement, and instead honor the spirit of the contract. Your father gave you to an Ormond, and you shall wed an Ormond—tomorrow."

Though she had expected something like this, the actual sound of it sent a shudder through her. She felt a momentary wave of panic as her mind scrambled to recall Guy's advice. Delay. She drew in a deep breath and willed her trembling body to relax.

"You do me a great honor, Sir Roger...." she began. A rustling in a shadowed archway caught her attention. Brother Guy, his hood once again concealing most of his face, glided into the room. Celeste relaxed her shoulders as she continued.

"But there is one thing that my mind misgives, Sir Roger."

"What?" he barked. The dozing wolfhound merely twitched his ear in his sleep.

Celeste lifted her chin a notch. "The marriage contract states very clearly that it is your *son* I am to wed. I must inform my father of the change in the terms and receive his permission to marry you, my lord. Surely you agree it is the honorable thing to do, *n'est-ce pas?*"

"The devil fiddle 'em!" Sir Roger bellowed. " 'Twould take till Candlemas to send a message to France and receive an answer. A plague on it, mistress! 'Tis wintertime. Haven't you noticed that there is ice in your pitcher in the mornings?"

Guy lightly rested his hand on her shoulder. His warm touch reassured Celeste. "*Mais oui,* Sir Roger. I have already had the pleasure of the snow down my back and in my shoes. But hear me out, I beg you—" To her dismay, her voice broke slightly. She hurried on. "I am sure that my father would be most pleased to agree to this new proposal." She cocked her head and allowed a coquettish smile to play upon her lips. "And perhaps he would even be disposed to send a larger dowry."

Guy squeezed her shoulder. Celeste drew strength from the warmth of his approval. Sir Roger sank into the chair opposite hers and leaned over to scratch the dog's massive head. The animal sighed with pleasure.

"A larger dowry, say you?" Sir Roger repeated, with a thoughtful look in his single eye.

Celeste released the breath she held. "*Oui,* my lord. To do you the proper honor, as you are lord of Snape Castle." She could almost hear the clink of the gold coins that danced in Sir Roger's greedy imagination.

" 'Tis a tempting thought, my lady, and one that I had not considered."

Emboldened by her first success, Celeste pressed on. "Also, my lord, my goodly Brother Guy reminds me that Advent comes apace. The time between now and Christmas would allow a message to be sent to L'Étoile. In the meantime, I could begin to learn my new duties as mistress of this house...." She cast a swift glance at the shocking disrepair of the great hall. It would take a decade to clean up the filth. "And I could practice my English, so that I would be more pleasing to my husband." She ended by fluttering her long lashes.

"Advent," Ormond rumbled under his breath. "Bestrew me! Another time of fasting and alms-giving. Fire and brimstone, mistress mine! So be it! Tonight we shall make merry over this new betrothal, and feast until bursting—enough to last us four weeks of wilted greens, brown bread and water."

Celeste turned her smile of triumph into one of pleasant acquiescence. "And come Christmastide, Sir Roger, we shall have a wedding feast and a tournament to celebrate our marriage!"

"Tournament?" Ormond bristled his shaggy brows. "Expensive."

"Oui!" Celeste agreed. If Brother Guy's miracle did not happen, at least she would have the excitement of a tournament. For one day, she would realize her dream of being the Queen of Truth and Beauty. After that, she could bear the weight of being Sir Roger's wife—and by the size of him, that weight would be heavy indeed.

"I would so love to see you joust in my honor, my lord." Cocking her head, Celeste laughed lightly. "Oh, la, la, I think you make a very handsome knight," she purred, again fluttering her lashes.

To her surprise, Sir Roger flushed red, like a schoolboy caught in his first kiss. "Aye, I have broken my share of lances in the past. Well, my lady, if your heart's desire is a tournament to celebrate our nuptials, then you shall have one—a small one, mind you.''

Celeste clapped her hands with glee. Arranging and practicing for a tournament would keep Sir Roger occupied for the weeks to come, and leave her free to clean up his house in peace. *"Merci beaucoup,* my lord. I shall be so proud of you!''

"Cease your tongue-wagging, mistress mine," he growled, though he smiled as he spoke. "So we have an agreement, eh? On the day after Christmas, Saint Stephen's Day, we will be wed and you shall have your tournament, I vow. Come now...Celeste, let us seal this bargain between us with a sweet betrothal kiss." He stood and held out his arms to her. "And you, monk, will be witness to the plighting of our troth."

Celeste fixed a smile firmly on her face, though inwardly she quailed. The only men she had ever kissed before were her father and brother. From observing her parents, she knew that a kiss was part of marriage, but until this moment she had not realistically considered who would be her partner in this new experience. Sir Roger's face, even softened as it was now, bore the fearful marks of several battles and a hard, angry life. She rose from her chair and advanced toward him, reminding herself that kissing the father was infinitely preferable to placing her lips against the thin, rotting ones of his son.

Sir Roger enfolded her in a crushing embrace and bent her backward over his arm, so that her slippers barely brushed the floor. Suppressing her initial instinct to struggle against him, Celeste tried to relax in his arms, though she felt she would crash to the flagstones at any moment. Before she could compose herself, he attacked her mouth, planting his thick lips around hers. His whisker bristle scraped against her chin and under her nose as he pressed himself hard against her. She couldn't breathe. When she opened her mouth in panic, Ormond's thick wet tongue pushed itself inside, and began sucking on hers. Celeste almost gagged. Tears pricked behind her eyelids. At long last, Sir Roger withdrew from her lips, though he still gripped her in his hands.

"Cupid have mercy, wench! You taste as sweet as a honeycomb," he rumbled. "'Twill be a penance indeed to wait four weeks afore I can dip into your honey pot. Once more, say I!" He swooped down on her bruised mouth again.

Celeste closed her eyes this time, held her breath and endured his shameful thrusts between her lips. This treatment must be part of what Aunt Marguerite had hinted at in such dire tones on their last evening together, in the priory. *Mon Dieu, good Aunt! I wish you were here with me now!*

Guy rattled the chair behind them. The grating sound broke through Sir Roger's eager occupation, and slowly he released Celeste, nipping at her lower lip as he did so. Celeste's head spun and she felt the first inkling of another headache announce itself. *Oui*, she would spend the rest of the morning locked in her room with a cold compress. The prospect sounded delightful.

"Your confessor has reminded me in time, my sweet ducky, or else I might not have waited for the holy words to make you mine in truth." Sir Roger's boisterous laughter rocked Celeste's fragile sense of balance, and woke the huge hound at her feet. "I bid you adieu, until we meet at dinner. Aye, and I'll want another one of those kisses for my sweet course!"

Snapping his fingers at the dog, Ormond turned on his heel and lumbered across the hall. He disappeared down the stairs to the courtyard, whistling out of tune. Celeste collapsed in his chair and massaged her temples. The headache rose up in full force behind her eyeballs.

"*Zut alors,* Brother Guy! I fear Christmastide will come too soon. If I must endure attentions like that, I doubt I shall last until Twelfth Night. By my heel, that man killed his other two wives with his...kissing!" She wiped her lips with her handkerchief.

When Sir Roger clasped the lady to his barrel chest, Guy had gripped the carved knob on the back of Celeste's chair to keep himself from snatching her out of Ormond's lascivious clutches.

His conscience had fired a warning bolt. *She is not yours. She belongs to Sir Roger.*

Nevertheless, the sight of her frightened expression as Ormond plundered his prize had almost torn Guy's voice out of his vow. By her quick wits and his advice, Celeste had bought herself four weeks of grace, but what then?

After Ormond left the hall, Guy knelt before his shaken lady. He dropped his hood back so that he could see her better. He wondered how long it would be before Sir Roger or the villainous Walter discovered the identity of Celeste's silent "confessor." No doubt they would evict him with unholy oaths in his ear, despite the fact that Guy's father was their overlord. For a generation, hot words, bitter accusations and occasional bloodshed had flowed between the greedy, grasping Ormonds and their liege lords, the Cavendish family. Guy longed to snatch up this poor, shaken flower and ride with her to the safety of his father's house. Only his honor, now fraying around the edges, kept him from doing it.

Celeste blew her nose into the handkerchief. Her lips quivered a smile at Guy, though her beautiful violet eyes shimmered with unshed tears. "Thank you for being here, good Brother," she whispered. "I do not think I could have persuaded him to wait, had you not come."

Guy bowed his head. She was probably right. Had Ormond not been bedazzled by the gleaming thought of more dowry, he would have realized he could marry Celeste tonight, before Advent began. Guy took her hands in his. They were hot and damp with her fear.

"And so, *mon ami,* I have four weeks to clean up this pigsty of a castle and to make a gown to be married in, since I lost my first one in the river two months ago. And yes, Brother Guy, I will pray, as you suggested. I will pray so much you will be astounded."

Guy took out his slate. *Why a tournament?* he wrote.

Celeste lifted her shoulders in her delightful little shrug, which he had come to love. "Why not? That is my wedding present, for I think after that, there will be no more merriment for a long time to come." She drew her wing-swept brows together. "There are times, Brother Guy, when I think I would like to be a man. This is one of them."

Despite the seriousness of the situation, Guy grinned. Personally, he was glad she was so utterly feminine. Then he chided himself. He must not regard Celeste as a seductive, beautiful, desirable, spirited woman, but only as a poor soul to save. *What a barrow of rubbish!* his conscience sneered.

Celeste placed her hand over his. "Brother Guy, I must make a confession to you."

Guy's stomach clenched with a sudden spasm of fear and guilt. For two months, he had hoped to avoid this predicament. Now he must tell her that he did not have the authority to forgive her sins—whatever they could possibly be. He started to fumble for his slate and chalk, but her hands stayed him.

"Fret not, good Brother. Do you think I could tell to you all my evil deeds? Oh, la, la! I should be a month of Sundays at it, and much ashamed to boot. *Non,* my sins I will confess to someone who knows me not. But to you, I must tell a secret of my heart."

She leaned closer to him. He closed his eyes and reveled in her sweet scent of musk roses. "I tell you true, for I know you cannot betray me, or scold me. I do not want to marry either Sir Roger or his son."

Guy opened his eyes and looked upon her with a mixture of relief and gladness in his heart. It cheered him to hear it, yet her revelation left a bitter aftertaste.

"*Oui,* I knew you would be shocked. Furthermore, I tell you, if a mysterious knight should ride into the lists on my wedding day and challenge for my hand in marriage, I swear I would jump on his horse's back and ride away with him. Such a man could not be any worse than the pickle barrel I am in now." She stared into the space over Guy's head, with a dreamy look on her face. "Perhaps that is the real reason I wish for a tournament. I wish for a handsome knight to save me."

She pondered the idea for a moment, then gave herself a little shake. "*Ma foi!* What am I saying? I am no longer a silly child who believes in magic wishes. Do not think me evil, Brother Guy. These are only my dreams of fancy, mere toys of the mind." She rubbed her temple again. "Pray, excuse me, good Brother. I have a headache and must rest before dinner."

Celeste stood and shook out her skirts. Guy couldn't help but admire the way her yellow satin gown displayed her tiny waist to such an advantage. 'Sdeath! His handspan would more than encompass her. Guy's palms itched to hold her. Instead, he stood aside to let her pass. As she did so, she spoke to him over her shoulder.

"Do you think Sir Roger will want to kiss me at *every* meal?"

I would do so, my heart.

Without expecting any reaction from him, she continued. "If that becomes his habit, I need to get more herbs for headaches. Adieu, Brother." She slowly climbed the steps to the upper gallery.

Guy watched her departure until the last wisp of her golden buttercup train disappeared around the bend of the stairs. With the firm intention of spending the rest of the day prostrate on the chapel's icy floor, he spun around and raced down the courtyard staircase. Surely God, in his divine wisdom and justice, would not let this ill-conceived marriage take place. If Guy prayed hard enough, fasted enough, subjected himself to enough physical torment, perhaps his prayers for Celeste's deliverance might be answered. Didn't Father Jocelyn say, time and again, that the good Lord hears all petitions? Hears, yes, but answers—?

In the center of the courtyard, Gaston was instructing Pierre and Émile in a bit of swordplay. Pip sat nearby on an upright keg and watched the lesson with open admiration.

"Zounds! Go creep back into the pond, you turtle!" Gaston railed at the perspiring Pierre, who was obviously getting the worst part of the exercise. "Your skill is as thick as dried Dijon mustard! Parry, parry, lackwit!"

Pulling his hood lower, Guy hid his grin. Gaston sounded much like his own master-of-arms in days gone by.

Gaston grabbed the sword out of Pierre's hand, then turned to face Émile. "Observe, mule-head!" Gaston moved with a speed that belied both his years and the girth of his waist. "Parry left, parry right, then attack, attack, attack, lunge, like so! Pah! You will never graduate from the stable loft!" Spying the monk, Gaston berated his winded wagoneer even louder.

"Mark you, Pierre! Even the good priest laughs at you. I think, perhaps, even you can best our Pierre with a sword, eh, Brother Guy?"

Without further preamble, Gaston lofted the naked blade into the air toward the monk. Acting on pure instinct, Guy extended his right hand and closed his fingers around the haft. The weight of the weapon felt at home in his grip.

Gaston chuckled. "Think you can pull your wool robe over my eyes, dissembling monk? Ha! I knew I spied a sword arm 'neath your sleeve. Come, go a round with Émile."

Reminding himself that he had sworn off his former warlike pastimes, Guy pushed the temptation aside. Peace must rule his life now. He held the sword out to Gaston, hilt first. Gaston stuck out his lower lip and glowered at Guy.

"You white-livered worm! Your reluctance does not sit well in my weak stomach, and therefore I must cast it up!" Gaston snatched Émile's blade from his hand, then waggled it at Guy. "I think you a coward, and by this hand will I verify it."

Guy tightened his grip around the sword. How dare this garlic-mouthed, snail-munching Frenchman call him a coward! Guy knew he could make mincemeat of the old soldier in three strokes. A hot, angry flush spread over his face.

Gaston danced lightly on the balls of his feet. "What say you, toad? Craven jackdaw? Think you so little of your honor? Perhaps you should retire to a nunnery! What say you, cowl-covered knave?''

Guy expelled short, angry bursts of air from his lungs as he listened to Gaston's taunts. Émile, Pip and Pierre gawked with amazement as Gaston launched into yet more invective. What had gotten into the old goat? Guy always considered Gaston the most sensible of Celeste's men. In his headstrong youth, Guy would have answered such rude comments with his blade. Even now, red spots whirled before his eyes as Gaston continued to describe Guy's courage, honor and manly parts in the lowest possible terms. The sword shook in Guy's grip.

Suddenly Gaston attacked. Guy parried the thrust and returned in kind. His long robe impeded his footwork. Without caring who might happen to be watching, Guy dropped back his hood and hoisted his robe with one hand, baring his legs to the biting wind. Gaston attacked again, forcing Guy to defend himself with more vigor than the monk intended. For several minutes the two fought in silence, save for occasional grunts from Gaston. Seizing an unguarded moment, Guy sent Gaston's sword flying toward the stable refuse heap.

Gaston threw up his hands in a gesture of surrender. A wide grin split his features. ''Peace, peace, good Brother! I did but test your mettle.'' He mopped his brow with his sleeve. ''By the Book, I have not had such good exercise in over a year!'' He grew more serious as Guy lowered his blade.

Sweet Jesu! What had Guy done just now? Why had he allowed Gaston to goad him into a bout of arms? A plague on it! Guy had forgotten his vows, forgotten the rule of his order, forgotten everything save the exhilarating clash and clang of tempered steel. Beads of sweat mixed with the dust rolling into his eyes as Guy took in deep drafts of the cold air. Hang it all! He was woefully out of shape!

"You, you and you!" Gaston pointed to his three pupils in turn. "The lesson is over for the day. Go give the horses some exercise! Be off with you!" He retrieved the sword from Guy's limp hand, then pulled him by the sleeve behind the stable. "I crave a word or two with you."

Guy drew his hood over his head again and hoped no one had recognized him for a Cavendish. Wondering what Gaston was up to, Guy followed the old soldier and accepted a dipper of cold water from the bucket by the well.

"You fight with skill." As Gaston complimented him, he took Guy's right wrist and pulled up his sleeve. "Ha! As I thought. This is the arm of a knight, not a cleric. So tell me, as best you can, why is a knight hiding in a monk's robe, eh?"

Guy started to turn away, but Gaston held fast to him. "Not this time, Brother Guy. You can pray later. Answer me first, why have you taken holy orders?"

I'm not a real priest and I am not hiding. To Gaston, he presented a impassive face. Guy's motives for joining the Franciscans were none of the old man's business.

"Think I am blind? Ha!" Gaston poured a dipperful of water over his head, then shook the drops off, like a large shaggy dog. "Think I do not see what has happened to you?"

In the shadowed protection of his hood, Guy regarded Gaston intently. What *had* happened to him? Guy folded his arms over his chest, hugging himself. Now that he had cooled down from his brief engagement, the wind that blew around the courtyard felt doubly cold.

Gaston chuckled. "I'll tender my point, before your privates freeze in this shrill-gorged weather. My lady deserves better than an old windbag for a husband. *Oui,* do not look so surprised that I know this, my friend. Our young Peep has long ears and a ready tongue. Lady Celeste is a jewel, agreed? Her father has sent a precious rose to a man who can smell nothing but money. It is a crime that she be left to rot in this miserable dungheap!" Gaston spat in the direction of the central keep.

Guy shifted uneasily. He curled his toes under his sandal straps, but found no warmth there. Gaston cocked his head, then tapped the side of his large nose with his finger and nodded.

"The long and short of it is this. My lady is full in love with you."

Guy stepped back and shook his head. It wasn't possible! It could not be! Gaston grinned, then winked his eye.

"You look thunderstruck, my fine fellow. Ah! That often is the case with love. *Non!* Stop shaking your head and unstop your ears. I have known Lady Celeste since the cradle. Indeed, it was I who helped her take her first steps and taught her how to ride a horse and climb trees. Not that climbing trees is a necessary part of a young lady's education, but it is a good thing to know if you wish to pluck the sweetest pear from the limb. Pay some attention, dolt-head!" He punched Guy on the shoulder.

Guy's agitated mind whirled. Gaston said Celeste loved him. Nay, it was too good to be true! Surely Gaston mistook. It was Guy who loved the lady.

Gaston continued, "And I spy the same love-light in your eyes. Fah! Do not think you have hidden it behind that sanctimonious mask of yours. The question is this— what will you do about it, eh? Tell me, are you a true priest?" Gaston narrowed his eyes at Guy.

Guy considered the question. There was no point in lying to the man, and lying was a sin. Slowly, Guy shook his head.

"*Sacrebleu!* I thought as much, since I never saw you offer the holy mass yourself. Are you a real monk? Have you taken your final vows?"

Again Guy shook his head. Why was his blood pounding in his ears? Why did Gaston's simple questions leave him feeling so uneasy?

"*Très bien.*" Gaston licked his lips, like a satisfied cat after a stolen bowl of cream. "Then I tell you this truth in plain French, so you do not mistake my meaning. The lady loves you. You love the lady. If you do not use the good sense that God gave you now, I think you should start running out that gate this minute and not stop until you are back in your safe little hole at the monastery. *Oui!* There you can hide your face—the face of an angel, my lady says—and pretend you don't care a whit about what happens to her here."

Gaston turned toward the main staircase. "I leave it to you, middling monk. You have four weeks to do right by my little one who loves you with all her heart," Gaston tossed over his shoulder. He paused at the base of the stairs. A blood-freezing smile broke across his weathered face.

"But if you don't make the right decision, silent knight, I will cut out your gizzard and feed it to the dogs for a wedding breakfast."

Chapter Twenty-Four

When Guy rose from his knees in the dark, frigid chapel, he did so with a glad heart and a wide grin. For the first time in months, he ended his prayers with sincere thanks to the Almighty above. He strode out through the low arched doorway with a light spring to his step. Finally he knew what he wanted to do with his life—and how to go about it. Four weeks didn't give him much time to prepare, but as Father Jocelyn used to tell the novices, God helped those who helped themselves.

Silently begging a piece of writing paper and some ink from the castle chaplain, who was too sleepy to ask questions, Guy sat down under one of the narrow lancet windows and by moonlight scratched out a hasty letter to his brother, Brandon. The quill's frayed tip caused the ink to spatter and blot. When he had finished, Guy reread his missive. There was no high praise for either the spelling or the penmanship, but Brandon would understand his request. Guy judged the time to be near ten o'clock when he stole into the stable and gently shook Pip, who slept in the loft with the French men-at-arms. Ormond did not overextend his hospitality when it came to foreign-speaking temporary retainers.

"God's mercy!" Pip squeaked as he rubbed the sleep from his eyes. "Brother Guy, you gave me the fright o' me life, to be sure! Methought I had died and 'twas the angel Gabriel come to fetch me home to heaven." The boy yawned, then shook himself all over, like a puppy come in from a downpour. "What's your pleasure?"

Guy put his finger to his lips, then nodded his head toward the sleeping Pierre. The moon's slanting beams reflected Pip's snaggle-toothed grin of understanding. Together the tall monk and the slim boy descended the ladder into the stable below.

"Have ye a secret now?" Pip whispered, wriggling with anticipation.

Guy returned his infectious grin. He remembered from his own boyhood the lure of midnight mischief. He nodded again, his answer increasing the boy's excitement. Knowing that Pip could not read, Guy proceeded to mime his request. It would have been easier to tell Gaston, but Guy wasn't sure Brandon would answer his summons, and Guy didn't want to get Gaston's hopes too high.

"Which horse do ye want me to take?" Pip licked his lips as he eyed Gaston's black stallion, in his stall.

Guy almost chuckled aloud. There would be hell to pay if he saddled the beast for Pip. Gaston would probably skin both of them alive, without so much as a by-your-leave. Besides, Black Devil was far too powerful for a lightweight novice rider like Pip to handle. Guy moved into the stall that held Pierre's docile mare. Next to her, Daisy snorted and flattened her ears. Guy took an extra moment to rub the disagreeable donkey's neck. He felt a good deal more charitable toward her, now that he had settled his future. Guy slipped the bridle bit into the mare's mouth, then backed her out of the stall. Pip, his eyes sparkling with delight, watched as Guy cinched up the girth of Pierre's saddle.

Together they led the patient horse out of the stables, around the storehouses and behind the blacksmith's, to the low postern gate in the wall.

"Yer blessing, Father?" asked Nicholas, one of the younger guards, who shivered at his lonely post.

Guy hesitated only a fraction of a second before making the sign of the cross over the bowed, uncovered head. Then he motioned to the guard to unlatch the gate.

"I'd earn a beatin' for sure, but seein' 'tis only ye and the lad, I'll do it, Father. Mind the path, 'tis steep past the gate till ye reach the road. 'Tis a fair moon tonight, so ye'll ne'er have trouble findin' it." He unbolted the gate. "Methinks 'tis a wee bit late fer a ride," the guardsman remarked as he watched Guy lead the mare out.

"Aye, but Brother Guy has a message I am to deliver," Pip confided importantly. Guy snatched the youngster by the collar of his shirt before he could elaborate any further.

"Godspeed," Nicholas responded. "An' stay in the middle o' the road. 'Tis far ye ride?"

"Nay!" Pip gasped as Guy dragged him down the incline. "D'ye think I'd miss breaking me fast in the morning?"

The guard chuckled in reply.

Once they had reached the roadbed, Guy took out his slate and drew a makeshift map. Now all business, Pip followed the unspoken directions with a serious mien.

"Aye, Brother, I follow the road..."

Guy held up four fingers.

"Four miles till I come to a fork. I take the left-hand road and ride until I reach..."

Guy spread his hands wide, to indicate *large,* then pointed to Snape's brooding keep.

"I reach a great castle."

Guy nodded, then handed the boy the unsealed letter. On the outside he had written *Brandon.*

"I give this to the porter to give to the person what's written on this paper. D'ye want me to wait?"

Guy nodded again. Brandon would probably need help carrying all the things Guy needed.

"D'ye think they might feed me there?" Pip asked with a hopeful expression.

Pointing to the name, Guy nodded. Of all people, Brandon would appreciate a growing boy's appetite.

"Then to it, say I!" Pip threw himself into the borrowed saddle, then gathered the reins in his small hands. "Will ye bless me, Father?"

Willingly, and may your guardian angel ride tightly on your shoulder. Guy traced another cross in the air before Pip and the mare.

Chirruping low to the horse, Pip flicked her rump with his reins, and they took off at a brisk trot. Standing in the roadway, Guy watched his young messenger until the horse and his rider disappeared over the rise. The countryside between Snape and Wolf Hall was dotted with farmer's cottages. Pip was close enough to civilization not to get into trouble. Guy sent a swift prayer to heaven for the boy's safety.

With a contented spirit, Guy climbed the narrow stairs to his small, sparse room by the chapel. Noontime should bring his answer—and Brandon, he hoped. Guy fell onto his straw-filled pallet. Sleep softly overtook him.

Brandon reread the smeared letter in his hand, then cocked one brow at the yawning stripling who hunched over a plate of cold meat and cheese in Brandon's quarters, high in the east tower of Wolf Hall.

"Is my bro— Does Brother Guy have all his wits about him?" he asked.

"Oh, aye, my lord, the last time I looked." Pip shoved another large wedge of cheese in his mouth.

"What does he mean by asking for a shield with three blue forget-me-nots painted on it?"

Pip shrugged as he wiped the bottom of the wooden platter with a heel of bread. "I know not, my lord."

Brandon admired his own shield, hanging above his hearth. The wavering firelight gave the painted wolf's head a certain fearsome animation. What was wrong with bearing the family's coat of arms? he wondered. Flowers, indeed! And winged hearts on the saddlecloths? Mother would be weeks sewing this new device.

"When you have quite finished licking the trencher clean, little man, you can roll up by the fire and sleep. There's a blanket in yon chest."

Brandon stared at the signature. Moonstruck or not, Guy needed him. After a half year's silence, Brandon couldn't refuse his brother's summons. Besides, if they could tweak Ormond's nose in the bargain, why not? More sauce to the dish made it tasty.

"Mass is at six. We shall ride as soon as the sun is up," he told Pip.

A gentle snore answered him. Brandon shook his head with amusement at Guy's latest stray pet. Gently lifting Pip off the stool, Brandon laid the boy near the fire. He placed a sack under Pip's head and covered him with a thick blanket, tucking the ends around him.

Hearts and flowers? Methinks there is a goodly tale to be told here, little brother, and one that involves a lady. With a grin of anticipation, Brandon blew out the candle.

* * *

The first week of Advent brought true winter to Snape Castle. Icy winds howled down the privy shafts and whirled glowing embers up the flues. Snow settled over the landscape and frosted the branches of the nearby forest into fanciful shapes, like a subtlety of spun sugar. Noble and peasant alike shivered and drew closer to their hearths.

Celeste ignored the unaccustomed cold. The day after her betrothal was announced, she plunged into a whirl of activity around the castle, drawing along all the servants in her energetic wake. Mistress Conroy grumbled as she oversaw the thrashing of the dust-laden tapestries and the scouring of encrusted pots, but Celeste soon discovered that under her perpetual scowl Mistress Conroy possessed a warm heart. In truth, the housekeeper was never so happy as when she grumbled the loudest.

Pewter plates, warming pans, bolsters and mattresses—nothing escaped Celeste's eagle eye, or the army of cleaners she commanded. Sir Roger roared fruitlessly at the upheaval of his home, then retreated to his accounts office in a fit of self-preservation. Walter initially impeded the work, taking perverse pleasure in baiting his lost bride.

One morning Celeste came upon him in the buttery. He had pinned a cringing scullion maid backward over a long table, with her skirts pushed high above her hips, baring her to the waist. Celeste covered her mouth with her hand, but her gasp of shock escaped before she could muffle it. Walter looked up and grinned, his gums bleeding.

"Good Morrow, my lady—or should I call you Mother? Nay, I think not," he snarled to the frightened girl who was trying to pull herself out from under him.

Celeste knotted her fists at her sides and gathered her strength into her voice. "*Sacre!* Let her go this minute. What do you think you are doing?"

Walter merely laughed in reply as he fumbled with the drawstrings of his codpiece. "Why, I am taking a bit of pleasure to while away this raw-boned morning. I am instructing young Polly here in the finer points of swiving."

"Help me, my lady!" Polly whimpered, struggling against Walter's body.

"Aye, my pet!" he crooned, with an evil undertone. "Wriggle around all you please. 'Twill make me grow hotter!" He reached into his hose and drew out his partially erect member.

Celeste gasped at the sight, and a deep red stained her face and neck. Walter was more than disgusting. He belonged in the kennel.

"Would you like to see how it is done, Lady Celeste?" Still pinioning the girl to the table, Walter caressed his shaft with his hand. "Perhaps after I have finished with Polly, you would like a lesson or two yourself?" He stuck out his tongue and waggled it suggestively at Celeste. "You may as well, Frenchie. Methinks I can raise my flag far better than my father. Aye, and sheathe it deeper."

He turned his attention back to the kitchen maid, who increased her struggles against him. Looking about, Celeste spied the butter churn. Wrenching the long handle from the tub, she whacked it across Walter's back. The blow knocked him to the floor, where he lay gasping for breath and filling the air with curses. Like a cat, Polly scrambled off the table and raced out the door.

"Fetch help!" Celeste shouted after her.

"Witch!" Walter screamed, rolling on the flagstones in pain. "You rag, you baggage, you polecat! Bitch! A plague of whoremasters take you!" He pulled himself to his knees. "I shall beat your beauty into a withered canker."

Celeste gripped the churn handle as she backed out the doorway. "Pah! You are not worth another word, except to call you a peench-'potted raw-beet sucker!"

Grasping the table for support, Walter pulled himself to his feet. His red-rimmed eyes burned stark hatred at her. "Most excellent and accomplished linguist, may the heavens rain dung upon you!"

Black fright gripped Celeste. With his hat fallen to the floor, Walter looked like a living corpse with sprigs of brittle hair sprouting out of his bald head. Sweet Jesu! Where was Brother Guy? Walter lunged. Celeste managed to sidestep him, but had to back into a side passageway too narrow for her to swing the wooden churn handle. Grunting with a mixture of pain and pleasure, Walter stalked after her.

"Come, wench, give me a kiss!"

"May your lips rot off!" Celeste spat at him.

With his slash of a mouth twisting in a smiling grimace, he grabbed for her neck. Celeste ducked, leaving Walter clutching only her cap and veil.

"The devil take it!" He threw the coif after her.

"The devil and his dam take you posthaste to hell, bawdy villain!" Sir Roger's roar reverberated down the stone passage.

Celeste sagged against the wall as the elder Ormond's thick figure filled up the archway behind Walter. For the first time since her arrival at Snape Castle, Celeste could honestly say she was very glad to see her betrothed. Half the servants followed at his heels.

"I but seek to instruct—" Walter began. His father backhanded him against the wall. Walter slid to the floor at Celeste's feet.

"By this hand, I shall rid you of some of your teeth. Get up, you sniveling worm!" Sir Roger hoisted his son by his clothing, then shook him like a rag doll. "Methinks I should laugh myself to death at this puppy-headed monster. What say you, scurvy monster? Shall I chain you to a post and beat you?"

Without waiting for Walter to answer, Ormond threw him at the guards behind him. "Lock him in his room! There you will languish until I may devise your punishment! Away with you!"

Celeste felt hot and cold all at once. She put her hand out to steady herself, but the passageway seemed to grow narrower. Reaching for Sir Roger, she collapsed into a deep faint.

When Celeste awoke in her bed, Mistress Conroy breathlessly told her that Walter had escaped, taking his arms and armor with him. Sir Roger had given orders that the gates be barred against his son, then drunk off a crock of the harsh aqua vitae that the Scottish called whiskey.

That evening after supper, Guy paid her a visit. Celeste thought he looked exhausted, though she had no earthly idea what he had been doing or where he had been keeping himself. He moved with an unaccustomed stiffness when he knelt beside her bed. As he took her hands in his, Celeste noticed fresh blisters on his palms.

"Oh, la, la, Brother Guy! Where did these marks come from?" Lightly she traced the injured skin with her finger. "I think perhaps you must be praying too much."

His answering smile kissed her heart with its enchantment and lit her soul with flame.

Chapter Twenty-Five

As Advent progressed, Walter's protracted absence went unmourned by the inhabitants of Snape, most especially by Celeste. Whatever Sir Roger might have felt about his son's perfidy, he kept silent as he threw himself into preparations for his forthcoming wedding, particularly training for the joust. From early morn until the last rays of the wan sun disappeared below the horizon, the courtyard rang with shouts and the clash of arms as Sir Roger honed his fighting skills.

From the solar window, Celeste watched her elderly betrothed ride against the straw-stuffed, counterweighted quintain. *Thank the saints he is occupied and gives little thought to me.* The midday dinner had turned into a hurried affair, as the master of the castle bolted his food before dashing outside again to practice his swordsmanship. Supper in the evening often found Sir Roger nodding over the dishes of stewed eels, shallots or baked cheese pie. More than once, Celeste had to nudge him hard with her elbow to wake him before he fell asleep into the lentil soup. Immediately after the evening prayers, Ormond staggered off to his bed, giving Celeste the merest peck on the cheek. This state of affairs did not dismay her at all.

What did concern her was Brother Guy's puzzling behavior. Like Sir Roger, he disappeared from the hall after the morning mass, but where he went, she had no idea. Likewise, Gaston could not be found, which amazed Celeste, as she knew the old soldier hated the biting-cold weather of Northumberland. When she asked Pip where everyone was, the boy merely shrugged and hinted about a surprise.

Christmastide! They must be making something as a gift for her. Celeste looked through her own meager possessions and wondered what she had to give anyone in return. When she wasn't busy supervising the cleaning of the castle and the preparations for the coming fortnight of seasonal festivities, Celeste spent painstaking hours before a roaring fire in her room, embroidering handkerchiefs for her loyal retainers. As for Brother Guy—what did one give a monk who had sworn a vow of poverty? Observing him one evening at prayers, Celeste realized that his robe looked even more decrepit than she recalled.

How had he torn the seam away on one shoulder? Why was the hem completely gone? And why on earth did he look so tired at night? Surely he wasn't up all hours praying. Celeste never saw him in the chapel, except at mass and vespers. That, too, was odd. Before arriving at Snape Castle, Brother Guy could always be found on his knees in whatever church or chapel was handy. At least his appetite had finally returned. In fact, he often asked for a second helping, which surely must be against one of his rules about fasting. On the few occasions when Celeste managed to corner him and ask him how he was, he had merely smiled that wonderful angelic smile, which had made her forget the question. She decided to fashion him a new robe. He would not turn down such a practical gift.

As she sewed and embroidered, Celeste deliberately ignored all thoughts of her forthcoming nuptials, on Saint Stephen's Day. Though she knew Sir Roger's messenger to her father could not possibly return by then, unless he sprouted wings, she realized she could not delay the inevitable.

To mask her unease over her future, Celeste threw herself, and the younger servants, into gathering pine, holly and mistletoe to deck the newly cleaned great hall for the holidays. Gaston suggested that her men be given leave to go into the forest for a hunt to supply the high table with the traditional boar's head and minced meat pies. When she did so, the entire lot of them disappeared for almost a fortnight, returning in excellent high spirits, but with very little to show for the effort, except a lot of cuts and bruises that none of them explained. By the third week of Advent, only Pip appeared, with cheerful regularity, at every meal.

The days grew shorter and the nights darker as the year wound down to await the birthday of Christ and the annual renewal of the sun's progress through the seasons. One evening, as Celeste turned to leave the chapel, an unfamiliar voice called to her from behind one of the pillars.

"Lady Celeste, I humbly beg a word with you," he said in a low, pleasant voice. Though he spoke excellent French, his accent was plainly English.

Celeste paused; a flicker of apprehension coursed through her. By now, everyone else had deserted the chapel, seeking the warmth of their beds.

"Who speaks?" she asked, half in anticipation, half in dread.

"One who has your welfare in his heart."

Celeste gathered her furred cloak tighter about her, preparing to run if necessary. "And who might this be?"

"I am the messenger of the Knight of the Loyal Heart," he answered, stepping farther back into the darkness of the chapel.

At the name of her dream hero, a warm glow flowed through her. "*C'est impossible!* You speak like a troubadour."

He chuckled, the sound easing her fear. "I pray you do not ask me to sing like one, my lady. I fear I have the voice of a frog."

She stepped closer to the figure, who was wrapped and hooded in a full-length cloak. *Tall, but not like Brother Guy.* "And what says this knight?"

The mysterious messenger moved around to the far side of the pillar. "I bring you his greetings—and his love," he whispered.

Her heart sang a hymn of delight. Celeste wet her lips. "Give your master my thanks, good messenger." *Who in this world is he?*

"There is more, fair lady. The Knight of the Loyal Heart begs that you not wed until the evening of Saint Stephen's Day."

Celeste peered around the pillar. The messenger had moved to a second one, still deeper in the shadows. "But Sir Roger has planned—" she began.

"Change his mind," the shadow snapped, with sudden vehemence. Then his voice softened again. "What mortal man could deny you anything?"

"Are you a spirit?" *Merciful saints!*

He chuckled again, the sound like honey in her ears. "Nay, my lady, I fear I am all too human."

"And your master, the Knight of the Loyal Heart? He is not a spirit?"

"Nay, my lady. His blood flows hotly in his veins for you. His heart beats a song of love for you."

Celeste stepped closer. "But I am pledged to Sir Roger."

The messenger retreated a step. "Aye, sweet lady. But you are not yet wed to him. My master told me to remind you that miracles do happen."

Celeste put her hand to her throat. By all the stars of heaven! Was she dreaming? If so, she prayed she would not awaken soon.

"And what will happen if I can persuade Sir Roger to delay the ceremony?"

He chuckled again. The knight had engaged a very cheerful messenger. "A tournament in your honor, Queen of Truth and Beauty," he answered. "Challenges made and received. And many will be unhorsed."

"And I?" Celeste whispered.

"If your knight should attend the tourney, joust for your hand and defeat Sir Roger, would you accept him?" whispered the warm voice from the darkness.

Celeste's heart skipped a beat. Was she being tested for her loyalty and honesty? But who knew of her secret longing for a knight to sweep her away—except Brother Guy? And this messenger certainly was not he. She must give her answer very carefully.

"Nothing shall ever cause my heart to go one way and my body another. I will never become any man's whore, nor will two men share my body. He who has my heart shall have my body. All others I reject."

The messenger did not answer at once. Celeste crept forward and heard him move away again.

"You have answered well, cherished lady," he finally said. "I bid you good night. Remember what my master has asked you to do. You will not rue it, I swear it upon my sword. You hold his love in your hands, my lady. Treat it as your own, and all will be well. Adieu, and may sweet dreams attend you this night."

"Wait!" Celeste's voice rang clearly in the cold air. "How do I know what you say is true?"

"For each part of love, there must be equal trust."

"When shall I know?" Celeste stepped around the pillar, but found the place empty.

"Come Saint Stephen's Day, we shall meet again."

A draft of freezing night air caused the single candle in the sanctuary to flicker wildly. Despite the fact that she could not see in the darkness, Celeste knew her mysterious visitor had departed through one of the side doors. Though his message, and the manner of its delivery, disturbed her, nevertheless a sense of euphoria settled upon her like a perfumed cloud as she carefully picked her way through the night back to her room.

"Well, little brother, I'll give you your due. You have chosen wisely this time," Brandon Cavendish said as he pulled off his heavy cape and tossed it on a low stool. Moving around the central pole of his pavilion, he crossed to the folding table where he poured two large cups of wine. "'Sdeath! 'Tis cold as a witch's teat out there!" He took a deep drink.

Guy sat up straighter on the edge of his brother's cot. *You spoke with her?* he wrote on his slate.

Brandon warmed his hands over a low brass brazier filled with glowing coals. "Aye, and she has a cat's purr in her voice."

Guy nodded, with a slow satisfied smile on his lips. *You told her you were from the Knight of the Loyal Heart?* he wrote.

Brandon laughed as he poured himself more wine. "Aye, and she rose to it like a trout on a summer's day."

Guy narrowed his eyes. His chalk flew over the slate. *You didn't engage her in wanton speech? You often speak with a silver tongue to women.*

Brandon held up his hands in mock surrender. "The devil can have me if I did! Nay, angel-face, I spoke to her only of your love for her. And you should have seen the look in her eye when I mentioned the Knight of the Loyal Heart!" Brandon laughed so that his wine slopped over the rim of his cup.

Guy held his impatience in check. He knew that his little masque amused Brandon no end, but he wished his brother would cease to call him "angel-face." In their youth, Guy had often bloodied his brother's nose for it. *Will she delay the wedding?* He underlined the words.

Brandon took another drink before answering. "Aye, I think she will try. It remains to be seen what Sir Roger will say."

Guy raised one eyebrow with amused contempt, then wrote, *The walls of this tent will quiver with his wind.*

Grinning, Brandon stretched out his legs. "Good for him, so long as he does not blow out my fire in the bargain. 'Tis a right cold time of year to be camping. Pour us another cup, Guy."

Guy returned his brother's grin. *Advent,* he wrote. *You are supposed to be fasting.*

Brandon shrugged as he wagged the cup under Guy's nose. "Pish, posh! 'Tis for medicinal reasons, since there is no wench around to warm my blood."

Guy shook his head good-naturedly as he complied with Brandon's request. As he handed the cup back to Brandon, his brother tapped Guy's slate.

"Why do you insist on keeping this ridiculous vow of silence?" he asked, a look of mischief dancing in his light blue eyes.

My honor.

"And how long must I endure your gnarling penmanship?"

Until Celeste's wedding day. Guy stared at the words he had written. Two weeks more. Would she find his voice pleasing?

Brandon grinned. "I pray I do not go blind afore then. By my troth, little brother, I've done more reading this fortnight than in the entire past year!"

Guy finished his wine, then stood, his head nearly touching the canvas roof of Brandon's lavishly appointed pavilion. He winced as he moved. How quickly his muscles had softened! He could barely raise his shield arm after the bruising exercise Gaston had given him today at the quintain. *I must return to the keep,* he wrote. *My absences are noticed.* He massaged his aching shoulder as Brandon squinted at the slate.

"By a pair of the most purple eyes I have ever seen, perchance?" Brandon stretched himself out on the cot that Guy had just vacated.

Hie you to a bog, brother! The chalk snapped in two. Guy lifted the tent flap and shivered anew in the penetrating wind.

"After you!" Brandon retorted with a broad smile as he handed the slate back to Guy. "And close the flap quickly, 'ere I freeze and can no longer play your squire!"

Guy hugged himself for warmth as he crossed the field to the postern gate, where faithful Pip waited to let him in. The snow covered his feet at each step.

Forgive my weakness, Lord, but I am looking forward to wearing boots again.

The next morning, Celeste met Sir Roger in the hall as he was pulling on his thick leather gauntlets.

"A word, my lord, I pray you?" She smiled as she rose from her simple curtsy, though a hard knot had formed itself in her throat.

"Good morrow, sweetheart!" Sir Roger boomed in French, an answering smile wreathing his thick lips. "You look well this day."

Celeste tensed. "*Merci,* my lord, as do you." Quickly! She must broach the subject before she completely lost her nerve. "I have a boon to ask of you."

Sir Roger looked pleased. "Say on!" He waved one gauntlet in the air. His squire, Grapper, withdrew a few paces.

"I have been thinking of our wedding day, my lord," she began.

"As I have." He stepped closer to her. She noticed that drippings from yesterday's dinner still stuck to the gray velvet of his short coat. She itched to wrinkle her nose, but restrained her natural inclination. "And your boon?" he asked.

Celeste moistened her lips. Lying did not come easily to her. She thanked her lucky star that Gaston was not within earshot. "Merely this—it is the custom of my family to be wed at night, my lord."

His thick brows furrowed. "How now?" he bellowed.

She lifted her shoulders in a little shrug. "It is very silly, I know, but all my sisters were married by candlelight. It is very romantic, my lord, *n'est-ce pas?*" She cocked her head, smiled as sweetly as she knew how, then fluttered her lashes as her sister Henriette used to do.

Sir Roger barked, "Bolts and shackles, wench! I said on Saint Stephen's Day, and by my head, 'twill—"

Celeste laid her hand on his arm and felt his muscles harden beneath the sleeve. "*Oui,*" she murmured softly.

"Saint Stephen's Day, at six o'clock—in the evening, my lord. Also, I think it will be better for you."

Sir Roger paused in his fuming. "How so?"

Celeste stroked his sleeve, much as she would do to a quarrelsome child. "I wish you to do well at the jousting, my lord. Indeed, I am sure every knight who comes is quaking in his greaves that you shall be riding in the lists against them."

Sir Roger nodded, stroking his mustache. "My skill is well-known."

"D'accord," she agreed, swallowing down her flutters of anxiety. "And I would be much grieved if you were injured on our wedding day—before the evening." She blushed as she thought of what the evening's activities were to be. Sweet Saint Anne! How could she do *that* with him? She pushed the disgusting thought away.

Sir Roger slipped his arm around her waist and drew her hard against him. "'Tis a consummation that I devoutly wish for, sweetheart." His breath reeked of stale beer and old onions.

Quelling her urge to gag, Celeste hurried on. "If you...that is, we...were married before the tournament, I fear you would be distracted, my lord, and not at your best."

"I am always at my best!" he roared. Her ears rang.

"Oui, but I fear that you may be injured because your mind is not fastened to the point of your lance, but on other...points."

Her skin burned with shame.

He waggled his bushy gray brows at her, then roared with laughter. "They do say that a wise husband will not disdain to hear his wife's advice, and follow it, if it be good."

Celeste adjusted her coif and veil, which his rough handling had knocked askew. "Then you agree? We will be married after the tournament, *n'est-ce pas?*"

Sir Roger whacked her soundly on the backside. The force of his affectionate blow nearly sent her spinning out of his embrace. "Aye, 'tis agreed, and to seal the bargain, I claim a kiss, for I have not tasted those cherry lips of yours in many a day."

"Pleasures grow sweeter by delay," she murmured. The ferocity of his passion frightened her.

"Nay, I would kiss your sweet mouth again and again, so that the mark of my lips would show for a month." Before Celeste could protest, his mouth engulfed hers; his tongue delved deeply inside, nearly causing her to choke. It seemed an eternity before he released her. "Now, there's a wench!" he shouted in English to everyone in earshot as he thundered down the staircase to the courtyard.

Her lips raw from the encounter, Celeste sank down on the nearest bench. Her skirts of burgundy velvet shielded her trembling knees. *Mon Dieu!* How was she ever going to survive this fearful wedding night? Aunt Marguerite's vivid description flashed across her memory.

Was last night's visitation a mere figment of her fantasy and not a real man? No matter now. The die was cast. If nothing else, she had just bought herself twelve more hours of freedom. She lightly touched her bruised lips, and shuddered at the memory of the encounter.

That kiss was as comfortless as frozen water to a starved snake. O Knight of the Loyal Heart, if you be real, come save me.

Chapter Twenty-Six

When Celeste opened her prayer book the next morning, a small paper fluttered to the floor. Curious, she picked it up and turned it over. By the dim light of the altar candles, she saw the device of a heart with wings sprouting on either side. It had been hastily drawn with a frayed quill, but the scrap buoyed her spirits. The Knight of the Loyal Heart had sent her a sign—but what cunning had gotten it into her prayer book?

The next evening, as Celeste shuffled her playing cards to while away the long hours between vespers and bedtime with a game of patience, another paper fell onto her table. It, too, bore the winged heart of the fascinating and mysterious knight. Over the remainder of the week, other hearts appeared in the most unexpected places: in her sewing basket, under her trencher at dinner, in her reticule, and even under her pillow. She carefully preserved each of them between the pages of her Book of Love, as a maid might press a may-flower in a heavy volume. But the question remained. Who had slipped these intriguing billets-doux among her private possessions, and who was the Knight of the Loyal Heart?

* * *

Advent came to an end at midnight on Christmas Eve, when the first of the traditional three masses was sung in the castle chapel. Despite the lateness of the hour, the usually dim, cold place of worship radiated warmth and light as the castle's family, guests and servants crowded in to celebrate with fire and music the birth of the infant Jesus. The familiar Latin songs, the reading of the age-old story and the smell of the incense reminded Celeste of many happy memories of the Christmas season at her home, L'Étoile. Clutching her lighted taper, she tried to banish her homesickness. At her side, Gaston lent her the comfort of his reassuring presence, and when she chanced to glance at him, he gave her a brave smile, as if he understood her feelings.

Celeste had hoped Brother Guy would stand with her, as well, but he lingered in the side aisle, in the darkest part of the nave. He prayed in his usual silence, though for once his head was uncovered. Celeste marveled at how long his bright golden hair had grown since the first time she had seen him. At the end of the mass, he flashed her one of his brilliant smiles before slipping out the side door with several other men swathed in dark cloaks.

Since the day before, knights and their retinues had been arriving from neighboring estates to take part in the tournament and the subsequent wedding celebration of the lord of Snape Castle. Tonight, the chapel had been filled with many of these visitors. Initially Sir Roger had growled at the huge expense of his impending nuptials, but with the colorful arrival of so many distinguished guests, he had discovered that his reputation was considerably enhanced in the eyes of the local nobility by the prospect of good food, kegs of beer, and a chance to crack each other's heads open on Saint Stephen's Day.

The second Christmas mass, at dawn, celebrated the arrival of the shepherds at the stable in Bethlehem. Afterward, Mistress Conroy directed the serving men to pass among the milling throng with steaming mugs of hot spiced cider, which would slake everyone's thirst for both drink and warmth until after the third mass was celebrated in the midmorning. Following the final amen, Talbott, the steward, would serve the nine-course dinner that the cooks had been preparing for days.

Celeste sipped her cider and looked over the noisy company with a contented pride of place. For once, huge fires burned in both the hearths of the great hall. Holly and ivy garlands wreathed the chimney hoods and festooned the trestle tables that Talbott had already ordered set up. Up in the minstrel gallery, a threesome—two recorders and a tabor player—began to lay out their music. One of the early arrivals, Lord Jeffrey of Brownlow, had brought the musicians with him for the tournament, and had graciously loaned their services for the prenoon feast. Sir Roger passed among his guests, roaring at each with gladsome bellows. If he missed Walter's presence, he gave no indication of it.

Celeste searched for Guy, but could not find him. In less than a day, she would be wed to Sir Roger and Guy would leave Snape forever. She had hoped to share a few private moments with him before the many events of the day overwhelmed her. Celeste swallowed back the hovering tears of disappointment at his continued absence. Perhaps it is for the best, she consoled herself. She had allowed Guy to become far too important to her. The stunningly handsome monk was not hers, no matter how much she longed for him. He belonged to God alone.

Skirting the company, Celeste made her way to the bay window that overlooked the field below the castle. Overnight, a colorful tented city had sprung up like magical mushrooms. The weather had been cold and cloudy, but it had not snowed for several days, which allowed a great many neighbors from far and near to hazard the journey to Snape Castle. More than one lord, upon meeting Celeste for the first time, had bowed over her hand and thanked her for alleviating the boredom of midwinter. The wives who had accompanied their husbands equally thanked Celeste for the opportunity to show off their colorful wardrobes to each other and for the pleasure of three days of gossip and news-gathering among themselves.

Above each tent flew a banner emblazoned with the owner's coat of arms. Though lions, bears, roses, cockleshells, greyhounds and French lilies filled the pewter gray sky in profusion, none of them bore the device she yearned to see—the red heart with golden wings of the Knight of the Loyal Heart.

"Sacrebleu!" Gaston rumbled beside her. "I have not seen such a display in a long time." His eyes twinkled with the excitement of a man half his age. "Lord Ormond will be out of pocket for a good time to come."

Celeste sighed and leaned her head against the stone window frame. "I am much amazed that the English would sooner give five or six ducats to provide an entertainment for a person than a groat to assist him in any distress."

Gaston cocked his head, an inquiring look on his weathered features. "How now, my lady? You are the one who wanted this tournament, *n'est-ce pas?*"

She nodded, though she did not meet his eyes. *"Oui."* She sighed again.

"Perhaps not enough company has come? Pah! There are over a dozen nobles of worthy rank here to do you honor in the lists."

"*Oui,*" she agreed, staring out again at the colorful flags. "It looks very grand."

"But?" The old soldier gently prodded her. When Celeste finally met his gaze, she saw him laughing at her.

"I was expecting..." She stopped. How could she explain to Gaston what she had hoped to see? He would be even more amused, or he would be angry at her hopes of delivery from the marriage her father had arranged.

Gaston chuckled. "Expecting what, my lady? That one of your knights would leap out of the pages of your book and come to joust for you?"

Celeste swallowed hard. Gaston was far too astute. She must be very careful not to betray her hopes for that very thing. "*Oui,* Gaston." She fixed a false smile on her face. "And I would like a dragon or two, preferably breathing fire. If we could tame one, he would do very well in the main fireplace. Please excuse me. I must see to my lord's guests." Ducking his mirth, she hastened to lose herself in the crowd of colorful swirling velvets, brocades, jewels and fur.

To Sir Guy Cavendish at Snape Castle, greetings and peace be with you.

In the small antechamber off the great hall, Guy read the neatly inscribed letter by the spill of light from the boisterous dinner. Only moments before, a travel-stained messenger had sought him out at the lowest end of the table and pressed the missive upon the monk. The young man's weary face had lit up with pure joy when Guy rose, gave him his place and heaped a trencher full of venison and roast capon for him. Guy had then slipped into the small alcove, where he stared at the red seal with an anxious thudding in his heart. He recognized the signet of the father abbot of the Saint Hugh's Priory.

May this letter find you and your charges in good health and excellent spirits and—if God be willing— celebrating the great Feast of the Nativity.

Father Jocelyn's timing was impeccable, as always. The younger novices had often wondered if the man possessed second sight or had an angel as his watchdog. The truth of either would come as no surprise.

If the messenger has found you, and you are reading this at Snape Castle, then I trust that you have arrived with Lady Celeste de Montcalm. It is to this matter that I wish to open my thoughts. When you came to us in the spring, you were filled with the love of God and good intentions. Yet your heart was weary, and no amount of prayer, fasting or hard work seemed to give you the joy and peace you so desperately sought.

Guy's mouth twisted in a rueful smile. Father Jocelyn also read men's souls, it seemed. He should be prudent, lest he be burned as a wizard.

You have been gone from our care for several months, and I have prayed that your journey reach not only a successful conclusion for your body, but for your soul. If now you find that your life's path lies not within the four small walls of Saint Hugh's, but in the hands and the heart of the Lady Celeste, then that is where our Lord wants you to be.

Guy closed his eyes for a moment. The blood pounded in his temples. When his breathing became more regular, he opened his eyes and continued reading.

If this then is the case, I heretofore release you from all your vows: those of poverty, chastity and obedience to me and to the rule of the Order of St. Francis, and that vow which I placed especially upon you—silence. If the lady is willing and you can claim her in honor, then I further bestow upon you my blessings and prayers for a long and happy life together. May you both rejoice in the love of Christ all the days of your lives. Written by my hand this 28th day of November, in the year of our Lord fifteen hundred and eight and twenty, Father Jocelyn Pollock.

Guy reread the letter, afraid he had misunderstood his superior's generosity. Once assured that Father Jocelyn had indeed returned him to the secular world with love and understanding, Guy sagged against the chill wall. For Celeste, he had been willing to dash his pride of honor to the four winds and literally abduct her. Now he held in his hands the permission to pursue his heart's desire with all the nobility that was his by birthright. How his father would roar with laughter over this turn of events! Guy thought.

He was tempted to fling back the alcove's curtain and shout his love above the music and the din, but he realized that seemingly scandalous action would not only break the good cheer of the guests and anger Sir Roger into a dangerous rage, but would, no doubt, highly distress the object of his desire, Celeste. Best to let his plans, conceived on the first day of Advent—in fact, on the very day

Father Jocelyn had written this letter—go forward. Guy interpreted the letter as a good omen. Tomorrow he would win his lady's heart and hand on the field of honor—or die in the attempt.

Fearing that his great joy might prompt him to speak to Celeste and reveal his identity to her, Guy stole away from the Christmas feast and hurried back to Brandon's secret camp beyond the forest. He never felt the cold wetness of the snow seeping through his sandals, or the bitter winds from the North Sea that tore at his ragged robe. His cheerful spirit warmed him as he crossed the frozen field, and his heart truly did possess golden wings.

The day's merry celebrations wound down early, as everyone wanted to get a good night's sleep for the tournament on the morrow. Sir Roger kissed his betrothed often during the evening supper, in full view of his guests, who urged their host with much cheering to even more public displays of his affection. Celeste bore his invasions of her mouth and person with as good a grace as she could muster in the face of the grinning horde, though as each hour passed her heart grew heavier. At last, pleading a headache, she excused herself from the company.

"Aye, there's a wench!" Sir Roger bellowed in English as Celeste started up the stairs to her room. "Tomorrow at this time, my friends, I shall wait upon that lady and forward her desire to lead a merrier life!"

Though shamed by his thinly veiled vulgarity, Celeste held her head high and pretended she had not understood a word he said.

"In truth, I am sorely tempted to experience her delights much sooner!" Clamorous banging on the tables greeted Sir Roger's remark.

After rounding the bend of the stairs, Celeste picked up her skirts of yellow satin and raced for her room. *Not tonight! Sweet Jesu! Please, not yet!*

Just as she reached her door, she heard Lord Jeffrey's voice. "Nay, be not so hot, old man, or you'll spend yourself in one volley. Save your strength for the lists tomorrow, for I intend to unhorse you before your fair bride."

"Think you so, prattling drunkard?" Sir Roger's roar bounced off every wall. "Nay, 'tis impossible that I should be brought low by such a varlet as yourself!"

"How low?" Lord Jeffrey retorted. "By my troth, I shall bring you low this night."

"Listen to the jackdaw croak! What weapons do you choose? Sword or broomstick?"

"Nay, by sack wine! Ho, churls! Fill our cups to overflowing, and let us see who falls first!"

Pausing with her hand on the latch, Celeste breathed a sigh of relief. Thanks to Lord Jeffrey's taunting challenge, Ormond had forgotten all about her. She flung open the door and rushed inside.

"My—my lady!" Pip jumped from where he had been kneeling by her bed. "Good evening to ye!"

Celeste eyed the red-faced boy. What manner of mischief was his intent? She crossed her arms over her breast. "Hey-ho, Peep! What is it you do here, eh? A frog to warm my bed, perhaps?"

Pip backed away from the canopied four-poster as if it had suddenly burst into flames. "Nay, my lady! Faith, no frog with any wit about him is out this cold night."

"*Oui,* so what have you put in my bed—a poor witless worm?" Celeste bit the inside of her cheeks to keep from laughing. Pip looked so deliciously guilty. He reminded her of her pranks at home. "Come, come. I have caught you—how you say?—fair and square. Show me this Christmas surprise.''

Pip opened his mouth, but his protest of innocence died on his lips when he saw Celeste pick up a switch from the kindling. Nearly tripping over his new shoes, he dashed for the bed and lifted the top bolster. Shyly he handed her a small packet tied with a red ribbon. Celeste softened when she saw his gift.

"Oh, Peep! It is not yet New Year's Day. Your gift is early."

Pip drew himself up. "'Tis nae mine to give. I am a messenger.'' His thin shoulders slumped. "An' a poor one, to be found out."

"I am the judge of that." Celeste untied the ribbon, and revealed a simple golden ring with the words, *Pencez moi,* engraved on it. The paper that had wrapped it bore no name, only the beloved sign of the winged heart. *Think of me,* her Knight begged her, with his golden circle signifying eternal love.

"Who gave this to you?" she asked, when she could finally speak without a tear in her voice.

"By'r Larkin!'' Pip breathed, ogling the ring. "'Tis a pretty piece o' work, that!''

"But where did you get it?'' Celeste slipped it onto the third finger of her left hand, and was pleased that it fit perfectly.

He backed toward the door. "Nay, I swear by the moon, I did nae steal it!''

"Little knave! Who gave you this ring?" She changed her tone into one of gentle wheedling. "Please tell me, Peep.''

The boy swallowed. "I would if'n I could, my lady, but I did swear upon a sword—aye, an' a sharp sword 'twas too!—that I would nae tell no one. Ye can rack me or hang

me in chains, 'twon't do ye nae good. I pledged me word.''
Despite his brave speech, Pip looked very nervous, as if he
feared Celeste might put him to some hideous torture.

"Then tell me this, Peep. Is the Knight of the Loyal
Heart ver-rey handsome?''

The relieved boy broke into a wide grin. "Bein' no lady
like ye, I am a poor judge, but I tell ye true—your knight
is the best man in the world for ye, my lady. An' he loves
ye full sore. Is that handsome enough?''

Celeste's only answer was tears of joy. The sight of them
rolling down her cheeks unnerved Pip. With a hurried wish
for sweet dreams, he bolted from the room.

Far into the magical night of Christmas, when all the
animals of the world were said to speak at midnight, Celeste sat before her fire and admired the flames' reflection
in the slim golden band around her finger.

Chapter Twenty-Seven

In the darkness of early morning on Saint Stephen's Day, Celeste awoke with a dull headache and a great lump in her throat. Burrowing deeper under the feather quilting, she listened to the wind whistling outside the window. Her wedding day had arrived—the most important day in her life—and Celeste wanted to turn the calendar either forward or backward. She grimaced as she thought of the next twenty-four hours.

The newness of the golden ring on her finger reminded her of the one ray of hope. The Knight of the Loyal Heart, no longer a figment of her imagination, would finally make his appearance today. Pip had seen him, talked with him. Whatever else happened to her, Celeste would treasure this dream come true for the rest of her days as the mistress of bleak Snape Castle.

"Dress warmly, my lady." Mistress Conroy bustled into the room, followed by Nan, who carried a steaming mug of spiced wine. "'Tis a day fit to shatter the devil's tail."

Celeste wished the housekeeper didn't sound so cheerful.

"Faith, my lady, I've ne'er seen such a crop o' handsome men as have come t' do ye honor," Nan rhapsodized as she poked up the fire into a roaring blaze. "More came in the middle o' the night. By'r Larkin, my lady! There's horses an' pages everywhere, an' the meadow looks like the grandest thing since…'' Nan paused, wrinkling her brow. "Since I've ne'er seen before," she finished.

Celeste's heart skipped a beat. Her knight must have come! Ignoring the chill of the room, she threw off the covers and dashed to the window. Clucking behind her, Mistress Conroy held out her furred robe. At least a hundred cooking fires burned in the velvet blackness of the field below the ramparts. Even at this distance, Celeste heard good-natured shouting, and the metallic jingle of harness for both the men and their horses.

"How many of the knights have come?" she asked breathlessly as Mistress Conroy guided her back to the warmth of the hearth.

"By my troth! 'Tis more'n we've seen in my lifetime." The housekeeper ran a brush through Celeste's hair, working to loosen the tangles after a restless night. "There's the Lords of Morpeth, Brownlow, young Sir Harry Percy from Alnwick, a-hiding from his shrewish wife, Rothbury, the master of Cheviot, an' even the Earl of Thornbury himself. He's Sir Roger's overlord, an' hasn't been here in a friendly manner for years. Brought his lady wife, as well."

"Is the earl a quarrelsome man?" asked Celeste as Nan dropped several woolen petticoats over her head before tying them around Celeste's waist.

Mistress Conroy pursed her lips before answering. "The earl has never liked the master, and Sir Roger returns the favor."

"Sir Roger's done a right lot to make his way in the world, my lady," Nan whispered. "He got himself married to a noblewoman with property—that be his first wife, more than twenty years ago, afore my time. Me da said that Sir Roger planted his crops on lands that weren't his—"

"Nan, watch that prattlin' tongue of yours, lest it get cut out!" snapped Mistress Conroy.

"*Non,* I wish to hear all." Celeste chewed on her lower lip. She knew she shouldn't be listening to the servants' gossip, but the tale they told explained a great deal about her bellowing husband-to-be.

Knowing she had Celeste's full attention, Nan preened. "Me da said that the master took bits of the earl's land over the years. Bits that the earl had ne'er used. Me da said that Sir Roger gained as much land in twenty years as his father did in an hour on Bosworth field. Aye, an' each year the taxes got higher for the folk what lives on that land. When his first wife died, straightaway he married again."

"Lady Edith, God rest her soul." Mistress Conroy crossed herself again, then tied on a second set of fur-lined sleeves over Celeste's tight red velvet ones.

"Aye, an' she brought my lord more gold for his coffers. The earl has threatened to make all right with the poor folk on the lands he claims, but Sir Roger has the sheriff o' York a-lickin' his codpiece, an'—"

"Nan!" Mistress Conroy shot the maid a murderous look. "You best watch your mouth, girl. Lady Celeste may not speak our English fair yet, but I reckon she knows a word or two."

Celeste knew exactly what Nan had meant, and the information troubled her. Sir Roger had made it clear that once she was married, Gaston and the others were no longer welcome at Snape. With only Pip as her guardian, she would be totally at the mercy of a rapacious, greedy man.

"If Sir Roger is so tight with his money, why does he have this tournament, eh?" she asked thoughtfully. Outside, the sky began to lighten with the dull gray of dawn.

"Lord have mercy, my lady! He expects your father to pay for that. I heard him say as much to Talbott, when the steward asked him that very question." Mistress Conroy brushed back the stray tendrils of Celeste's hair before adjusting the red-and-black French hood on her head.

Icy flutters spread themselves through Celeste's empty stomach. She knew that her father would not send another sou after her. His troublesome, mischief-making fifth daughter was locked up tight in a castle at the coldest end of the earth, and there she could stay, in whatever state her husband pleased to keep her. Though her lips quivered at the thought of Sir Roger's ire when he discovered the empty lie of an enlarged dowry, Celeste lifted her head proudly. At least this one day was hers. Today she was the Queen of Truth and Beauty, and she planned to savor it to the dregs.

Before descending the stairs, she looked out once again at the encampment. The colorful pavilions and banners snapped in the brisk north wind. Though she searched each heraldic device in turn, nowhere did she spy the beloved symbol of the winged heart. Instead, an old familiar one caught her eye.

"*Ma foi!* Mistress Conroy, who is that with the wicked wolf's head?"

The housekeeper squinted in the direction where Celeste pointed. "Aye, that is the one I was a-tellin' ye about, my lady. That belongs to the earl of Thornbury."

Memories of another tournament, on a windy summer's day in France, welled up inside Celeste's mind. Memories of a tall knight on a dark gray war-horse—one who hadn't seen her outstretched favor. "Oh, la, la! I think perhaps the earl will notice me today, *oui?*" she murmured, more to herself than to the two women beside her.

"He won't help but t' notice ye, my lady," Nan pronounced. "Ye look fit for a king."

Sir Roger, garbed in his padded jacket and thick hose for the joust, greeted his bride in the hall, bestowing on her a long, lusty kiss. His male guests approved with a mixture of amusement and envy.

"Give over, Ormond!" Jeffrey of Brownlow called. "For tasting such sweetness, you might have broken your fast before mass."

Let the dog bark! Roger had them all by the tail this day. Aye! Even that priggish Thornbury had to dance to his tune. Sir Roger slid his arm around Celeste's waist as they went into the chapel together.

A pox on it! He and his little bride should be saying their marriage vows this minute, instead of waiting until after supper! Roger's eye ran hungrily over the raven-haired beauty. What a delicious morsel awaited him this evening! He cared not who knew it. Let the rest of them lust after her all they wanted. Aye, let every dog of them whimper for her, and so fail in the day's sport. This tournament idea of hers was not such a bad one after all. Never had Roger seen so many of his enemies under his roof at the same time. He looked around the chapel and chuckled. Every last one of the rump-fed rogues envied him this day! Roger pulled Celeste tighter against him.

What was the matter with the little minx now? He cast her a look meant to quell, but she didn't see it. Instead, she seemed to be looking around the filled chapel for someone, while the dithering old priest droned through the Introit prayer. What knave had caught her fancy already? *No*

*more of that, mistress mine! I'll imprint myself so deep in
you this night, you'll never wish to look for another.*

At the conclusion of Saint Stephen's mass, the great hall
erupted with the loud calls for bread and meat. Dogs
barked and fought with each other over the scraps. Serving men and wenches waded through the noisy, jostling
throng holding heaped platters over their heads. Everyone ate standing up. As soon as the knights finished and
rinsed their hands in the proffered ewers, they dashed off
to the encampment beyond the walls. Their ladies, attired
in every hue made possible by the dyer's art, took a little
more time, their mouths moving constantly, either to chew
the cold beef or to chew on juicy pieces of gossip.

Celeste stood slightly apart, not knowing quite what to
do next. She did not feel confident enough in her grasp of
the English language to sally forth among the ladies and
join in their talk. And none of them made a move toward
her, though every so often one stately matron would look
up and smile at her.

Gaston pushed his way through a pack of quarreling
hounds. "*Zut alors!* For a miser, the master of Snape puts
on a good show." He flashed Celeste a wide grin. "The day
is a good one for breaking a number of thick heads!"

Celeste smiled up at him with gratitude. In two sentences, he had made her feel much better. "*Oui,* my good
friend. And I suppose you would like to do some of the
head-breaking yourself?"

Gaston gestured dismissively. "Blasts and fogs, my lady!
I but give way so that there will be some one or two left
standing by supper! Puppies! Whelps! What could an Englishman learn that a Frenchman hasn't already practiced, eh?" He offered her his arm. "But come now—away

with you. The heralds have been told to form for the parade, and you must take your place.''

Celeste slipped her hand around his muscle-knotted arm. How strong and reassuring he felt! "Gaston, have you seen Brother Guy?" she asked as he led her down the stairway.

"The priestling?" The old soldier's lips twitched. "I think he is gone, my lady."

Celeste pulled him to a stop at the bottom of the steps. Tears pricked at her eyes, though she would not give them her permission to fall.

"How can that be? He did not even say goodbye to me!" She bit her lower lip.

Gaston's eyes dared to twinkle though he spoke to her in a gruff voice. "Brother Guy is a man of honor. He promised to guide you until your wedding day, and *voilà!* Today is your wedding day, so—pffft! He is gone—as if he were never here."

How could Guy have done this to her? Didn't he know how much he meant to her? She had expected him to bless her in her marriage. She had hoped to hear him finally speak a few words to her. Now he had flown away like a freed lark.

"*Courage,* my lady! Hold your head up high," Gaston gently admonished her. "The monk is gone, as he should be. But—" his brown eyes twinkled all the more "—who knows what this day will bring?"

The Knight of the Loyal Heart? Yes, she hoped he would come, and yet... Celeste swallowed back an enormous lump. She realized now, with stunning finality, that the greatest knight she would ever know was the one who wore a plain brown robe of wool tied at the waist with a frayed rope and only sandals to cover his poor feet in the snow. She thought of the new robe she had made for him, folded away in the chest in her room, waiting for the gift-giving time on New Year's Day. If she had only known Guy was leaving, she would have given him her present earlier.

"Lady Celeste de Montcalm!" Gaston gave her arm a little shake. "What are you? A crybaby? Do you intend to shame me in front of these knavish peasants? Hold your head up—and remember who you are!"

Celeste blinked away the tears that threatened, then squared her shoulders. How many times had Gaston said those very words when Celeste had been summoned into the presence of her unsmiling father to face retribution for her latest piece of mischief? She flashed him a brave smile, though her heart felt dead within her.

"*Allons-y,* my good Gaston! Let us march into the fray together."

His smiled widened. "*Très bien, ma petite!* This day, I think the English have met their match!"

Despite the cold blustery weather, the meadow filled with every manner of folk enjoying the first of the twelve days of Christmas. Even though she ached with the emptiness of Guy's absence, Celeste's spirits could not help but lift at the gladsome sights and sounds around her. After four dark weeks of fasting and penance, the holiday revelry was infectious.

As she walked through the tented village, Celeste saw squires and pages dashing hither and yon, with lances, swords and bits of armor in their hands. Occasionally they passed by a pavilion whose flap was tied back and Celeste saw the knight inside, standing patiently while his squire fastened him into a complicated array of hauberk, leg harness and breastplate shined to a silver gleam. One young gallant saw her and winked as she passed.

"Insolent pup!" Gaston growled under his breath.

Children, squealing with excitement, ran underfoot, heedless of the crowds. As Gaston and Celeste drew closer to the makeshift tiltyard at the far end of the meadow, they saw vendors of hot nuts and gingerbread doing a brisk trade among the nobility and the common folk alike. A *jongleur* played a sprightly tune on his recorder, while a boy and girl—brother and sister, by the look of them— whirled and danced. The onlookers applauded and tossed small coins into the mud at the musician's feet.

Gaston pulled Celeste out of the way as a squire led a huge war-horse past them. Red and green ribbons festooned the stately animal's mane and long tail, and his hooves gleamed with some sort of black polish. Celeste had never seen one of these huge horses so close before, and she marveled at its size.

Gaston snorted. "Pah! I would have my Black Devil any day, rather than sit astride one of those plow horses." But Celeste noticed a wistful look in his eye as he said it.

The frozen cattle pond provided another source of entertainment. A large crowd had gathered to watch a young man who appeared to fly like a bowshot across the ice. Gaston shouldered a path for Celeste, so that she might better view this marvel.

"Isn't that Nicholas?" she asked Gaston, recognizing the young castle guardsman. "How does he do that?"

Gaston squinted. "The devil take it! He's tied shank bones to his feet. The knave will break his neck in due time."

Catching sight of the new mistress of Snape, Nicholas executed a quick twist. The crowd applauded as he skated backward past them, a huge grin on his face.

"*Quelle merveille!*" Celeste applauded loudly with the rest. "Is that not a wonder, Gaston?"

"*Oui,*" he conceded gruffly. "But you'd best pray, my lady, that Pierre does not see him. That scamp would steal the bones off the platters at dinner to try such a harebrained trick himself. And who would have to put back the pieces after he breaks his arm or leg, eh? *Moi!*"

Through the crisp air, unseen trumpets blared their golden notes of invitation. Gaston jerked Celeste away from the icy entertainment.

"*Sacrebleu!* They are about to begin the tournament without the Queen of Truth and Beauty!"

Chapter Twenty-Eight

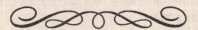

Celeste rode her palfrey into the tiltyard beside the beaming Sir Roger Ormond. Despite the gray overcast of the sky and the chill wind whipping the banners straight out from their poles, a goodly crowd hung over the double palisade wall that separated the godlike combatants from lesser mortals. The good cheer of the crowds, the golden-throated trumpets, the bright colors worn by all the guests and the eager expectation of the sport to come did much to lift the pall shrouding Celeste's spirit.

As she proceeded slowly past the stands that held the families of the knights, Celeste vowed to forget her earlier pique over Guy's sudden departure. Gaston was right. The good monk had done all he was commanded to do—and more—to ensure her safe arrival at Snape Castle. Now, true to his honor, he had retired. She must accept that fact and go on with the life she would begin this night.

When Celeste drew abreast of the main reviewing pavilion, Talbott descended the stairs and helped her down from her saddle. Then he escorted her to one of the raised chairs on the dais. The empty place on her right was reserved for Sir Roger after he had jousted.

"My lady of Thornbury, I have the honor to present Lady Celeste de Montcalm, betrothed to my lord Ormond." Talbott bowed to the dignified woman seated on the other side of Celeste. "My lady Celeste, may I present the countess of Thornbury, the honored wife of our liege lord?"

The countess smiled as Celeste dipped a curtsy. *Ma foi,* thought Celeste as she rose and took her seat. The countess had the same smile as— No! She mustn't think of the monk. He was gone.

"'Tis a cold day, my dear. Please share this lap robe with me, and perchance we shall keep each other warm." The countess possessed a warm, musical voice, and she spoke French with a delightful accent.

"*Merci beaucoup,* Countess." Though Celeste recognized the charming, tall woman beside her as the one who had smiled at her in the hall earlier, she couldn't shake the feeling that they had met before. There was something so very familiar about her.

After Talbott tucked the thick white fox fur robe around the legs of both ladies, he withdrew behind his master's chair. Celeste burrowed her gloved hands deep inside her hanging sleeves, under her cloak. The day would indeed be a cold one. Perhaps she would be so numb by this evening, she would feel nothing during the dreaded wedding night. She fervently hoped so.

The countess leaned closer to Celeste. "Since we are to be neighbors, I hope we may also be friends. I am Alicia Cavendish."

At the sound of the name, Celeste turned to the lady with a wide-eyed stare. "*Mon Dieu!* Cavendish! That is the same name as Brother Guy, who escorted us here."

The lady smiled. "The very same indeed. Guy is my second son. My eldest, Brandon, is one of the knights who jousts in your honor this day. See? Here he comes now!"

Her face glowed with motherly pride as a tall golden-blond man entered the tiltyard astride a massive war-horse.

Brandon paused before the ladies and bowed from his saddle, his mouth curving into a mischievous smile.

"Is he not handsome?" his mother whispered to Celeste. "But I fear he makes a wide swath among the unmarried ladies with those devilish good looks."

"Mais oui," Celeste agreed. Though not as tall as Guy, and not possessing Guy's angelic face, Brandon Cavendish bore the same family stamp as his brother. His light blue eyes twinkled when his gaze rested on Celeste. Raising his fingers to his lips, he blew her a kiss before moving on.

Lady Alicia chuckled. "Do you see? He is such a rogue! I pray he soon falls to the charms of a young lady and is wed. He is much too handsome for his own good."

"As is your other son, Brother Guy," Celeste remarked softly as she watched Brandon proceed down the palisade. His red banner with the wolf's head crest snapped in the breeze. Could Brandon be the knight who had ignored her favor so long ago in France?

The countess sighed. "My Guy was made too beautiful for this world. I suppose that is why he took to the church."

Under Lady's Alicia's soft tone, Celeste detected a note of sorrow. "You do not approve of Guy's vocation, eh?"

The countess's blue eyes, so like both her sons', regarded Celeste for almost a full minute before she answered. Then she smiled. "Guy has always been ruled by two things—his honor and his firm convictions. His honor has remained constant, and of that I am proud. His firm convictions, however, tend to change with each season. However, I think he has, at last, found what he wants. I pray he can attain it."

Celeste merely nodded.

"You seem troubled, my dear," Lady Alicia continued. "Are you taking a chill?"

Celeste shook her head. How could she possibly explain her disappointment at Guy's hasty departure and her fear of the nuptial bed to Guy's mother without sounding disloyal to Sir Roger, who was her husband in all but ceremony and deed? "I think I am one of those nervous brides, my lady. And I had hoped Brother Guy would stay to see me married," she added.

"Guy has always been abrupt in his leave-taking," his mother remarked. "Not because he has so little care for those he leaves, but because he has too much."

"Ah," Celeste murmured. She hoped that was true. She would like to think she meant a little something to her handsome guardian angel.

"And here is my husband, the earl of Thornbury," the countess announced as she applauded her husband's entrance into the arena. "Thank all the saints, he does not joust today. He is to act as the king of arms and judge the contests." She lowered her voice to Celeste. "He adores jousting, but his eyesight is not what it used to be. It has taken me these past two weeks to talk him out of challenging Sir Roger."

Celeste smiled into the folds of her cloak. Though she had just met the countess, she hoped they would become fast friends.

The parade of knights ended. Celeste hid her disappointment behind a smile. None had entered the tiltyard wearing the winged heart. Perhaps her mysterious knight was already here, and would reveal himself later. Just then, a multi-pronged tip of a lance appeared at her feet. When she looked up, she saw Sir Roger extending it toward her.

"Your favor, mistress mine!" he bellowed.

While dressing, Celeste had tucked a small blue veil inside her sleeve—the very same she had proffered to the Knight of the Wolf many years ago. But that cherished favor was for another—if he ever came. Instead, Celeste stripped off her veil of black gauze from her coif and twined it around the lance head. Sir Roger roared his pleasure, waved aloft Celeste's favor, then tied it around his right arm.

Brandon rode up to his mother, his lance fluttering with many ribbons, veils and sleeves. "Methinks I will start a true war if I chose one of these favors to wear." He eyed his bedecked lance with a rueful smile. "Perchance you would honor me with your favor, Mother, so that I will be able to joust in safety."

Laughing at her eldest son's amorous difficulties, Lady Alicia extracted a long green ribbon from her sleeve. "You do me a great honor, my son."

"Nay, you are saving my life, good Mother." Brandon turned his attention to Celeste. "As always, I fight for the honor of the queen of the joust, Lady Celeste," he told her in French. "Though if I should beg for your favor, I fear Sir Roger would unhorse me in earnest."

"Then ride with my blessing," Celeste replied, smiling at him. His voice! Where had she heard it before?

Bowing to both ladies, Brandon spurred his great bay destrier to the gate where he would retire until his joust was called.

"My son will need all your prayers, Lady Celeste," his mother remarked watching his exit. "Brandon jousts to the point of sheer recklessness."

Celeste wondered what sort of a knight Guy would have been, then chided herself for thinking of him. Guy had returned to his monastery. The entrance of the pursuivant ended her further musings. In a loud, high-pitched voice, the brightly clad man announced the beginning of the tournament. From outside the ring, the horn of challenge sounded from the Tree of Honor, on which hung the wooden shields of the participating knights. The crowd grew still as the pursuivant introduced the first defender, Lord Jeffrey of Brownlow, and the first challenger, hot-headed Percy of Alnwick.

Lord Jeffrey, his destrier clad in black-and-gold caparisons, burst through the arena's gates amid much cheering and took his position at the far end of the tiltyard. Sir Henry Percy, in green and white, made an equally exciting entrance, applauded with unabashed enthusiasm by many of the ladies.

"They say young Harry Percy fights to ease his wounded heart," Lady Alicia murmured to Celeste.

"How so?" Celeste watched the young lord lower his visor and hoist his lance.

"He was betrothed to the king's new mistress, Anne Boleyn. When the king turned his eye on her, Harry was sent north to marry Shrewsbury's nagging daughter. 'Tis not a gladsome match, I fear."

"I am sorry for him," Celeste answered, thinking of her own unhappy marriage to come.

After three thunderous passes and several shattered lances, both knights retired from the field, with the honors going to Sir Henry.

Sir Roger entered the lists as the next defender. As he raced his horse past Celeste, he shouted out his war cry, "Ormond to me!" Grapper, acting as his master's squire, followed, bearing the Ormond banner of three black crows on a gold background. Sir Griffith, master of the Cheviot, followed as the challenger.

Celeste held her breath as the two men, clad in full armor, wheeled their horses into position at opposite ends of the long arena, then spurred their mounts into a full gallop toward each other. The pounding hooves of the massive destriers shook the ground as they drew closer on opposite sides of the six-foot wooden barrier. On the first pass, both lances missed their mark.

Lady Alicia chuckled. "I do believe Sir Griffith is pulling up his thrust. Watch on the next pass, my dear. The Cheviot will allow your betrothed the honor of striking his shield."

As the countess predicted, Sir Roger shattered his hollow lance against Sir Griffith's shield. The household and villagers of Snape cheered their lord.

"It would not do for the host to fail in the lists, especially on his wedding day, would it?" Lady Alicia arched one eyebrow in a very knowing manner.

"Mais non." Celeste burrowed deeper into her cloak. How utterly embarrassing for everyone to see that Sir Griffith had given that point to the older man!

On the third pass, Sir Griffith leveled his lance across his horse's neck and cleanly struck Ormond's wooden shield, shattering his lance. Sir Roger swayed in the saddle from the impact, but managed to stay upright until he exited the yard. Sir Griffith followed at a leisurely pace, accepting the acclaim of the crowd.

Lady Alicia rolled her eyes. "I am glad for your lord's sake that he did not fall. 'Twould have given Sir Griffith the highest score so far."

Celeste merely nodded. Talbott appeared with a small tray of mulled cider and sugared nuts for the ladies.

"Is Sir Roger well?" Celeste asked the steward.

Talbott pursed his lips. "He'll be a bit sore this night, but methinks 'tis his pride that is badly bruised. He will seek satisfaction anon. Fret not, my lady," Talbott added in an undertone. "He will be well enough to do his duty by you this night."

Celeste colored. That wasn't what she had meant at all!

Lady Alicia held her cup gingerly. "'Tis good to hold this hot drink against my fingers," she remarked with a smile.

"I am sorry to hear you suffer from aches in the joints," Celeste murmured politely. She prayed Lady Alicia was not the type who took pleasure in cataloging her ills.

The Countess shook her head. "Not that affliction yet, thank the Lord. I have been most busy these past four weeks, sewing saddlecloths and banners for my son." She nodded with satisfaction. "A few pricked fingers is a small price to pay," she added. "You shall see my handiwork anon."

As Celeste sipped her hot drink, her gaze swept over the crowd across from her. She smiled when she saw Gaston and four of her men, clustered around several buxom maids. From the look of it, her men were more interested in the tournament of love than in that of arms. Farther along the high palisade she spied Pierre. Next to him, Pip rode on the shoulders of a tall peasant. Both boys shouted and whistled as the next two combatants charged into the ring. Lucky for little Pip to have such a fine vantage point. Celeste tried to see who was the poor soul who bore the excited boy's weight, but his head was hidden in a large green hood. She must try to find the kind man later and give him a penny for his burden.

In the ring, the challenger neatly unhorsed his opponent on the second pass. The defender hit the ground with a resounding crash. Immediately his squire raced to his side. The fallen man didn't move. The crowd grew quiet. The squire knelt and spoke to his master. The defeated lord groaned, then sat up. The squire helped him remove his fluted helm. With a wave of his hand, Sir Thomas of Rothbury conceded the contest to Sir Robert of Morpeth. Then his squire helped the injured knight out of the arena, while Sir Robert rode around the perimeter of the palisade, accepting the accolades of the crowd. He bowed to Celeste as he passed by her.

When she next looked for Pip and Pierre, she could not find them. Their place at the wall had been taken by Nicholas and several of his fellow guardsmen.

Inside Ormond's tent, Grapper tossed a bucket of cold water over his master's bowed head, then wiped him dry with a thick piece of toweling.

"God's teeth!" Roger bellowed, shaking the drops from his eyes. "A pox on Cheviot's innards! He'll yield the crow a pudding one of these days!"

Grapper eased his irate lord onto a stool and began to massage Sir Roger's shoulders. "Will you issue him another challenge, my lord?"

Ormond chewed an end of his mustache as he considered the question. The devil take that churlish Griffith! Made Roger look the fool in front of his own people—and the French girl. Aye! That blow would have unhorsed him, if he wasn't the better rider of the two. On the other hand, there was no point in inviting another public humiliation. Act the chivalrous knight now—and catch the knave in his cups later. Then transform the fat villain into an ape. Besides, Ormond had another challenger to meet before dinner. He must save his strength for Lord Jeffrey—and, later, for the wench in bed.

Roger closed his eyes and pictured himself thrusting a lance of a different sort into that soft, yielding body. *Tonight, Celeste, you'll be mine at last!*

*   *   *

A pair of deep sapphire eyes observed Celeste from under the shelter of an oversize hood. He had always admired that red gown with the black fur edging the hem and sleeves. He well knew how it hugged her breasts and outlined her slim waist. Celeste made a beautiful Queen of Truth and Beauty, to rival any illustration in her Book of Love. He just wished her dark eyes didn't look so haunted. No matter, he would soon make them sparkle with joy.

Tonight, my love, you'll be mine at last!

Red-rimmed eyes glowered at the figure in crimson sitting to the right of his father's empty chair. Let her laugh and simper now; she'd dance to a different tune anon. His tune, the way it should have been—the way it would be again. The old dog might have his morning, but the sun had not set. Walter ran his tongue along his teeth. A plague on it! He tasted the salt of his bleeding gums. At least he had used these past few weeks wisely, and not in wine. He felt fitter than ever. Strong enough for both his sire and the French minx.

He licked his lips again as his gaze lingered on Celeste's breasts. Even through the thick cloak, they jutted out like a wanton's. Aye, and he would make her play the whore—maybe even share her with his men. That sight might make him hard.

Tonight, bitch, you'll be mine at last!

Chapter Twenty-Nine

At midday, Sir Roger allowed his guests only a brief respite, instead of the usual lengthy dinner. The knights had to make good use of the few remaining hours of winter daylight. In a tent beside the tiltyard, serving men laid out a repast of meat pies, cheese tarts, roast duck and chicken, hard-boiled eggs, bread, butter and ale. Everyone, even the ladies, ate standing up, which encouraged the speed of the meal. At least the tent and the press of steaming bodies helped to warm Celeste's chilled skin.

Mon Dieu! Why did the English live so far to the north? Celeste held her hands over a smoldering brazier. She doubted she would ever be warm again. Having broken several more lances before dinner, Sir Roger appeared in good spirits.

"There's a wench!" he roared, catching sight of her amid the jostling crowd.

Celeste cringed inside, though she presented him with a smile.

"A kiss, mistress mine, for luck this afternoon!" her betrothed bellowed, while the onlookers cheered. Before Celeste could protest, he took her lips with his chicken-greased ones and saluted her with loud smacking noises.

Celeste wanted to wipe her lips and chin with her handkerchief, but decided to wait until she could do so in private. She had no desire to irritate her lord.

Her lord! Celeste clenched her teeth when she thought of Ormond as her husband. Whatever dreams she might have entertained last night showed no promise of coming true today. The sun had traveled over half his course across the pale sky. A few more hours, and all her hopes would be forever locked away in the secret place of her heart.

Plainly, the Knight of the Loyal Heart, whoever he might be, had played her a cruel jest. Tomorrow or sometime there after, she would take a switch to Pip for his part in the rogue's masque. With a leaden spirit, Celeste resumed her seat on the stand, shivering under Lady Alicia's fox fur rug. On her right, Sir Roger took his chair, from which vantage point he shouted at all and sundry.

The next hour blurred in front of Celeste's eyes. The crashing of the jousters as they rode headlong at each other grew dimmer in her ears. Retreating behind her fixed smile, Celeste permitted the luxury of self-pity to wash over her.

Duped! She had been duped by everyone—beginning with her own father. How he must have chuckled when she rode so bravely down the beech-shaded lane from L'Étoile in August! He must have known exactly what sort of family the Ormonds were, and exactly how far away they lived. How satisfied he must have been to finally see the last of his most unwanted, and meddlesome fifth daughter!

Duped by the holy monks of Saint Hugh's into thinking she was going to a good home. Duped by her aunt, who surely must have had some inkling as to what a horrible place they traveled to! Duped for three hundred miles by smiling faces who robbed her blind at every public house in England. And, most of all, duped by that handsome archangel himself, Brother Guy, who had brought her to this cold place, then fled, taking her heart with him, and leaving the rest of her to face her fate alone.

Lady Alicia's cry of pleasure mixed with concern pulled Celeste from her dark brooding. Brandon and Harry Percy had entered the lists. Both young men gave no thought to saving their limbs, according to the countess, and they had chosen to fight both on horseback, and on foot with blunted swords. As she watched the long contest, Celeste had to admit that the men fought exceedingly well. In the end, the judges ruled in Brandon's favor—the call greeted with an equal mixture of cheering and disapproval from the onlookers.

After Brandon and Percy retired from the arena, the pursuivant stepped forward and began to read the accumulated scores.

"The grand melee is next," Sir Roger rumbled beside Celeste, his one eye shining with anticipation. "You'll like that, my lady. A lot of color, a lot of noise."

Celeste nodded, her smile even more frozen than before. Another one of her headaches began to form behind her eyes. *Ma foi!* In all her years in France, she had never been ill. Now it seemed not a day passed when she didn't suffer a headache or an upset stomach.

The pursuivant rolled up his paper. He had opened his mouth to announce the main event of the afternoon when a blast of the challenger's horn interrupted him. Startled, he looked first to the king of arms, then to Sir Roger.

"Oh, ho!" the host of the tournament chuckled. "An unknown knight, I surmise! Nice touch! I wonder who thought of it?"

Celeste felt her blood rush to her cheeks. Her Knight of the Loyal Heart had finally come! Headache banished, she sat up straighter in her seat and craned her neck to see who entered the ring.

The gates at the far end opened wide, to admit four riders, looking as ominous as the Four Horsemen of the Apocalypse. The leader wore a colorful *jupon* emblazoned with the Ormond crows over his breastplate. The other three riders, ruffians all, were dressed completely in black. Sir Roger half rose out of his seat. A strangled choking sound came from his throat. Recognizing one of the squires as the hideous Deighton, Celeste collapsed against the countess, moaning softly.

Lady Alicia took Celeste's clammy hand in her warm one. "What ails you, my dear?" she asked with a worried frown on her face.

Celeste's heart hammered against her rib cage. "Sweet angels protect me," she murmured. "It is Walter Ormond. I recognize his henchmen."

Sir Roger stood, his thick legs braced apart, as the lead rider reined to a halt in front of the stand. "Most villainous knave! How dare you enter the lists! You have no right to wear the arms of a knight since you were denied that honor by the king. Begone!"

Walter lifted his visor. The silver metal framed his pale face, though his red-rimmed eyes burned like those of a maddened boar. "Salutations, Father!" Walter made an exaggerated bow to his enraged sire, then turned his disgusting visage toward Celeste. His lewd expression reminded her of illustrations of a grinning death's-head. She shivered, and Lady Alicia's fingers entwined with hers for comfort.

"And greetings to you, my bride, on this, our wedding day," Walter continued. The crowd stilled and pressed closer to the palisade walls.

A wave of nausea swept over Celeste. Was this pestilent caricature her Knight of the Loyal Heart, for whom she had longed and hoped? This was the cruelest jest of all.

"*Your* bride!" The makeshift walls of the stand shook with Sir Roger's fury. "You are a prattling fool! And therefore, being a fool, your suit should be a jester's motley, not armor. Away with you, Sir Maggot! Your presence offends my eyes!"

Far from being angered, Walter snickered. "Methinks the winds blow a fetid stench hereabouts," he remarked to Deighton.

Sir Roger motioned to the guardsman at the base of the pavilion's stairs. "Escort this . . . this carrion in borrowed feathers from the field of honor!"

Deighton drew his sword and leveled it at the man. The flustered guard looked from the sharp point of the weapon to his master's mottled face.

"See how fine this tyrant tickles!" Walter remarked smoothly. "But to the matter at hand. I have come for my rightful property—the Lady Celeste—betrothed to me eight years ago." Raising his voice with each word, his complaint carried to the ends of the now-silent arena. "I demand justice for the theft of my wife! I challenge you, Roger Ormond, to combat. God will award justice and the lady to the victor."

"You have no right to this place of honor!" the earl of Thornbury called out from his judgment seat above the spectators. "You have not taken the oath of knighthood."

"True, my lord!" Walter shouted back. "But this is a family matter, and I choose to settle it here, in public. If my father is afraid to meet me in fair combat—"

"Grapper! My horse!" Sir Roger practically hurled himself down the stairs. "No unlicked pup is going to call me a coward and live to see the sunset!"

"What weapons?" asked the earl, though his expression made it plain that he disapproved of the proceedings.

"Pointed lances and sharpened swords," answered Walter. He practically licked his lips as he said it.

"First blood?" The earl inquired.

"To the death!" shouted Walter, shaking his lance in the air.

"Sir Roger Ormond, do you agree to these terms?" The earl could barely contain the rage in his voice.

"I will begin at the varlet's heels and reveal his poxed innards by inches!" the father thundered.

"I am going to be ill," whispered Celeste to Lady Alicia.

"Not now!" the lady whispered back, squeezing Celeste's hand. "Now, of all times, you must stiffen your spine. Chin up! Show the people you are worthy to be the prize."

"*Sacre!* I am no piece of chattel!" Celeste's fury almost strangled the words in her throat. Her anger quelled the green-sickness in her stomach.

"Tell that to a man!" Lady Alicia snorted. The vehemence of her words surprised Celeste. "You must show that you are better than all of them! Look the part, even if you don't feel it."

Celeste stared deeply into Lady Alicia's blue eyes, which now sparkled with icy fire. In them she saw Guy's eyes staring back at her.

"For better or for worse, it will be over soon." The countess had softened her voice.

"I fear it will be the worst. Sir Roger is tired, and has suffered several grievous blows." Celeste tightened her jaws together to keep her teeth from chattering. Sweet Jesu! Walter Ormond could yet be her husband!

Celeste drew herself up in her seat and assumed a cold expression. Inside, her stomach rolled and bucked with icy fear. Without seeming to move her head, she searched the crowd for Gaston or one of her men. None could be seen.

In the arena, Grapper helped his master into the saddle of his war-horse. Before lowering his visor, Sir Roger flashed Celeste a smile and roared, "There's a wench worth fighting for!"

The crowd cheered. Celeste continued to grip Lady Alicia's hand, and she prayed for the elder man's safety and success. On him alone rested all her chances for a decent future.

The pursuivant scampered out of the way, and the two combatants, clad in identical heraldry, took their positions at the opposite ends of the field. Like twin bolts from a double crossbow, the two horses suddenly charged down the list on either side of the frail barrier. The thudding of their massive hooves echoed Celeste's heartbeats as father and son drew closer. With a ringing clash, they met and dashed on. Walter's lance splintered at the tip, where it had struck against Sir Roger's shield. At the bottom of the turn, Walter threw down the damaged lance and took up a second that Deighton handed to him. Both Ormonds wheeled at the same time, and urged their horses down the course again.

The second pass knocked Sir Roger sideways in his saddle. He fought to regain his seat, but his feet slipped out of the stirrups just past the barrier. Celeste covered her mouth with her hand to prevent her scream escaping. Grapper dashed forward to catch the horse, and to snatch the fallen lance out of the way. Sir Roger staggered to his feet and drew his sword as Walter dismounted and advanced toward him.

The audience grew quiet again as the two men in the ring traded blows with their long doubled-edged blades. The resounding clang of each strike set Celeste's teeth on edge. Her head throbbed anew. Forcing down her quaking nausea, she gripped Lady Alicia's hand tighter. The freshening wind blew colder under her long skirts.

Walter proved lighter on his feet than Sir Roger. He danced from one side to the other, occasionally lunging to make a hit. Most of the time, he fended off his father's more practiced swings. As the contest wore on, Sir Roger grew visibly tired. Walter landed a hard blow to Sir Roger's helmet. Stunned by the concussion, the older man sank to his knees, though he did not drop his guard. Celeste moaned into her handkerchief.

Circling behind his father, Walter struck him hard between the shoulder blades, at the base of the skull. Amid the shouts of the crowd and calls of "Foul!" from the judges, Sir Roger fell onto all fours. Both Celeste and the countess rose to their feet. Walter hesitated a fraction of a second; then, rounding on Sir Roger's blind side, he wedged his sword tip into his father's unprotected armhole and drove the blade deep.

Sir Roger pitched forward onto his side. Before either the squires or the marshals could reach him, Walter leaned his weight on the hilt of the sword, forcing the point deeper into the inert body. Then, placing his foot on his father's hip, Walter yanked the sword out and held it aloft. A red stream of blood ran down the length of the blade. Overcome with dizziness, Celeste swayed. Lady Alicia caught her in her arms and eased the stricken girl back into her seat.

Walter raised his visor, then pointed toward Celeste with the bloody tip of his weapon. "I claim the Lady Celeste as my rightful wife, as God is my judge!" he shouted. Throwing back his head, he laughed like a demented crow.

"Doomed," Celeste whispered, squeezing her eyes shut against the horror before her. "I shall be worm's meat before this year has turned."

Chapter Thirty

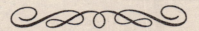

The jarring note of the challenger's horn again pierced
the ice-chilled air. A murmur ran through the crowd. Lady
Alicia's body relaxed around Celeste.

"Who comes?" whispered Celeste, lifting her head and
sweeping the hair out of her eyes.

"Another knight," the countess answered, her voice
strengthened with pride. "A true knight."

"*Non!*" Celeste shook her head. "I don't believe in
them anymore."

"Then unshackle your disbelief and observe!" Lady
Alicia pointed toward the gates.

As they swung open, three new riders dashed into the
arena at full speed. One held high a lance to which was affixed a streaming white banner. A bloodred heart flew
across the silk on a pair of golden wings. The crowd went
wild with approval.

Celeste stared at it mutely, not daring to move or speak,
lest the apparition disappear. Walter Ormond stood over
the body of his father in angry disbelief as the trio drew
abreast of him.

The tall central figure, clad in brilliant silver armor,
wore the winged heart on his fluted helm. On his war
shield, three blue forget-me-nots gleamed with new-painted

brightness. His charcoal gray destrier pranced, flapping his trailing saddlecloths, on which a legion of winged hearts took flight. The two squires on either side of the knight, one almost as tall as his master, wore short white satin doublets, with the winged heart on their chests, and tight white silken hose. Most amazing of all, both squires were masked.

The Knight of the Loyal Heart pointed his lance tip at Walter, then turned to Celeste and bowed to her from his waist. Trembling, she returned her savior's salute.

"Who comes upon the field of honor?" the earl of Thornbury called across the arena. The crowd stilled again, eager to hear what the mysterious knight would answer.

The squire holding the banner replied. "I have the honor to present the Knight of the Loyal Heart. He has come to do battle for the hand of the Lady Celeste."

"No!" screamed Walter, shaking his sword, which still dripped with his father's gore. "She's mine! She has always been mine by right."

"Silence, Walter Ormond!" roared the king of arms. "Is the stranger knight a true knight?" he asked the mysterious squire.

Under his half mask, the first squire smiled. "Aye, my lord. He swore the oath of chivalry eight years ago. Our noble king, Great Harry himself, buckled on his spurs and dubbed him Knight of the Realm."

"Then you are welcome, Knight of the Loyal Heart," replied the earl.

"And doubly so," murmured his countess in Celeste's ear.

"No!" shrieked Walter. "This tournament is dissolved! Everyone depart this place! Begone!"

"'Tis not your right to dissolve this day's proceedings, Walter Ormond." The earl's deep voice rolled over all present. "That right belonged to your father. And passed from him to me. You are challenged by this knight. What say you?"

"I say you may be damned to hell!" Walter shouted back.

"Mark me, Ormond," boomed the earl. "If you deny the challenge, then I, as your overlord, will place you and your minions under arrest for the unlawful death of your sire, here witnessed by me and by these other judges, and your lands will be forfeit to me." The four judges on either side of the earl nodded their agreement. "For you slew your father unfairly from behind and on his blind flank. As one who is not a knight and therefore has no noble rank, you will be punished as a commoner and I, as your judge, will see that your execution will be long and painful."

Walter's knees trembled at this pronouncement, though he stood his ground. For the first time today, a spark of hope lit up Celeste's soul.

The earl continued in his deep voice. "This knight does you more honor than you deserve, varlet. If you accept his challenge, you might escape your just punishment. The decision is yours, but make haste. The pallid sun waits for no man."

Walter licked his lips as he stared up at the imposing, silent knight astride the restless horse. He cast an evil glance at Celeste, then threw down his gauntlet next to his father's cooling body. "I accept the challenge," he snarled.

The first squire then spoke to Celeste. "Lady Celeste de Montcalm, if the Knight of the Loyal Heart is the victor, will you accept him as your husband and lord, and will you wed him this night?''

Everyone around the palisade and in the stands looked at Celeste. She ran her tongue over her dry lips. She glanced down at Sir Roger's body, then at his murderer, above it. Finally she returned her gaze to the heart-helmed knight before her.

Celeste cleared her throat, so that all the world could hear her answer. "*Oui,* I accept this knight if he wins," she proclaimed. *Please win!*

The knight extended the tip of his lance to her. Its sharp point glinted wickedly.

"Your favor," prompted the countess beside her in a whisper.

From her inner sleeve, Celeste withdrew the scrap of blue silk and attached it to the lance tip. With it went her silent prayer. The knight bowed again as he withdrew the lance.

"*Merci,* my lady," the first squire responded in French. "As you see, I have kept my promise. We have met again on Saint Stephen's Day, though not under the conditions my lord expected. For the death of Sir Roger Ormond, we are sorry."

Celeste could not trust herself to speak, lest she disgrace herself by bursting into tears. Instead, she nodded. The three horsemen saluted her, then wheeled their mounts to the far end of the ring. As Celeste watched them, she recognized the second squire's horse. Black Devil! *Mon Dieu!* Could that be Gaston hiding behind the mask of the second squire? She wished she had looked closer at him.

Talbott, his face wet with tears for his slain master, hurried down the steps and directed the solemn removal of Sir Roger's body. As he passed Walter, the steward spat in the mud at his feet. Walter appeared to be too perturbed to notice the insult. Deighton grabbed him by the arm and hauled him toward his horse, at the near end.

"What weapons?" the king of arms called across the arena.

The challenger remained silent. The spectators turned toward Walter.

"Sharpened lances and swords, and may the devil take the hindmost!" Walter swung himself into the saddle.

"First blood?" intoned the earl, this time looking at the silent knight.

"Agreed!" answered the first squire.

"No!" Walter screamed. "I crave his heart, with or without wings, for my supper!"

"First blood only," ruled the earl. "Commence at the sound of the trumpet."

Sweet Jesu, protect my knight, Celeste prayed. *Please deliver me from Walter Ormond.*

"Walter will try to kill him," she said aloud to Lady Alicia.

"I know," the countess answered grimly, never taking her eyes off the mysterious knight. "We must pray that God rides with your champion."

Walter took up a fresh lance, then snapped his visor shut. At the other end of the arena, the mysterious knight tucked Celeste's veil inside his gauntlet, then raised his lance to signify his readiness. Walter lifted his lance in the air, and the heralds blew a three-note tattoo. Both horses sprang forward.

Celeste wanted to close her eyes, but didn't dare. Beside her, Lady Alicia drew in her breath as the two opponents thundered down the course, along the barrier. On the first pass, Walter ducked under the knight's lance. The crowd hissed and booed at him as he rounded the far turn. On the second pass, the knight aimed his lance lower, almost under his shield.

Celeste's breath caught in her throat at the moment of impact. The jarring sound shimmered the air in front of her eyes; then it seemed to crack into a spider's web of pieces. When her vision cleared, she saw that Walter lay on the ground. Deighton and one of the marshals ran up to him. The challenger retired to the far end of the ring and waited.

Standing, the marshal faced the king of arms. "There's no breath left in him, my lord, and blood springs from his mouth and nose."

Celeste pulled herself up to a standing position. She gave Lady Alicia a weak smile as the matron joined her. Be a worthy prize, the countess had told her earlier. The cost had been high, and it was one Celeste knew she would never forget. She prayed God that the price had been worth it.

"First blood has been drawn, and justice served by the hand of the Almighty," the earl intoned as Walter's body was dragged away. "Sir Knight, you may claim the lady."

As the Knight of the Loyal Heart rode to the base of the stand, Celeste swallowed hard. All her life she had dreamed of something like this happening to her. Today she had discovered that dreams could turn into nightmares. What would the next few minutes bring?

The squires helped the knight dismount, then held the reins of his magnificent charger as he walked slowly up the stairs. Celeste's knees quivered as he drew nearer. Oh, la, la! The man was a giant! The golden tips of the wings on his helm scraped the top of the pavilion.

The knight pulled off one gauntlet, then the other. Dropping to one knee before her, he took her left hand in his. The warmth of his skin calmed her skittering nerves. His thumb gently caressed the golden ring on her finger.

Without lifting his visor or removing his helm, he murmured in French, "Sweetest Lissa."

Celeste gasped at the sound of her pet name. "How did you know that?"

He did not answer her question, but continued to speak through the slit in his visor. His deep voice resonated from within as he spoke. "I have known you in my heart all my life. This day, I have won your hand in honorable combat, though I regret the outcome and will pray for the souls of both father and son. But now the sadness of this day has come to an end, and we should turn to happier thoughts. Heart of my heart, will you give me your heart in return for mine?"

Celeste tried to see into the visor. She wished she could look at his eyes and read his soul. His hand continued to caress hers in an oddly familiar way, suggesting more pleasant, more personal encounters to come. Her heart fluttered in her throat, as if longing to join its mate kneeling before her. Her flesh prickled and burned at the knight's touch. Blood raced through her like molten wildfire.

"My lady?" he implored.

"Do what your heart tells you," whispered Lady Alicia behind her.

Celeste lifted her chin. "My lord knight, you have won my body, and you hold my hand. I think you had better take my heart to make the package complete." Having uttered the boldest words of her life, Celeste drew in her breath and wondered what would happen next.

The knight released her hand, then lifted his helm from his shoulders. When he raised his golden head, he smiled that unearthly, beloved smile at her. His sapphire eyes probed hers with shimmering pools of love.

"Brother Guy!" Celeste gasped, taking an involuntary step backward. She fought to keep the earth and sky from spinning around her head. "This cannot be! It is blasphemy! You are a priest!"

His mouth quirked slightly. "Never that."

"But you are dedicated to the church! You took your vows. You cannot marry me!" She had to escape this awful situation, but there was no room to run, no place to hide her mortification.

Guy took her hand in his again. "Listen to me, sweetest one. I was only a novice at Saint Hugh's. I have never taken final vows. Two days ago I received a letter from Father Jocelyn, releasing me from the Franciscans. It seems he knew me better than I knew myself. And I *have* kept my last vow. You notice I did not speak to you until your wedding day." Guy kissed her cold fingers, his warm lips stirring her already befuddled senses. Now fully hearing his voice, Celeste found it velvet-edged and strong.

"Celeste, as my mother behind you is my witness, I will make you a new vow. I shall not go again to court. I have done with the sham of courtly life. And I have done with the celibate life of a monk as well. But, sweet mistress mine, I vow I shall never be done with you. I love you. Will you trust me with your love and happiness now?" The blue depths of his eyes promised volumes more.

Her fingers tightened around his. "*Oui,* Sir Guy Cavendish, minister to lost souls and flying hearts, I give you my love to keep. I fear that is all the dowry I have to offer."

Guy's laughter floated up from his throat. "Your dowry is your own sweet self. Your hand in mine is all the riches I need or want." He kissed each finger in turn, pay-ing special honor to the one his ring encircled. Then he stood and swept Celeste off her feet into the enveloping protection of his embrace. The forgotten crowd roared back to life with their deep-throated cheers of approval.

"Shield your eyes, Mother," Guy warned the countess. "I fear my next behavior may shock you."

"By my troth, nothing you do shocks me anymore, my son," she replied calmly.

Dipping his head, Guy sealed his betrothal with the most passionate, loving kiss Celeste had ever experienced. Her world ceased to sway and spin. It stopped moving altogether.

Epilogue

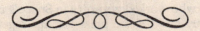

October 1529
Snape Castle, Northumberland

"*Voilà, mon cher,* I win again!" Celeste laid her cards down on the polished tabletop, then reclined against the high-backed cushioned chair, her hands folded across her bulging abdomen. She regarded her husband, across from her, with eyes shining in violet triumph.

Guy added up the scores on his well-worn slate. By the Book! The sly minx had done it again. By now, after ten months of marriage, he should know better than to think he could ever best his little wife at her favorite card game. In fact, ever since Celeste had learned his manner of play, she had been beating him by wider margins. Running his fingers through his hair, Guy glanced up at her.

"There's no need to chew your lips so, my sweet." Leaning across the table, he traced his finger across her lower lip. She kissed it in return. "I will pay my just debts. How much do I owe you now?"

Celeste shrugged one shoulder in an offhand manner. "Crowns and pounds, who knows? Indeed, I have lost count since midsummer." Her black brows knitted together, as if she recalled something distasteful from her memory.

Puzzled by her expression, which belied the lightness of her words, Guy flopped against the back of his chair. He drained the rest of the wine in his cup. One added benefit of having a French wife was the excellent wine she imported from France—at a ruinous tax—as well as the French chef who worked wizardry in Snape's refurbished kitchens. Guy saw Celeste press her lips together into a thin, tight line.

Had he displeased her since supper? Since she'd become pregnant, Celeste's moods swung in a wider arc, if that was possible—usually for the better. The coming babe seemed to have given her an increased energy that she used to transform grim old Snape Castle into a warm and cheerful home for Guy and his growing family.

Growing? Aye, there was the rub. In the past month, Celeste's middle had ballooned so that he wondered if she harbored twins. Twins, he mused. Mother would like that. Did twins run in the family?

A muted gasp snapped him out of his reverie. Celeste sat straight in her chair, gripping the lion's-paw arms. Though the light from the blazing fire turned the room into dancing reds and oranges, Celeste's complexion had taken on a shade like new parchment.

"My love, is there something amiss?" The stewed eels at supper had been a trifle rich.

She held her breath for a moment longer, then relaxed. A ghost of a smile flitted across her lips.

"The babe," she murmured.

Guy's heartbeat doubled and pounded against his chest. "Sweet Jesu!" he murmured. "You mean . . . now?" His mind, usually so clear in a crisis, befuddled itself. He could only stare at her as if she were some mysterious creature come to rest at his hearthside.

Celeste relaxed against her cushions. Her face resumed its normal look—one that hinted of untapped mischief.

"*Non,* our child will not pop out this next minute. But, I think, you will be a father by the morrow." She giggled. "*Mon Dieu!* I can see you are not quite ready for this blessed event. In truth, you look like a landed trout, my love."

The impact of her words galvanized Guy as a call of the trumpets would have sent him plunging into the lists in an earlier time. He shot out of his chair, knocking it backward with a crash. "In the good Lord's name, Celeste! Why did you not tell me before this?"

With one impatient hand, Guy swept the table aside, sending wine, cards and cups clattering to the clean-swept floor. Gaston, dozing on the settle by the fire, jerked awake.

"The devil take it!" he thundered, scrambling to his feet. "Are we attacked?"

"The babe!" Guy responded with a strange hoarseness in his throat. "'Tis time." He knelt by his wife's side. How could she possibly smile and look so calm at a time like this, when every nerve throbbed in his body and the stewed eels danced a galliard in the pit of his stomach?

"*Sacrebleu!*" With a colorful oath, Gaston lumbered across the hall, calling for Mistress Conroy, maids, fire, water and wine.

Several hounds took up the cry, adding to the growing commotion. Servants peered through several doorways, then scurried off, only to return moments later, carrying all manner of things and heading for Celeste's lying-in chamber, above the hall. In the midst of this early-evening chaos, Celeste smiled serenely at her husband. Obviously, the pain had unhinged her mind.

"Why did you not tell me sooner?" Guy asked again, gently placing his hand over her tummy. Her full roundness was tight under his touch.

With playful fingers, Celeste brushed a wayward lock of hair from his eyes. "Because, you great loud bear, I was winning. I couldn't cry off until we had finished the game."

Guy could only gape at her. He had heard that birthing sometimes turned women to madness. Dear God! Not his own sweet Celeste! He would offer a thousand masses, light ten thousand candles. . . .

"Such a face!" she chided, stroking his cheek. "Are you going to be ill?"

The food inside him considered the question seriously. "Nay!" He swallowed with difficulty. "Can you put your arms around my neck?"

Celeste leaned over and kissed the tip of his nose. "*Oui*, as long as you promise not to drop me."

"Drop you?" As if Guy could possibly do such a thing. Yet, as he gently lifted Celeste from the chair, he discovered a certain weakness in his knees. "Lean your head on my shoulder, my heart, and I will have you in your bed in no time."

The rest of his consoling murmurs died in his throat as Celeste stiffened in his arms. Head bowed over her, he held her tight against his chest as her pain peaked and then ebbed.

"My lord?" Pip's large eyes peered through the mat of his perpetually uncombed hair. "What will you have me do?"

"Get my lady mother!" Guy instructed as he strode toward the staircase. "And my father. Send a messenger to Wolf Hall at once."

Pip spun on his heel. "I'll go myself!" he replied, running for the stairs that led down to the courtyard. "I'll be there and back with them afore the moon rises."

Guy didn't trust himself to caution the young scamp about temperamental horses and the holes in the road between Snape and his father's home. The boy knew the way well enough, and Guy's only thoughts were for the precious burden in his arms.

"Peep need not hurry to get there," Celeste murmured as Guy carried her up the winding stairs. "They tell me that first babies take a long time coming."

"I would share your pain." Guy kicked open the door, narrowly missing Nan, who hurried in front of him, bearing a large basin of warm, scented water in her hands.

Celeste's answering laughter sounded like bells on a May maiden's wrist. "*Non*, my brave knight. I do not think so."

Guy laid her on the thick feather bed. Was the chamber very hot, or was it him? "I will be with you every moment." He kissed her fingers, one by one.

Celeste merely rolled her eyes at him before another pain seized her. Guy winced as he watched helplessly. Someone shook him by the shoulders.

"Ye do Her Ladyship not one whit o' good by being here, my lord." Mistress Conroy pried his fingers loose from Celeste's moist hand. "A birthing chamber is no place for a man, Sir Guy. Now be off with ye, and let us get on with our work."

Stung by the housekeeper's callousness, Guy wheeled on her, but that good lady merely fixed him with a stare that would have frozen a charging bull on the spot. "Take good care of her," he managed to mumble. His mouth was dry. Wine—he needed a lot of it.

"Aye, to be sure, my lord, as soon as ye've gone. I'll not be having ye swoon on me and clutter up the floor. Now out with ye!'' She flapped her apron at him, as if he were a schoolboy caught red-handed with an almond tart.

"Go on, Guy,'' Celeste added as Nan helped her out of her furred *robe de chambre*. "I am in good hands here.''

He leaned over the bed and took her pale face between his hands. How tiny Celeste was! How big his child within her! Too big. He traced each beloved feature with his thumb, trying to memorize every part of her. Sweet angels in heaven! What if he should lose her now? Not that. They had only enjoyed a year together. One scant year of happiness. *Pray, let Celeste live, and I will give up...swearing! Aye! And drinking wine, and...*

"Hey-ho, Brother Guy!'' Celeste caressed his hand with hers. "If you are planning to prostrate yourself on that cold chapel floor all night, I pray you not to do it naked. It will shock the maids, and you'll catch a chill. It would vex me sore to have you sick at a time when I need you. Come, give me a kiss to remember you, then go away. All shall be well.''

"I shall kiss you forever and a day,'' he murmured as his lips closed over hers, drinking in her sweetness. She clung to him for a moment longer, then pulled away as another pain took hold of her.

Feeling like a craven cur, Guy turned and fled the chamber. Gaston greeted him at the bottom of the stairs with a brimming cupful of unwatered wine.

"You look like the devil's own whoreson,'' the old soldier remarked with gruff affection as he pulled Guy toward the hearth, which the pages had piled high with fresh logs. "Sit down, man, before you fall down. This birthing business!'' Gaston quaffed his own generous portion of wine. "It's slower than a teasing virgin and frays a man's nerves just as badly. Nay—worse!''

By the time the earl and countess of Thornbury arrived, Guy had his head down between his knees, trying to blot out the piercing cries that came from the chamber above.

"How long has it been so?" Lady Alicia asked Gaston as Pip took her cloak and gloves.

Gaston replied with a crooked grin. "For my lady, I think it has been close to four hours. For your son here, it seems much longer."

"Eternity," Guy moaned.

"Pull yourself together, Guy. Babies are born every day."

Lady Alicia dropped a kiss on the top of his head as she swept toward the stairs. "Thomas," she called to her husband over her shoulder, "do something with him."

Guy stared at his father. "Was it thus with Mother when she had us?"

Thomas stretched out his hands to the blaze. "How should I know? I was a-hawking when you were born, and hunting the stag when Brandon came."

Guy's jaw dropped. He bit back the disrespectful words to his father that bubbled to his lips. His parents were a most loving couple. How could his father have abandoned his wife so cruelly?

Sir Thomas smiled at his son. "Hunting was invented for fathers-to-be, I think. You did not plan this babe well, son. Night is a terrible time to go thrashing about in the woods. You should have done it like me—labor pains at dawn, and 'twas off with the hounds an hour later. By the time I got back with a buck—and an eighteen-pointer, I confess—Brandon was all cleaned up and howling for his supper. And speak of the devil . . ." Thomas turned as his eldest son staggered into the hall under the weight of a keg.

"Greetings, little brother!" With a great heave, Brandon placed his burden on the floor. "I see I've come in good time with medicine for you." He winked at Gaston and his father.

"Medicine for me?" Guy repeated dully. Had Brandon gone horn-mad, as well? Was he, Guy, the only sane man among the lot of them? Just then, another one of Celeste's cries pierced the air. Guy winced.

" 'Tis killing her," he groaned.

"Nay." Brandon pulled the bung from the keg and poured a stream of amber liquid into Guy's empty wine cup. "But methinks 'twill kill you. Here, drink this."

"I've had wine enough," Guy muttered.

"Wine? Wine is for children. This is a man's drink—whiskey, straight from a goodly shop in Edinburgh. I've had it laid by since August, just for this occasion." Brandon grinned at his own foresight. "Father? Gaston?" He offered to fill their cups.

"Just the thing—if you can't go hunting," replied Sir Thomas. Gaston shook his head and mumbled a number of foul things in his best gutter French. Celeste cried out again. The four men shuddered as one.

"There's no sound quite like it, is there?" Brandon remarked in the silence that followed.

"By Saint Luke, if Celeste lives through this, I swear it will never happen again." Guy balled up his hands into fists and drove them into his eyes, as if that action could blot out the unearthly, horrific sounds from above. "I will never let her bear another child."

"Oh, truly?" Brandon poured his brother another drink. "And do you plan to renew your vow of chastity? Forgive me, little brother, but methinks you are moonstruck. I have seen the look in your eye when Celeste smiles at you. You have about as much control as a bantam rooster in a well-stocked henyard, and—"

Before Brandon could continue his observations, Guy leapt at him, hurling them both to the floor. They rolled about on the flagstones, trading blows. Sir Thomas looked on his sons with fond amusement.

"Always thought a little exercise was good at a time like this," he remarked to Gaston. "If you can't go a-hunting, that is."

Night waned, and the new day broke with a rare show of crystal blue sky. Only Guy remained awake, every cry of Celeste's ripping him apart. The whiskey had only made him chilled, not numb. Brandon, sporting a split lip, slept on the floor in front of the low-burning fire. Gaston and Sir Thomas snored in company on the settle.

Like a terrier sniffing the wind, Guy lifted his head and listened. Nothing but silence. She's dead! He dropped his head into the crook of his elbow. Tears stung his eyelids. He cried as he had not done since he was ten.

"You are a grand sight." Lady Alicia's voice chided him through the haze of his grief. "Drunk and blubbering." Guy looked up at his mother, waiting for the final blow— her confirmation of what he knew was the truth. Instead, she smiled at him.

"What is your poor little daughter to think, if the first sight of her father is a red-eyed, unshaven giant—with a black eye, no less? How now, Guy?"

Only the word *daughter* penetrated Guy's consciousness. He moistened his dry lips. "What say you, Mother?" he croaked.

Lady Alicia stroked his hair, as she had done all the years he could remember, when he was in need of comfort. "I say you have sired a fine baby girl this new day," his mother crooned. "Forsooth, she's the first dark-haired Cavendish, and—"

"And Lissa?" Guy could barely whisper her name. *Sweet angels, be kind.*

"Safe, but tired, as well she should be."

With a war cry last heard some five years ago, Guy leapt up, grabbed his mother with him and twirled her about the hall, waking dogs, servants and, finally, her husband.

"Unhand my wife, you rascal!" Laughing, Sir Thomas joined in their mad capering. "I take it we have a Cavendish heir?"

"Girl," Guy blurted out as he kissed each parent in turn. Then he bolted for the stairs, giving Brandon a brotherly kick en route.

"She needs to sleep," his mother cautioned him as he took the stairs two at a time.

Inside the stifling chamber, Celeste greeted him with a wan smile.

"Have you seen our daughter?" she asked softly, gazing up at him with those huge purple eyes he loved so well.

"Nay," he murmured, kissing her again and again, each kiss not half enough to slake his thirst for more. "I can only concentrate upon one lady at a time. How fare you, sweetest Lissa?"

Celeste sighed with contentment. "Most marvelously sleepy, and very happy."

"My lord." Mistress Conroy nudged him. "Will ye look upon your child?" She held out a small, tightly wrapped bundle to him.

Guy looked from the housekeeper to his smiling wife. "In there?" he asked, pulling back the edge of the swaddling blanket. His new daughter regarded her father with solemn eyes that hinted at a lavender color. A halo of fine black silk crowned her head. Without a doubt, the youngest Cavendish was the the prettiest, tiniest creature he had ever seen.

"Ye won't break her, my lord." Mistress Conroy smiled widely, showing a loss of several teeth. "Just hold her head thus."

Without quite knowing how, Guy found himself cradling his child.

"You're not disappointed, I hope?" Celeste asked, watching him closely.

Guy glanced at his wife. His poor sweetheart must still suffer some of the madness from her pain. "Disappointed? Nay! She's a beautiful miniature of her mother."

"Aye, an' healthy too," Mistress Conroy put in. "Has all her fingers and toes. I counted."

"We'll have a boy next year." Celeste yawned.

Guy trembled at the thought. He couldn't put her through that hell again. He knew for certain, *he* couldn't go through it again. "One girl is enough. No more, my darling."

Celeste's eyes grew larger, then sparked with a glimmer of fire. "Then you are displeased with me, *oui?* You don't want any more of my children, *oui?* Who blackened your eye, eh? I must reward him well. Perhaps I will blacken the other."

Mistress Conroy rescued the baby when Guy almost dropped her. She tactfully withdrew, for which privacy he thanked assorted saints. The whiskey began to take its delayed effect. He could tell he was due for a monstrous hangover.

"Not so, my sweet. 'Tis only that I cannot bear to be the cause of such pain for you." He knelt beside her and slipped one hand under her, gently drawing her closer to him. "I love you too much to lose you. I think I died a thousand times this night." He buried his face in her damp hair.

Celeste said nothing, but stroked the back of his neck in the way she knew would send shivers of pleasure down his spine. "You let me be the judge of what I can bear and not bear," she murmured in his ear. "I say next year a son. Tonia will need a playmate soon."

"Tonia?" Guy looked at her and tried to focus his whiskey-soaked brains. What sort of a name was that? "You want to call her Tonia?"

"*Oui*," Celeste purred, still stroking his neck. "For short, of course."

"Short for what?"

Celeste ran her pink tongue across her lips, a sign Guy had come to recognize when his wife was up to something. "Tonia is short for someone who has never had a child and who craves to be a godfather. One who is very dear to me—Gaston. But Gaston is a boy's name, so she must be Gastonia, *oui?*"

Guy answered her beguiling smile with a broad one of his own. "You have just doomed that poor man, my sweet. He will be as wet clay in her little hands—and she's not yet a day old. Aye, Tonia it is."

Celeste pulled his face closer to hers. "And do you know what you are for suggesting we have no more children, my archangel?"

Guy brushed his lips across hers and chuckled when she sputtered at the bristles on his chin. "Nay, my heart, what am I?"

"You are the most peench-'potted raw-beet sucker I have ever met," she pronounced, drawing him into a deeper kiss. Guy had neither the breath nor the desire to debate the matter.

* * * * *

HARLEQUIN®

Scandals

A passionate story of romance, where bold, daring characters set out to defy their world of propriety and strict social codes.

"Scandals—a story that will make your heart race and your pulse pound. Spectacular!"
—Suzanne Forster

"Devon is daring, dangerous and altogether delicious."
—Amanda Quick

Don't miss this wonderful full-length novel from Regency favorite Georgina Devon.

Available in December, wherever Harlequin books are sold.

SCAN

Weddings by DeWilde

Since the turn of the century the elegant and fashionable DeWilde stores have helped brides around the world turn the fantasy of their "Special Day" into reality. But now the store and three generations of family are torn apart by the separation of Grace and Jeffrey DeWilde. Family members face new challenges and loves in this fast-paced, glamorous, internationally set series. For weddings and romance, glamour and fun-filled entertainment, enter the world of DeWildes....

Watch for *WILDE MAN*,
by Daphne Clair
Coming to you in January, 1997

The sophisticated image and spotless reputation of DeWilde's Sydney store was being destroyed by tacky T-shirts and unmentionable souvenirs! And Maxine Sterling was not going to let swaggering DeWilde Cutter get away with it! He'd have to take his gorgeous looks and puzzling name and find another business. And she was certainly *not* going to fall in love with a man whose life-style symbolized everything she'd fought so hard to escape!

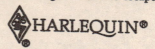

HARLEQUIN®

Ring in the New Year with babies, families and romance!

NEW YEAR'S RESOLUTION:

BABY

★

Add a dash of romance to your holiday celebrations with this delightful, heartwarming collection from three outstanding romance authors—bestselling author **JoAnn Ross** and award winners **Anne Stuart** and **Margot Dalton.**

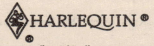

1997
Reader's Engagement Book
A calendar of important dates
and anniversaries for readers to use!

Informative and entertaining—with notable
dates and trivia highlighted throughout the year.

Handy, convenient, pocketbook size to help you
keep track of your own personal important dates.

Added bonus—contains $5.00 worth of coupons
for upcoming Harlequin and Silhouette books.
This calendar more than pays for itself!

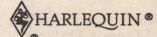

Available beginning in November at
your favorite retail outlet.

HARLEQUIN ® **Silhouette** ®

The collection of the year!
NEW YORK TIMES BESTSELLING AUTHORS

Linda Lael Miller
Wild About Harry

Janet Dailey
Sweet Promise

Elizabeth Lowell
Reckless Love

Penny Jordan
Love's Choices

and featuring
Nora Roberts
The Calhoun Women

This special trade-size edition features four of the wildly popular titles in the Calhoun miniseries together in one volume—a true collector's item!

Pick up these great authors and a chance to win a weekend for two in New York City at the Marriott Marquis Hotel on Broadway! We'll pay for your flight, your hotel—even a Broadway show!

Available in December at your favorite retail outlet.

NEW YORK
Marriott
MARQUIS

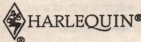 HARLEQUIN®  *Silhouette*®

NYT1296-R

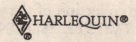

Not The Same Old Story!

 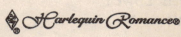

You are cordially invited to a

HOMETOWN REUNION

September 1996—August 1997

Bad boys, cowboys, babies. Feuding families,
arson, mistaken identity, a mom on the run...
Where can you find romance and adventure?
Tyler, Wisconsin, that's where!

So join us in this not-so-sleepy little town and
experience the love, the laughter and the
tears of those who call it home.

WELCOME TO A
HOMETOWN REUNION

Sheila and Douglas are going to spend their
honeymoon in a wigwam, by choice. But rumor
has it that Rosemary Dusold may be *forced*—by
runny-nosed babies—to live in one if the new
pediatrician follows through on his intention to
renovate her home as an office. Don't miss
Helen Conrad's *Baby Blues,* fifth in
a series you won't want to end....

Available in January 1997
at your favorite retail store.

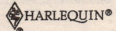

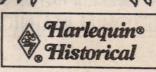

Harlequin® Historical

If you're a serious fan of historical romance,
then you're in luck!

Harlequin Historicals brings you
stories by bestselling authors, rising new stars
and talented first-timers.

Ruth Langan & Theresa Michaels
Mary McBride & Cheryl St. John
Margaret Moore & Merline Lovelace
Julie Tetel & Nina Beaumont
Susan Amarillas & Ana Seymour
Deborah Simmons & Linda Castle
Cassandra Austin & Emily French
Miranda Jarrett & Suzanne Barclay
DeLoras Scott & Laurie Grant...

You'll never run out of favorites.

Harlequin Historicals...they're too good to miss!

HH-GEN